Coyote
Healer,
Coyote
Curandero

Books by Mariana Ruybalid

Daring to Write (1999)
A Pattern of Silent Tears (2003)

Coyote
Healer,
Coyote
Curandero

by
Mariana Ruybalid

Permissions

Acknowledgments

Judith Barrington and Ruth Gundle provided two scholarships to Flight of the Mind, a women's writing camp, which led me to Flight Stanby, an online women's writing group where I got to know Cathleen Kirkwood who told me about Barbara Sjoholm and the Author-Editor Clinic in Seattle. Sjoholm introduced me to Marta Tanrikulu who was a great resource for the last two re-writes and in helping to finalize the book.

Richard Neagle gave me confidence and wise council.

Leona Benten gave me encouragement and advise during a re-write.

Joseph Alvarez Jr. provided good conversation and support.

Dave Baker did the final copy editing.

To

Autumn Dann,

a good friend

Part 1

Chapter 1
March 15, 2026

Martin chuckles. His grandfather, Sigún Gonzalez, has discovered his secret.

"What do you mean Martín knows how to read? M'ijo soon will turn five, but he doesn't talk or hold up his head, and he still wears diapers." The boy's beautiful mother, Sofía, a petite Latina with almond shaped eyes, argues with her dad.

He glances at her. Men turn their heads to look at her in the street.

"I'll search for a way for him to signal when he wants to use the toilet. He kept looking me in the eye like he wanted to tell me something, so I went to his school every day this week and brought him home on BART. I tell you, he knows how to read." Abuelo, his grandfather, a short swarthy man in his mid-sixties but in great shape, came from both Manchurian and Peruvian parents.

"I'll settle this, once and for all." Sofía finds a piece of paper on which she prints in large letters, "If you know how to read, blink your eyes three times." She holds it in front of Martín, who is strapped into a high chair in the kitchen. The room smells of red chili and cinnamon. A lavender plant sits on the window sill.

He blinks three times and giggles. He doesn't weigh much, maybe twenty pounds. He works hard to sit upright in his high chair, and when he gets tired he leans to the left. His body, an odd combination of muscle spasms and flaccidity, makes uncontrolled random movements.

"Wow, Papá, how did you figure it out?" Sofía picks up her son and gives him a hug. She runs her hand through his thick black hair. An old photo taped to a kitchen cabinet catches Martín's dark brown eyes. He sees four people.

"First, I saw his teacher training him to look up to the right when he wanted to indicate 'yes,' and down to the left for 'no.' On BART, I started asking him questions, easy ones at first, ones he could answer with a yes or a no. Like 'Does that woman wear blue shoes?' Then, when I made sure he could see the sign, I would inquire if I stood on a certain street. Or if we passed Rigo's body shop, I would ask him if the sign read 'Diego's body shop.'" Sigún sighs. "It took me the whole week, but I feel glad to know your beautiful son possesses great intelligence. He looks no bigger than a two-year-old, but his brain..." Sigún taps his head proudly.

Martín hoots. He sounds a little like an owl. Abuelo takes him from his daughter and supports his head. "Next week, I'll take him to the Kwoon."

"What would he do in a kung fu school? You sound too ambitious. I don't want m'ijo getting hurt." She wipes a blob of saliva from her son's chin with his bib.

"His physical therapist said he could learn from watching the other students. She showed me how to work on him, turning over from his back to his stomach, as part of his training." Abuelo turns to his grandson with a gleam in his eye. "You want to study Kung Fu, don't you?"

Martín looks up to the right and giggles with anticipation.

Martín sits near the window in the front room and looks at a wall covered by books in both English and Spanish. The room doesn't seem overcrowded with the small sofa and four easy chairs with lamps near them. He hears his grandfather step out to the front porch of his brown-shingled house and take a deep breath. "Even though so many live here, I feel happy. Now that Sofía and Martín came home, I can do no more to keep you safe.

The small boy hears his Tío Juan comment. "Papá, does it seem better now the War on Terrorism has ended?"

"No, of course not. It has become even worse. The Brotherhood demands passports to go to San Francisco." Martín can hear Abuelo's sadness.

Tío Juan snorts. "They pretend all their damn rules will bring back the East Coast." He takes off his backpack and it thumps as he puts it down on the porch.

Abuelo whispers, "No, no bomb can undo another bomb's damage."

Tío Juan pinches his arm. "Who would ever believe brown skin could be so powerful? They act as if we bombed away entire countries just by speaking Spanish!"

"Be careful with your anger, m'ijo. Look at your son, Esteban. He carries this anger with him and got suspended for fighting."

Tío Juan looks a lot like Abuelo. "How long ago did you come here, Papá?"

"It seems ironic. We moved here from Peru to escape the authorities' battle against El Sendero Luminoso, a true terrorist group. We found your uncle Pablo shot dead. Our father did nothing, but they thought he belonged to the terrorists. They said they would shoot me, just ten. We enjoyed Berkeley when we got here, but look at it now. The Pure White Brotherhood made us enemies of the state. Sofía came, and now all my children live together."

Martín's uncle whispers. "The damn white racists don't care when people of color die. They want us dead. We can't earn money. There aren't enough ration coupons to feed our kids. This time they covered only one package of rice, beans, and powdered milk."

"I don't know what we'd do without the water tanks and our garden."

Martín sees Abuelo tap his pocket to make sure he put his I.D. Pass there. "I'll go to the BART station. I get bored checking each person who gets off the train. Who cares whether or not they do business in Berkeley?" Sigún scratches his head. "After work I will go to the Kwoon. I want to include Martín. First, I will talk to the other teachers. One, a true person of vision, includes people with physical disabilities in her classes."

Three weeks later, Martín feels surprised to see his grandfather come into the bedroom where he sleeps with three cousins. His mother usually gets him ready in the morning. He awoke remembering his dream about a coyote. Then he daydreamed about Superboy, an extraordinary boy without cerebral palsy but with marvelous powers. He shakes his head to re-enter reality.

"Happy birthday, m'ijito! I brought you a present. First, I'll take you to the toilet." Abuelo carries the small boy into the bathroom and sets him on the special toilet chair he had made for his grandson.

Abuelo takes a bright yellow baseball cap from his back pocket and puts it on Martín's head. "Let's see you get the cap off."

He lowers his head and hits the brim with his left fist. On his third try, he sends the hat flying.

"You did great!" Sigún puts the yellow baseball cap back on the child's head. "M'ijito, do you think you can knock the cap off when you want to use the bathroom?"

The five-year-old looks up and to the right, signaling yes.

"Good, then I'll tell your mother and teacher." Abuelo carries Martín back to the bedroom and gets him ready for school. "You like your new school better, don't you, Martín?"

Martín signals yes.

"I feel so glad I got you transferred to Berkeley, once you let me know you could read." Sigún knows the whites made the old school into a dumping ground for developmentally disabled children whom the Brotherhood would kill later.

Martín wakes up the next morning. He remembers his stint at the developmental center in Oakland. He thinks about the white government loading them on a bus and taking them somewhere to kill them. He imagines Superboy stopping the bus, hijacking it, and overpowering the driver and the two guards. He uses his kung fu to kick all three in the head. He drives the bus to

Arizona and safety. Just before Santa Barbara, Superboy encounters a roadblock. He guns the bus and zooms right through.

"Time to get up!" He hears his mother and shakes his head to return to his room.

Martín wonders what happens to people with developmental disabilities right before they turn eighteen.

Chapter 2
May 8, 2026

A month later, in nearby San Leandro, the screen door slams as Lark throws her backpack down on the slip-covered couch. Muddy footprints go from the door to the dining-room table, where her mother sobs.

"Mom?" Lark sees her parents' half-eaten pork buns and a spilled cup of tea on the table. "Mom, what happened?"

Her mother, a small, slim forty-year-old whose parents came from Viet Nam, looks up and wipes her nose. "Tommy, they took Tommy."

"Who did, Mom?"

When her mother doesn't answer, Lark screams. "Did the White Brotherhood come? Where did they take him? Where's Papa? Mom! Where did they go?"

"They took him to the hospital."

"I will stop them!" Lark pushes open the door and runs down the street toward the hospital. *No!* echoes in her head. She will stop them. She thinks, *They can't kill my brother. He's fabulous. They just don't know anything. The damn white government thinks they can do whatever they want.*

She runs into St. Luke's Hospital in San Leandro, up the steps to the second floor, and bursts into the waiting room, which smells of antiseptic and perspiration. At first she does not recognize her father, a slight man whose grandparents came from China. In his face she can see what they had done to Tommy. She had arrived too late. The white bastards had given her brother the fatal injection.

Twelve-year-old Lark fights to keep her body from collapsing on the floor. She must not attract more attention. She stumbles over to a wall and leans against it. She takes a deep breath and notices the two soldiers walking through the crowd of angry Asians and Latinos. Their machine guns look ready to shoot. Lark recognizes some of the angry people. Fathers and brothers of Tommy's classmates in the Special Education Class at San Leandro High mill around the room. The damn white government had killed all fifteen students in Tommy's class! She feels horrified.

Lark sees one father signal another with his oldest son. On cue, six men rush the two guards. In the chaos, Lark runs toward her father, grabs his arm, and pulls him toward the door to the hallway. "Let's get out of here!"

At first her father stands still as if he is asleep or does not see her. Lark tugs harder. At last her father shakes his head and his eyes clear. He looks around, taking in the horror. "I don't want to lose you, too. Come." He runs to the door pushing Lark ahead of him.

They scramble down the stairs. They hear two shots fired, groans and screams. Her father shouts, "Go home!" and stumbles in front of a soldier who runs up the steps.

Lark, slightly built but wiry and strong, steps around them and joins the stream of people running out the front door. Her legs pump down Mono Street. She ducks behind a hedge as she sees a jeep-load of soldiers turn the corner, slam to a stop, and the soldiers rush inside. She feels torn between wanting to help her father and wanting to escape. But what can she do? She takes a deep breath and runs home.

Chapter 3
October 11, 2026

Six months after his transfer to the new school, his *pri-ma,* first cousin, Susana, a heavy-set sixth grader with dark hair who enjoys helping others, brings him into his classroom. She takes off her cousin's worn coat and parks his wheelchair in front of a computer. Martín shakes his head to end his daydream where Superboy had robbed a grocery store and gave the food to his classmates. Susana takes off his yellow baseball cap and puts a band around his forehead. Tío Juan had attached a laser wand to the band. Martin activates the computer with the laser and types "Thank you" on the screen. Tío Juan had modified the old computer to receive impulses from the boy's laser wand.

Susana replaces the yellow baseball cap. "I'll come back at lunchtime and feed you. And I'll remind Alex to come at half past ten and take you to the bathroom."

"Hi, Martín, how do you feel today?" His teacher glances at the computer screen. A tall woman, in her forties with light brown hair and green eyes, she had felt hesitant to include such a disabled child in her class until she had seen how quickly he learns and how Susana takes care of him.

"I feel great and I enjoy reading The Last Battle. I'll finish it today," he types out on the computer screen.

His teacher sighs. She had put the whole series of Narnia books by C. S. Lewis on Martín's computer so he could turn the pages electronically. Although only five and a half, Martín reads much better than the other second graders, including even his *primo*, cousin, Esteban, seven, who grows more and more jealous of the younger boy.

"Don't worry. I found a series of books by Lloyd Alexander for you to read after this one. Martín, can I send a reading group to you to listen to?" The teacher also had discovered Martín can use the talking mode of his computer to help the other students with their reading.

He types, "Sure, but not Esteban. He gets angry when I correct him." Martín remembers the shove his jealous cousin gave him the day before. He doesn't want to squeal on Estebán, and he wants to learn how to defend himself. He'll talk to his grandfather.

He blinks and looks at his teacher. He wants to ask a question and wonders how to put it. "You can live outside this ghetto and earn more money teaching white kids, yet you teach us children of color. Why?"

She looks around the room. "I lived in Berkeley a long time and I enjoyed our past freedom. Just because I'm white doesn't mean I agree with the Brotherhood's racist policies. I can oppose them by giving you children the best education I can."

He feels curious. "Do you know many people like you?"

"Yes. Many of us combat the Brotherhood's lies."

At recess, Martín remembers two older students at the Kwoon had stated that a kick in a certain part on the male body could feel very painful. He imagines Superboy getting caught by a White Brotherhood soldier after giving away the groceries. Superboy kicks the soldier in the balls and gets away. That afternoon, Martín writes a note to Alex requesting he unfasten the Velcro straps on his legs when Alex takes him to the bathroom.

"Sure, no problem." Alex, a sixth grader, big for his age, twelve, gentle with dark curly hair, had struck up a friendship with Martín. His father, an Afro-American, met his mother in Japan. He asks whether Estebán bullied him. The small boy signals yes.

When school ends, Susana pushes Martín home and feeds him a snack. Then she puts him by the window in the front room and goes to her room to change her clothes.

Estebán, a broad-shoulder boy with short black hair who can easily carry a twenty-five-pound sack of beans, slams the door, stomps into the front room, and yells, "You big show-off! You get all the attention!" He rears back to shove Martín again. At just the right moment Martín leans forward and bangs his head against his cousin's face. At the same time, Martín visualizes hitting him in the groin with his mind.

"Ow, that little bastard kicked me in the cojones!" Estebán howls, holding both his head and his groin.

Martín feels surprised. Did he really hit Estebán with his mind force?

Their grandfather runs into the room, dressed in Kung Fu clothes. "That's a funny place for cojones. What were you doing to Martín? He wouldn't just kick you in the balls!"

"Oh, nothing!" Estebán grumbles.

"Did he hurt you, Martín?" Sigún glances at the small boy, who signals no.

Estebán can feel his grandfather's eyes upon him. "I didn't do anything. Why do you always think I did wrong?"

"Estebán, you weigh forty pounds more than Martín and are two years older. You stay here and think. I'll take Martín to the Kwoon, where we will develop his self-defense skills. I would become friends with him."

Sigún undoes the Velcro straps on the wheelchair
and picks up the tiny boy. "Wow, Martín, you learn to
defend yourself faster than I can teach you. We'll work
on your kicking skills today." He starts for the door with
Martín's head against his shoulder.

"I want to come to the Kwoon. How come he gets to
go?" Estebán whines.

"No, Estebán. You will stay home until I know you
won't use what you learn in Kung Fu to hurt someone
smaller than yourself. I'll talk to your parents tonight."

"Why does the bastard get everything?" Esteban
yells as Sigún goes through the door, down the steps,
and walks the four blocks to the Kwoon at Fulton and
Parker.

"Esteban doesn't understand he condemns himself
with his own words." Sigún Gonzalez notices Martín
staring at the pocket of his own shirt. "Did Alex put
something in your pocket you want me to see?"

He signals yes with his eyes.

Abuelo squats in a grassy area and reaches into the
pocket of the little boy's shirt and unfolds the paper.

Dear Abuelo,

I keep having the same dream over and
over. We live in a blue house with a wood-
en ramp in front, in a town in the desert.
I go to the Prescott Public Library by
myself and the librarian helps me check

out books. Do you know what the dream
means?

                              Martín

Sigún puts the paper in his pants pocket. "No, I don't
know what the dream means, but I will think about it."
He picks up the boy, walks to the Kwoon, squats again,
and places his grandson on the mat.

Alex and Pedro, Martín's cousin, come rushing over.
Pedro is a short, stocky thirteen-year-old who, like his
sister Susana, eagerly took on Martín's care. They both
salute Sigún, who gives the two-handed salute back to
them. They belong to a six-person team. Sigún had giv-
en scholarships to the six in return for their labor.

"I want you three to practice rolling. Martín can
work on rolling from one end of the mat to the other.
Then he'll practice creeping. Five minutes, or he'll wear
himself out." Sigún walks toward another group of students dressed in black Kung Fu uniforms.

The boys put Martín at one end of the mat and encourage him to roll to the other. Then he rolls. He concentrates to get his body to do what he wants it to do.
On his stomach, he releases the muscles in his right arm
and pulls it above his head. Then he focuses on his left
knee, pressing it into the mat at the same time he presses down with left arm. The left side of his body rises.
He lies on his right side. Throwing his left arm behind
him, he flips to his back. He releases the muscles of his
left arm and drags it above his head. Then he brings his

right arm and leg across his body at the same time. The momentum turns him on his left side. After ten minutes he reaches the other side of the mat, and crows. The muscles in his shoulders feel tired and yet a lot looser. But his head hurts from concentrating so hard.

Pedro rubs his cousin's shoulders. "Wow, you gone farther than ever! Take a break and then we'll work on sitting up." He and Alex lie down beside him.

Martín resists the temptation to go into his daydream because he enjoys training with Alex and Pedro. His headache lessens as he breathes in and out.

"Let's get back to work." Pedro winks at the younger boy. "Do you want to try sitting on your own?"

Martín uses his eyes to signal a reluctant yes.

Pedro arranges his legs Indian style, sits him up with his back leaning against the wall, and takes his hands away from his shoulders. His shoulders slide to the left. Pedro catches Martín before his head hits the mat. "I guess you can't sit on your own yet. Let's try your creeping." Pedro lays him down and disentangles his legs.

Martín rolls over to his stomach and extends his arms in front of him. Alex puts slight pressure on the tiny boy's arms, and he pulls his body forward three inches. Alex lets go of his arms so he can extend them again. Martín becomes more aware that to move, he must let go of some muscles and tighten others at the same time. The pain in his head grows sharper.

Martín wakes up and looks around the small bedroom. He recalls having hit Estebán in the groin the
day before. As he looks around the room, he projects his
mind force at the curtain and brushes the curtain aside.
He can see the clear fall day outside. Pedro sleeps in
bed next to where his crib mattress lies on the floor. He
uses his mind force to brush the hair out of Pedro's face.
Pedro sighs and turns over, still asleep. Martín turns to
Estebán, beside Pedro. He doesn't like this cousin who
always bullies him, so without any compunction he gives
Estebán a harder brush. Nothing happens, so he does it
even harder. Estebán sits up, "Ow!" and rubs his face.
Martín works hard not to giggle and give himself away,
but he feels happy. Now he can get even with Estebán.

Later in the week, Sofía, Martín's mother, starts cooking
dinner with her sister-in-law, Sara. Susana walks into
the kitchen pushing Martín in his wheelchair. She parks
him near the stove. "What can I do to help?"

While the women start the meal, Martín takes a
good look at the room. He notices the bright orange
cabinets. Dark smudges show where people have opened
and closed them. He glances at a collection of old pho-
tographs on the cabinet nearest him. He sees a much
younger face of Abuelo and wonders about the identity
of the pretty Thai or Vietnamese woman standing beside him. After some thought he concludes she looks
a lot like his mother but not so tired. He decides to

call her Abuela when he sees her picture with a younger
Abuelo and Martín's mother and Tío Juan. They all sit
on the front steps of the house. Tío Juan looks about
fourteen and his mother looks like just a little girl.

"Susana, mi corazón, how did school go today?" Sofía
rinses the rice.

"It went well. We learn to do hard word problems in
math. I always enjoy math."

"Please put the bright blue tablecloth on the table.
We could use a change. Then set the table. It looks like
everyone will eat dinner." Sofía drains off the water and
pours the rice into a pot. Sara cleans the pinto beans.
Her light brown fingers push the beans across the table
until she stops to tuck in a wisp of white hair that escapes from her black bun. She looks Indian, short, and
heavy-set. She thinks nothing of carrying a fifty-pound
sack of rice six blocks from the food distribution center.
They plan to soak the beans to cook for tomorrow's supper.

"Sure, Tía." Susana walks into the dining room.

Martín feels his muscles soften in the warmth of the
kitchen. He shuts his eyes and imagines Superboy learning to kick in his kung fu class.

As Sofía starts making the salad, Sara gathers the
beans into a pot. She murmurs, "At Susana's age, I
walked from Tijuana to Santa Barbara with my parents
and four brothers looking for work. We came up from
Oaxaca. We found conditions in the Mexican camps so

bad, my parents decided to come farther north. Did you walk all the way from Denver?"

Martín shakes his head to come out of his fantasy and listen.

Sofía thinks back to her trip to Berkeley. "What a horrible time! I opened this damn notice the Wholly Aryan Government would terminate Martín when he turned five unless I could show he'd contribute to society." As she looks at her son, who feels warmer and a wave of relaxation passes through him, she remembers the tenseness of her body and the sick feeling in the pit of her stomach. She hadn't seen any options. But then she had decided they would never kill her son.

"Should he hear this?" Tía Sara looks worried.

"Yeah, he already knows." Sofía realizes she had never told anyone. "I didn't want to lose him. How could they know what a five-year-old might contribute or who he would become? At first I didn't know what to do. But then I kept thinking about my dad and this house where I grew up. We stayed out of contact. The *pinche* government wouldn't allow us to use personal phones and they monitored the pay phones. All of a sudden I knew I wanted to come to California to live with my dad. Here people of color with physical limitations can live until they turn eighteen before they confirm their worth to society. When the governor's daughter became disabled, they changed the law."

Tía Sara inquires, "Did you feel scared? I'll get you some water."

His mother glances at him and whispers, "I felt terrified, but what could I do?"

Susana comes into the kitchen and opens the silverware drawer.

Sofía's body trembles. "For six months, I saved the money from my waitressing job. My husband and I didn't pay our last month's rent. We sold our furniture and even our clothes. He called himself Gil Sanchez, a widower. On Saturdays, he took Martín on long walks to give me a break. He put us on the bus to Antonito. When I checked the envelope with the money, I realized he didn't keep a dime for himself even though he'd not get paid again for two weeks." She takes a sip of water.

"When the bus stopped at a checkpoint in Romeo, I felt so scared; I didn't know what to do. I walked away from the bus into the small town and ducked behind a garage." Sofía takes a deep breath. "Then I met an angel."

"A real angel, Tía?" Susana wonders.

"A real angel in a light blue work shirt with frayed cuffs. Now, every time I see frayed cuffs, I remember the angel and I know everything will turn out okay.

"He didn't ask any questions. An older Hispanic man invited us into his small wooden house. I can never forget that house. From the outside it looked tiny, no more than a small cottage. But when inside, I saw three large rooms filled with many plants. How strange to see so much green. His wife appeared with big plates with beans and tortillas. She put a bowl with red chili on the side. The food felt warm as if she expected us. When we could eat no more, she packed us some food and water. The angel took us to his truck. He drove down narrow roads without signs, and no cars passed us. He drove us south past the last checkpoint in Antonito." Sofía remembers. "Do you know when he drove away; I saw no dust and his tires left no mark."

"Then you met an angel." Tía Sara shakes her head.

"Yes. Oh, I almost forgot. As I climbed out of his truck, he handed me a twenty dollar bill. 'Por favor, take this. Your little one will stay safe.'" Sofía takes a sip of water.

"Twenty dollars equals a fortune these days, when nobody can earn cash!" Tía Sara stares at her.

"And as I walked south into New Mexico, I used his words as a mantra: 'My little one will stay safe. Martín will stay safe.' That night I dozed by the side of the road cradling my sleeping son to keep him warm. When we woke, m'ijo's muscles felt stiff; the only time he cried on the whole long trip, I massaged his arms and legs until he stopped. We ate a good breakfast from the food the angel's wife gave us. I walked south. The deep blue sky, the clear and crisp air, and the awesome quiet filled me with hope.

"In the late afternoon I came to a small village, called Tres Piedras, just an old rickety Mustang gas station, where I stopped to buy us sodas. I saw a young Pueblo man in a battered pickup stop for gas and requested a ride. He drove too fast and dropped us off at a rundown hotel in Taos, where we spent the night." Sofía pauses.

Tía Sara looks at the boy by the stove. "How did Martín do through all this?"

Sofía looks at her son. "M'ijo did well. He cried that one time. I just made sure he could see everything, and he seemed content."

Susana shakes her head, amused. "He still wants to see everything."

Sofía continues. "In the morning, I got up and walked out to a café on the highway to buy us both a good breakfast. I struck up a conversation with a young Filipino truck driver, who wanted to drive a beautiful woman down to Albuquerque. He didn't charge us any money but he flirted with me, a little."

Sofía shakes her head. "He went out of his way to drop us at the café truckers use, west of the city, on I-40."

Susana inquires, "How come all the drivers are Filipinos and Chinese? I thought they lived in ghettos like us. If they drive all the trucks, why don't they just drive away?"

"I don't know, m'ija, that's a good question. I paid a driver to take us to Los Angeles. Los Angeles felt like a weird place. As I walked to the bus station downtown, I saw very little traffic and no children playing in the street." Sofia scratches her head.

Susana looks worried. "Where did all the children go?"

Sofía responds. "Most died. The truck driver said even though Los Angeles was fifteen hundred miles from Mexico City, the wind blew the wrong way. One-fourth of all the children died soon after the bomb decimated Mexico City, and another quarter died of leukemia. Many older people died of cancer." She grimaces.

Tía Sara wants to know. "Why do you frown?"

Sofía shakes her head. "He said, 'The whites never took over Los Angeles because they didn't want to deal with all those people lacking medical care.'

"He warned me to hide most of my money, because rival gangs rule Los Angeles. They would demand a tax for passing through their territory. I paid four different taxes. After walking all day, I found a hotel near the bus station. I felt so tired and the bed looked so good, I didn't care what the room looked like. We stayed an extra night. Martín and I sponged off and collapsed on the bed. I slept for twelve hours.

"On our third day in Los Angeles, I managed to catch a bus to Ojai, just south of Santa Barbara. I felt scared to call my dad."

Tía Sara pipes in. "Why did you feel scared?"

"I don't know. I felt frightened for my son during the whole trip. Dad told me to wait there; he'd call me back. A long six hours later he phoned and said to stay in Ojai for three days. The fourth day we should start walking toward the gate into Santa Barbara. Sara, he told me, 'Your little one will stay safe,' just like the angel said."

Sofía takes a deep breath. "When I arrived at the gate, Dad held the right papers to get us through the checkpoint. Once I walked through the gate, I collapsed into Dad's arms. At last I felt safe. I said, 'M'ijo, your Abuelo will take us home.' I remember looking straight into my son's eyes. 'Dad, I call him Martín. He turned four and a half.'"

Susana interjects, "I bet Abuelo felt happy."

"He beamed when he told Martín he felt glad to meet him." Sofía glances at her son, who smiles back. "Martín felt safe in his grandfather's strong arms and cooed. We combined our money and paid a San Francisco-bound truck driver for a ride. I didn't speak much but I did tell him we lived in Denver and I wanted to keep Martín safe."

Sofía continues. "For most of the trip, Dad held and cuddled his newly-found grandson. They giggled together and connected.

"At one point, when my son fell asleep, Dad said, 'I miss your mother. I will miss her until I die.' He remained silent awhile. I squeezed his hand. Then he said, 'Juan and Sara walked down from Portland last year with their four children. With you two the house may seem crowded. We'll get along fine. They ration food and they put an electric fence around Berkeley. They require written permission for us to go to Oakland or El Cerrito. I remember when all the cities ran together.'

"Dad looked me in the eye. 'But at least now you and Martín will stay safer.'"

Back in the kitchen, Sofía realizes she had got caught up in her storytelling. She looks at the unchopped vegetables. "I won't make this salad tonight."

"I'll hurry and set the table." Susana runs to the dining room.

"I feel so glad you two came." Tía Sara gives Sofía a warm hug.

A week later, Martín hears an alarm go off; Pedro and his older brother dress in the dark and leave. He remembers they train in an advanced class at the Kwoon with Abuelo. Soon Tío Juan shakes his youngest awake. "Get dressed. I want you come to with Sofía and me to get our rations. It takes three people and Susana is finishing a book report. You can carry a lot."

"But, oh, yeah, maybe this will help me get off probation." Esteban puts on his clothes and runs after his dad.

Before long, Tía Sara turns on the light. "Buenos días, cómo amanaciste? That means, 'How did you wake?' Did your mother tell you I'll get you ready this morning?"

Martín remembers his ma saying something and signals yes.

"Please tell me what to do. I never did this before." She grabs his clean clothes, carries him to the bathroom and sits him in his special toilet seat. "Did you know I met your Tío Juan when I picked apples in south-

ern Washington? He taught at the night school where
I went to get my G.E.D." She takes off Martín's T-shirt
and wipes his face as well as his upper body with a wet
cloth. "Juan did everything carefully even then. He
waited to ask me out until I graduated."

Martín feels fascinated by her story. Yet he can't help
noticing how deftly she dresses him, puts him in his
wheelchair, and takes him to the kitchen. She didn't
ever do this before, but he feels reassured by her skill
and tenderness. His muscles relax.

As she feeds him oatmeal, Tía Sara continues speaking. "After a year of getting to know each other, we got
married in Olympia. Your grandparents and Sofía came
for the simple ceremony. She still attended high school.
Your abuela, a beautiful woman, welcomed me into the
family. I miss her. You never met her, but my children
loved her, particularly Pedro.

"After our honeymoon, we moved to Portland, where
Juan taught math in a high school and I worked as a
nurse's aide on a burn-unit."

Susana rushes in. "I'll take Martín to school, but I'll
leave now." Before they leave the kitchen, Tío Juan,
Sofía, and Esteban come bustling through the back door
loaded with groceries. Martín feels thankful his youngest cousin didn't see Tía Sara feeding him. He doesn't
want any more trouble with Esteban.

Martín survived one journey. He'll soon take a different journey toward independence.

Chapter 4
January 10, 2029

Tony McNamara, a twenty-one-year-old engineering student with dark brown hair, worries about keeping his own secret. He takes too many risks. He has worked in the rehab center at Stanford for two years, designing and testing a headband with microchips that operates an electric wheelchair with a built-in communication device. He has tried the device on five quadriplegics. The headband integrates the client's mind waves, sends them through the computer, and activates a speaker in the wheelchair.

Tony thinks about his own stepfather. No one "official" knows that Mike McNamara had adopted him. When the Pure White Brotherhood had come to power, they had forced everyone to register. Tony had checked the "White" box for racial group. He knew he could pass if no one looked too closely. He had passed all his life even with his olive complexion. He had wanted to continue his research and help people of color from the inside. Only he had helped too many.

The Latino nurse opens the door and peers around it to make sure Tony works alone in the room before wheeling in a young mixed race man, his third lesson on using the special headband. He had become quadriplegic from a diving accident. Tony wonders how the nurse keeps his job in the white ghetto.

Tony had smuggled this guy into the program because he wasn't white. In five years from the date of his accident he must prove he contributes to society. The other five quadriplegics were white, so the Brotherhood automatically allows them to live and gives them a generous monthly grant. Tony knows if the young man can drive his own electric wheelchair and speak, he can prove he can function independently.

Tony puts the headband on the fellow. "How do you feel today?"

After three minutes, he says, "I feel fine, thank you."

Tony undoes the brakes. "Do you want to try driving the electric wheelchair?"

The young guy responds, "Yes, and I hope I don't drive into any walls like I did last time." He clicks the headband into driving mode and starts maneuvering the chair out the doorway and down the hall. The chair moves jerkily but doesn't hit a single wall.

"Hey, you do better this time." Tony jogs to catch up with him.

The quadriplegic clicks the headband into conversation mode, "Yes, I seem to get the hang of it." He then clicks the headband back into the driving mode. He goes five feet, stops, and states, "I sure hope I can prove I can work productively enough to meet the Brotherhood's standards."

Tony scratches his head. "Can you live with your family in Berkeley?"

"Yes, they'll support me. My dad even learned how to change my catheter."

"And now you can drive an electric wheelchair, you meet the criteria of getting around by yourself. So then you just find a job you can work at four hours a day."

"I know a lot of people in Berkeley, but it won't be easy to find a job now."

"We'll see." Tony opens the door to the empty gymnasium so the young man can go through it.

He drives the chair around the large room. After fifteen minutes, he heads back to Tony's workshop. "I got tired. Concentrating so hard gives me a headache."

Tony holds the door for him. "You did much better today. I wonder if age and habit impact learning this. Do you think someone younger could learn even faster?"

The quadriplegic clicks the headband into talking mode. "I know a kid you could try it on, my kung fu teacher's grandson with cerebral palsy. I saw how fast he learns."

"He isn't white, is he?" Tony looks at him as he shakes his head and winks.

"Nope. You'll slip him into the program, taking all your favorite risks. I'll give you his number. Sigún teaches at the Kwoon every afternoon."

The next day, Tony calls the Kwoon and explains the project to Sigún Gonzalez.

Sigún speaks with a melodious voice. "Sounds great for my grandson, but I'll say no thank you. We don't earn enough to buy a computer so he can communicate at home."

Tony knows he can find funds to get the boy the equipment. The legislature had devoted an entire budget line for equipment for disabled quads when the governor's daughter had jumped out of a second story window, breaking her neck. Tony had appreciated the money, but had felt unsatisfied with the explanations as to why a twelve-year-old would jump out of a window naked. "When I can get the money together, would you come down to Stanford for a week so I can train Martín to use the headband?"

"Dr. McNamara, this sounds wonderful and I thank you for this offer, but neither of us can register as white, and they declared Stanford an all-white enclave. I'll hope for the best, but I won't share this with Martín until you give us more details." Sigún sighs.

He replies, "It will take me a few months to order the electric wheelchair for your grandson. I hear Martín learns quickly. I feel eager to test my device on someone so young. And please call me Tony." He shakes his head and wonders about the risk.

Martín sighs as he thinks about the five months since he first heard about the headband for the electric wheel-chair. Abuelo had felt too excited to keep the possibility a secret. He works at turning over to his stomach on his crib mattress, which lies on the floor in the bedroom he shares with his cousins.

Sofía raises her voice. "I want Martín to stay safe. Going to Stanford will put him in danger. Don't pretend you don't know the Brotherhood declared it a white enclave."

He has heard this argument for a week now.

Abuelo sounds exasperated. "You did not take so many brave risks just so he could die in Berkeley unable to prove his value to society, did you, m'ija? Now I must take risks to take advantage of this great opportunity."

Sofía doesn't hesitate. "I don't want him to attract the authorities' attention. They kill people of color with developmental disabilities. I brought him here to stay safe."

Sigún enunciates each word. "Enough other people live in Berkeley who use electric wheelchairs for Martín to be safe driving one here. I want to take advantage of this great opportunity for him. He won't get this chance again!"

The next morning, Martín feels tense and excited. He had celebrated his eighth birthday two weeks ago. Today he and grandpa will go to Stanford so he can try a new headband that will enable him to drive an electric wheelchair. Abuelo will take him without his mother's permission. He feels guilty disobeying his mother. He also worries because his family can't earn the money to buy him the chair.

After Sofía leaves for work, Sigún Gonzalez attaches two backpacks to Martín's wheelchair, and again pats his pocket with directions to the lab. They take BART to the San Francisco Airport, where a truck driver picks them up and drives them to Palo Alto through the evening traffic.

As the truck heads south, Martín imagines Superboy applying more gas as he drives and makes the truck go very fast on the freeway. He feels powerful. The wind blows in his face. He notices a police officer standing next to his motorcycle on the side of the road. The truck swerves and sends the policeman flying. Superboy roars with satisfaction. He sees a sign stating "Palo Alto" and starts slowing down the truck.

Abuelo stares at Martín. "I wonder where you go in your head."

Tony waits for them when they get off the truck. "I feel glad you two could make it. Here, let me carry your packs for you. It's a bit of a walk to Stanford Medical Center."

"Thank you." Sigún pushes Martín's wheelchair, walking beside Tony along the dark path.

"It took me four months to get the equipment. I feel eager for him to try the headband. I ordered an adult narrow electric wheelchair, which will give him room to grow. Tonight we'll work on a seat I will mold to his body. The chair will provide stability and Martín can concentrate on learning to drive. Tomorrow evening we'll try the headband. You two must stay out of sight during the day." Tony trudges along.

He slows by some bushes covering a hole in the chain link fence. "We'll go through here." Together Tony and Sigún maneuver Martín through the opening.

The next evening, Tony has just finished attaching the special seat for Martín's new chair when he hears Abuelo walk into the workshop. Although he is being pushed ahead of his grandfather, Martín looks ready to fly. "He buzzes with excitement," Abuelo explains.

"I feel excited myself. I want to see what Martín, the youngest person to try the headband, can do. We will soon see the true possibilities of this device." Tony looks at Martín with a twinkle in his eye. "Tonight, you could jump into this chair by yourself, but I'll just ..." He places him in the new seat and fastens the Velcro straps. Tony puts the headband on the boy.

With few instructions and fifteen minutes, Martín figures how to use it. "Abuelo, this device works like the talking computer at school, easy! Now do I get to drive?"

Tony laughs. "Slow down, eager beaver. Give yourself five minutes to rest and feel proud of what you figured out already. It takes me four or five evenings to teach an adult what you just learned in twenty minutes. Practice some of your breathing techniques while I prepare to teach you to drive."

Within the hour, Martín drives the electric wheelchair around the empty gymnasium. After he made his first two rounds, Tony stops the boy. "How do you feel?"

With no hesitation, Martín clicks the headband into talking mode. "I love driving myself and I feel jazzed, but why does my head hurt?"

"You work so hard. You learned in an hour what some can never master. Come, let's take the electric wheelchair to my workshop and you can rest until tomorrow. You made phenomenal progress."

Tony jogs ahead to open the door. As he looks out, he sees the Latino nurse and the hospital security guard walking down the hallway. Tony looks back at Sigún, winks, and turns off the light in the gymnasium and walks into the corridor.

As the two approach, his colleague points toward the physical therapy room. "I heard a noise coming from there," he says to the security guard.

Tony hurries to his workshop. He perspires even though the night feels cool.

The security guard opens the workshop door and steps into the room with the Latino nurse right behind him. "You sure work late. Did you hear anything strange? It looks like someone moved the equipment down the hall."

Tony nods. They leave. Tony lets out a huge breath.

Martín imagines Superboy taking a flying leap and knocking the guard flat.

Tony waits another five minutes before walking back to the gymnasium, where the kung fu master and his grandson sit in the dark. "The coast seems clear. My colleague distracted the guard. Let's get the wheelchair back to my workshop."

Abuelo follows Martín out of the darkened gymnasium. "You take great risks for us. Thank you."

"Please. I do this for Martín. He learns so fast, in no time he will live much more independently. But I do this for myself too. And the risk just makes my resolve much stronger." Tony wipes the back of his neck. "Let's stay focused, and by the end of the week, Martín can take the chair home."

"I know we discussed this over the phone, but Tony, I can't earn the money to buy either the chair or the headband. And now that I see the conditions you work under, we must discuss this." Abuelo doesn't sound happy.

"There's nothing here to discuss. I found funding. True, it is for white people. I discussed with you I found enough to pay for both devices. At the end of the week Martín can take them home." Tony wipes the perspiration from his forehead.

"Alright, we'll repay you someway. Thank you." Abuelo glances at his grandson.

Saturday morning, a Filipino drives his truck to the loading bay behind Stanford Medical Center. He uses his hydraulic lift to load Martín's electric wheelchair.

Martín activates his communication device, which from now on he will use to speak. "Tony, thanks. I can do anything now."

"Hey, Martín, you could always do anything; I just provided a chair. I feel glad I could do it. You taught me a great deal. Younger people learn to use the headband more easily, giving me great hope. I'll come to visit you in six months to make sure you do okay. By then, I hope I can share my new idea." Tony sighs.

Abuelo shakes Tony's hand and climbs into the back of the truck. "Thanks again, Tony. I'll keep your secret."

Tony waves as the truck pulls away. He wonders to which secret Sigún refers.

Sofía rushes out the door to greet them. "You, sin virguenza! You act without shame! I worried about you two all week. You took Martín to Stanford against my wishes! How could you do that to me?" Sofía's voice gets louder and louder.

"M'ija, please, calm down. I did what I thought right. Let's not fight. We both know I did it for Martín." Sigún struggles to keep his voice even.

All at once, Tío Juan, Tía Sara, Pedro, Pedro's older brother, Guillermo, and Susana come outside.

"He's my son, father. I brought him out here to keep him safe, and you put him in danger. Who gave you the right to decide for Martín?" Sofía sobs.

Martín activates his communication device. "Mama, please, we came back safely. Look, I can talk to you. Mama, I wanted to go."

Sofía's mouth drops open and tears flood her eyes. She had never heard her son speak out loud. "Martín, how did you do that?"

Martín takes a minute to key in his message. "I feel sorry you felt worried, please stop crying. Yes, I can talk now, but I can do so much more."

Sofía shakes her head, takes a deep breath. "My beautiful son, you can talk. Here, let me take you into the house."

Abuelo looks at Martín and holds his breath.

"Mama, look." Martín twirls the chair around on the sidewalk.

Now Sofía holds her breath.

"Mama, I can drive into the house myself with a ramp."

"Excuse me, hermanita, but for now we will all lift Martín. And don't worry about a ramp. Susana found a deserted garage in South Berkeley. We scavenged wood from it all week, a piece at a time. All the students from the Kwoon helped. We'll build Martín a ramp this week." Tío Juan puts his arm around Sofía.

Pedro walks over to the small boy in the electric wheelchair. "Wow, now you can go wherever you want."

Tío Juan raises his voice. "Let's get Martín inside."

They gather around the chair and lift it to the porch.

Chapter 5
October 2, 2029

On a sunny Saturday morning, Martín waits for Alex to walk up the ramp. They have both enrolled as freshmen at Berkeley High even though Alex has turned fourteen and Martín has just turned eight and a half. Martín drives his electric wheelchair all over town. The two friends have planned all week to go exploring the streets of Berkeley. Estebán, now ten years old, watches the two boys from a bush near the side of the house. He feels angry and jealous because Martín does better in school. Also, he won't forget the day Martín embarrassed him by banging him on the head.

"Let's roll." Alex taps the younger boy's shoulder.

"You bet. I want to see how far I can go." He clicks his headband into driving mode, and heads down the ramp.

"Thanks for recommending *The Fellowship of the Ring*. I just finished reading the last one, *The Return of the King*. I enjoyed it." Alex walks fast to keep up with him.

While they talk, Esteban takes off running to gather his friends to ambush them.

"I feel glad you liked it." Martín remarks, "I love how hope always appears. In the trilogy, even when all seems lost, good happens. Plus, I felt surprised to find out the identity of the king. I never guessed Strider."

"Yeah, Strider acted nobly all along. I like Legolas. He never says much, but he sacrifices for his friends." Alex moves his hands while he talks.

"You act a lot like Legolas, a great friend to me. I'll call my new electric wheelchair Shadowfax."

Alex recalls, "Gandolf called his horse that."

The two boys head toward Telegraph Avenue. Esteban and five other boys wait behind a building as the two unsuspecting boys start to cross the old UC Campus to get to University Avenue. Three boys get ahead of the two friends and three boys spring out of the bushes behind them, cutting off their retreat. Alex looks at Martín. They rush the three boys ahead. At the

Kwoon, Martín has trained in using his wheelchair for self-defense. He drives into his cousin, using his foot plate to hit Estebán's shins and his mind force to make the larger boy's fall hard while Alex kicks the other two boys. When Martín and Alex turn to fight the others, the bullies run away.

The two friends take off full speed toward University Avenue. Once sure no one follows them, Martín stops his chair. "Wow, that felt rough. Did they hurt you, Alex?"

Alex stops and wipes the sweat from his forehead. "I feel fine. I don't think Estebán realizes how much we learned in the past three years. And you?"

"I feel scared about tonight. I still share a bedroom with Estebán. My other cousins treat me well, but he scares me."

"Martín, now you beat him in a fight. Do you still feel afraid? You can catch more flies with honey than with vinegar." Alex tilts his head. "You two could become friends."

"Do you know how?" Martín rolls alongside Alex.

"Next Saturday we'll invite Estebán to come with us when we go exploring. I know he feels jealous of you, but maybe if you paid attention and listened to him, he'd open up and you could find out what makes him tick." Alex taps Martín's shoulder.

Martín stops driving his wheelchair. "It just might work. I'll think it through." He starts rolling alongside the older boy again. Martín realizes he can use his mind force against him if becoming his friend doesn't work.

Later, after Esteban goes to bed, Martín experiments. He can turn his mind force into a blue light and explore a person's inner body, bones, blood vessels, and nerves. But what happens if he focuses on an injury? He locates the bruise on one of Esteban's shins, the right one. The bruise begins to dissolve.

The next Saturday, Esteban waits with Martín when Alex comes up the ramp. Esteban looks at Alex. "Do you feel sure you two want me to come with you after what happened last week?" He bends down and rubs his left shin, but not the other.

Alex replies, "Yes. Martín?"

Martín looks down at the ground. "Yeah, I guess."

"Alright then, I'll come along." Esteban looks at Alex, then at the ground and scuffs his shoe. "But I still don't think it seems fair," he mutters almost to himself.

"What doesn't seem fair?" Alex insists.

Esteban looks right at Martín. "Why do you get to go to special places with Grandpa?"

"Esteban, don't you know I'd much rather dress and feed myself like you do, than get to go places with Abuelo?" Martín clicks his headband into driving mode and rolls down the ramp with Alex walking beside him.

"Yeah, okay, but no one ever built anything for me." Estebán kicks a stone, which rolls down the handmade ramp.

"Esteban, do you want them to build you a ramp? Don't you get it? You can *walk* up and down. Martín's wheelchair doesn't climb stairs."

Esteban stops, his hands in his pockets. "I'll go now. I feel tired of Martín and all his specialness." He walks away.

As the two friends walk north on Fulton Avenue, Alex glances at Martín. "Don't worry. He won't change overnight, but he'll think about what we said."

Chapter 6
June 15, 2030

Nine months later during the summer, Martín wakes up in a strange hospital bed in a strange room smelling like antiseptic. When he moves his head, it hurts like hell. Bandages pad it. To keep still, he uses a relaxation technique his grandfather has taught him.

Tony McNamara trudges into the room. "I feel glad to see you awake. I know your head hurts, but the pain will lessen and in a couple of days it will leave. Would you like some water?" The rehab engineer raises the little boy's head with one arm as he holds a glass with a straw with the other.

A wave of pain floods over Martín and his face pales. He shuts his eyes until it passes. He sips water, which feels cold and refreshing in his dry, parched mouth. He remembers Tony's nurse and the trip to the guy's mother's house in San José.

Tony and a brain surgeon had asked Martín to come to San José for an experimental procedure. They had implanted three computer chips inside Martín's head to replace his headband. One chip interfaces with his computer and his communication device. The second chip allows him to drive his electric wheelchair, and makes the chair more responsive. They had experimented with the third chip. It allows him to reduce the tension in his muscles in small increments when he triggers it. But Martín can't receive surgery at Stanford Medical Center, so he stays at the Latino nurse's house in San Jose.

Martín takes another sip of water and closes his eyes. As he falls asleep, he feels aware that Tony puts down his head and tiptoes out of the room. He doesn't see the look of admiration Tony gives him before shutting the door.

A week later, Abuelo comes to Martín's room in San José. "Buenos días, I made it down. My supervisor wouldn't give me time off." He gives his grandson a hug.

The nurse had removed most of the bandages. "Hola, Abuelo. Glad you could make it. I'll go see Coyote Yakushi, a healer and meditation master. I want you to come with me." The boy watches to see his grandfather agree before he heads down the street.

"Hey, wait up. How do you feel? You drive the chair much more smoothly." Abuelo jogs to catch up.

"I feel fine. My head hurt a lot the first few days. Now I feel jazzed because I can control the chair and the communication device more easily. Now I'll work with Coyote on keeping my body more mellow." The small boy drives three blocks until he comes to a small wooden house.

"I could only get two days off, so I'll head back to Berkeley tomorrow night." Sigún shakes his head. "The Brotherhood gets more and more repressive." Coyote opens his front door and leads them into the house, which smells of incense and curry.

When Coyote, a Shin Jin Jitsu teacher in his thirties, wearing crisp khakis, a yellow sports shirt, and a red ribbon woven into the single black braid down his back, greets them at the door, Martín sees recognition pass between Abuelo and the healer. He assumes they have met before and sees a similarity about them making them seem like brothers although they look nothing alike. Coyote lifts him with such gentleness his headache disappears. Coyote puts him cross-legged on a mat with his back against the wall. "Martín accomplished a great deal with this simple pose.

"Today you seem to sit more easily than you did yesterday. Someday you'll sit without leaning against the wall. You learn fast."

Did he hear the healer add, as quietly as his footsteps, *and then one day, you shall walk?*

Coyote turns to Sigún. "Like most people with cerebral palsy, your grandson's body gets very tense and his muscles get hard, which hurts. I teach him relaxation techniques to use in conjunction with the chip in his head, a meeting of the old and the new. Since you teach Kung Fu, you can continue training Martín." He bows with his two palms together.

"Yes, Martín wanted me to come with him today for that reason." Abuelo sits cross-legged on the mat. "I hope to learn as quickly. I'll head back tomorrow."

"Then let us make it so Martín can go home with you." Coyote kneels on the mat and lights a candle, which he puts four feet in front of his small student. "Now, Martín, as you watch the candle flame, imagine yourself entering the flame, becoming one with its gentle light. As you feel its warmth, let your breathing slow down."

Five minutes pass. Abuelo and Martín both relax.

Coyote's voice sounds calm and steady. "Now, find the place in your body where your muscles feel the most tense, visualize that place, see its color, and breathe right into that spot. At the same time, click the muscle tone reducer. Feel how that changes the tension in your muscles. Do you see how much more effective it functions when under your control?"

He nods.

Coyote works with him for an hour. "With this breath, move outside your body and back into the room. Feel yourself leaning against the wall, and notice the floor supporting you. For now you finished your work. Bring yourself to us in the present."

Martín sighs and focuses on the electric wheelchair on the other side of the room. Practicing what his operation made possible, he activates the built-in communication device from the mat. "Wow, Coyote, my body feels more comfortable."

"You must not trigger your muscle tone reducer automatically but use it with your breath intentionally." Coyote squats beside him. "You accomplished a lot today." He picks up the boy.

Martín laughs as his wheelchair arrives beside him. Coyote puts him in the chair.

Abuelo stands with delight. "Look at you, Martín, you can call your wheelchair to come to you without sitting in it."

"Wait until you see all the things I can do, Abuelo."

As he and his grandfather leave, he hears Coyote say, *And you will become less of a good boy and more human to become a healer.* Martín wonders what he means.

Chapter 7
July 10, 2030

"Can Martín come, too?" Alex looks at Guillermo, Martín's oldest cousin, a heavy-set, twenty-year-old with black curly hair, dark brown eyes, and olive skin.

Guillermo, with a fierce grin, squats down and looks his cousin in the eye. "Martín, you can't tell Abuelo. Whether or not I let you come, do you promise not to tell him anything?"

Martín responds, "Don't worry, Guillermo. I won't tell either way."

Guillermo looks at Alex. "We'll take a risk. Will you carry him and care for him?"

"Of course. No sweat." Alex turns to Martín.

"And I'll help, too." Pedro messes up Martín's hair with his hand before lifting him. He slides him into the special backpack with holes for his legs Alex holds. Pedro supports him in the backpack as Alex turns around and puts his arms through the straps. "Here, Alex. You better take this." He hands him a baseball cap. "No, not for Martín, estupido; it's for you. You look too black to pass for Latino in San Leandro. This should help you stay invisible."

Alex adjusts Martín on his back and whispers, "I know you hate leaving your electric wheelchair, but I figured you'd want to come."

"Yeah and just so you know, they could arrest you. I hold papers to go to San Leandro, because of my job, but you three don't." Guillermo leads the way down the steps to the BART station on Shattuck Avenue.

"No big deal. The Brotherhood reserved San Leandro for Asians and Latinos. Since we belong to both groups, we'll fit right in, except for Alex." Pedro smirks. As they reach the BART platform, a train to San José pulls into the station.

Guillermo lifts Martín out of Alex's backpack and sits down, holding him in his lap. "I worry about leaving the BART station. Once we hit the street we'll blend in fine."

Martín takes a deep breath and scans his own body. Most of his body appears lavender. An orange glow mirrors his excitement about the journey, and a red spot shows tension in his neck and right shoulder. The older guys hadn't ever included him in their adventures. Except for Alex they wouldn't include him now. He triggers the relaxation chip, which sends attention to his neck. After a few moments he still feels excited but the red became magenta and the orange glow toned down to peach blossom.

Pedro sits next to Guillermo. "How did you meet these people in San Leandro?"

Guillermo glances at Alex, who sits in front of them. "I work with a guy at the hospital, Sammy Manzanares. We help each other out when things get crazy. His mother, a master of these arnís sticks, teaches this class."

Soon the boys exit the BART station. Pedro carries Martín on his back. A crowd jostles to get out. Guillermo flashes his pass, and the busy guards wave the four of them through the exit gate. He leads the way at a fast pace through the outdoor market to the Catholic Church. On this Saturday the plaza bustles. Winding their way through the worshippers, they go through the church, walk several blocks and arrive at the gym.

A group of twenty-five young men and women—Filipinos, a few Chinese, and several Latinos—train, dressed in street clothes or black T-shirts and black cotton pants.

Sammy Manzanares steps forward and grasps Guillermo's hand. "I feel happy you came. Let me introduce you to my mother." He steps toward a stocky Filipina woman in her forties dressed in black pants and a black gee. "Ma, Guillermo Gonzalez works with me."

"Welcome. I call myself Maestra Manzanares. You must be one of Sigún Gonzalez's grandsons." She extends her hand.

"Yes, and let me introduce you to Pedro and Martín, two more of his grandsons, and our friend Alex Mori-Brown." Guillermo points toward each person.

Maestra Manzanares stares at Martín a second before turning toward her senior student. "Will you work with Pedro and Guillermo? Teach them the first four arnís points and blocks."

"Yes, Maestra. Sammy brought extra arnís sticks." The student bows.

Maestra Manzanares signals Sammy, and they both take a step toward Alex, who lifts Martín out of Pedro's backpack. "Sammy will teach you the first four arnís points and blocks."

Nearby, two students face each other. Martín feels surprised to see his friend Tony McNamara. They beat out an intricate pattern of strikes and counter-strikes in a quick rhythm. The clicking sound of the sticks sounds soothing and musical. Maestra turns to a heavy-set boy. "Son, use this opportunity to work on control."

"Yes." Sammy bows toward his mother.

"Great, just let me set Martín down so he can watch us." Alex places Martín on a mat with his back against the wall, and arranges his legs in a cross-legged position. He stands and steps toward Sammy.

Sammy salutes Alex. "I feel honored to teach you." Alex returns the salute. Then Sammy hands Alex two eighteen-inch arnís sticks, keeping two for himself.

Tony runs over to Martín. "Hey, Martín, I feel surprised and glad to see you here. We'll talk after class. I should get back to sparring."

Maestra Manzanares checks whether each student trains with a partner before she squats in front of Martín. "I'd like to work with you. May I see you signal yes."

As he looks up and to the right, a thrill runs through his body. He expected to watch and now this great arnís master will teach him.

"Would you like to work with me?" She sits on the mat.

Martín signals yes.

"Do you hit people or project force with your thoughts?"

He hesitates a few seconds before signaling yes.

She searches his eyes. "I felt the force of your thoughts when Guillermo introduced you. Does your grandfather know you can hit people with your thoughts?"

He looks down and to the left, signaling no.

"Don't worry; I'll keep your secret. I'll let you tell him when you feel ready." She holds up her open hand. "Go ahead, hit it."

He looks at the hand. A thick and silent path seems to weave itself between him and the maestra. Energy passes through it, and the teacher's hand moves.

"You hold a most considerable gift. Let's work so you become the master of it. It can assist you the rest of your life." She reaches out and gently cups his head. "We'll practice today turning it off and on so it will not take control of you."

On the way back to Berkeley, Alex holds Martín in his lap. "You worked with Maestra Manzanares a long time. Do you feel tired?"

He signals yes and leans against Alex, feeling warmth and love from his friend's beating heart.

Alex looks at Guillermo and Pedro, seated on the other side of the door, and continues speaking to Martín in a low voice. "I feel tired, too. Sammy knows how to teach. A couple of times I hit him too hard. He laughed and told me we seem the same, very powerful but we want to learn control. I can't imagine how it would feel to work with his mother. She and his dad began the school years ago. When the Brotherhood shot her husband dead, she decided to keep it going."

Martín feels tired. He wants to learn this control Maestra spoke about. And he wonders how Superboy would use his mind force.

"Okay, Martín, what did you do?" Guillermo squats beside him the next Sunday morning. "Sammy said his mother wants you and Alex to go to the gym this morning. The master never invites anyone."

Martín declares, "I didn't do anything. Maestra helps me develop my special gift."

Guillermo looks Martín in the eye. "What special gift?"

"I don't feel ready to tell you. Even Abuelo doesn't know."

Guillermo shakes his head. "You seem like one weird dude. You look like you can't do much because you appear crippled and stuck in that wheelchair. Hell, you don't even talk. But one day, you'll do something great no one else can do. And the stupid white government won't even suspect you." Guillermo's hand brushes Martín's shoulder. "I'll feed you breakfast. Alex will arrive in half an hour. Pedro will come, too."

Soon the four boys make their way through the worshippers in the Catholic Church near the San Leandro BART station.

Pedro whispers, "Why do we always come through the people attending Mass instead of going around the building?"

Guillermo speaks in a low voice. "Sammy told me to come this way for security."

"Ah, so." Pedro bows toward his brother and laughs, as they exit through the side door.

Inside the gymnasium, Maestra Manzanares, her senior student, her son, and a young girl wait for them. Maestra steps forward. "I feel happy you four came." She gestures toward the petite girl. "My student, Lark, will help me work with Martín while these students teach you three the next set of arnís points and blocks."

Martín realizes he missed the rhythmical clicking of the sticks. His hands begin to tingle when the boys spar. All at once he sees Superboy standing, arnís sticks in his hand. Legions of White Brotherhood try to pass, but Superboy's elegant blows stop them.

Lark steps toward Martín and bows. "May I take you out of the backpack?"

He signals yes.

Lark deftly lifts him out of the backpack and carries him to a mat near the back wall. She sets him down where he sat during his first lesson.

Sammy bows toward Alex, hands him two arnís sticks. They stride toward one corner as if they had sparred together for years. The head student bows toward Pedro and they walk toward a different corner.

Guillermo tags along behind, skipping backwards as he stares at Lark. "She's beautiful. How come Martín gets to work with her?"

Pedro taps Guillermo on the shoulder. "C'mon. We got a lot to learn." The young man hands out the sticks.

When satisfied, Maestra joins Lark on the mat. "Martín, I thought about your gift. Your ability to project force with your thoughts will make you powerful and put you in the path of danger. You are still a young boy and we must take responsibility for your safety. I must tell your grandfather about this skill. I wanted to tell you first."

He feels relieved.

"So, do you agree that I tell him?"

Martín hesitates. If Abuelo finds out then he must use his mind force for good, but then he signals yes.

"Good. Let us get on with the lesson. Lark gained experience working with people with developmental disabilities. She'll help me teach you the first eight arnís points. You will focus on these particular points, and aim for them when an opponent attacks you. Instead of sticks, you will use the force of your thoughts."

Lark sees him staring at her skin, the color of honey, and her hair in a long braid down her back. "Do you wonder why I do this? My brother Tommy..." She stops and places a hand on his shoulder. "You don't seem so different, but you must learn to defend yourself. After I saw my brother killed, I made this my work."

Lark reminds Martín of the statue of Kuan Yin on an altar at the Kwoon. She told him a small part. She looks like a graceful crow feather in her black T-shirt and pants.

Maestra inquires whether he can read.

Martín feels amused, and signals yes.

"Good. Then I will give you an assignment. You must get hold of a book on human physiology and study the nervous and circulatory systems, also, one on Chinese pressure points. I will meet with your grandfather and bring Coyote, a Japanese-Mexican healer, or curandero, from San José." Maestra feels Martín's thoughts flow toward her. "Do you know him?"

He signals an emphatic yes.

"Good. He will tell us if you can use your gift for healing as well as for protecting yourself. Lark, please teach Martín the first point."

Lark, on her knees, bows toward the older woman. "Yes, Maestra." She turns to the small boy. "First a warning: I will teach you these points. You may touch them with the lightest tap, unless you find yourself in a life or death situation. Agreed?"

He thinks about killing some Brotherhood soldiers then looks up to the right.

Lark sees him pause before answering. "Martín, does your hesitation mean you can imagine killing white soldiers?"

He answers yes with his eyes.

"All of us who care think those kinds of thoughts. You will soon get to the point where you could kill someone, but sooner or later you would get caught. They would torture and kill you and your family." She waits a few seconds then adds, "Right after they killed Tommy, I wanted to kill all the white soldiers I could find. After Coyote, the healer, came to visit my father in the hospital, he suggested we take a walk. He told me I would become just like what I hate. So I would become brutal and callous like the soldiers who just follow orders if I continued to hate them. He also said I must never kill except in self-defense. Killing a person wounds the soul. We're too young to understand, but I trust Coyote."

Martín also knows and trusts the healer.

"This is the first arnís point," she points to her left temple.

On the way to the BART station, Martín ponders the sentence "Killing a person wounds the soul." He realizes he doesn't know what a soul is. Who can he ask?

On BART, Pedro holds him in his lap. "I don't mind holding you. I'll practice for when I raise children. I want to become a good father like Abuelo and my dad."

Martín wonders whether he'll become a father. He hopes so. He questions the identity of his father. He knows the man his mother had lived with in Denver, Gil Sanchez. But she does not talk about him. Martín remembers that Gil had taken him to a movie about dolphins. He had felt amazed seeing the creatures swimming. He looks at his own skin. He decides his father would look darker than Gil.

Guillermo hits Martín's shoulder none too gently. "I hope you enjoyed working with that beautiful girl."

Martín, startled, hesitates before signaling yes.

Alex pipes in. "Guillermo, cool it. Sammy looks out for her. He loves her and you don't want to tangle with him. I spar with him, I should know."

"What's he like?"

Alex thinks. "Sammy feels things intensely and gets focused. He seems patient and gentle, but I wouldn't want to fight him because he's strong and knows his stuff. I'd like to become his friend."

Pedro wonders, "Do you think he'll turn into a good parent?"

Alex considers. "Sammy will grow into a good parent because his own mother seems like one. Maestra Manzanares wants the best for her son and her students, besides treating them with firmness and patience. Pedro, what's this good parent stuff?"

Pedro blushes. "I dated girls. They get serious too fast, like they want to get intimate. I don't want to do that. What if she gets pregnant? I don't know about getting married. Hell, I don't know if I'll survive re-education. How would I support a kid?"

Guillermo turns to him. "Slow down. Don't do anything before you feel ready. I know just what you mean. I feel scared Susana might get pregnant. The law's crazy. If she's not married, she's a whore and they'll kill her. Here's our station."

Martín rests his head on Guillermo's shoulder. He wonders when he'll ever meet his father.

Martín feels nervous because his mentors will come together. As he approaches the Kwoon he sees two of the people he respects the most and wonders how they will answer his questions.

Sigún shakes Maestra Manzanares' hand. "I feel delighted to see you."

"Sigún, I met three of your fine grandchildren."

"And you raise a wonderful son." Abuelo bows toward Coyote and opens the door. "Please come inside where we can talk safely."

She sees Martín drive up the ramp. "You hold many skills. I didn't realize you get around so well."

Martín beams, "Yes, and I learned how to make this machine talk for me."

"That explains your great focus."

Martín turns toward Coyote and bows. "Hello, I feel pleased seeing you again."

"And I feel great joy seeing you. Maestra told me you practice with your muscle tension reduction chip."

"Yes, I experiment with reducing the tension in my muscles. I challenge myself to relax without becoming too floppy." He pauses. "Abuelo, I wonder about something."

"Sure, Martín."

The little boy responds, "Coyote, Lark told me you said, 'Killing someone wounds the soul.' What did you mean?"

Coyote pauses. "Yes, but who do you want to kill?"

He declares, "For a start, all White Brotherhood soldiers."

Coyote starts to speak but Maestra interrupts, "Excuse me, but Martín showed me he can hit people with the force of his thoughts. This can develop into a dangerous gift, and I taught him how to turn it off and on." She looks at Abuelo. "Very soon, I decided to tell you. Forgive me for waiting. As for you, my friend," she looks at Coyote, "I feel curious whether Martín could also use the gift for healing."

He speaks, "Yes, you, Martín, hold potential to become a great healer, all the more reason you cannot kill. Your sacred gift would become corrupted if you killed anyone even in the extreme case of self-defense.

"But to get back to your original question, Martín, we consist of our body, mind, heart, soul, and spirit. As you grow older and become an adult, you'll integrate those five elements. Whenever we kill a person, we do serious damage to our souls. The younger the individual is when they kill their first person; the harder it is to recover. Studies show few child-soldiers in Africa reintegrate into society." Coyote sighs.

Martín furls his eyebrows. "I'll find a way to put people to sleep quickly."

Sigún speaks quietly. "My daughter brought him to California just before his fifth birthday because the authorities scheduled him for termination in Colorado. My grandson, even with severe cerebral palsy, learns faster than anyone I met. That he holds other gifts doesn't surprise me. I ask for all the advice you can give me on how to help him develop these talents and grow into a whole person. Also, we'll protect him from killing anybody so he can mature."

After a minute of silence, Coyote relates, "When I taught Martín to use his muscle tone reduction chip, I saw he can project both a positive healing force and a negative defensive force with his thoughts. He uses that healing force within his own body."

Maestra adds, "I suggested he study the nervous and circulatory system."

After another period of silence, Coyote adds, "I'll move to Prescott, Arizona, in three months. I want Martín to study with me."

A shiver runs down Martín's spine at the mention of "Prescott, Arizona." He feels glad he told Abuelo about his dream.

Sigún muses. "Prescott may prove the answer to keeping my grandson safe."

Coyote continues. "In the meantime, although he could study with old Master Alex Fong here, he could better use his time to study on his own and keep a low profile. Martín, with so much potential, can't defend himself yet. He must do nothing to attract attention. Do you agree?"

Abuelo and Maestra nod. A few minutes pass in silence. Then Abuelo salutes the group and lifts the small boy into his chair. He instructs Martín. "Go on home and eat supper. Tell your tía to keep some food for me."

"Yes, Abuelo." Martín bows to the three teachers before wheeling out. As he rolls away, he wonders if he's hearing Coyote whisper, *Martín, you hold a dark side which can do mean and cruel deeds. When will you talk about it with your grandfather?*

Martín still feels excited five days later. He rolls toward the Kwoon to meet Lark. Maestra Manzanares decided it seemed safer for her to come to Berkeley than for Martín to go to San Leandro. Sammy and Lark wait when Martín rolls up the ramp.

Martín doesn't know Sammy and decides to check him out. "Welcome to the Kwoon."

Both teenagers stare at him, but Sammy recovers first. "How did you do that?"

Martín grins. "Tony McNamara put some computer chips inside my head, which I use to drive my chair and talk with my communication device."

Lark exclaims, "That's super."

He glances down. "Sammy, Tía Sara put the key to the Kwoon in the pocket of my shirt. Will you open the door for us?"

Sammy bows. "Y'know, I'll gladly do it." He finds the key, opens the door, and puts the key back in Martín's pocket. "I'll keep a watch out here while you two work.

Martín sees Sammy fade into the shadows before he rolls in and salutes Lark.

Lark scratches her head. "Martín, does the force you use to hit my hand seem different from what you use to drive your chair?"

He thinks a minute. "As long as I can remember, I held the force I use to hit people and I can use it for other things, but I just now learn to control it. They put the chips in my head about seven weeks ago. Both Coyote and Maestra recognized I hold the other force and started training me to use it. So they seem separate."

She looks at him. "Today, let's work on using the force to avoid blows. I'll hit you with this arnís stick and I want you to block it." She draws the arnís stick out of a pocket in her pants along her calf. She starts to strike him, and he sends the stick soaring.

She says, "You threw a great block, but try preventing the arnís stick from hitting you without sending it flying. When the Brotherhood attacks, you want to send their weapons airborne, but when you just spar, practice deflecting blows without people knowing you do it."

Martín concentrates on keeping the stick from hitting him.

About twenty minutes later, Sammy carries a boy about twelve into the Kwoon. "This fellow tells me he knows you."

Martín sees tears fill Esteban's eyes, his clothes torn and one leg injured. Sammy puts him down on the mat.

Martín rolls his wheelchair over. "Yes, that's my primo, Esteban. He's Pedro and Guillermo's younger brother." He does a quick scan of his cousin's body. Except for the knee, Martín just finds minor scrapes and bruises. The joint starts to swell.

Esteban groans. "I threw boxes of food off the back of a truck when the driver hit the gas and I went flying. I figured I would rest here before trying to get home." He looks around at the young people. "Do I know you?"

Sammy looks at him. "Excuse me. I call myself Sammy and she calls herself Lark. Y'know, I work with your brother Guillermo."

Esteban groans again. "My knee hurts a lot."

Martín takes a deep breath. "I can do something, but each of you must promise never to tell anyone."

Lark looks him in the eye. "I see you as one of the Special Ones like my brother, Tommy, so I'll never tell."

Sammy states, "My ma taught me to value everyone's gifts and she says you hold some special ones. So, y'know, I won't tell."

Esteban clears his throat. "I don't like you. Abuelo gives you all the attention and you do better in school than I do. But you're my primo, so I'll never betray you."

Martín sighs. "I'll go into a trance for a while."

"I'll go outside and keep watch. You never know whether someone followed Esteban here." Sammy bows and goes out the door.

Lark takes a small vial of pills out of her pocket and shows it to Martín. "Arnica reduces swelling. Shall I give Esteban one to put under his tongue?"

"Sure." Martín goes into a trance. He heals other kids' cuts and bruises without telling them just so he can figure out how to do it. He brings his blue light to Esteban's knee and stops the bleeding, and then he starts the healing process in the torn tissue. He drains the blood, but soon his blue light grows dimmer. When he comes out of his trance, he feels very hungry.

Estebán says, "I don't know what you did, but it doesn't hurt so much. I owe you."

Martín shakes his head. "I can do no more for now. I feel weak from hunger."

Lark seems pensive. "Sammy can carry Estebán home. I'll go get him." She motions for Martín to follow her. Outside, she turns to Martín. "Do you use your gift in another way?"

"Yes, but I want to get to Prescott, Arizona. Coyote will move there. He can teach me how to use it."

A couple days later, Sofía runs up to Lark, who watches a building on Allston Way and Shattuck Avenue. Lark informs her, "An hour ago, a refrigerated truck stopped in front of the whites-only clinic and soldiers took a box inside. Then they left."

Sofía catches her breath. "My informant said they would deliver it today. We'll steal the vaccine this evening. The Brotherhood spreads a new flu and we want to vaccinate our at-risk-people, like Martín and our older folks. Do you want to help me?"

Lark grins. "Sure, but can you find another person to keep watch?"

Sofía looks at the sky and opens her backpack. "I made you some sandwiches. I'll return in a couple hours. I'll ask my sister-in-law. I wanted to get her involved for a while."

Lark opens the bag. "Guillermo said his mother's okay, but his dad seems to put safety first."

"Yeah, I can't believe he's my brother. I'll see you later." Sofía runs off.

Lark bites into the sandwich and realizes she feels famished. She remembers to savor each bite. She doesn't miss school. She'd dropped out right after Tommy died, when she realized her teachers no longer were trying to teach. She feels glad she joined the martial arts school. Maestra Manzanares requires that her students write book reports, do study projects, and participate in a weekly discussion group. She grins inwardly. Between Sofía and Maestra she learns a lot, just not the old-fashioned education.

After dark, Sofía returns with an older Latina. Susana looks like her. Sofía introduces her. "Tía Sara will keep watch for us." Lark and Tía Sara shake hands.

Lark whispers, "Four people left at six o'clock sharp, and I saw no one go in. So hopefully we'll get out okay." They walk toward the clinic, a block away.

Sofía turns to Tía Sara at the corner. "Take this whistle to blow if you see anyone enter the clinic. After you blow it, use a roundabout route back to your house and we'll meet you there." Tía Sara nods.

Lark and Sofía run to the back of the clinic, and Sofía jimmies the door with a tire iron. They close the door behind them and run through the clinic to the pharmacy. Lark sees a refrigerator. Again Sofía uses the tire iron to bust the lock. When Sofía takes off her backpack, they hear Tía Sara blowing the whistle. Sofía crams two boxes of vials into her backpack. Lark hands her two packets of syringes. "Here take these."

They hear men at the front door and head toward the back door, where a man stands with a flashlight. Before Lark takes a flying leap, she tells Sofía, "Run, I'll take care of him!" As the two crash together, Sofía takes off running.

Lark, stunned by a blow to her face, manages to stay right against the guy until her head clears. She knees him in the groin and pulls the flashlight away from him, as he folds at the waist. She hits him with it several times in the back of the head and takes off running east to the old UC campus.

As she runs across campus, she realizes she still grasps the flashlight and so she throws it into a dumpster. Tía Sara and Sofía wait on the front porch of their house when Lark collapses in their arms, out of breath. She gasps. "Please go get Martín."

When Sofia carries him out of the house, Lark whispers, "Martín, I'll let them know your secret. I want you to check me out. My face hurts."

He nods okay and looks at his mother and Tía Sara before going into a trance as Lark sits on the steps. She decides to meditate on her breath until she feels a tingling on the side of her face and then in her left shoulder. He comes out of the trance and moans.

Lark whispers, "Wow, I feel better already. Thanks, Martín." She turns to Sofía. "When he does this work, he gets very hungry. I suggest you make him a milk-shake."

Sofía looks at her son. "Okay, I'll see what I can find." She carries him into the house.

Tía Sara turns to Lark. "You live in San Leandro, right? I'll ride BART with you and make sure you get home."

On BART, Tía Sara and Lark find themselves seated in an empty train car. Lark confides, "I fought for the Resistance two years. I joined after my thirteenth birth-day. A year after my brother got killed." Tears fill her eyes. "He got terminated for living with a developmen-tal disability."

Tía Sara puts her arm around the teenager. They ride in silence for a few minutes until Lark asks, "When did you join the Resistance?"

Tía Sara answers. "Tonight I did my first action. I just live in a house with other involved people. I suspect my oldest two sons and my father-in-law. My young-est son steals food with a gang. I don't know about my daughter. My husband does all things way too cautious-ly." Her voice trails off until she inquires, "How did you join?"

She responds, "Maybe I shouldn't tell you this, but I feel like I can trust you. I started training at a martial arts school, where I met my friend, Sammy. His mother runs the school. She asked me to join the Resistance when I seemed ready. Seven months ago, she paid me the honor of assigning me to Sofía's crew."

The BART train pulls into San Leandro. Lark feels relieved when she hears Sammy's whistle as she leaves.

Martín ponders his questions for another ten days. He just ate breakfast, when he sees his grandfather sitting on the sofa reading a book. "Abuelo, can we go for a walk?"

Sigún looks up. "Sure, let's go." Using a bookmark to designate his place, he puts his book on the end table and strides to the front door. "What a beautiful day."

They stroll for a few minutes in silence. Abuelo inquires, "What's on you mind?"

The boy stops and changes from driving mode to talking mode. "Two things. First, more and more, I want to go to Prescott and study with Coyote. But I don't know how I'll get there. What do you think?" He starts his chair rolling.

Abuelo scratches his head. "I don't know, I can't predict the future. But if you want to go there, I'll do my best to get you there, even if I carry you on my back. I don't know when, though." After a few minutes, he sits down on a bench. "And the other thing you wanted to talk to me about?"

He hesitates. "Did you know I enjoy an active fantasy life?"

His grandfather responds, "Ever since I met you, I noticed you go somewhere inside your head. I assumed you get pleasure from a rich inner life."

The boy pauses. "I created a person I call Superboy, who does the things I want to do but can't. He protects children with disabilities, steals food to feed the poor, and fights White Brotherhood soldiers."

Sigún takes a minute before asking, "Does Superboy ever kill the soldiers?"

Martín agrees, "Yes, and that worries me. As I learn to use my mind force to defend myself, I could kill someone. Coyote said killing would hurt me."

"Maestra taught you to turn your mind force on and off to teach you control. Did you ever deliberately hurt anyone?"

Martín watches a squirrel run up a tree. "I experiment healing the cuts and bruises of my cousins and the kids at school. After one boy beat up a smaller boy, I made the bigger kid's bruises worse. Would you call that 'deliberately hurting' someone?"

Abuelo doesn't hesitate: "What do you think?"

His grandson feels nervous. "I felt good when I did it. But, well, since I didn't do it in self-defense, I did wrong."

Sigún shakes his head. "You're so young; but believe us. For now, you can neither kill nor injure anyone. We can't enforce this or watch you all the time. But you tend to keep your word. I want you to promise me you won't kill or intentionally hurt anyone until we move to Prescott or find another Master Healer."

The boy thinks a minute. "It could take a couple years, right?"

The older man assents.

"What about sparring and my lessons with Lark?"

Abuelo responds, "The White Brotherhood exterminates us. You can defend yourself. You can spar and you can learn from Lark. I want you to take a couple days and figure out the difference between defending yourself and your people and deliberately injuring someone. In a week, I will ask you. You can make the promise then."

Martín looks at his abuelo and nods.

Chapter 8
August 12, 2030

Martín explores on his own near Bush Junior High, which used to be called King Middle School before the white apartheid. He goes full speed down Josephine Street. As he slows down near Vine Street, he notices an army truck stop in front of his friend's house and four white soldiers climb out. His pal lives with muscular dystrophy and uses a power wheelchair. He is African-American and just graduated from Berkeley High.

The officer approaches the house. Martín notices a Diné, standing behind a tree. He looks familiar but

Martín cannot remember how he knows this man belongs to the Navajo people. No time to consider. His school friend comes roaring down the ramp in front of his house. A stone hits the officer in the head and he falls. The Diné takes off running. The boy heads toward him. "Run for the Kwoon! My Grandpa will help you," Martín manages to cry out as his friend wheels by.

Out of the corner of his eye, Martín sees his pal's younger sister run out of their house, dump a sack of sugar into the gas tank, and drop the sack. Without drawing any attention, she walks toward the junior high.

Two white soldiers sprint after his pal, who just rammed a third soldier in the shins. Martín knocks the fourth soldier down. The other boy turns left on Vine while Martín flees down Josephine Street. The downed soldiers rub their bruises. The soldiers can't match the two disabled boys and the clever girl.

Martín takes a roundabout route. He tries to remember where he saw the Indian. At home, he feels nervous and can't focus. He wants to stay clear, but struggles not to go into his fantasy world where the Resistance always beats the soldiers.

At six fifteen, Sigún walks up the steps and over to his anxious grandson. He seems calm. He whispers, "Your friend remains safe. I'd rather you didn't know where he went. They target your group."

Martín groans. "Do they target us even before we turn eighteen?"

"As soon as anyone graduates from school, they become vulnerable. Young people go to re-education camps, but you with physical limitations…" He puts a hand on Martín's shoulder. "We didn't organize before, but we organized ourselves now."

Martín feels sad. "I feel honored to be targeted. But it seems foolish that they bother educating us, only to kill us when we graduate."

His grandfather squats. "Our city is known for its great education. But outside Berkeley the Brotherhood stopped educating people of color. They closed down all the high schools, and the colleges in Oakland. But none of that matters. Many of us work on ways to keep you safe. Your pal's escape gave us a chance to test our plan, along with the three others with physical disabilities who just graduated." He grins at Martín's puzzled look. "Your friend told me where they live."

The boy feels eager to tell him, "This afternoon I figured out the difference between defending myself as well as our people and intentionally hurting someone else. Those soldiers wanted to capture my friend. I slowed them enough so we could get away. I didn't create any permanent damage which might cause them to look for me later."

Abuelo agrees. "I like the way you put it. Slow them enough to get away, but leave no evidence which would cause them to hunt you later."

Tía Sara walks out to the front porch and sees Martín and Sigún talking. Pedro and Susana arrive home and hug their mother, who asks, "Does anyone else dream about Prescott, Arizona?"

Martín jumps out of his seat. "I do."

"So do I," Pedro and Susana say in unison.

Tío Juan, overhearing the conversation, joins the others on the porch. "I wonder what the dreams mean and why Prescott, Arizona. I hope we don't move there. I would hate to give up this old house."

Later, Martín sees Alex come through the kitchen and go up the stairs. Then Pedro and Guillermo excuse themselves too. As he gets back into reading, he notices three older kung fu students going up. Then he feels surprised to see Lark and Sammy go upstairs. How many people fit in Abuelo's room? He feels curious.

The next morning a rough hand shakes Martín awake. Esteban whispers in his ear. "Help me. Grandpa told me to get you dressed and feed you breakfast. He wants us to run some errands. Tell me what to do."

Martín groans. "Esteban, are you the only person around who can give me a shower? You don't even like me." He flounders, tangled in the sheets.

Esteban grimaces. "I know I felt jealous of you in the past, but I want to grow up. Give me this chance to show you I can change."

Martín feels nervous but says, "Okay."

Esteban holds the sheet as Martín rolls away from it. "There. You did your first job. Now let's try the shower.

I feel hot and sweaty." Martín rolls toward the bathroom.

"I still don't like you, but you did heal me, when I hurt my knee. So I'll do this as gentle as I can. I want to learn to do this right. Something is going down. I want to pull my share of the load." Esteban sounds serious. Martín takes a good look at him.

Esteban slides the younger boy into the shower chair, takes off his grimy T-shirt, and rolls the chair into the shower. "Do you feel ready for shampoo?"

Martín signals yes. His cousin pours a dipper of water and shampoo on his head. Esteban massages the suds into his hair, taking care to avoid the eyes. He shampoos his own hair before squirting a washcloth with liquid biodegradable soap. He soaps Martín's body, then his own.

"I know neither Grandpa nor your mother get in the shower with you, but I saw both Pedro and Alex do it this way." Esteban turns on the shower and uses his hands to make sure all the shampoo and soap get rinsed from both bodies. Turning the shower off, he wraps Martín in a large towel before grabbing one for himself. The tanks on the roof collect rainwater. From the shower the water drains to the backyard garden.

"You do great."

Esteban blushes.

Susana washes dishes as Martín rolls into the kitchen. "Good morning Martín. I'll feed you breakfast while Esteban eats."

They can hear Estebán whistling as he wipes the shower chair and the bathroom floor before hanging up the towels. He runs into the kitchen, where he sees Susana blending a bowl of granola for Martín. "Thanks for doing that, Susana. I'll come right back. I'll put our dirty clothes in the basket and make our beds." He hurries.

Susana puts a towel across Martín's chest and shoulders and places a spoonful of granola into his mouth. "What's got into Estebán?"

Martín feels happy eating. His new muscle tone reducer chip made swallowing easier for him. And even though he still adjusts to the change, he already gained two pounds. "Estebán says he wants to change and grow up, and he seems to mean it."

As Estebán returns to the kitchen, Abuelo rushes in the back door. "I feel glad you two seem almost ready. Don't go too near their houses, but show Estebán where your friends live, the ones who just graduated from high school. Keep watch while Estebán goes to the back door. He will tell each family the teenagers left Berkeley safely. Talk face-to-face with them. Leave nothing in writing!" He wipes his forehead. "If you find no one home, go back later."

Estebán looks Martín in the eye and turns. "Okay, Abuelo. You can count on us."

Martín adds, "Don't worry. We'll get the job done."

Two mornings later, Martín notices his mother, wearing a yellow cotton sundress and over-blouse, seems excited, so he follows her. She leaves their house earlier than usual and walks toward Shattuck Avenue and Channing Way, where she enters a small restaurant. The dark-skinned Diné he saw at his pal's house, dressed in a worn denim jacket and navy-blue T-shirt, waves her over to his table, where she gives him a long hug. Her hand brushes the top of his crew cut. Neither sees Martín take a good look. He's surprised to see the Navajo with his mother. They seem to know to each other well.

Right after lunch, his grandfather catches Martín's eye. "Let's go for a stroll."

"Sure." The small boy feels eager as he rolls out the front door and down the ramp. "Abuelo?" The older man nods and the boy continues, "I saw this Diné guy hiding from the white soldiers in front of the house when I helped my pal get away. This morning, I noticed Mama seemed super-energized, so I followed her to the café on Shattuck Avenue. She met the same Diné for breakfast. They knew each other well. Do you know who he is?"

Abuelo looks dismayed. "Don't follow any of us. We each guard our own secrets. But I know who you mean. I saw him around for three weeks. When I questioned your mother, she vouched for him as one of ours, but she wouldn't tell me more. She fought in the Resistance for years, and she still knows many contacts. I guess we just trust her."

The two stroll in companionable silence past the Y and the post office to the park opposite the high school. Sigún sits on a bench. "You gave a lot of thought to my request you not kill or hurt anyone on purpose. What did you decide?"

The boy watches a group of children walking toward the Y. "I wonder whether you see a difference between deliberately injuring someone and slowing them down, like I did in front of my pal's house, so they don't capture us."

Sigún hesitates. "Yes, I understand the distinction; however, can you slow them down without drawing attention to yourself?"

His grandson thinks a minute. "Can I start practicing slowing people down and even putting them to sleep while I spar with them?"

Abuelo concurs. "Yes, that would be the safest place for you to develop control. But I don't want the whole Kwoon falling asleep.

The boy shakes his head. "No, I wouldn't do that."

The two sit until Martín says, "Abuelo, I won't kill anyone except in extreme self-defense until we can find a healer or curandero I can learn from."

Sigún gives Martín a hug. "I'll work hard to keep you safe."

During the next three weeks, Martín notices the older students don't come to the Kwoon. Even his good friend Alex went away.

Six days later, Tía Sara comes into the bedroom, waking up the four boys. "Buenos días, cómo amanacieron?

Pedro, will you give Martín a shower and get him dressed?"

"Sure, but where's Tía Sofía?"

"She decided to take a break and went away with an old friend for a couple of days. I told her we would all do our share and care for her son." She turns to her youngest son. "Come help me with breakfast right away."

Martín knows from her tone she's serious and knows he won't miss his ma while she's away. He wonders whether his ma calls the guy in the denim jacket her old friend.

Esteban fastens his pants and dashes to the kitchen. He too knows his own mother means what she says.

As Pedro gets him ready, Martín can hear his tía's voice but he can't make out her words. In no time, Pedro puts him in Shadowfax and he goes to the kitchen.

Susana puts a towel under his chin and a spoonful of scrambled eggs in his mouth. Ma gave us all jobs, which we feel happy to do."

Tía Sara finishes stirring the powder into the milk and pours him a glass. "Martín, when your mother returns, I will ask you how Esteban treated you; depending on your answer, he'll get to return to the Kwoon.'

Esteban grins and Martín says, "He'll do fine. He told me he wants to grow up."

The next day, Susana and Martín come home together and enter the kitchen. She sits down to eat her snack.

Tía Sara gives him a bite of peanut butter cookie and hands her daughter another. "I made them this morning. Martín, what did you do in school?"

He responds, "My teacher lent me a book by Howard Zinn. I enjoyed reading it for an hour during history."

His tía gives him another bite. Esteban walks in and yells, "That's not fair!"

Tía Sara grabs her son by the shoulders before he can leave. "What's not fair?"

He squirms but then gives up. "He gets a cookie and I don't."

She lets him go, opens a cupboard, and takes out a platter of cookies. "I made plenty for everyone, and you saw me feed him before. What's really going on?"

He collapses into a chair and takes a minute to look inside. "I gotta read ten pages of social studies, and I can't read all the words. He can read anything. I just feel jealous."

She sighs. "I understand your feelings, but you can't let them control your actions."

Susana puts a gentle hand on her brother's shoulder. "I can study later. Would you like me to read you those pages and go over the difficult words?"

"Yes. My teacher promised us a quiz tomorrow." He gives Martín a bite of cookie.

That evening, Abuelo Tío Juan and Esteban go for a walk. Tía Sara tells her nephew, "Come. I'll give you a special massage before I put you to bed."

As Martín rolls into a very warm kitchen, he sees the table covered with a sheet. His tía undresses him and puts him on the table face down, arranging pillows until he looks comfortable. She pours warm oil and kneads his back. "Even with your muscle tone reducer, your muscles feel harder than rocks."

He sighs and falls asleep.

The next afternoon, the two boys stroll home together. Martín asks Esteban, "How did you do on your social studies quiz?"

"I got an 84. Thanks for asking." Sticking out his chest, he strides up the ramp and opens the door for his primo. The two race to the kitchen, laughing.

Tía Sara washes vegetables. Esteban hugs her and then takes a page out of his pocket. "Look, Mamacita, I got a B."

She dries her hands on her apron and beams. "Excelente! I feel so proud of you. I wonder whether a reading difficulty slows your progress. I will write a note to your principal to get you tested."

Martín chimes in. "Don't worry, Esteban. We'll find you a special teacher. Then you can call yourself exceptional like I do."

His primo frowns, and then smiles. "I love you, too!" He turns to his mother. "Can you give us some cookies?"

"Your dad ate the last one."

"Oh, I'll come right back." Estebán runs from the kitchen, colliding with Susana. "Sorry. Thanks for your help. I earned a B on my test." He continues to his room.

She enters and sits at the table. Her younger brother returns with a chocolate bar. "I saved this for a special occasion. We can share it four ways."

Later, Martín feels happy with his mother home, and he recognizes Tía Sara cared for him well. Abuelo's voice startles him. "Please come with me."

He sees Tío Juan, Estebán, and his ma already seated at the kitchen table; Tía Sara looks nervous. "Martín, I made a mistake when I said I would ask you how Estebán treated you, and depending on your answer, he would get to return to the Kwoon," Tía Sara says. "Abuelo and Estebán will make the decision, not us. I apologize to you."

"I accept your apology. It didn't feel right for me to make the decision."

Abuelo inquires, "How did Tía Sara treat you while your mother went away?"

Martín grins. "She did great. I felt well taken care of and I barely missed my ma. I enjoyed the special massage she gave me last night."

Tío Juan looks him in the eye. "And how did my youngest son treat you?"

Martín pauses. "He and I develop very different gifts. We learn to enjoy each other. I want to see him get more support with his reading so he won't feel jealous."

Abuelo asks, "Do you object to his returning to the Kwoon?"

"Not at all. I see him changing and growing."

Sigún looks at Estebán. "Tomorrow you can return, and we'll make getting support to improve your reading part of your training contract."

"Thanks, Abuelo."

Chapter 9
November 23, 2030

She slips the lovely magenta dress over her head. Her mother pulls the soft silk down over her daughter's hips and zips it. Lark steps in front of the mirror. "Mama, it's beautiful."

Her mother smiles. "I know you'd like to wear pants, but for tonight I wanted you to wear a pretty dress, yes."

They hear a light knock at the door. Her father inquires, "Is my birthday girl ready?"

Lark sees her mother glance at the mirror and pull down the hem of her own black wool dress. Her mother's bun had turned white. Lark never noticed before tonight. She pulls open the door. "Mama made me the most beautiful dress." She twirls.

"Yes, you look great." Her dad hesitates in the doorway. "We better go. I made reservations for seven o'clock."

Lark watches her father help her mother put on her coat. She takes a good look at her father. He had shrunk in the four years since the white bastards had killed Tommy. Her father looks like an old man. He had never come home that night. The following day, she had found her father lying in a bed in a crowded hospital room. His face full of bruises, he had suffered three broken ribs, a fractured arm and a damaged spleen. It had taken him more than a year to heal. But since then his body had imploded on itself and he had shrunk.

"I'll get my coat." Lark ducks her head so her parents won't see her tears.

Sammy Manzanares stands and waves when they enter Pho's Vietnamese Restaurant. The stocky seventeen-year-old helps Lark take off her coat and holds her chair. "You look so beautiful, y'know," he whispers as he picks up a white box from the table. "I give this to you. You don't turn sixteen every day."

Lark looks around the table at her friends as she opens the box. "Sammy, the beautiful orchid goes with my dress so well."

Sammy looks at the well-dressed Filipina seated at the table. "My mother tells us to pay attention to details.'" He leans over and pins the orchid to Lark's dress.

Tears fill Lark's eyes as she squeezes Sammy's hand.

About a month later, on a cold December evening, Lark arrives in Berkeley on BART, nods at Sigún Gonzalez, who checks IDs at the station, and heads north on Shattuck Avenue. She walks faster as a chill wind hits her. Since she joined Sofía's crew, they meet with a growing group of women in a different place in Berkeley every two weeks. According to Sofía, their job, besides taking part in actions, requires organizing women into a base of support and teaching them to defend themselves.

Lark turns right on Vine and walks one block to the Quaker Meeting House, which she enters through the nursery. Sofía chats in the main meeting room with six women. A white woman in her late thirties dressed in a dark wool sweater and pants acts as their liaison to the main Resistance. Other women arrive. Lark feels pleased to see Tía Sara come to her first meeting with Susana, who attends regularly. Lark shakes hands with Tía Sara. Susana winks as she shakes her hand so Lark won't tell Tía Sara they know each other. Susana wears a too-big, old, torn, and battered jacket she had borrowed.

When twenty women and girls arrive, Sofía calls the meeting to order. After several reports, a Latina in her late thirties stands. "Mis'ijos suffer from the cold. They grew out of last year's jackets and sweatshirts. The White Brotherhood won't issue warm clothing this winter. Does anyone know where we can liberate some warm clothing?"

A mixed-race woman informs them, "My kids get sick from the cold, too. I earn a little cash cleaning rich people's houses. On my way home from work, I noticed truckers delivering a shipment of warm clothing at the clothing distribution place on Piedmont Avenue yesterday, just in time for the holidays. Before coming tonight, I went by there and watched them close at five o'clock."

Sofía suggests, "We'll meet at 40th and Broadway tomorrow at 7 pm. I'll create a diversion. How will we get home with our loot?"

The liaison speaks: "I'll arrange for two trucks to arrive on Piedmont and 40th at 8 pm. Don't come late. And don't forget to rough up the jackets before you wear them. We don't want the Brotherhood connecting your kids with tomorrow's action."

Lark, Sammy, and three friends meet Sofía and four white fighters near the distribution center at 6:30 the next evening. Sofía explains the job and gives out assignments. When Sofía finishes speaking and the few questions are answered, Lark hurries to the meeting place on 40th. Sammy will watch her from the shadows, alert for trouble.

Lark hears a series of explosions, her signal. Fifteen women and girls, including Tía Sara and Susana, follow her as she jogs through the back door of the distribution center. They hear sirens and shots in the distance. One woman passes out large plastic garbage bags. Lark spots some tables with handy items and takes two bags, filling one with long-sleeved black cotton T-shirts and the other with six black cashmere sweaters.

She looks at the clock on the wall and yells, "Hurry, we got to leave!" As she reaches 40th, two trucks arrive; Pedro Gonzalez drives one, so she feels safe. She helps the women climb into the trucks. She spots Susana and her mother. Sammy arrives with two stragglers and helps them into a truck. She gives the signal and the drivers leave.

Sammy picks up one of her bags and the two take off running.

Chapter 10
February 12, 2031

On a Saturday afternoon, Martín and Alex, a block from the Kwoon, see an army truck full of Pure White Brotherhood soldiers pull up in front of it. Alex turns to Martín and says, "Take a long way home; I'll go see if I can help our people."

"Don't get caught." Martín watches his friend run to the back of the Kwoon, open a window, and shout. Pedro, other senior students, and then Abuelo climb out the window and start fighting the soldiers, while Alex and Estebán lead the younger students running from the Kwoon. When he sees some of the soldiers following,

Alex shouts, "Go in different directions! Get away any way you can!" He runs back.

Martín remembers to leave. He goes west on Carlton toward Shattuck and wanders around downtown until he knows no one follows. Once home he heads for the kitchen. Abuelo, Pedro, Esteban, and Alex sit at the table. He sees bruises on Abuelo's right hand and head. A bad cut on Alex's forearm oozes blood.

Abuelo stands. "Martín, I feel glad to see you. Those bastards didn't realize we could fight and didn't send enough soldiers. By the time reinforcements came, we all vanished. We can't use the Kwoon anymore, so we'll train in a different place every day.

"Can you look at Alex's cut? It won't stop bleeding."

"Sure." The little boy goes into a trance and uses his blue light to disinfect the wound and then stop the bleeding. When he comes out of the trance, his head hurts so he groans. "I can't do any more right now. I feel too hungry!"

"I keep a chocolate bar in our room," Pedro says, racing out of the kitchen.

Alex turns to his friends. "Thanks for stopping the bleeding."

Abuelo adds, "Alex, your quick action enabled all of us to get away. Thank you."

Late one evening, about two months later, Martín hears a noise in the backyard, quickly gets into his wheelchair, and heads for the kitchen. As Abuelo opens the back door, Pedro stumbles into the house with a big bruise on the left side of his face. The whole Gonzalez family trickles into the kitchen while Pedro catches his breath.

Sigún motions to Susana. "Run upstairs and get some arnica ointment." She races out of the room. He pulls a chair from the table and moves it toward Pedro.

Pedro collapses into it. As his shoulders touch the back of the chair, he flinches and leans forward and looks Abuelo in the eye. "I stopped at Maestra Manzanares and told her what happened. She helped me get cleaned up so I could get back here." He hesitates as Susana returns to the room and places a jar on the kitchen table, and then he continues speaking in a voice harsh with pain and anger. "The white soldier-bastards got Guillermo, Sammy, and Lark. I met Guillermo after he got off work in San Leandro. We went to an ice cream place where our arnís class hangs out. We saw Sammy and Lark, so we joined them. I just finished my hot fudge sundae, when I heard a lot of trucks drive up, whistles blowing, and heavy boots running."

Martín feels anger pour through him, causing his body to tighten. He takes a deep breath and triggers his muscle tension reduction chip. It does not do much good.

Pedro shakes his head and winces. "An officer burst through the front door yelling, 'Everybody drop! On the floor now! We'll take you to re-education camp.' We four ran to the back door, but soldiers with clubs waited there. Sammy, Lark, and I got out our arnís sticks and tried to defend ourselves while Guillermo tried to kick his way through. We fought hard, but we couldn't do much against so many. Sammy and I saw a break, but they hurt his leg. He told me to run for it and tell his ma. I yelled for him and Lark to drop their sticks. If soldiers catch us holding sticks, they shoot us on the spot. Then I took off running. I wish I could do more."

Sigún speaks from a very deep place. "You did all you could. At least this way, we know what happened. But those kids don't stand a chance." He shakes his head and turns toward Pedro. "Let's get you to bed."

Tío Juan helps him up. "I'll go downtown and leave a message for Maestra Manzanares at the Catholic Church in San Leandro, so she won't worry about you, too."

Sigún signals Tía Sara. "We'll take you to your room and put some arnica on those bruises." They both help Pedro to the bedroom. Martín and Esteban follow.

Once in the room and leaning against Tía Sara, Pedro winces as Sigún lowers Pedro's jeans and removes his sweater. Tía Sara helps her wounded son lie down. Martín gasps as he catches a glance of the bruises on Pedro's shoulders, arms and thighs.

Sigún kneels by the bed and spreads arnica on Pedro's shoulders. "Those bastards beat you good. How did you make it here in this condition?"
Pedro winces. "I wanted you to know what happened. Neither Maestra nor I realized how badly they hurt me. I felt so angry, I just kept moving. I didn't feel any pain until I sat down on BART."

Tía Sara removes the shoes, pants, and socks. "I'll go get him some aspirin."

Esteban helps Martín into bed and plugs in Shadowfax.

When Tía Sara returns, she and his grandfather help Pedro sit up. After he takes the pills with a long drink of water, they help him lie on his stomach again.

Esteban gently covers his brother. "Pedro, if you want anything, just holler."

Sigún turns out the light. "I want to get you all to a safe place," he says as he walks out.

When Martín hears Pedro's breath become more regular, he projects his force toward Pedro's body and does a quick scan. He sees no broken bones or serious internal injuries, but several bad bruises. He senses two very angry red places: one on Pedro's left shoulder and one on his left thigh. Martín projects a blue light to the bruise on Pedro's shoulder. The angry red turns purple, and then, after a few minutes, lavender.

Martín takes a deep breath. His head begins to hurt and he feels hungry. He returns his focus to Pedro's left thigh and projects the blue light to the bruise there. The angry red becomes purple and then lavender. Martín takes another deep breath. His headache pounds worse and he feels famished. He groans. He can do no more.

A little later, Tío Juan comes into the room and crouches. "Maestra Manzanares stayed at the gym. She felt relieved to know you made it here."

Pedro speaks softly. "I feel much less pain in my left shoulder and thigh, but I heard Martín groan."

"I'll check him." Tío Juan picks up the small boy, carries him to the hall and shuts the bedroom door. He takes a good look at Martín's face in the light of the hallway. "You appear paler than a ghost. You did something and Pedro feels better already." Tío Juan walks to the kitchen. "Do you feel hungry?"

Martín signals an emphatic yes.

Tío Juan whispers, "I'll keep your secret, though soon we won't find it so easy to do." He searches the cupboards. Sofía walks into the kitchen. He thrusts him into her arms. "Hold your son while I look for food. He seems gray from hunger."

Sofía cradles Martín in her arms. "You healed your primo." She turns to her brother. "I don't think you'll find much. We ate the last of the rice and beans at dinner. We won't get the next allotment of food for three days."

Tío Juan looks Martín in the eye. "Sorry, Martín. I found nothing to eat."

Martín's head hurts and he whimpers.

Sofía looks sad. "I'll take him to my room and hold him until he falls asleep."

Tío Juan says, "I didn't know. I'll talk to Esteban and see if he can come up with anything. I hate to encourage him to steal food, but we require groceries."

Once upstairs, Sofía sits in an easy chair. "I know you hunger. I feel sad. Please try to sleep."

He whimpers again and then sighs. He imagines Superboy stealing a truckload of food and passing it out at the high school.

A month later, Martín hears Estebán calling him. He'll take a break from his studies, which he enjoys. Although he's still a lot younger than the other students, he passed them. Since the Brotherhood doesn't allow students of color to go to college, Berkeley High School's principal made other arrangements for this very bright little boy. So Martín studies Calculus and Differential Equations with a math teacher, advanced anatomy and physiology with a biology teacher, and a special tutorial with an acupuncturist. His primo calls again, and Martín hurries outside.

Martín follows Estebán and four of his friends down Fulton. The group turns right on Stuart toward a food distribution warehouse formerly called Berkeley Bowl. One boy runs forward to reconnoiter. This is the first time Estebán requested he accompany them on a food expedition; he hopes he can handle his end of the action.

The boy who ran to scout ahead reports back that he saw one guard on the northern door. "He sits drinking out of a can wrapped in a paper bag."

"I bet it's a beer." Estebán turns to his to his younger cousin. "How close do you want to come to put someone to sleep?"

"I don't know, maybe ten feet." Martín wishes he'd stayed home. "Since he sits he won't wake himself up falling down."

The guys laugh as they cross Shattuck Avenue and enter the parking lot. They amble up to the guard. Esteban sounds confused. "Do you give out the rations today?"

The soldier shakes his head. "No. We give food to you, rice eaters, on Monday mornings between 5 and 6." He laughs at his less-than-clever lie. Five seconds later, his head rolls forward. He sleeps.

Martín hesitates before he follows the guys inside.

Esteban motions him over to some protein drink cases. "How long will he sleep?"

He answers, "Ten minutes, tops."

The older boy says, "This stuff will come in handy. Do you want chocolate?" When Martín nods yes, Esteban fills the large backpack on the rear of Martín's chair with the cans, protein bars, dried fruit, and four bags of chocolate chips. Esteban packs his own backpack with cans of meat and chocolate bars.

Esteban signals and the boys leave. Passing the sleeping guard, they sprint toward the corner. Crossing the street, they hear yelling and a soldier running after them. Esteban tells the other boys, "I got to get Martín away. Slow him down." He turns to his younger cousin. "Follow me!"

For ten minutes, Esteban leads Martín away from their house. He hides his backpack behind a tree. When he knows no one follows, he stops to catch his breath. "Abuelo will kill me. They can't stop me from taking risks, but involving you will get me in big trouble."

Martín notices his body feels tense, so he activates his chip and breathes deeply. His ability to put white soldiers to sleep and all the resulting possibilities excites him.

The two cousins circle back to pick up Esteban's pack. Tío Juan waits for them on the porch. "If you think you can pull a stunt like that in Berkeley without us knowing, think again! Wait in the front room in complete silence, now!"

Martín rolls into the house. Esteban catches his eye and gives him a thumb's up. They both grin and shake heads. They hear a heated discussion in the kitchen. Martín giggles when he realizes no one has figured out how to discipline him. He triggers his muscle relaxing chip.

The older adults stomp into the front room. Abuelo, Sofía, and Tío Juan show serious concern on their faces, but Tía Sara, with a gleam in her eye, grins. Tío Juan turns to Esteban and says, "As the oldest, you'll go first. What do you say for yourself?"

Esteban stands and speaks hesitantly. "We felt hungry. I didn't think it through. My friends and I run risks when we go on our food expeditions, but I did wrong taking Martín. He seems too identifiable, even though his gifts made robbing the warehouse a lot easier. We felt hungry."

Tío Juan roars back, "I don't accept your excuse. We all hunger all the time. The damn White Brotherhood keeps us hungry so we can't fight back."

Abuelo interrupts, "Esteban didn't go alone. Martín, what about you?"

He responds, "I could have said no when Esteban asked me to come with him and the guys, but I didn't. So, I don't blame Esteban. I did want to try putting a white soldier to sleep, so I used this opportunity. I tried it and it worked. Think of all the possibilities!"

Sofía sounds alarmed. "Between your gifts and your electric wheelchair, you run great risk, and I don't know how to get that through to you! I admire your spirit. I don't know how to discipline you, so you stay out of danger. Do you even begin to understand the danger?"

Martín shakes his head. "Mama, I lived ten years and you and Abuelo taught me to fear nothing. So, no, I don't get it!"

Tía Sara clears her throat. "We find you both difficult to discipline for different reasons, but after much discussion, I choose to take responsibility for doing it." She turns to Esteban. "First of all, I want a commitment from you that you will not include Martín in any of your escapades!"

Esteban replies, "Don't worry, I learned my lesson. I won't include Martín in anything dangerous, ever."

Tía Sara continues, "For the next month, you will visit Abuelo's old friend in Redwood Garden for an hour every day, and you will invite him to help you with your reading. And you will do any chores he requires you to do."

Estebán groans. "Ah ma, he stinks." He notices her stern expression. "Okay, I'll do it."

"You'll do it without complaints." His aunt turns to Martín. "And you, every day for the next month, I will separate you from your electric wheelchair for an hour. You'll meditate on the risks you run putting white soldiers asleep. Every day at four o'clock I'll take you out of your chair, and remind you of what you will meditate on."

Martín moans and murmurs, "Okay." He hates getting separated from Shadowfax, his electric wheelchair. He realizes he met his match in Tía Sara.

Tía Sara looks at her watch. "It's ten to four. You can both begin today. Go use the bathroom, and come back here at four on the dot."

The boys groan and race out of the room.

When they return, Tía Sara escorts her younger son out the door and turns to Martín. "I suppose you feel hungry. Can I find something in your backpack for you to eat?"

"Yes, Tía Sara. Can I drink a can of protein drink?"

She finds a can, opens it, and holds it for him. "Don't think I condone your actions, but I know you do get so hungry."

When he finishes she undoes the Velcro straps, takes him out of his chair, and deftly puts him on the floor with his back against the wall. "Now you will meditate on your mother and how much you love her. Then you'll think about what would happen to her if you get caught stealing or putting white soldiers to sleep. I'll return in an hour."

Martín realizes how much he loves his mother. He also realizes he has never thought about her suffering as a result of his actions, and he feels humbled.

Three weeks pass, and Martín reports to Tía Sara for his daily meditation practice. He won't admit it to her, but he enjoys both mediating and their interaction. She greets him: "I know you ate a snack, so we'll get you started." In no time he sits on the floor.

She explains, "Today you will reflect on your healing gifts and ways you want to use them in the future."

An hour later, Tía Sara lifts him to his chair. "Tell me some of your thoughts."

Martín grins. "I enjoy your questions. I want to take time to imagine my future. I plan to study healing with Coyote and get a degree in biology with emphasis in anatomy and physiology. I hope Coyote will teach me to heal myself. I don't imagine getting rid of my cerebral palsy but rather doing more for myself with it. I want to get married and raise a family. I know I want to deepen my connections to friends so I don't spend so much time in my fantasy world. I got that far and I want to imagine more."

Tía Sara hugs him. "Wow, I feel amazed by how seriously you take my questions and how well you use this time. In the beginning I felt afraid you would escape into your fantasies for an hour, but I see real growth in your thinking. I feel proud of you for using this time well, and I hope you will continue to meditate after this month ends."

"Thank you for asking great questions. I met someone who could discipline me by giving me the opportunity to develop discipline."

He wonders whether they can get enough food in Prescott, and how he will get there.

Chapter 11
April 9, 2032

Almost a year has passed since Guillermo disappeared. Tío Juan asks, "Why does the Diné still watch our house?"

The family gathers in the living room at the end of Susana and Martín's junior year in high school. Martín will soon turn eleven, and Susana will soon turn sixteen.

Pedro inquires, "Do you mean the one with the crew cut who wears blue denim?"

Tío Juan responds, "Yes, him."

Sofía says, "Don't worry about him. I'll vouch for him."

He persists. "Yes, but who is he?" She shrugs.

Abuelo clears his throat. "I called this meeting because too much time passed since they captured Guillermo. Let's figure out how to keep the rest of us safe. I don't want more of my grandkids to get re-educated or terminated." He looks at Martín.

Tía Sara jumps in. "I dream about going to Prescott, Arizona."

Tío Juan frowns. "I don't want to leave this house. I don't want to lose it."

Pedro adds, "I dream about Prescott, too. I'd attend a great four-year college."

Abuelo affirms, "The Brotherhood will come for you when you graduate. You and Susana could go to college and Martín could study healing with Coyote Yakushi."

Tío Juan repeats, "I don't want to lose this house or leave Berkeley."

Tía Sara speaks. "I'll walk to Prescott this summer with Pedro and whoever else wants to come. I'll find us a house. I don't want to lose another child."

"Can Miguel Lopez come with us?" Pedro asks. "Miguel risks death because of his blindness, but he can out-walk all of us."

Tía Sara responds, "I already talked with his grandmother, who feels desperate."

Susana sighs. "Then maybe if all goes well, Abuelo can bring Martín and me after we graduate next year. Alex may want to come with us."

Tía Sara turns to Estebán. "What do you want to do? You are my youngest, but in this you must make your own choice."

He takes a minute to think. "I don't know. I'd like to stay here with Susana, Martín, and Dad, and then come to Prescott with Abuelo."

Tía Sara puts a hand on Estebán's shoulder. "That seems okay with me if your father agrees. He'll take responsibility for you." Tío Juan nods.

She turns to her father-in-law. "It's a long walk to Prescott. What about your heart?"

Abuelo answers softly, "Oh, I'll do okay."

Martín comments, "Mama, you keep so quiet. What's up with you?"

Sofía clears her throat. "I gave our future a lot of thought. I want to stay here with my son until he graduates from high school. After that, I trust you to look out for him."

Sofía gives Martín an intense look and searches his eyes. "Before Martín's birth, I belonged to the Resistance. When I became pregnant, I married a kind man from the movement and settled down in Denver. Dave More, the doctor at the hospital, put Gil Sanchez on the birth certificate, even though he knows Martín's real father."

"Gil wasn't my real father, was he? He treated me well, but I figured my real father was someone else." Martín smiles as he remembers Gil holding him carefully so he could watch a soccer game. His stepfather had figured out very early Martín wanted to see everything.

"No, he wasn't." Sofía looks at Abuelo. "I want to return to the Resistance, Dad. I know you and I don't always agree, but we both want the best for Martín." She looks at Martín again. "You'll grow into a great person and you'll do fine."

Martín feels a frog in his throat and wants to cry. "I'll do okay, Mama."

Abuelo caresses Sofía's head. "We'll take good care of him when the time comes."

Tío Juan almost whines, "And what about me?"

Tía Sara answers, "Unless you figure out the lives of your children remain more important than some house, you'll stay on your own when Abuelo and the kids take off."

Tío Juan remarks, "And will you just leave me?"

"No, I'll reside in Prescott, caring for our kids, and Martín." Tía Sara sounds sad.

Eleven months later Sofía says, "Let's talk." The others left the house.

Martín glances at his mother. She seems sad and serious. "Now, I feel curious."

"Something came up, an invitation to go to Durango next week. There's a job I want to do for the Resistance. If I do this job, I'll go underground. I can't come back here. What do you think I should I do?"

Martín cocks his head and takes a good look at his mother. "I'll miss you. In kung fu, I learn to take charge of my own path. You also must take responsibility for yours and do what your heart tells you to do." He pauses. "Will you come visit us in Prescott?"

His mother cries and wipes tears from her eyes. "Like I said before, I trust Abuelo and Tía Sara to keep you safe, though I will miss you. You taught me to live to my fullest. You can feel sure I will come to Prescott when safe and possible."

"Does Abuelo know?"

"No, I wanted to talk to you first. I kept you as my priority for twelve years."

"I love you, my wonderful mama. But will you tell me one thing? What about, Gil Sanchez, the guy in Denver? Tell me about him."

She pauses. "Gil, a kind man, agreed to marry me when I found myself pregnant. Your real father, a leader in the Resistance, with a price on his head, couldn't live with us. He still carries a price on his head. If Gil didn't marry me, the fascist government would label me a "whore" and kill me. When you were born with cerebral palsy, he agreed to provide us with a stable home. He treated you with great tenderness and spent Saturday afternoons with you to give me a break. He fell in love with me, but he acted a gentleman and did not take advantage of our situation."

Martín thinks a minute. "Who is my father?"

"Soon after you get to Prescott, your father will visit you and introduce himself. While you reside in the Brotherhood's territory, I will keep you safer by not telling you."

Martín squints at his mother a minute.

"Martín, I love you so much." Sofía picks up her small son and hugs him.

Chapter 12

May 10, 2033

Twenty-eight young people march into the crowded barracks. The white sergeant stands at the door. "Dinner at 1800 hours. We'll show a special movie at 1930 hours at the base theater. At ease."

Lark glances at the clock on the wall and Guillermo's empty bed and resists the urge to collapse onto her bunk. Keeping her light cotton jacket zipped, she follows Sammy out the door.

Sammy scans the area before giving her a hug. "Y'know I love you."

She kisses him on the cheek. "And I love you, even more." She steps apart and leads the way. She hears him murmur, "That's impossible."

Rounding the corner, they get hit by a blast of wind and sand. Lark shivers and stumbles. Sammy catches her in his strong arms, but lets her go with a gentle squeeze as soon as she regains her balance. They will shoot him for touching her.

"You keep me alive; you keep us all alive." She leads the way into the infirmary and finds Guillermo asleep. The officer had beaten and drugged him. Lark gives him water.

An orderly comes into the room and speaks to Sammy in a low voice. "If you value his life, get him back to your barracks tonight. I overheard the word 'Ludlow,' whatever that means."

Sammy thinks a minute. "We'll come back after the movie."

The orderly hands Sammy a small package. "Here, take his papers. I'll also give you some painkillers and super-Neosporin."

Lark takes the orderly's hand. "Thank you."

She and Sammy head toward the dining hall, where they spot friends from their unit, Tomás and Juanita. Tomás looks taller than Sammy, about five feet eight inches, but he doesn't weigh as much. Lark recalls his constant helpfulness and cheerfulness over the last six months. He used to work in his parents' grocery store and was the oldest of five children. The four take their food trays to a corner table.

Juanita eats a couple of bites. "Something will happen. In the nine months we survived here, this is the first a decent meal they gave us."

Lark notices how efficiently her friend consumes her food, wasting neither a movement nor a grain of rice. She admires Juanita's take-charge attitude and her dark curly hair. Lark remembers her friend telling them about the farm near Stockton where she had grown up. Juanita's father had bought it after he migrated from Japan. White soldiers shot her mother ten years ago.

Sammy clears his throat. "Y'know, I want your help. I don't know what will happen tonight. I do know we must get Guillermo to the barracks and pack our things."

Juanita looks at Tomás, who nods. "Thanks for the warning. Sure, we'll help. Maybe we should pack our things now while no one can see us."

Lark stands. "Good idea."

They bus their trays and follow Juanita back to the barrack. Lark packs her small duffle bag then helps Sammy with Guillermo's meager belongings.

Tomás looks out the door. "We better get back to the movie."

Sammy realizes, "Wait a minute. We run low on supplies." He passes each a roll of quarters. "Take the last of my stash. Buy all you can from the vending machines."

The four arrive back at the dining hall as an officer calls their unit to muster outside and takes roll. Lark shivers and then groans inside when the officer orders them to run to the theater. Once in the lobby each buys five cans of soda and five candy bars.

Dismissed after the movie, Sammy leads the way, jogging toward the infirmary. He stations Juanita and Lark outside. "Tomás, please help me carry Guillermo."

Lark feels an odd tension in the air. She doesn't see even one white soldier as the guys carry Guillermo back to the barracks and lay him on his bunk.

Juanita passes the word, "Best sleep in your clothes and fill your canteens."

A nineteen-year-old mixed-race guy notices they carried Guillermo back. "You and Sammy saved my ass many times. Something is about to happen. How can I help?"

Tomás takes him aside. "They may take us away in trucks tonight, the way Unit Seven vanished last week. We want a diversion as we load Guillermo."

The other boy taps Tomás' shoulder. "Will do."

Lark covers herself with her blanket and falls asleep.

Several hours later, the squeal of brakes wakes her. An officer opens the door and shouts. "I give you five minutes to get on the truck or I'll shoot you."

Sammy and Juanita pause to tie their shoes before they sprint out the door with their gear, loading it way inside the truck against the cab. Lark and Tomás follow. Tomás passes Guillermo's bag and two blankets to Juanita.

A fire starts in the restroom on the other side of the building. As the officer and two soldiers rush there to put it out, Sammy and Tomás pass Guillermo to Lark and Juanita, who put him down on the blanket. They both stay outside the truck helping their unit board. Tomás' friend winks as he climbs over the tailgate.

Tomás whispers, "Great job!"

The officer blows a whistle. Tomás and Sammy help two stragglers before jumping onto the moving truck.

A week later and a month before Alex, Susana, and Martín were due to graduate; Sigún wakes the boys without turning on the light. "We leave now. Esteban, dress yourself and Martín in warm clothes. Use the light in the hallway. I don't want to attract attention."

Both ready, Martín turns to Esteban. "You know those pictures in the kitchen?"

Esteban nods.

"Will you get them for me?"

Esteban runs out of the room and comes back with the photos. "I'll keep these for you in my backpack."

Alex crouches beside the small boy. Martín sighs in relief "Hey, Alex, I feel relieved you could make it."

He takes off his pack. "I wouldn't miss this trek for the world."

Soon Alex helps Esteban put Martín into a special backpack with holes for his legs. His grandfather squats as they put Martín on his back. Esteban, Susana and Alex follow Sigún out the back door. He leads them in a light jog up Russell Street, to Ashby, then out Tunnel Road. He whispers, "Martín, you still don't weigh sixty pounds."

Martín feels naked and vulnerable without his electric wheelchair. He wonders when he'll see it again.

Alex and Susana pull back a small section of chain link fence as Esteban helps his grandfather climb through. Sigún speaks to the Filipino-American driver of a truck hidden behind some bushes. The teenagers put their packs in the truck and help Sigún with Martín. Esteban and Abuelo climb on the back and reach over the tailgate for him. In the brief moments he dangles in the air, Martín spies the man in worn denim. The Diné stands watching them from among some eucalyptus a hundred feet away. Martín wonders. Susana bangs on the side of the truck three times to signal they climbed up. The truck speeds south to Hayward, then east to Pleasanton.

They trade off holding Martín against themselves so he doesn't get hurt when the truck hits rocks and potholes. The first half hour, the little boy feels tense and excited by their escape. He spends the next hour doing yoga breathing exercises and using his chip to relax his body. He daydreams. Superboy grew and looks more and more like the Navajo with the crew cut. Today, as part of the Resistance, the hero hijacks a bus of deaf schoolchildren and drives them to safety near Albuquerque.

Five miles shy of Barstow, the truck driver pulls off
the road, goes south two hundred feet, and stops behind a sand dune to them let out. "I can take you no
farther."

"We thank you," Sigún says as his grandkids put
Martín on Alex's back.

"If you stay about five hundred feet from the road,
you'll get past the checkpoint," the driver tells them.
"When you get to Newberry Springs, walk north until
you get over the railroad tracks. You don't want to run
into the Zombie Marines who train south of Ludlow.
Follow Highway 40 to Needles and then on to Flagstaff."

"Thanks again for the ride." Sigún joins the others
and puts on the backpack full of supplies he shares with
Alex. They head east.

"Let's get ourselves past the checkpoint and then
look for a shady place to wait for evening." Sigún wipes
his forehead with a handkerchief.

Soon they stop to strip down to their shorts and tank
tops.

"Susana, can I give you the job of making sure Martín
drinks enough water and puts on sunscreen?" Sigún
holds him while she spreads lotion on Martín's face.

"Sure, I'll gladly do it. None of us feels used to all
this sun."

Martín squints until his eyes adapt to the bright-
ness. He feels Alex assume an easy walking rhythm.
After an hour, Abuelo switches with Alex. The per-

son carrying him will set the pace. His grandfather's rhythm seems jerkier, but Martín can feel him use his breath to steady himself. His own body feels warm. He uses the chip to relax, easier in the heat. He puts his head on Abuelo's shoulder and dozes.

Alex wakes Martín as he lowers him to the ground. Susana gives him water and reapplies sunscreen. The lotion feels cool on his skin. He recalls Esteban stole of box of it and several canteens for the trip.

Sigún takes a minute to catch his breath. "Susana, I want you to scout and make sure we passed the checkpoint and we do not stray too far from the road."

"Okay. I'll make sure no one sees me. I assume you'll keep walking east."

"Yes, you won't find it hard to catch up." The older man turns to his fourteen-year-old grandson. "Esteban, can you scout ahead and find us a shady place to rest?"

"Sure. About how far shall I go?" Esteban stands and wipes his forehead.

"Go three miles. Don't overdo it on our first day." Sigún walks over to Martín. "Before you leave, help me put Martín on Alex's back."

Martín feels reassured by Alex's steady rhythm. He resists the temptation to go into his fantasy. Too young, he hadn't noticed the desert when his mother had walked with him to Berkeley. Now he looks around at the sparsely treed, rolling landscape. He sees no people. He watches an eagle soaring in the wind. The bird catches an updraft and glides out of sight.

Half an hour later, Susana jogs up to them and shrugs off her pack and pants until she catches her breath. "Six armed soldiers guard the checkpoint, two miles back. The road lies about six hundred feet from here."

A little while later, the group walks up to Estebán, sitting in the shadow of a boulder. "Let's walk ten minutes that way to a place a little shadier than this," he says, standing up and pointing southeast.

"Great. I want to rest soon." Alex takes a deep breath and walks in the direction Estebán indicated.

Later, too warm to sleep, Martín leans against Alex. He misses his electric wheelchair, he misses talking, and he misses sitting comfortably.

Quiet, Martín notices the first stars come out, many more than he ever saw in Berkeley. The few cacti make shadows, reminding him of Superboy. Martín wants to keep company with Alex, his cousins, and Abuelo. He misses his mother and wonders if Alex misses his parents.

Estebán clears his throat. "Abuelo, tell us about your parents."

Sigún sits. "My father taught Latin American literature at the private high school in Lima, where my mother taught English. My parents did translations from Japanese literature. Grandmother learned the language in Manchuria and taught it to my mother. We lived in a modest apartment, where I shared a bedroom with my older brother."

Abuelo remains silent for a few minutes. Martín hears crickets in the distance and the hoot of an owl.

Everything seems so different. His fatigue keeps him from worrying.

Abuelo continues, "Protesters and rioters marched during the seventies and early eighties. The police suspected my father as a leader of the Sendero Luminoso, a Maoist terrorist group. My father formed no connections with them, but he wrote a letter published in a progressive newspaper. It said neither the oppression by terrorists nor the repression by the government produced democracy or long-term benefits."

Susana interrupts, "Abuelo, did the Peruvian government seem as repressive as the Brotherhood?"

"Repression equals repression wherever. The Peruvian government silenced everyone who expressed opposition to its policy of killing those suspected of supporting the terrorists. Two days after my father's letter published, we found my brother's tortured body dumped outside our apartment building with a note."

The young people wait for Abuelo to continue.

Sigún swallows hard. "It said, 'We'll kill your other son!' My father photographed the body with the note attached. In less than a week, my parents sold our apartment, furniture, even our books, cashed their retirement, took all our money out of the bank, and we caught an airplane to Los Angeles. A few days later, we rode the train to Berkeley, where my father bought the house on Fulton Street and enrolled me in public school so I could learn English."

Alex pipes in, "You speak English so well; I didn't know you spoke Spanish first. But why did your parents want to live in Berkeley with all the repression there?"

Abuelo furls his eyebrows. "You may not believe it, but in the seventies and eighties in Berkeley, a progressive place, people from all races could live freely." He looks at Martín. "People with physical disabilities lived independently there."

The morning of the third day, Martín notices flashes of light followed by explosions of dust, to the east. He signals them to his grandfather with his eyes.

"That must be the old Marine Corps Training Grounds. We better head north and avoid them." Sigún's voice sounds less than certain.

On I-40, they see a group of fifty young men and woman dressed in camouflage, standing at attention motionless on the asphalt in the hot sun. Martín's body jumps when he hears a gravely voice snarl, "The next can of shit that moves a muscle will pull guard duty for a week!"

The little boy feels himself lurch forward and drop as Alex goes down on his hands and knees at the verge of the road. Alex lets him catch his balance before he crawls behind a bush where he can sit up. Estebán whispers, "Grandpa says to wait."

Martín can see a tough-looking white man with a gray shirt scan each conscript's face. He holds a small black box. The faces of the recruits seem much darker. Is this what happens to the young people of color who survive the re-education? One looks so familiar. Could it really be … ?

After what seems like an eternity, the man barks. "Follow me, you foul-smelling, crap-encrusted rice eaters. We'll run all the way back to camp. The last five scumbags to arrive will do ten laps around the perimeter! But first maybe you bags of trash require a little rest."

Martín watches as the gray-shirted man presses a button on his black box. All the recruits fall to the ground, moaning and holding their heads. Before they struggle to their feet, the commander takes off running east on the steaming asphalt. The group trails behind him.

As soon as the marines leave, Sigún walks over to where the guys sit and extends a hand to Alex, who stands, careful not to dump Martín out of his backpack. "Let's get across the road and into those hills." He points north.

Martín feels Alex take a deep breath, step up, and jog across the road. Alex doesn't stop for fifteen minutes until he descends an arroyo, shielding them from the road.

Susana holds up a canteen with a straw so Martín can drink while Alex catches his breath. "Fifty to one. Why don't they just kill the white bastard?"

Alex pants. "Didn't you see them all fall down? The guy controls them with that black box. That's what the truck driver meant when he said, 'You don't want to run into the Zombie Marines!'"

Grandfather's voice sounds low and desperate. "We must get over the border and into Arizona. We must get you four to Prescott."

Susana and Esteban switch Martín to his grandfather's back. Susana mutters. "They will never re-educate me!"

Alex speaks in a low voice. "None of us would survive it, but you, Susana, would get yourself killed real fast!"

Later she goes off to pee. When she doesn't come back, Alex worries. "Susana left a while ago. I wonder where. I hope the Zombie Marines never catch her."

Abuelo responds, "I feel worried, too. She said she'd come right back."

Alex wipes the sweat from his brow. "Shall I go look for her?"

Abuelo shakes his head. "No, I want your help with Martín. If anything happened to you, I couldn't get him to Prescott."

Esteban offers, "I'll go look."

Abuelo looks sad. "No, thanks Esteban. I want your help, too. We'll just wait."

It grows darker and darker, much blacker than any night Martín can remember. Abuelo takes three food bars and a can of protein drink out of the backpack. He gives Alex and Estebán each one bar. "I don't think we should light a fire. Give Martín the drink since I don't suppose he can chew these food bars." He pokes a hole in the top of the can with his pocket knife. Martín still feels hungry after he finishes drinking.

When they finish their tiny meal, Estebán pleads, "Abuelo, please tell us a story. Tell us about how your Manchurian mother got to Peru."

Martín doesn't know where Manchuria lies. He thinks it must be somewhere near China because Abuelo talks about Shanghai and Manchuria together. Peru lies south, below Mexico. But Martín doesn't know whether it still exists because the catastrophe wiped out Mexico and he doesn't know how far south the destruction extended.

Abuelo speaks into the darkness. By now his voice is as soothing to Martín as his mother's arms when she rocked him to sleep. "We come from strong people who make their own decisions. Remember, just like we fight a war now, your grandmother survived a terrible war while still a young girl."

Crack! A stick breaks in the darkness. They all hold still. Martín takes a deep breath and uses his chip to reduce his high muscle tone. Hearing no further sound, Abuelo continues. "During wars, soldiers do terrible things. They often do terrible things to women." He pauses. "And then they punish the women for something men forced them to do, and they even punish little babies though they did nothing wrong. After my grandmother gave birth, she decided to take my mother to a place where she wouldn't carry so much stigma.

"They took a ship to Shanghai. My grandmother ended up in Peru, where she became a seamstress."

A voice startles them. "Your grandmother sounds like a very strong woman to leave Manchuria and settle in Peru." Susana appears.

Abuelo says nothing for a few seconds. Then he sounds angry. "Where did you go? We worried."

Susana runs into his arms. She cries.

"When the Zombie Marines went by us on the road, I thought I saw Sammy Manzanares. I didn't even think. I just walked to the camp."

Martín feels a jolt of excitement. He'd seen Sammy, too.

Alex sounds angry. "Susana, you can't take off without telling us. We all worried to death, and nobody could come looking for you."

"I just went. I didn't think about it. That worked better, less dangerous than with more people. Sorry I made you worry. Anyway, I waited for a while and then Sammy came out on guard duty."

Abuelo sounds amazed. "You saw Sammy? Did you talk to him? What did he say about your brother? Does Guillermo live, too?"

"I managed to distract Sammy's partner by throwing a rock. I talked to Sammy for a minute. He told me the bastards planted chips inside their heads. When the black box gets aimed at them they obey or they suffer agonizing pain. He can still think for himself, but many of them seem too far gone. He keeps Guillermo and Lark safe. They beat Guillermo many times because he continues resisting. Sammy begged me to tell you to get them out. He got nervous and freaked out."

Abuelo felt furious. "We'll get them. As soon as we get to Prescott, I'll call the Maestra, Tony McNamara, and your dad. Sammy got freaked out? He remains strong enough to resist. He breaks all his conditioning just talking to you."

Martín never imagined the Pure White Brotherhood would use computer chips to torture people. But after all the other atrocities they had committed, he didn't feel shocked.

Alex sounds worried. "Wow, I feel surprised they still live. Sammy impressed me as a very special person, almost magical. What did you do next, Susana?"

"I heard footsteps, so I told him we'd come get them. Then I took off running."

Abuelo holds her face. "You do brave deeds like all your ancestors. You took a terrible chance, but I feel glad you did. Now we know they live and where to find them."

He touches Martín's shoulder. "We'll want you and Tony to figure out a way to deactivate the chips inside those poor souls' heads. We'll free our people."

Martín's heart pounds as he imagines using his blue light to free Guillermo, Sammy, and Lark from their torturing chips.

Chapter 13

May 20, 2033

The fourth morning, Grandpa wakes Martín. "The nights get pretty cool, but the days feel too hot. We'll walk in the mornings and late afternoons."

From his perch on Alex's shoulder, Martín sees someone sitting on a rock. As they draw closer, he sees the guy in the denim jacket stand up. He feels elated and excited! The Indian looks tall, maybe five feet ten inches, with a slender, wiry body. Martín guesses the dude is around forty because of the touches of gray in his single braid.

The man gazes straight into Martín's eyes. "I hold the honor of guiding you." He turns to Sigún and extends his hand. "I call myself Mateo. And yes, you all have seen me around Berkeley. I know Sofía. For your safety, I won't say more."

Martín's grandfather takes his hand. "I call myself Sigún Gonzalez."

Mateo speaks. "I understand you go to Prescott. Is your food running low? I can hunt, and teach you to find water."

Sigún bows. "I welcome your help." He searches Mateo's dark eyes.

"We best keep going before it gets hot," Alex says, heading east. Mateo and Estebán take the lead, but then Mateo falls back to walk beside Alex.

Martín sees the group wondering about Mateo and how he had found them. When Alex stops to shift Martín to Sigún, Susana gives him a long drink of water. Martín sees Mateo observing him the same way he watched him back in Berkeley.

That afternoon, something startles him awake. He feels hot and sticky from his nap; the guy in denim kneels beside him. "You want to know who I am, but I won't tell you yet because of security. I'll tell you in Prescott. I know a creek not far from here. May I take you there?"

He nods.

The Indian picks him up and follows a slight depression to an arroyo leading the stream. "Water collects at the lowest point of the terrain." Mateo breaks a sprig off a little bush near the water and holds it for Martín. "Smell some desert lavender. If I cross your legs, can you sit up by yourself?"

Martin feels unsure he can do this without a back-rest, but he signals yes anyway.

Mateo puts the little boy on the ground and arranges his legs. Martín relaxes a bit as he realizes he can sit up by himself, at last. Mateo removes Martín's clothes and places him in the cool water. The Indian rinses out the boy's clothes. When Martín signals, Mateo takes him out of the water and puts him on a towel. Mateo dries him off, rubs sunscreen on his body, and dresses him in the clean outfit he takes out of his shoulder bag. "I bet you get tired of just signaling yes and no."

Martín looks upstream and notices Sigún watches them from the shade of a shimmering green cottonwood tree.

Mateo offers to take a shift carrying Martín, easily walking with him on his back.

At sunset, they eat some rabbit Mateo killed with his slingshot. Martín sits in front of his grandfather, who massages his neck and shoulders.

Mateo speaks. "Seeing you carry Martín on your back reminds me of The Night Way[i], a nine-night healing chant the Diné sing. Would you like me to tell the story?"

Martín feels a thrill of electricity go through his body when he hears the words "the Diné." He wants to shout, "Yes!" so he signals it with his eyes.

Both Sigún and Alex, aware of his excitement, agree.

"I can tell you this because you yourselves seem ready to hear this old story with powerful words. The wise ones say each time we tell the story a healing comes for every soul in the world. Those who hear it carry it with them, healed each day anew.

"This story happened in Canyon de Chelly in North-east Arizona near where I live. Ages ago, when the gods still spoke directly to humans, there lived a poor family, a grandmother, father, mother, son, and daughter. They hold no sheep or corn but eat seeds, wild fruit, and wood rats.

"The granddaughter, who is fourteen and not quite a woman, goes out to hunt for yucca fruit. She hears a strange voice. When she returns home she tells her family, but they don't pay attention to her. This happens again the next day and the next.

"On the fourth day when she gathers fruit under a ce-dar tree, she notices a man, Talking God, standing beside her, dressed in a mask and fine buckskins. She feels shy and does not answer when four times he asks her to marry him, but she worries about what her family will say. Fi-nally she consents and they make a mutual vow of secrecy.

"The young girl keeps their secret well, but her family begins noticing the changes in her body. They say nothing and do not ask her questions. After four months, she feels unusual movements within her.

"Nine months after her meeting with Talking God, she gives birth to twin sons. She doesn't answer her family's questions about the father. When her grand-mother threatens her, her brother defends her, saying,

'She knows more than she tells us. Our numbers are few. We can use two more men in the family.'

"When the boys turn nine years old they look handsome and quite similar. Despite the family's vigilance, one day they wander off. The family searches for them for days. On the evening of the fifth day, the twins enter their home, the older carrying the younger on his back; one became blind and the other became lame."

Mateo sits. Martín watches him.

"Let's get some rest. I'll tell you more tomorrow." Mateo beds down near the fire.

Martín wonders why the boys became blind and lame and what caused these ailments in children, half-gods. A picture of the twins flashes through his head as he falls asleep.

The next evening after a hard day's walk through the mountain just north of Highway 40, in the quiet as they finish eating, Alex looks from his young friend to Mateo. "Martín and I found your story fascinating. We wonder if you will tell us the healing chant itself when you tell the story. How does the healing happen?"

Mateo scratches his head. "I rephrase the chant as I tell the story and all of it contains the power of healing. But yes, I will tell you a portion of the chant just as I heard it as a child." He laughs. "Of course I will translate it into your language first. Give me a few minutes to compose my thoughts."

The group waits in silence.

House made of dawn.
House made of evening light.
House made of the dark cloud.
House made of male rain.
House made of dark mist.
House made of female rain.
House made of pollen.
House made of grasshoppers.

Dark cloud is at the door.
The trail out of it is dark cloud.
The zigzag lightning stands high upon it.
An offering I make.
Restore my feet for me.
Restore my legs for me.
Restore my body for me.
Restore my mind for me.
Restore my voice for me.
This very day take out your spell for me.

Happily I recover.
Happily my interior becomes cool.
Happily I go forth.

My interior feeling cool, may I walk.
No longer sore, may I walk.
Impervious to pain, may I walk.
With lively feelings may I walk.
As it used to be long ago, may I walk.
Happily may I walk.
Happily, with abundant dark clouds, may I walk.
Happily, with abundant showers, may I walk.
Happily, with abundant plants, may I walk.
Happily on a trail of pollen, may I walk.
Happily may I walk.
Being as it used to be long ago, may I walk.

May it be beautiful before me.
May it be beautiful behind me.
May it be beautiful below me.
May it be beautiful above me.
May it be beautiful all around me.
In beauty it is finished.
In beauty it is finished.
'Sa'ah naaghéi, Bik'eh hózhó[ii]
Mateo stops chanting. Silence fills the evening.

A picture fills Martín's mind, so clear it seems real.
He sees a beautiful house in the desert and he sees himself walking into the house, walking on his own. Once
inside he kneels at an altar and offers his own blue light.
He wonders can he request the healing he learns to give
others. Martín stands. Hands rest on his shoulders. He

turns to the right and there stands Abuelo. To his left Mateo. Mateo's mouth moves, but his voice comes from outside this picture. Martín opens his eyes and sees Mateo, cross-legged beside the fire.

"Please allow me to carry on where I left off last night.

"The family welcomes the twins and questions them about what happened; what caused their blindness and lameness? The boys reply they didn't wander far, when the rock shelter they sat under collapsed upon them and closed them in darkness for four days and nights. When a god opened the rocks and let them out, they found themselves to be disabled, but they found a way to come back to their home; the blind one carrying the lame one, the lame one guiding the blind."

Martín identifies with the lame one. But he doesn't feel wise enough to guide those who don't see what he can see. He wants to become wise like Abuelo and Mateo. And he remembers his dark side and wonders if he will ever become wise.

Mateo continues the story. "Their people try to heal the boys. They use herbs and other means until they understand it is hopeless. After a few days, the family recognizes it is too poor to feed two extra people who can't help out. The twins cannot gather food. Their relatives tell them, 'Go away, go wherever you want. Go die somewhere.'"

Estebán interrupts. "It seems cold! It isn't the twins' fault they became disabled."

Susana yells at him, "No, it's not, it's not cold. The family earned too little to feed them; if they tried all the others would die. Our mother's family walked away from starvation too. They left their *ejido,* their community, their whole country so they would not starve." Martín senses in the dark Susana blushing from the anger her mother's situation causes her. "Sorry," she says, bowing her head, "please continue."

Mateo speaks. "I welcome your comments. I find it beautiful how you relate to this story so deeply.

"The twins spend the next four days wandering near their family's dwelling, hoping their relatives will change their minds. Their father, Talking God, provides them with food every morning and a warm covering of darkness every night. Once they see their family means to abandon them, they decide to go appeal to the gods. Their father, who already gave them a magic bowl of mush, listens to their tale and instructs them on how to get into the house of the gods. He does all this without revealing his identity.

"Once the two brothers travel to Tse'intyel and touch the rainbow according to their father's instruction, they enter the fourth room of the house, where the gods gathered. Each god, even Talking God, denies giving them the secret of entry. The twins tell their story and request healing from the gods. The gods lie and say they can't help the twins and send them to another dwelling place for gods. They ask the twins whether they brought the required sacred offering. The boys say no because they remain very poor and can gather no offering. The gods refuse to help them. The twins' quest continues through a long cycle of refusals by the gods, in the middle of which the twins try to return home but their relatives reject them again.

"As the twins continue to seek out the gods, they receive a test where they choose from four sets of bows and arrows. By their choice, the gods realize Talking God is their father. Finally a one-day healing ceremony begins for the twins, but the boys forget their instructions and talk during the ceremony. The gods put a stop to it and tell the twins to leave, unhealed. As the twins leave crying, their crying turns into a song.

From the white plain where stands the water,
    From there we come,
Bereft of eyes, one bears another,
    From there we come,
Bereft of limbs, one bears another,
    From there we come,
Where healing herbs grow by the waters,
    From there we come,
With these eyes you shall recover,
    From there we come,
With these limbs you shall recover,
    From there we come.

From meadows green where ponds are scattered,
    From there we come,
Bereft of limbs, one bears another,
    From there we come,
Bereft of eyes, one bears another,
    From there we come,
By ponds where healing herbs grow,
    From there we come,
With these limbs you shall recover,
    From there we come,
With these eyes you shall recover,
    From there we come.[iii]

"The gods so impressed by the twins' song they took counsel and decided to give the boys four bundles, each with a magic object the twins could use among the Hopi and Pueblo Indians to gain the offerings they required to get healed."

Mateo pauses and breathes deeply. He looks into the night sky and bows as if communing with the stars. "Yes, I'll stop. Tomorrow I will tell some more."

Alex comes to himself, puts Martín in his bedroll, and gets into his own.

Martín hears his grandfather and the others get ready to sleep. He remembers some of the words of the chant. He gazes at the stars and wonders whether the Navajo gods can see him and if he will ever gather the required offerings.

The next day, Martín notices the closer they get to Needles, the hotter he feels. His grandfather feels the heat,
too. He carries his grandson for shorter periods; Mateo
makes up the difference.

With his friend on his back, Alex strides ahead. "Mateo, please tell us the words to the last part of the first
chant about beauty?"

Mateo's expression softens as he seems to translate in
his head. "Do you mean,

May it be beautiful before me.
May it be beautiful behind me.
May it be beautiful below me.
May it be beautiful above me.
May it be beautiful all around me.
In beauty it is finished.
   In beauty it is finished?"[iv]

Alex takes a deep breath. "Yes, we wonder what you
mean by 'beauty?'"

Mateo looks from Martín's eyes to Alex's. "I see how
you two communicate. But more than just that, how
can you respond without him speaking to you?"

"I knew him since he turned five. I look into his eyes,
get an idea of what he thinks, and then I ask him." Alex
glances at Martín. "Do you want me to tell him I say
what you think too often for it to call it a guess?"

The smaller boy signals yes.

Mateo continues, "You two formed a beautiful relationship. I see beauty when a strong person can speak for someone less able than himself without patronizing."

Alex shakes his head. "I see beauty in our friendship, but not because Martín seems less able. He gives me the benefit of his intelligence so generously, I feel privileged to call myself his friend."

Mateo lowers his voice even more. "She told me about Martín." Then he says out loud, "I'll take a shift carrying your friend."

As the temperature drops, Susana feeds Martín some lizard jerky. He notices his grandfather seems too tired to eat supper.

Mateo squats beside Sigún. "I know an abandoned shack with a well about five miles from here. I'd like to take Susana and Esteban into Needles to get some supplies while you rest. I'll make some phone calls."

"Okay, I could use the rest. Just leave Alex with Martín. In case anything happens, they can get away." The old man takes a deep breath.

"Try to eat something." Mateo reaches under his shirt into the small leather bag he wears around his neck, and brings out a few pinches of dried herb. "I will make you a tea with these. You won't require your heart to work so hard."

Martín finishes eating. Esteban and Alex squat as they rub the battered tin plates with sand to clean them. They place the dishes in the backpack and arrange themselves around the small fire.

Mateo stands up, walks toward the fire, and clears his throat. He begins his tale where he left off the evening before.

"The twins travel to the Hopi and Pueblo towns on a rainbow. They carry with them the four magic objects, which also correspond to four plagues: kangaroo rat, worm, talisman to produce wind, and grasshoppers. The other Indians tease and revile the twins, refusing them food. The two boys set out the pests, which eat or damage the corn crop. The town elders come to the twins for help to save the crops, offering them costly treasures. After the two boys remove the pests, the town reviles them again. The twins repeat the procedure thrice more, each time acquiring more of the items required for the sacred offering. By the fourth time, the Pueblos suspect the twins set the pests themselves. They plan to kill the boys and regain their own wealth, but the twins use the rainbow to escape."

Mateo looks at Martín, who meets his eyes with an attentive look.

"The twins return to the Navajo gods with their offerings and tell their story. The gods suggest the twins visit their family because the healing ritual will begin in four days.

"The twins go through the nine-day healing ritual. After the gods heal them, the daughters of Hastse Hogan shape the boys to look beautiful. The gods decide to send the formerly blind one to Tse'desdzai (you might know this place as the sandstone pinnacles near Fort

Defiance), where he would become the god of thunder and where people can pray to him when they want rain. They plan to send the formerly lame one to Tse'nihoki'z (this place lies near Navajo Springs), where he would become the god who watches over the animals. Before the gods send them to their new homes, the twins spend time with the People of the Earth teaching them the nine-day-healing ritual, which ends with the chant:

In the house made of dawn,
In the house made of evening twilight,
In the house made of dark cloud,
In the house made of rain and mist, of pollen, of grass-
hoppers,
     Where the dark mist curtains the doorway,
The path to which is on the rainbow,
Where the zigzag lightning stands high on top,
Where the he-rain stands high on top,
Oh, Father God!
With your moccasins of dark cloud, come to us,
With your mind enveloped in dark cloud, come to us,
With the dark thunder above you, come to us soaring,
With the shapen cloud at your feet, come to us soaring.
With the far darkness made of the dark cloud over your
head, come to us soaring,
With the far darkness made of the rain and the mist over
your head, come to us soaring,

With the far darkness made of the rain and the mist over your head, come to us soaring.
With the zigzag lightning flung out high over your head,
With the rainbow hanging high over your head, come to us soaring.
With the far darkness made of the dark cloud on the ends of your wings,
With the far darkness made of the rain and the mist on the ends of your wings,
come to us soaring,
With the zigzag lightning, with the rainbow hanging high on the ends of your wings, come to us soaring.
With the near darkness made of dark cloud of the rain and the mist, come to us,
   With the darkness on the earth, come to us.[v]

The chant echoes in Martín's head. He sees himself walking into the dark cloud house. The darkness speaks and the zigzag lightning makes its way through his tired body. He feels both wide awake and ready to release into sleep. Before dozing off, he scans Abuelo's body. He sees two grayish masses in the tubes, leading to his grandfather's heart and the heart itself appears a bright red bruised color. Abuelo's heart looks very tired. Martín doesn't know what to do about the grayish masses, so he brings the blue light to the heart itself. After a few minutes, he stops. He feels too hungry to do more, but Abuelo breathes more easily.

The next morning, Mateo points down a dirt road. "Walk two miles that way. We may not get back until tomorrow. I'll take good care of your grandchildren."

"Or they will take good care of you. See you soon." Sigún watches them walk down the highway and then follows Alex.

Once Abuelo falls asleep, Martín scans his grandfather's heart. While he feels too hungry to do much, he brings the blue light to the bruised, tired areas. Martín hopes Coyote can show him what to do about the gray spots.

Around five in the afternoon on their third day at the shack, Mateo, Susana, and Esteban trot down the dirt road.

"Pack up and hide all signs you stayed here. I brought some canned food to replenish the supplies you fellows used. People walking out of California use this way station." Mateo puts down his two shoulder bags.

Susana walks over to where Alex and Martín share a mattress. She shrugs out of her pack and opens it up. "I brought you each a can of soda. Here."

Alex takes the cans. "Wow, they still feel cold. Thanks. They'll hit the spot."

Soon Mateo leads in a southeasterly direction. "Let's get across the river as soon as we can. A Mojave friend will meet us on the road in the morning."

Martín sees a line of cottonwood trees from his
perch. Alex carries him all night. Mateo leads them to a
ford. They follow Mateo across, careful to watch where
he steps.

"Many patrols watch this section of the river during the day, so I didn't want to wait." Mateo pauses and
squints, searching for the best path.

"Agh!" They hear a splash as Sigún goes down behind them.

"I'll go back and help Grandpa," Esteban says, turning around.

Alex stops to catch his breath on the other side of
the river. Martín glances as his wet grandfather leans on
Esteban, steps from the last rock to the bank.

"Let's rest here until dawn," Mateo says. "That will
give us two hours to get to the road by eight." Mateo
spreads a blanket on the ground and then helps Susana take Martín out of Alex's pack and lay him down.
Martín feels the hard ground. His eyes droop shut as he
hears the others settle.

Too soon, Martín feels a gentle hand on his shoulder.
Susana arranges him in cross-legged position and helps
him sit. "It's way too early to say good morning. Here,
drink this." He drinks. The water feels cool and delicious. He notices the sky, a wonderful pink and yellow.

Mateo replaces Martín's sweaty T-shirt with a dry
one.

Soon Martin dozes off with his head on Alex's shoulder, a blissful two-hour nap.

"There's Franklin." Mateo points to a pickup.

Martín sees a dust cloud approaching. He squints and makes out the old truck.

A heavy-set man with a black crew cut with a hint of gray leans out the window. "Welcome to Arizona, the land of the free. I hope you like it hot."

Soon Mateo holds Martín on his lap inside the cab of the truck. Martín feels the warm air coming through the window and the perspiration pooling where his back meets the Navajo's stomach. His grandfather sits between him and Franklin, who drives north. The thirty-year-old Mojave wears blue jeans, a short-sleeve blue shirt, and running shoes. He doesn't seem very tall, and his stomach sticks out over his belt buckle. His eyes twinkle and his smile lights up his whole face.

After a quick stop for breakfast, Franklin looks at the sky. "I don't mean to rush you, but if we start soon, we can eat dinner in Prescott. I want to go back to work tomorrow morning."

Soon the truck reaches the highway to Flagstaff.

Abuelo speaks. "Franklin, I appreciate all you do for us. I'll request one more thing. When we camped near the Marine Base, we saw some recruits. Susana recognized one of them. Later, she managed to talk to him. My grandson, Guillermo, and two other dear friends remain captured at the camp. How we can get them out of there?"

Franklin responds, "I'll give it some thought. I know my way to the camp, so you can count on me as a guide. When we rescue three people we'll want two large trucks and twelve people we can trust. I made a contact inside the camp. After we make our plans, I can get one message to your folks."

Mateo announces, "I'll supply a truck and six warriors. Also, I know a safe place where we can all rendezvous and go over the plans."

Abuelo tells them, "It will take me a week to get some people out here from the Bay Area. As soon as I get to Prescott, I'll call the Filipino pipeline. We can count on my grandson."

They discuss logistics and plan to meet again in ten days.

Six hours later, the truck pulls up in front of a light blue wooden house on East Goodwin near the public library. Martín feels thrilled when he sees his cousin Pedro stride out of the house and down the ramp. They had built a ramp! Martín wants his electric wheelchair more than a cold drink, more than anything. Tony Mc-Namara had arranged to ship the electric wheelchair to Prescott. Martín mentally calls Shadowfax, which rolls down the ramp and stops two feet from the truck.

Tía Sara follows Shadowfax out of the house. Covered with dust, Susana and Esteban tumble from the truck, run to their mother and their brother Pedro and hug them. Alex scrambles down and dusts himself off before hugging Pedro.

Mateo jumps in surprise as he hears the chair say, "Put me in my chair, now. I want to sit in Shadowfax." He gets out and places Martín in the electric wheelchair.

Franklin and Abuelo climb down. Pedro hugs his grandfather. Tía Sara hugs Martín, and tears roll down her cheeks. "You arrived; all of you. I feel so happy." She looks at the motley crew. "Each one of you looks skinnier than the next. Come inside; I'll heat food." She runs her hand over Susana's hair. "And all of you must want a shower."

Susana touches her mother's shoulder. "We ran into some Zombie Marines on the highway. I saw Sammy Manzanares. I followed them and got to talk to him for a minute. Guillermo and Lark remain with him."

Tía Sara stands still, her hand on the screen door.

Martín speaks. "It's okay, Tía. Abuelo, Mateo, and Franklin will rescue them."

Abuelo gestures. "Mateo and Franklin, please meet Sara, Esteban, and Susana's mother, and their brother, Pedro."

Martín notices Mateo and Tía Sara exchange smiles as if they knew each other.

After a round of handshakes and hugs, Abuelo suggests, "Let's go inside."

The house feels cool and comfortable. Besides the large living room and kitchen, there are two bedrooms and a bathroom downstairs. Later, Martín hears about the four bedrooms and the large bathroom upstairs.

Chapter 14

June 3, 2033

Pedro puts a spoonful of scrambled eggs and salsa into Martín's mouth. A bit of egg escapes and falls on the towel on Martín's chest. "Oops, I used to do this better," Pedro says.

Alex laughs. "Just practice." He wipes his own plate with a flour tortilla. The kitchen smells of garlic and cinnamon. Eight people can easily sit at the round table. Tía Sara put up cheery yellow curtains on the windows above the sink.

Even though Martín chews, his communication device remarks, "You do fine but I want more chocolate milk."

Pedro laughs as he holds a glass up. "Martín can talk clearly with his mouth full."

Tía Sara hands Alex a doughnut. "Ever since you four arrived a week ago, you do nothing but eat and drink. And Abuelo does nothing but sleep." She puts a doughnut each on Esteban and Susana's plate. She looks at Pedro and puts one on his plate, too.

Susana swallows. "Thanks, Mama. And Martín won't stop talking either."

They hear a knock at the front door. Tía Sara stands and says, "I'll get it."

Mateo and Tony McNamara follow Tía Sara into the kitchen. Miguel Lopez, who walked to Prescott with Tía Sara and Pedro, also comes in. He and Mateo lean against the counter while Martín introduces Tony.

Mateo clears his throat. "Alex, did you completely recover from your trek across the desert?"

Alex responds, "I feel fine. I still drink a lot of fluids, but I feel great. Why?"

Mateo speaks in a low voice. "Sigún Gonzalez doesn't recover as quickly as you."

Martín's device tells them, "I think Abuelo's heart sustained damage."

Mateo looks at Martín, raises his eyebrow, and then turns his gaze back to Alex. "The young recover more quickly than the old. Alex, we want you to take Sigún's place in the raid."

Alex says, "I'd feel honored to go as long as you don't require me to tell Sigún I'll take his place."

Mateo's eyes twinkle. "No, I'll do it. I can talk a rattlesnake out of her rattles."

Everyone laughs.

Mateo waits for quiet. "Pedro, I assume you want to go." He receives an eager consent and continues, "Would you team up with Miguel? We want his listening skills."

Martín sees Miguel straighten his body and cock his head.

Pedro replies. "We walked across the desert. He fights better, so definitely."

Mateo taps Miguel on the shoulder. "I assume you'll come with us. We want someone who can warn us of approaching trucks. The marines bring them down the highway without lights, so you'll hear them before we see them."

Miguel responds, "I can do that, and I'd feel honored to go."

Mateo lowers his voice. "We'll leave at two this afternoon, which will give us tomorrow and the next day to practice with the other teams before the action on Wednesday night." He shifts his weight toward Tía Sara. "It's your turn."

She turns toward the table. "Susana and Estebán, m'ijos, I would like your help. Today, we'll look for a quiet motel and reserve two adjoining rooms for Wednesday. Then we'll buy food and medical supplies. You two will scout various routes from here to the motel. Once the action goes down, you'll serve as runners. We don't want to compromise this place."

Mateo speaks again. "Martín, I'll give you three important tasks. This afternoon, you and Tony will take your grandfather to see Coyote, to get his heart checked out and to discuss how you two deactivate the control chips. Secondly, after our meeting with Coyote yesterday, he agreed you will assist while he heals the injured. But, thirdly, in the next few days, I want you to eat all the carbohydrates and protein you can. Supplying Coyote with extra healing force will require a lot of energy from you."

Martín responds, "I'll learn a lot working with Coyote. I'll feel honored to help."

Mateo lowers his voice, "Now I get to tell Sigún about the change in plans."

Tía Sara says, "Suerte, Mateo. I feel glad you'll do it and not me."

Around one, Martín rolls into Coyote's backyard. Both Tony and his grandfather follow him through the gate.

Abuelo feels unhappy. "I want to go with them, this afternoon, not come here to see a healer."

Tony looks Sigún in the eye. "We each make sacrifices to ensure the success of this action." He pauses. "You know, Sigún, I gave up my job in Stanford."

"But you help so many people…" Martín says.

Tony cuts Martín off. "The authorities insisted on adding an agent to my team. And many of the people I help, like you, don't come from lily white families."

Martín adds, "But why would a white man like you leave such a good job?"

Abuelo whispers, "Tony isn't white. He can pass, but not if they look too closely. Why do you think he helps you and other people of color?"

Their conversation stops when Coyote clears his throat and steps forward. He shakes the men's hands and squeezes Martín's shoulder. "Please, sit down, gentlemen." He laughs and looks at his own bronze hand. "I could never pass; my mother comes from the People, Diné, and my father's parents came from Japan." He turns to Tony. "What do you know about the chips they put in the heads of non-white prisoners?"

Tony responds, "The chips I put into Martín's head give him freedom. The chips they put into the young people's heads they control with a radio signal. And it would take major surgery to remove them from their heads."

Martín inquires, "Can we turn off the chips so they can't receive radio signals? Would leaving them in place cause long-term problems?"

Tony marvels. "Martín, how did you get so smart? Yes, there's a small, almost imperceptible on/off switch. I'll draw a picture of a chip and show you. No one has studied the long-term effects of leaving the chips in the brain, but I don't see an alternative."

"Martín understands the chips better than I ever will," Coyote says. "If I help you locate them, do you think you can turn them off?"

Martín mutters, "Yes."

Abuelo's eyes open wide. "Martín," he exclaims, "I've never heard you talk before. You just spoke, m'ijo."

Martín signals yes, and with his device states, "So far I can say one word at a time." He pauses. "And it takes a lot of energy. But I also gain more control over my body. I found out I can sit cross-legged on the ground without back support."

Coyote grins. "I'll teach you more ways to heal your body now that I see how far you came on your own. But first we'll heal those who escape."

Abuelo speaks. "The Brotherhood injured my grandson Guillermo badly for resisting their control."

Tony frowns. "Maestra always said, 'It is better to survive and resist later.'"

Coyote responds, "I will bring my trusted assistant. She, Martín, and I will examine those you rescue and will work on healing them. It may take as long as six months or a year for them to function completely. Once we know the white agents don't follow them, we can move them here. I can't promise to heal all the damage. The White Brotherhood wounds people in ways difficult to treat."

Abuelo worries. "Martín just turned twelve. Should he know about such injuries?"

Martín answers, "When I become a healer, I'll find out the worst about what people do."

Coyote puts his hand on Martín's shoulder. "And I will teach you ways to shield yourself so you don't take any evil into your soul.

Martín declares, "I do deeds I wish I didn't do, so I will work hard to become more integrated. Coyote, how do you feel about teaching me to heal?"

Coyote thinks a minute. "You seem so young and so powerful already, you scare me shitless. I'll define my task as watching your moral and psychological development. I hope your growing up with cerebral palsy grounded you in connecting to other people."

Martín nods his head, remembering the story Mateo told them about the blind twin and the lame twin. He thinks about his friendship with Alex, his twin. "I want to learn so much. Coyote, please take me on."

Coyote grins. "Consider yourself my student until we agree you can move on."

Martín grins, too. "Thanks," he says aloud.

Three nights later, Alex feels excited and nervous as he rides with the older warriors in the back of the truck. Sweat runs down his back. He has enjoyed training with this group and has learned a lot. When this is over, he'll ask Mateo about becoming a warrior in the Resistance.

The truck stops. Alex climbs down, takes a second to orient himself and sees the lights of the camp. He follows Tío Juan to the front gate, and sees Sammy. When Alex gives him a hug he can feel Sammy's ribs. They must not feed the detainees. He follows Tío Juan and Franklin as Sammy leads them down a dark hallway to a small room where Lark, Guillermo, and two other detainees wait. Guillermo seems to be unconscious.

Sammy grabs Franklin's arm. "These two gotta come with us."

Franklin appears to want to stick with the plan. "Well, I don't know."

Alex hears Pedro shouting, trucks arriving, and heavy boots coming their way. Sammy seems quite agitated when he says, "They are my friends. She's scheduled to be shot in the morning. They gotta come with us."

Alex hears shots, shouts, and people running. Franklin speaks loudly, "Okay, but we must move fast. Juan and Alex, you two carry Guillermo and get everyone back to the truck. I'll go see what's going on." He runs out the door.

Tío Juan tells Sammy, "You lead the way" as he and Alex pick Guillermo up. Alex senses how light Guillermo weighs. He feels nervous as they follow Sammy and the other three to the back of the truck. But he gradually becomes aware of a circle of dark clad warriors ensuring their progress through the chaos.

Strong hands lift Guillermo into the back of the truck. Tío Juan sits on the floor and holds his oldest son against his chest. Alex climbs into the truck and sits against the side. The truck starts. Pedro shouts, "Hey, wait for us!"

Alex rushes over to help Miguel climb up and finds him a place to sit. Miguel's clothes drip with blood, but he doesn't appear wounded.

Alex makes himself comfortable, breathes to release the tension in his body, and promptly falls asleep on the long ride back to Prescott.

Martín dreams the next morning about Superboy rescuing teenagers from a prison when he feels a gentle hand on his shoulder shaking him awake.

Tía Sara whispers, "Mateo says to eat a good breakfast and come to the motel. The action succeeded. Coyote wants your help with five rescued ones."

Martín rolls to a sitting position. Shadowfax moves over to him.

Very soon, Tía Sara knocks on the door of a motel room. A Diné warrior opens the door and Martín rolls in ahead of her. She hands a bag of doughnuts to the Diné. Several other young men and women dressed in dark clothing seem tired yet elated. Pedro motions his mother and Martín into the adjoining room.

In the crowded room, Coyote's assistant, a young Pueblo woman, works on a warrior, wounded in the shoulder. Mateo gives first aid to an unconscious woman, and Sammy Manzanares holds Lark while his mother bandages his arm. Coyote crouches to examine Guillermo, motionless on a bed. Tía Sara moves toward Guillermo.

Coyote stands when he sees Martín. "We just got here. Your Tío Juan went to rent another room where we can deactivate the chips inside these young people. Guillermo doesn't look good. I find his pulse thready and his breathing too rapid."

Tío Juan comes through the door from a third adjoining room. "The manager told me we can use this room, too." He strides over to his wife and gives her a hug. "Amor, I finally left the damn house in Berkeley. Friends will stay there."

Coyote speaks up. "Let's move Guillermo so Martín can turn off his chip and I can get him stabilized." He and Tío Juan carry Guillermo into the other room. As soon as Martín rolls through the doorway, Coyote motions Guillermo's parents to leave and shuts the door.

Martín moves closer to Guillermo, who appears very pale. "He doesn't look good."

Coyote whispers, "We'll just do the best we can. I'll lead you into his brain so you can deactivate the chip."

Soon Martín's blue light follows Coyote's yellow light through a mass of red bruised brain. Martín sees the chip and looks for the on/off switch. He finds the tiny switch. He takes a deep breath and taps it with his force. Nothing happens. Martín taps it a little harder and the switch shifts into off-position. He and Coyote withdraw their healing forces. Both perspire and breathe hard. Guillermo looks even paler. The bruised tissue felt both fragile and slippery like tiptoeing on banana peels in a dark room.

Coyote looks at Martín. "I'll start healing him or he'll go into shock. Can you do the next one yourself?"

When Martín agrees, Coyote opens the door and tells Maestra Manzanares, "Please bring Sammy and Lark in here. And then help Martín drink something now, and then get him a high-protein shake. The work he does demands a lot from him." Coyote turns to his assistant. "Please come in here."

Coyote and his helper stabilize Guillermo and restore his blood pressure. Martín, using his blue light, searches for the chip in Lark's brain. He finds the on/off switch, and turns it off. The red area surrounding the chip seems less bruised than in Guillermo's brain. Martín feels deep affection for Lark and takes time to bathe the bruised area in a blue, healing light. She takes a deep breath and her hands unclench. Martín withdraws his force. Not surprised, he finds his own body starving and his T-shirt drenched.

Both Coyote and the Pueblo woman focus their healing on Guillermo, whose face looks less gray. Maestra holds a chocolate shake. Martín can't drink it fast enough. He drinks half the shake, shuts his eyes, and breathes deeply for five minutes before turning his attention to searching for Sammy's chip. He can't get inside Sammy's head, so he withdraws and his device speaks, "Please let down your shields."

Sammy whispers. "What shields?" He turns his attention inside himself. "Oh, yeah, y'know I did that automatically. I protected myself. You can go in now."

Martín uses his blue light to enter Sammy's brain and turn off his chip. He sees almost no bruising in the area. "You did a great job shielding yourself. Please show me how you did that. I look for ways to protect myself, too."

Sammy speaks wanly. "Y'know I'd feel honored to teach you anything I know. But, right now, I just want to sleep."

Martin agrees. "Sure, we both feel tired, and I want to turn off two people's chips."

Coyote, his assistant, and Guillermo drink tea. The three look exhausted, but at least now Guillermo seems semi-conscious.

Maestra leads Sammy and Lark to the other room. She returns with a young multi-racial couple unknown to Martín. The injured woman looks less alert than the wound would merit.

Coyote recommends, "Martín, rest a few minutes. Then I'll help you locate their chips. You look exhausted."

As Maestra holds the shake so Martín can finish it, she turns to the young man and inquires, "What do you two call yourselves?"

"I call myself Tomás Rodriguez, and she calls herself Juanita Yamamoto. Your son befriended us. When they came to get him, Sammy knew they would shoot

Juanita today for refusing to service an officer, so he got them to bring us."

Maestra mutters, "Those damn bastards!"

Tomás continues speaking. "They beat her up when she kneed the officer in the groin. We lived in Stockton. The Brotherhood picked up our class as we graduated from high school. They loaded us into trucks as we left the auditorium, still in our graduation robes with our diplomas in our hands."

Coyote turns to his assistant. "Check out her injuries while I help Martín deactivate his chip." He glances at the small boy in the electric wheelchair. Yellow and blue lights trace the path to another chip.

Tomás shuts his eyes but starts talking again. "In the three years since they captured us, the officers killed most of our classmates. If not for Sammy, we would be dead too. Last year, an officer transferred us into his unit. Somehow he managed to keep people alive."

After shutting off Tomás' chip, Coyote and Martín turn their attention to Juanita. Coyote leads the search for her chip.

Tomás continues speaking. "It took me a while to figure out someone caused the officers to calm down when they came around us. They would come into our barracks ready to punish us and then forget all about it. One day I saw Sammy closed his eyes and concentrated. Then I saw the officer didn't notice Guillermo, like he looked right through him. The officer didn't like Guillermo, so the officer always tried to break him down.

Sammy saved Guillermo from quite a few beatings by making him invisible. Sammy kept him alive; he kept all of us alive.

"Once I questioned Sammy about why he protected us. He said, 'Y'know one day we will get out of here. And we can't fight back if they kill us.' I didn't believe him." Tomás' voice trails off into the silent room.

Coyote, his assistant, and Martín breathe deeply with their eyes shut. Perspiration soaks their clothes. Coyote rouses himself. "Martín, you did a great job. Go home and sleep for at least twelve hours." He turns to his helper. "I'll get some sleep and return in four hours. Can you handle things here for a while?"

"Sure, everyone seems stable. I'll just take a shower and put on some dry clothes." His assistant picks up her backpack and walks toward the bathroom.

Coyote speaks. "I worry about Guillermo. Call me if he changes." He opens the door and turns to Tía Sara. "Please take Martín home and feed him."

Martín, so tired, can't drive his electric wheelchair. He falls asleep in the shower.

Alex shakes Mateo awake. "I can't find Martín."

Mateo yawns and sits. He pulls on his pants. "Let's find him."

Alex follows him. "I suspect Martín feels a lot of pressure."

"Yes, I know, but it's dangerous." Mateo stops and whistles four times.

A young warrior in black steps out of the shadows and points west. She speaks in a low voice. "Martín went that way. One of the Filipinas keeps an eye on him."

Mateo looks at Alex. "He may want the time alone. What do you think?"

Alex meets his eyes. "I didn't realize you have everything under control."

"I set up a watch to make sure the soldiers didn't follow us."

"Let's go back to bed?"

Mateo yawns. "I can use the sleep. And thank you for keeping an eye out for Martín. He will always be more vulnerable, but don't tell him."

"Of course not. We're friends." Alex winks before reentering the house.

The living room seems crowded when Martín rolls into it later that morning. Everyone sits wherever they can fit, on the couch or the floor. Abuelo gives Martín a hug. "Hey, sleepyhead, we waited for you. Your Tío Juan will tell us about the rescue."

Maestra puts a hand on Martín's shoulder. "I watched you yesterday. Your gift grows by leaps and bounds. You have just the right touch."

He blushes and says aloud, "Thank you."

Tío Juan laughs. "You spoke."

Martín tells them, "As I learn to heal other people, I also learn to heal myself."

Alex fills Martín in. "Coyote took Guillermo to his house. He seems better but still not out of the woods. Sammy, Lark, Tomás, and Juanita will stay at the motel. Maestra and Sammy will look for a house to rent in this neighborhood. Sammy will run it. Coyote wants them to stick around while he finishes healing them. The others involved either still do guard duty or went home."

Tío Juan holds Tía Sara's hand. "As I told you before sleepyhead joined us, the week before I got the message to come out here, my friend came to inquire whether they could live at our place. His son recently became quadriplegic, and he couldn't find an accessible house. So their whole family moved in and will keep it up for us." He looks at his wife, who shakes her head. "In case we ever return," he adds.

Maestra continues the tale. "I got a ride for Juan, three students, and myself. Easy, since we Filipinos drive half the trucks in the west. Needles felt so hot. We spent a day training with everyone. We rested a day, and that night we headed out in two trucks toward the Marine Training Camp, more of a prison than anything else."

Tío Juan resumes speaking. "I'd call it a concentration camp. Those white bastards want to get rid of all the non-white people in their territories. I felt amazed to see my friend Sammy guarding the front gate. Franklin got word to him, so he volunteered for extra guard duty. Sammy helped us locate Lark and Guillermo. He insisted we bring Tomás and Juanita, too. He became so agitated Franklin agreed."

They hear a knock at the backdoor. Tía Sara opens it. "Welcome. Come on in."

Sammy leads the way. "We wondered where everyone went until I saw the note Ma left me." Lark, Tomás, and Juanita follow him and they all sit on the floor.

Pedro speaks up. "We recount the action. Everything went smoothly until Miguel told me he heard some heavy trucks coming. He and I stayed on the perimeter. By the time I found Franklin, three Marines' trucks arrived."

Miguel talks. "I heard brakes, boots running, and shots. I squatted so I'd be less of a target, and I pulled my knife. A soldier stumbled over me. We grappled, but he weighed more so I stabbed him and he fell on top of me. I stayed under him until I heard Pedro whistle. When we climbed in the back of the truck, some thought the soldiers hurt me, but I felt okay."

Tío Juan recounts, "When pandemonium broke out, Franklin told me to load all the people we rescued into the back of the first truck. Alex and I carried Guillermo. The other warriors mounted a rearguard action while we picked up Miguel and Pedro."

Mateo talks in a calm voice. "I spoke with Franklin this morning. They managed to slash the tires on all three trucks. They left our truck in Las Vegas and vanished within seconds." He turns to Martín. "When you dress, take Sammy, Lark, Juanita, and Tomás to Coyote's house. He wants to continue your training this morning. I'll meet you there at four. I want to talk to you."

Maestra turns to Tía Sara. "Will you, Susana, and Esteban help Sammy and me find a house near here and buy furniture and the things Sammy will want?"

Tía Sara responds, "Sure, just let Esteban help Martín get showered and dressed."

Tío Juan says, "Pedro and I will continue a patrol perimeter around the houses."

By mid-afternoon, Martín feels wrung out. While Coyote's helper works on Guillermo, Martín and Coyote heal the other four.

Someone knocks. Coyote leads Mateo into the room. He asks, "How does it go?"

"Martín learns faster than anyone I ever met. Sammy just lacks good food and rest. Lark, Juanita, and Tomás require more healing. We can handle it, easy." Coyote turns to his assistant.

She seems sad. "We can keep Guillermo alive, but with this brain damage, I don't know."

Mateo turns to Martín. "I want to talk to you. Do you feel ready to roll?"

Martín turns to Coyote and bows.

Coyote bows. "Namaste. We will continue our work in the morning."

Mateo opens the door and leads the way. Martín quips, "What's up?"

Mateo sets an easy pace. "You arrived in a safer place, so I'll tell you about your father."

Martín feels excited. His weariness drops. He blurts, "I wanted to know forever."

The Navajo puts his hand on Martín's arm. "First, let me say, I feel proud of you. You grow into a fine person, kind, gentle, and a true curandero. You live with constant difficulty. You are too intelligent to feel sorry for yourself. I feel proud of the way you develop your gifts. I feel proud... to be your father." He picks up Martín and hugs him.

In the middle of the hug, Martín exclaims, "Oh, my. Oh, my! I knew we had a connection when I first met you, Dad, but this feels even better than I imagined."

Mateo puts him into Shadowfax. "For security reasons, continue to call me Mateo."

"Sure." Martín takes a breath. "Ever since I saw you I wanted to call you 'Dad.'"

"You can't tell anyone, not even Abuelo. I serve as an officer in the Resistance. You came to a safer place, so I wanted you to know. That day at your pal's house I threw the stone at the officer."

"I felt so glad he got away. I always wondered why you watched me so intently."

Mateo ruffles his son's hair. "Yes, I wanted to know all about you and keep you safe. I feel so proud of the way you learn to heal. I always loved you and I always will."

Martín hesitates. "I love you, too." He wishes he met his dad earlier.

Mateo speaks. "You also have an uncle and cousin who live north of here on Navajo land. Your cousin, Vela, just turned three. Let's get back to the house before they miss us."

Later, Susana wonders, "What's got into you, Martín? You seem so spacey."

Mateo answers. "He feels worn out from learning to heal."

Martín sighs in relief. Before Susana can ask why Mateo answers for him, Tony rushes through the door. "I just got back from Albuquerque with good and bad news."

Sammy stands and hugs his old sparring buddy.

Tío Juan motions for Tony to take a seat. "What's the good news?"

Tony sits. "My friend who works at Sandía Labs showed me how to program the chips with a virus. He gave me this black box, which will free all the kids with chips in their heads."

Abuelo's voice sounds sad. "And the bad news?"

Tony looks at Tía Sara. "A person with a chip must physically carry the virus back."

Sammy speaks. "Y'know they couldn't hurt me the first time. I'll go back."

Tío Juan catches his wife's attention, and she nods back. Her eyes fill with tears.

Tony frowns, "Whoever goes in won't come out. White soldiers will destroy that person."

Tío Juan stands. "Must the person who goes be conscious?" He steps toward Tía Sara and puts a hand on her shoulder.

Tony whispers, "No, he doesn't."

Tía Sara speaks with tears rolling down her face. "The white bastards destroyed our son. Let's make his death count for something."

Tío Juan holds his wife. "Guillermo would appreciate the irony of the situation and would want to strike this blow."

Abuelo sighs, "Sammy, thanks, but Guillermo will infect the chips."

Sammy solemnly acquiesces.

Mateo stands. "I'll call Franklin."

Tony inquires, "Martín, will you come with me and help me program the chip?"

Martín murmurs, "I can't. I love him." He starts sobbing. He never realized the seriousness of the stakes. Abuelo picks him up.

Tony catches Martín's attention. "Sorry; I forgot you're only twelve."

He cries harder. Susana, Estebán, and Pedro hug Abuelo and Martín and wail.

The next morning, Tío Juan and Pedro help Guillermo to a car outside Coyote's house. Tía Sara sits in the back seat and cradles Guillermo. Estebán joins his father and Pedro in the front seat, while Susana climbs in the back seat on the other side of Guillermo and grasps his hand. Abuelo and Martín watch as they drive away.

Several days pass; one evening Martín feels tired. He scouts around the house for someone to help him get into bed. Tía Sara sits in the kitchen drinking tea. He doesn't see anyone else, so he rolls up to her. "How do you feel?"

She seems so sad. "I feel devastated, losing my eldest son. I miss him so much. At least you and my other three kids and Miguel arrived here safely."

Martín says, "I'll miss Guillermo the rest of my life. He saw me as a person and he introduced me to Maestra, who changed my life. I missed him the last year, but I thought I would see him again. But now you sacrificed your son. He won't come back."

Tía Sara, with tears in her eyes, picks him up and hugs him. "I always thought I would see m'ijo until last week, and yes, I feel glad we broke Sammy and Lark out, but I miss m'ijo." She puts Martín back in his chair. "You look tired. Shall I help you to bed?"

"Yes, please, but before we do that, I saved a chocolate bar in my backpack, from the trip. Will you share a piece with me?"

Tía Sara nods. "Yes, I'll get it out. Since you arrived in Berkeley, I always thought of you as one of my own. And now that Pedro and Miguel seem inseparable, Miguel becomes one of my own too.

Martín looks at her. "I like Miguel, and he seems so capable. He'll do well as a massage therapist. I notice his blindness less and less each day." She digs in his backpack and finds a chocolate bar. She breaks off two pieces and puts the rest back. "Thanks for sharing this with me."

"Sure, I figured you loved chocolate."

Tía Sara turns toward the door. "Come Martín, I'll put you to bed."

Six days later Sammy runs into the library and spots Martín. "Coyote wants you to go to Flagstaff with us. Y'know he waits outside with the van. Your tía told us where you hang out. Shall I put your things in your backpack?"

Martín blinks. "Yeah, sure."

Sammy takes the book out of the automatic page-turner. "Martín, why do you read this microbiology text? Our summer classes don't start for two weeks."

Martín blinks again. "I signed up for a heavy load. And I never can tell when Coyote will want me, like now."

He rolls out of the library with Sammy and sees the van with a ramp sticking out.

Martín bows. "What's up, fearless teacher?"

Coyote laughs and returns the bow. "Franklin called. Several warriors watch the river, and six young people from the marine camp crossed over. He'll drive them to Flagstaff, but they want medical care for all the beatings, starvation, and dehydration."

Martín's eyes fill with tears. "That means Guillermo's sacrifice worked."

Sammy whispers, "Yes."

Martín closes his eyes, squeezing them shut. Tears roll down his face.

Part II

Chapter 15
April 17, 2039

Martín walks into Coyote's clinic using his walker. He has grown in the last six years and now looks the same size as a ten-year-old. Four families linger in the waiting room. He knocks on the door to Coyote's office, goes in, and sits down. "Hi, is our afternoon busy?" The room feels cozy. Both Eastern and Western medical texts fill the small bookcase, and a well-used poster showing Shin-jin-jitsu points hangs above them. Martín can see the tranquil rock and cactus garden through the window. The office smells of ginger and green tea.

Coyote looks up from his notes and seems sad. "Yes, and I want you to look at this one patient because I can't do anything for him."

Martín looks him in the eye. "If you can't help him, what can I do?" Both wear T-shirts and cotton shorts. Martín wears a battered pair of Converse sneakers.

"We have different gifts, and sometimes you can help people I can't and vice versa. Besides, we can't heal everyone."

Martín feels frustrated. "How do you know we can't help everyone?"

"I know, but you'll learn for yourself." Coyote stands. "Let's go to Exam Room 3, where he waits."

The two enter the exam room. An older Indian lies on the table. Coyote speaks. "I would like my assistant to scan your body."

The man nods. Martín, using his walker, sits in a chair and scans the man's body. As they leave, Coyote says, "Thank you."

The Indian responds, "I know I'll die soon. But if you could take some of the pain from my lower back, I'd feel relieved."

When Martín reaches the office, he collapses into the chair. "Whew, I feel terrible. The cancer started in his liver and spread through the lymph nodes. I can't do anything. But I'll see if I can ease the pain in his lower back. Too bad he didn't come sooner."

Coyote seems even sadder. "Yes, please do whatever you can for him and let me know when you finish. Many patients wait for us."

Later, Martín returns to the office. Coyote's other assistant brings them both protein drinks. He sighs. "I hate it. I hate it. I hate it. I hate death. I hate not helping everybody. I hate illness. I hate pain." He bursts into tears.

Coyote holds him. "I learned this most difficult lesson over and over. I hate death too. We want to understand the limits of our healing power and not take on everything."

Martín sniffles and wipes his nose. "If we didn't care so much about people, we wouldn't do good healing. But it's hard not to feel like a failure when someone dies."

"Yes, I know what you mean. We can accompany someone as they die, and ease their pain, but we yearn to do more."

Martín looks at his teacher. "What do I do with this sorrow?"

"I remember all the people I do help, and I swim everyday. I encourage you to do the same." The two rest in silence. Coyote adds, "I wish we could do more for your Abuelo besides prolonging his life. I wish we could heal his heart."

Martín sighs. "Yeah, but we'll keep him alive as long as we can."

The following Saturday, Estebán carefully avoids a pothole as he drives his old car on a dirt road. "We'll get to your dad's place soon."

Martín, sitting beside him, shakes his head to come out of his trance. "Thanks for the warning. I gave strength to Abuelo's heart."

Abuelo stirs and sits up. "I feel stronger. I enjoy seeing the next valley from your dad's place."

Esteban stops the car in front of two hogans. Vela, nine years old, black hair in braids, wearing jeans and a clean blue T-shirt, races up to the truck and gives Martín a hug. "I feel so glad you came. My mother went to buy supplies in Gallup. Tío Mateo and I just killed a ewe."

Mateo comes out wiping his hands on a rag. "Welcome. I feel glad to see each of you." He gives Martín a hug and shakes the other two's hand.

Martín asks his dad, "How's Ma?'

"Sofía seems okay. She drove to eastern California for some action. I'll feel relieved when we both get back to Santa Fe."

Mateo and Esteban help Abuelo walk from the car to an easy chair placed where he can see the mountains on the far side of the valley. Mateo asks, "I know Vela wants to visit with Martín. Esteban, will you help me with the ewe?"

"Sure, just tell me what to do."

Vela, tall and sturdy, steadies Martín's walker as they walk on the rough path to the river. "I miss my dad a lot since he died last year. I feel lonely when just my ma and I stay here. Tío Mateo comes when he can and does whatever chores he can."

Martín frowns. "I still miss my ma since she rejoined the Resistance when I turned twelve, but losing a parent would feel devastating."

Vela gets tears in her eyes. "Yes, when I first heard, I felt like I couldn't breathe. I don't remember the next three days. Mother said I went into shock, and she rushed me to the clinic."

"How do you feel these days?" Martín sighs as he sits down on a log.

Vela takes a minute to watch the river. "I love this spot."

"So do I."

Vela speaks quietly. "I feel sad and out of kilter. I noticed that I get angry a lot, more than before."

The two observe the river in a companionable silence for a while before Martín asks, "Can I do anything?"

"Come see me more often, and bring books."

Martín inquires, "Books?"

"I attend a one-room school not far from here. A group of five of us read everything we can get our hands on. But we can't find many books out here."

Martín smiles. "I love to read and I feel glad you enjoy it, too. No one prints decent books any more, so they are getting scarce. Last week I packed a box of books and graphic novels I already read, books like The Count of Monte Cristo, V, and The Watchmen. I planned to trade them, but I'll bring the box next time I come."

"Great, I'll share them with my reading group."

A week later, Lark enters an activity room behind the Catholic Church in Lone Pine, California, deep in Owens Valley, the driest place she has ever seen. A group of warriors enter with her, including her good friend and commander, Sofía, and a new recruit, an eighteen-year-old herbalist from northwestern Arizona who calls herself Blue Feather. She seems a little taller than Lark and broader across the shoulders, but more feminine. She wears long skirts and only during actions does she wear pants. She smiles when she cracks a joke.

The warriors come into the room, where a group of Timbisha fighters waits. Everyone drinks water, and a Timbisha combatant refills their glasses.

Halfway through the meeting, they hear a whistle from the lookout. Sofía yells, "We gotta go!" She rushes out the back door following the others. She yells, "We gotta get to our meeting at DeLaCour Ranch, where our people can cover us." They pile into a battered pickup truck and take off. A mile from the ranch, Lark hears a shot, and the front tire blows. They jump out. A soldier shoots Blue Feather in the back of the head. Lark covers Sofía as she and another warrior pick up the wounded girl.

Despite one soldier's persistent shots, they manage to carry Blue Feather to one of the cabins at DeLaCour Ranch and take her inside. Lark stays with Blue Feather while Sofía rushes outside. Through the open door, Lark sees a grenade land near Sofía's feet. *Boom!* Lark feels a horrified scrunch in her stomach. Sofía died, blown into pieces.

Lark stops the bleeding at the back of Blue Feather's head. Once the soldiers drive away, the group puts Blue Feather and the other wounded in the back of the truck and rush them to Blue Feather's mother's clinic near Lake Havasu in Arizona. Lark holds her hand during the ride and wishes Martín could see the injured.

A few days later, Coyote pounds on Martín's door. "You stayed in there for two days; I will come in." He rams the door with his shoulder. He finds Martín lying on the bed, very pale and hardly breathing. He scans his assistant's body and finds nothing wrong, so he shakes him.

Within his mind, Martín dwells in a cave with many rooms and cells. In one cell a Pure White Brotherhood officer with blond hair and blue eyes lies attached spread-eagle to a table. The man, about forty-five years old and in good shape, wears no shirt and shivers. Martín sits in an easy chair next to the table and attaches electrodes to the officer's brachial plexus. Increasing the voltage, Martín sends repeated shocks through the soldier's body. The soldier convulses in pain and stops breathing for a few seconds. When he starts breathing again, he screams in terror. Martín, the bereaved young man, feels a thrill of power each time he sends a jolt and sees the body convulse. Now he feels someone shaking his own body.

He moans groggily. "I don't want come out. I like going in my cave, where I can torture the white bastards who killed my mom."

Coyote, feeling exasperated, picks up Martín with a grunt, carries him to the shower, and turns on the cold water. Martín sputters. "You can't do this to me."

The older man yells, "You call yourself my apprentice. You stayed in the damn cave for two days. I will do whatever it takes to get you out."

The boy sputters again. "But this water feels so cold. Let me out of here."

Coyote growls back, "Take off your wet things, and I'll turn on the warm water and get you some clean clothes."

Later, Martín lurches into Coyote's study. Coyote frowns and says, "You can't even walk. What do you say for yourself?"

"You don't understand! My ma died. I feel deep grief. I'll do what I freakin' want."

Coyote makes a visible effort to control his frustration. "You hold this wonderful gift, and I want to help you grow into a responsible healer and a mature adult. You feel angry at the white soldiers, but withdrawing into the damn cave fantasy won't bring your mother back, nor will it help you develop your gifts. Do you want to shrivel away or do you want to become the person your mother raised? Don't answer now, but get a good night's sleep and come back tomorrow after breakfast and give me your answer."

Martín staggers out and slams the door. He slams the door to his room and collapses into bed.

Later, he dreams of chaos, explosions, shots, screams, and smoke. He stumbles over a pile of body parts and gags. All of a sudden, the noise stops, until a coyote howls in the distance. He can't take his eyes off the body parts, which reassemble a ghoulish, bleeding version of his mother with only one eye. She looks at her son. "M'ijo, I love you. No, you can't heal me. You can't heal everyone. Heal all our people you can. And find yourself a companion and soul mate. Find someone to share your joys and sorrows." The coyote stops howling. The chaos and noise of battle resume. Sofía's body falls apart and turns into dust. Wind disperses the dust. Martín wakes, weeping.

The next morning, Martín knocks on Coyote's door. When he responds, Martín, using his walker, strides in. He feels calm. "I dreamt about my ma. She told me to heal our people. I can heal. I want you to teach me to grow into a responsible adult and stay out of that damn cave."

Coyote speaks humbly. "I'll do my best. You hold a deep connection to your mother. You feel so much pain, you forget you hold links to the rest of us."

Coyote knows he will work hard to guide his apprentice, and he wonders how Martín will deal when his grandfather dies.

Chapter 16
March 8, 2041

Two years pass, in which Martín works hard both as a healer and taking responsibility for himself. The two healers labor in the office. Coyote asks, "How did your date go last night?"

"It bummed me out." Martín frowns. "She went out with me to satisfy her curiosity. She doesn't want to see me again. She wanted a good meal, but she doesn't want to date 'a skinny string bean who thinks he knows more than anybody else.'"

Coyote says, "So keep trying. I dated for a while before I met my wife. And then I courted her because she didn't want to date me. We both heal, so that helped."

They work in companionable silence until Tío Juan rushes in. "Coyote, your wife said you two were working here. My dad fails. Please come by the house as soon as you can."

Coyote frowns. "We'll come right away."

Tía Sara opens the door minutes later. "Come right in. Martín knows the way. He doesn't seem alert but very weak. I hope you can do something."

Martín leads the way to his grandfather's bedroom and knocks on the door before entering. "Hey Abuelo, how do you feel?"

The older man lies in bed. He speaks very softly. "I don't feel so hot but like a fifty-pound weight crushes my chest."

Both healers sit on the floor. Coyote inquires, "May we scan your heart?"

Abuelo nods. "Yes, you two operate that way. You kept me alive the last eight years, longer than I expected."

Martín and Coyote go into a trance. Ten minutes later, when they come out of the trance, Coyote looks at Martín. "I want to talk to you outside."

Abuelo says, "Stay. I know I'll die soon. You can speak in front of me."

Coyote frowns. "Hey Martín, I saw the heart muscle giving out and the lungs don't get enough oxygen. Did you see that?"

Martín speaks soberly. "Yes, I saw we can keep you alive for four or five days, tops." He starts crying. "But I don't want you to die."

Abuelo seems calm. "I feel ready to go. I feel so tired. This will give me a chance to say goodbye to each of my grandkids."

The following Sunday morning, Tía Sara calls each of Abuelo's grandchildren into the room. Finally, she calls Martín. His grandfather breathes very shallowly. Martín gets close to the bed and kneels so he can hear.

Abuelo seems quite peaceful. "I feel so glad your mother brought you to California and I discovered your intelligence. You brought me great joy. You became a phenomenal healer, and I feel so proud of you. I enjoyed watching you grow into a man. I know of your struggles to stay out of the cave at Tierra Oscura. Yet you do better these last eighteen months. The future will give you many challenges. I hope you can find a partner you can love and respect.

"I love you so much. You must integrate your healer side with your warrior side. Also, you must not leave out your playful coyote side. I leave you my spirit.

"I won't live long, and I want to give you my blessing. May you enjoy beauty and delight and learn to share both pleasure and sorrow with others. May you listen to the voice of your spirit. May you love deeply without expectations."

Martín and Abuelo sit in silence until Abuelo whispers, "Please go get the others."

Tío Juan, Tía Sara, Estebán, Pedro, and Susana gather around Abuelo's bed.

Abuelo whispers, "I love you all."

Susana says sadly, "Guillermo's not here."

Tía Sara whispers, "Y Sofía."

Tío Juan murmurs something that sounded like "Y Helena."

Martín holds Abuelo's hand when he hears Abuelo's last breath. All of a sudden a grey owl comes out of Abuelo's chest and strikes Martín's heart.

When Martín comes to, the world looks magical. Lines of energy connect everything.

A month later, after the family cremated Abuelo and scattered his ashes over the Grand Canyon, Susana leads Tony and Martín into her living room.

Tony grins. "I'll pour us some agua fresca."

Martín sits down at the table. "Did you invite us with a purpose in mind?"

Susana puts down her glass. "Yeah, ever since Sammy and Lark moved to Chimayo, I wanted to move closer to them. I did research. Santa Fe's healer died, and the heirs put the clinic up for sale near the plaza.

Tony can administrate the clinic and you two can live with Mateo until you find your own place. Lark already found me a tiny house four blocks from the clinic. I want to watch Swallow and Tommy-tres grow up. Lark said they both hold special gifts and could use Martín's guiding hand."

The two men think about Susana's proposal. Tony clears his throat. "The move would require a big change. I would enjoy administering a clinic, and if it means I get to spend more time with you, Susana, I'll do it. What do you think, Martín?"

Martín swallows. "I feel ready to work on my own with your support. I felt afraid that when Abuelo died, I would go into the cave at Tierra Oscura and not leave. With Abuelo's blessing and spirit, I stayed out, and I feel much stronger.

"When we visited Chimayo, I enjoyed seeing the mountains and feeling the crisp air. I want to live close to Swallow and Tommy-tres. Maybe I'll meet my future partner."

Susana grins. "Then it's unanimous. How soon can you two get ready?"

Tony sounds eager. "I can get ready in a month. I'll just give notice."

Martín speaks. "I want to give Coyote warning and I want his blessing. I want to go in three months. I don't want to leave the clinic in a bind. I'll act responsibly."

Susana sounds happy. "Then we agree; we will go to Santa Fe in three months."

Two months later, Martín sees Vela get out of an old truck in front of Coyote's house. He opens the front door. "I feel so glad to see you. I meant to get out to your place to tell you my news." He gives her a hug. "Let's go out to the back yard."

Once they sit on two comfortable wooden chairs, Vela says, "Tío Mateo brought me. He just came to talk to Tía Sara and Pedro. We'll go back this evening. What news do you want to tell me?'

Martín sighs. "I felt surprised since my Abuelo died and I received his spirit; I felt calm and positive. So when Susana invited Tony and me to move to Santa Fe, I said yes. I'll join a clinic, which Tony will manage. Coyote gave me his blessing, so I feel very excited.

"Wow, that will be a big change, and yet I feel so glad for you."

Martín glances at her. "I feel sad that I won't see you very often. Perhaps Mateo can bring you to Santa Fe for visits."

Vela looks wistful. "In three years, I'll be ready to go to high school. I keep asking my mother to move to a town with a good one. But she feels safer out where we live."

"A lot can happen in three years."

Martín wonders about his practice in Santa Fe and how he'll integrate Abuelo's spirit into his life.

Chapter 17

May 1, 2043

Two years later, Franklin and Lark wait outside a bank on East Main Street in Barstow, California. Lark wipes the perspiration from her brow and wonders how Franklin can stand waiting in his hot truck. She hears an explosion followed by gunshots and then an alarm. She glances at Franklin, who gives her a quick nod.

Lark takes a deep breath and rushes inside. She feels worried. Their plans did not include any shots. Alex stands on the other side of the bank with his hands in the air. The guard stands with his back to her. Sammy, wounded, groans, "Let's get out of here." Alex winks and starts singing loudly to distract the guard.

Lark helps Sammy stand. His right shoulder bleeds. He holds the money bag as she assists him outside. Franklin takes Sammy's other side. They get him into the back of the truck; a jeep full of soldiers arrives with a siren blaring. Sammy grunts, "Hopefully, the Brotherhood won't figure Alex as one of us before we get him out."

Lark sees all the soldiers hurry inside as she climbs into the back of the truck beside Sammy. Franklin covers them with an old, patched blue tarp.

Nine days later, Martín notices the deep blue sky and the crisp cool air as he walks across the plaza and turns up Washington Street. He stumbles on the curb cut but catches his balance. He giggles, remembering Alex telling him he walks like a drunken sailor. He wants to work on his gait, but when? He has come such a long way. Sure, he speaks slowly, but who cares? He feels happy he just went through a growth spurt and stands 4'8" tall and weighs 85 pounds. He turns just before the library and walks into the building he shares with an alternative healing group. The building used to be a hotel before the war on terrorism cut off the flow of tourists.

Three families wait. Martín glances at the receptionist and strides into the airy conference room. Two old-style blankets hang on the yellow walls. Along one wall stands a bookcase with toy bins on the bottom two shelves, books on the next two, and pottery and jewelry, given to the clinic by grateful clients, displayed on the top two shelves.

Tony stands. "Good morning, sleepyhead, I scheduled a full day. Shall I get you some tea?" He walks over to the counter with a built-in sink and small refrigerator.

Martín nods. "Tony, I meditate in the morning. You left the house so early."

Tony puts a large mug of tea with a straw in it on the table. "I ate breakfast at Susana's. We dated more than eight years, and I wish she'd marry me."

"At least she loves you. I keep wondering if I'll ever find someone. Look at me. Who would want such a big brain with such a little body?"

Tony suggests, "Give yourself time. You still can grow. But that doesn't mean you would describe yourself as a little boy with severe cerebral palsy. Your self-image will catch up with the rest of you."

Martín takes a sip. "How would you describe me? A short string bean who stumbles a lot?" He shakes his head and laughs.

"No. How about a remarkable curandero who gave me the opportunity to train him to drive an electric wheelchair and talk through a communication device, yet now stumbles wherever he pleases and never stops talking." He pours himself water.

Martín asks, "How's Susana?"

"She seems fine. She took Lark to Albuquerque for a break while Sammy watches the kids."

Martín gets serious. "How do his wounds heal?"

"Okay, but not fast enough for Sammy. He wants to go break Alex out of prison before the Brotherhood figures out his connection to the Resistance." Tony shakes his head. "People keep arriving in our reception area. We better get to work."

Martín scratches his head. "I'll go by Sammy's after work and check him out."

"That'd please Sammy." Tony opens a file. "You put a chip in our first client's head four months ago. Shall I bring his family in?"

Martín agrees. Since he and Tony invented a biodegradable chip a year ago, people flock to see them. If he remembers right, cerebral palsy had locked up the two-year-old's muscles to the point of rigidity, and he had grown more and more emaciated because he couldn't suck or swallow. Martín didn't see how his parents had kept him alive so long.

The father strides into the room cradling his son, and his wife follows holding the hand of a small boy. Tears fill his eyes. "Thank you for giving our son a chance."

Tony takes the two-year-old, gets down on the ground, and starts playing with him. Martín closes his eyes and scans the boy's brain with his blue light.

The mother clears her throat. "The first week, I didn't see any changes. Then I noticed he ate more and cried less. After three weeks, he started sleeping all night, and then his body seemed to get more relaxed." She looks at her husband.

He starts speaking. "After that it seemed like our son made up for lost time."

Martín finds two troubling spots and brings his healing force to one near a language center. Tony rolls a ball toward the two-year-old, who crows and bats it back.

The man continues. "Every day he goes after a new skill and keeps at it until he masters it. I never saw anyone so tenacious. First, he learned to turn over, creep, and then sit up. I felt amazed to see him crawling. I told my wife not to carry him inside."

Tony puts two hands out to the tiny boy, who uses them to pull himself to standing and take a few wobbly steps before collapsing on his bottom. Martín shifts his focus to the other troubling spot near the cerebellum.

"He wants to do everything his older brother does. Only six, my older son seems super patient." His mother shakes her head and laughs. "Two weeks ago, I caught them holding a peeing contest in the bathtub. Since then, my youngest refuses to wear diapers. He started to feed himself. He doesn't say a word, though."

Martín opens his eyes. "Whatever you did, keep doing it. He made great progress." He turns to the six-year-old. "I wish more older brothers cared for their younger ones like you do." The little boy grins from ear to ear.

Mariana Ruybalid193

Martín continues, "Make him a small walker, and label everything in your house. You know, put a sign saying, 'Bed' on his bed. Tony can show you how."

"But he is too young to read," the woman says.

"Yes, but we'll give him this insurance in case he doesn't learn to speak. It will make it easier for him to communicate if you surround him with written language."

The parents nod. The man adds, "I'll read to both my sons every night."

Martín states, "Remember: your son still lives with the challenge of cerebral palsy. We'll support him and leave as many opportunities open as possible." Martín gets on the floor. The toddler crawls to him, gazes into his eyes, and hugs him.

The father interjects, "You gave him a chance, and he'll make the most of it. I just want to thank you for that."

Martín blushes. "I feel glad I can help."

Tony stands. "Let's go to the reception, and I'll show you how to label your house."

The nurse strides in and waits for a nod before she opens a file. "Six months ago, a white soldier shot this eighteen-year-old, paralyzing him from the waist down. Two months ago, you and Tony put an experimental chip near his spinal cord."

Martín responds, "Bring them in. I feel eager to see what the chip did."

A broad-shouldered young man pushes his wheelchair into the room, followed by his parents. He looks at Martín. "Like you said, not much happened at first. Then I noticed I slept all night. Then I got sensation in my butt. Then I got control over my bladder. I hated the catheter." He looks at his father.

Martín shuts his eyes and scans the region near the eighteen-year-old's spinal cord. New nerve cells grow around the chip. Using his blue light, Martín heals a couple of bruised spots and removes damaged cells.

The father speaks. "For the last two weeks, he eats and eats. I figure his body wants the fuel to heal itself."

Martín blinks his eyes and withdraws his healing attention. He feels content. "Please continue this group process. The whole family goes through the healing, each in her or his own way. Everyone must stay strong; don't let him do all the eating for you." He looks at the father. "Will you excuse us for a moment; I want to see your son alone."

As soon as the others leave, Martín smirks. "Did you get back more than just control of your bladder?"

"I sure did. I feel full sensation in my penis and can get an erection. Thanks for not asking me that question in front of my parents."

"Well, yeah, some questions are like that. Just act responsibly."

"Don't worry. I feel so glad to get that back, I won't take any chances."

Martín opens the door. "I want to see you again in two months."

For a few seconds, the curandero thinks about his own lone-liness and starts to go to the dark place he calls Tierra Oscura. Then he shakes his head, coming back to the present.

Martín sees three more families. Then he takes a much-desired swim in the old hotel swimming pool, which the healing group refurbished soon after they moved in. Martín walks back across the plaza to the small restaurant. His stomach growls. Since he'd healed the owner's wife eighteen months ago, Martin gets free lunches from Rubén.

The slightly rotund owner leads Martín to a small table. "I know you always work up a healthy appetite, but feeding you keeps you on a retainer."

Martín gives up telling Rubén he doesn't require payment to heal people, and glances at the blackboard before sitting. "I feel hungrier than usual. Give me the meatloaf platter, ice tea, and a hot fudge sundae for dessert."

Rubén looks delighted. "I suppose you'd enjoy an extra slice of meatloaf."

He admits, "Yes, please. I do get hungry."

Martín glances around the room. He sees an older couple at one table and a young couple at another table. He winces inside as he recognizes the younger, petite Hispanic woman with beautiful brown eyes. About a year ago, Martín had invited her out twice. The first time, she'd said something noncommittal. But the second time, she'd rudely said, "Leave me alone. I'd never date a skinny cripple like you."

He shakes his head. Rubén brings his ice tea. He takes a sip.

Later, a friend drops Martín off near Chimayo. As he walks down a dirt road through an orchard, he hears someone chopping wood. He feels sad as he thinks about the increasing pull to enter Tierra Oscura and wonders how to cut down on the time he spends there.

"Sammy, what will I do with you? Rest and allow your shoulder to mend. Let Lark or Tony chop the wood." Martín looks serious as he walks to the large adobe house surrounded by sage and cactus. He glances around. "I enjoy seeing those mountains."

"Y'know I get so restless." Sammy walks into the house and leads the way into the kitchen, where two children play checkers.

"Just take it easy and contemplate the, uh…" He sees the six-year-old and groans.

Tommy-tres looks up from the game. "Hi Tío, what does 'con-tem-plate' mean?"

Martín thinks a minute. "Contemplate means look at from all angles or consider carefully, like meditate."

"Oh." Tommy-tres beams. "When I contemplate this game, I think I'll win."

Swallow looks up and winks at her dad.

Sammy winks back at her and heads into the den. "I want to talk with your Tío."

Swallow laughs. "Daddy, you mean Tío will tell you to cool it, like I told you to cool it."

"Sammy closes the door after Martín. "She gets more like her mother every day."

Martín relaxes in an easy chair. "You and Lark raise wonderful kids." He inhales deeply, breathing out slowly. "Swallow will become a wise one. But now let me scan your shoulder." He focuses his blue light on Sammy and notices two small black spots and much inflammation. He puts his attention on one black spot until it vanishes.

"Do you remember when you taught me how to use shields, and I taught you how to scan your body? I want you to scan your shoulder and tell me what you see."

Sammy focuses on his own body. "I see a bunch of red warmth and a dead spot."

Martín speaks. "Build a shield around the dead spot." A minute passes.

"I did it."

Martín scans again. "I want you to examine your shoulder every few hours and keep building shields around any dead spots. Drink a ton of water, and whatever you do, don't use you right arm."

"Okay, Martín, whatever, but I mostly use my right hand."

"Consider it a challenge."

They hear a knock. Sammy checks with Martín. "C'mon in, honey."

Swallow walks in. Martín looks at her. "Did you scan your body like I showed you?"

"Sure, Tío, I do it every night." She stops speaking and looks at her dad.

"And you check your father's shoulder." He raises his eyebrows. "I know the temptation. As soon as I learned to inspect my own body, I looked into everyone else's."

Swallow sits cross-legged on the floor and looks at Martín. "I scan other kids and practice curing their cuts and bruises."

Martín shakes his head. "Except for real little kids and unconscious people, please get a person's permission before you heal. Otherwise she won't know what's happening and might freak out."

Swallow thinks a minute. "Oh, yeah, Tío."

Martín looks from Sammy to Swallow. "Please follow my blue light into your dad's shoulder and watch how I clear up the redness. I'll leave a quarter-sized patch for you to work on." The room remains quiet for a few minutes. "Well done. You do it naturally. How do you feel?"

She shakes her head. "I feel very hungry."

Martín looks at her. "I want you to clear up a quarter-sized patch every morning, no more, no less. Do you understand? And call me at the clinic if you see any black or yellowish-white. You won't, but call me if you do. Got it?"

She stands taller and walks toward the door. "Okay. Every morning before I eat a big breakfast, I'll clear a patch."

As soon as she closes the door, Martín raises his hand to stop Sammy from speaking first. "I know you don't want her healing you, but she'll do it no matter what we tell her, and this way I hold some control over what she does."

Sammy grimaces. "No, I don't like it; she's a little girl. And she's my daughter. Do you think it's right for her to see inside my body?"

"I understand your concern. But think of it like you give her a beautiful, loving place to practice her skills, like a teacher would."

Sammy meets his friend's eyes. "That makes sense. Besides, the sooner I get better, the sooner we can rescue Alex."

"What do you mean by 'we?'"

Before Sammy can respond, they hear the door. Lark calls out, "Anyone home?"

Minutes later, Martín finds himself drinking his milkshake in an old battered van as Susana drives him to his house on Galisteo.

Susana sounds intense. "Martín, I know you want a ride, and I want to talk to you. I didn't mean to interrupt your visit with Sammy."

"That's okay. I finished healing him, and I think he wants to talk me into going with him to rescue Alex. What's up?"

Susana pulls the car over. She faces him. "I worry because you seem too busy healing other people. I saw you receive his force when Abuelo died two years ago, but I don't see you integrating his gift into your own power. Take some time to do that."

He takes a deep breath. "You know me too well. I feel compelled to heal anyone requiring healing. I do want time alone, but I don't know how to get it. Also, keeping busy helps me avoid facing certain issues."

"I know what you mean, but just stay open." She starts the car and pulls into traffic.

"You know me. I'll remain open. Do you know something I don't know?"

"You take care of everyone but yourself. And yes, a dinner guest arrived." She winks as she stops the car.

Martín gets out. "Thanks for the ride and the advice."

He walks into the house he shares with his father and Tony. He smells the comforting aroma of pinto beans and red chili. Living with Mateo, absent during his childhood, still feels weird. But when he and Tony had decided to move after Abuelo had died, Mateo already had owned a home in Santa Fe, where he had lived with Sofía before her murder. Martín and Tony had welcomed the idea of living so near the plaza.

He hears voices and follows them into the kitchen. He gives Pedro a hug and nods at his father, who kneads tortilla dough.

Pedro steps back. "You look tired and hungry."

Tony comes in. "Martín works too hard." He opens a silverware drawer.

Mateo puts another tortilla between the folds of a dishtowel. "You just came from Sammy's. How long before he can go get Alex?"

"Maybe two weeks."

"Let's give him three." Mateo looks at Pedro.

Pedro announces, "I came to invite you on a hike. We'll go to the Grand Canyon. I'll carry your gear."

Martín looks at Tony. "Can you spare me for two weeks?'

Mateo says, "It may take a month. We want him to come with us to rescue Alex."

Martín starts, "I don't see why you want me to go with you to rescue him."

Tony interrupts, "We can spare Martín for a month. I talked it over with the others."

Mateo adds, "Of course, Martín, just go with Pedro. Don't worry about the action."

Martín laughs. "I'll go as long as I can spend some time alone."

"Yes, of course," Pedro responds. "Can you leave tomorrow morning?"

They each look at Tony, and Martín sighs, "You guys figured it all out, didn't you? I just want to get a message to Swallow."

As Pedro drives the next morning, Martín meditates. He figures out how to use the walk down the canyon to improve his gait. Scanning his own brain feels surreal. He makes connections that will ground his feet. Then he uses his healing and yoga to loosen muscles so he can extend his hips better.

By the time he completes this healing, Martín feels hungry again. The truck stops. He asks Pedro, "Estebán turn up, yet?"

"No, since he disappeared a year ago, Mama prays for him every night. I hope he is still alive."

Martín inclines his head. "Between your ma and me, we'd know if he'd died. He got stuck in some prison.

"Miguel and the kids?"

Pedro asserts, "He gets wiser and the kids grow more beautiful but oh so fierce."

Martín pictures their four adopted children with disabilities.

On the trail, he stares down the gorge. "These reds and browns feed my soul."

Pedro stops. "Wait until we get down to the river. How do you feel?"

He answers, "I never walked so far in my life. I enjoy this new experience."

Pedro glances at his cousin. "Don't overdo it, but if you can last another hour, I know a great place to camp."

"I built up decent endurance from the swimming," Martín assures him. "I do enjoy the rhythm of walking for the first time. But what a great place! The last long trek I took with Alex and Abuelo carried me out of California."

Pedro clears his throat. "That happened a long time ago. While you became a great curandero, I get the sense you could develop in other ways."

Martín looks Pedro in the eye. "What do you mean?"

"I brought you here so you could go inside and explore for yourself."

Ten days later, Martín sits in a shady spot by the river. The green-blue water surges past. He looks up at the reddish tan walls of the canyon. A pair of eagles soars and frolics in the deep blue sky. He finishes his morning meditation and decides to allow himself to enter Tierra Oscura.

He nods at his old friend, Superboy, who guards the entrance to the cave.

Superboy poses a question: "Do you want to enter this realm?"

Martín hesitates. "But I didn't indulge for a while."

"But you feel an addicted pull to this place and to your own fantasies."

Martín sighs. "Yes, I know I still feel the pull. I know I avoid something."

Superboy frowns. "Martín, you avoid doing the hard work of mourning."

The young curandero groans, "But it feels so painful and I get so lonely."

"Go back to the river."

He finds himself sitting on a rock, no longer in the shade. He weeps and weeps.

Two days later, Martín sits on the same rock, his safe space to think and visualize. A small lizard scurries among the nearby rocks. The air smells faintly of water and sage. He watches the river flow; the same river etches its own path through this canyon for thousands of years, relentlessly. The sun's rays penetrate his back, warming his bones and his inner being. Sweat streams from his body, dampening his cotton shorts.

He takes a long drink. The sun shines persistently. Tears run down his face. How he misses his mother, Abuelo, and Guillermo. He even misses Alex. Their paths took them in different directions. Alex trained as a warrior while he trained as a healer. Now Alex endures prison. Yes, he misses them, though he carries so much of them inside.

He hiccups. Sofía, there for him the first twelve years, loved him and kept him safe. She had even given up the Resistance and had moved to Berkeley to keep him safe.

Abuelo: Coyote had kept him alive with his damaged heart for eight years, seeing him more the last two years. Without his Kwoon or his part-time job, Abuelo had worked at a home for orphans and had taken extended walks as long as his heart permitted. He had made it a priority to spend time with each of his grandkids every week. Martín knew little about what his primos had done with Abuelo, except Pedro and Miguel had seen him together.

Martín and Abuelo had spent Sundays together. Abuelo sometimes helped Martín heal the way he

moved, and Martín also used Abuelo's wisdom as a martial artist to apply techniques (learned from Coyote) to
his own body. Sometimes Abuelo had borrowed a car.
They had traveled to the Grand Canyon or to Mateo's
hogan, where Martín had spent hours listening to both
men telling stories. Toward the end, they had spent
Sundays talking in Abuelo's room. Sometimes Pedro
had driven them out to the desert.

Abuelo had gotten weaker and weaker. The last week,
Tío Juan had lifted him into an easy chair during the
day. Martín's eyes fill with tears, as he remembered the
last Sunday morning. Abuelo had blessed him, and as his
grandfather died, Martín had received Abuelo's spirit.

But Martín couldn't find time to integrate all that
power and wisdom. Now Pedro gave him time to process that discipline. He thinks about his grandfather
and his love.

Guillermo, so young, had accepted Martín as a person. He'd connected him to Maestra Manzanares, who
had opened the door to Martín's using his force for healing. Guillermo had fought the Brotherhood, and it had
cost him his life.

Martín and Alex experienced some great adventures,
like the time Esteban and his friends had ambushed
them, or the time they had found themselves lost in San
Francisco. Alex had helped Abuelo carry him to Arizona. Hell, toward the end of the journey, Alex had done
it almost single-handedly with Mateo's help. Yes, he'll
go rescue his friend.

Martín glances at the river. He feels more at peace. The air feels cooler, so he puts on a sweatshirt, eats some dried fruit, drinks some water, and lies down on his bedroll, listening to the gurgle of the water. Before he knows it, he sleeps.

He dreams he turns into a coyote living in a cave in the desert near a stream. A pup wakes him and he wrestles with three pups while a fourth watches. One pup yelps when he nips it a tad too hard. The pups' mother arrives with a rabbit, which she tears apart. He eats just enough to awaken his appetite. He wants more.

He searches the dry landscape as he walks away from the cave and growls at two pups who ignore him and continue in his footsteps. He spies a small ground animal, and chases it down. The scent of blood causes him to salivate. As he rips it apart, he hears a metal clang. A pup shrieks, howling, high-pitched. He snarls, picks up the carcass and runs toward the yelping. One pup squeals, its paw caught in a trap. After repeated tries to get the foot out, the coyote gnaws through the pup's foreleg, freeing him from the trap. He signals the other pup to follow him with the fresh kill, picks up the wounded one with his mouth, and runs back toward the cave.

The next morning, Martín sits cross-legged on his rock. He'd dreamed he had become a coyote before. He'd always felt an affinity for them. He likes the idea of having a mate and children. He wants deeper connections. He makes a commitment to himself and the universe to stay open to whoever comes his way, including a partner. He eats dried fruit.

Watching the flowing water reminds him of a Chi Gung form he saw done by Coyote. He closes his eyes and feels surprised he remembers the whole form. He pictures it again, then stands up, does the first movement, and then the next. Then he picks up his right foot and stumbles. He tries the move again and lurches off balance, but catches himself before he falls. He sits back down on the rock. He pictures the movement once more and discovers the weakness in his left hip. He takes his blue light inside and strengthens those muscles.

He stands and begins the form, this time getting several movements further. He stops when he feels his right hand move too jerkily. He sits and searches his cerebellum and heals a tiny synapse. Again, he gets to his feet and starts moving more smoothly.

He rests on the rock, feeling content, exhausted, and hungry. He drinks water and eats more dried fruit, and then he dreams: Coyote doing the Chi Gung form in slow motion, so beautiful. Then Abuelo joins Coyote on the rock and they do the form together. Martín wakes up weeping. He watches the river flow by and the shadows deepen. He drinks water and eats jerky.

That night he dreams again. His mother feeds him breakfast in the kitchen. His small body starts to grow. He grows too big for his electric wheelchair and keeps growing until he can just squeeze through the doorway. Someone calls at the front door. "Martín, come out and fight like a warrior." Outside, Maestra Manzanares hands him two arnís sticks. They start sparring and fight for a long time. Several times he feels like he can't fight anymore. He keeps going until Maestra drops her arnís sticks and tells him, "Enough. You did well. Remember to use all your gifts." She gives him a long hug.

Chapter 18
May 29, 2043

Four days later the camping trip ends and the practical plans for the rescue of Alex begin. Martín finds himself crawling through a concrete pipe in Franklin's yard. It feels impossible, and he adds up a list of his aching body parts.

Mateo yells, "You got to get through faster, Martín!"

He sticks his head out. "Stop yelling at me. I do my best. Why must I go through the damn pipe?"

Mateo looks at his sweaty son. "We keep telling you only you can fit through the damn pipe."

Martín feels exasperated. "I'll take a shower. Get me some knee pads."

"I'll put them on the list." Sammy exhales. "That's your fifth shower today."

Martín grabs a towel from the clothesline and stomps into the house. "I'll take all the showers I want. It's ninety-five degrees in the shade!"

He doesn't hear Sammy say, "But there's a water shortage."

Mateo winks at Sammy and follows Martín, who tries to shut the bathroom door. His father walks in after him. Martín growls, "I want some privacy."

Mateo stands his ground. "Son, I want to talk to you."

Martín shouts, "You call me your son when you want me on an action. I never knew you growing up."

Mateo grabs Martín's shoulders, turns him, and looks into his eyes. "I chose to fight in the Resistance rather than raise you, but don't think about me. Alex requires you, now, as a man, not a hurt little boy. Pull yourself together and act like an adult. You belong to a team now." Mateo strides out and slams the door.

Once again Mateo had walked out and Martín can't tell him all he feels. He feels angry. His clothes feel sticky and he shrugs out of them, steps into the shower, and turns on the cold water. His brain clears, and empties. Then thoughts of Alex flood his mind. "I'll go rescue Alex. I'll even learn to act as part of the team."

These words become his mantra as dries himself with a towel, and slips into clean, dry shorts and a T-shirt.

He stops at the refrigerator on his way and drinks cold water. Franklin motions for him to follow when he steps out the door. He climbs into Franklin's truck, the same truck Franklin drove ten years ago when Alex carried Martín across the river. He shakes his head as he remembers the Mojave's first greeting: "Welcome to Arizona, the land of the free. I hope you like it hot."

Franklin starts the truck. "I sent the others on a five-mile hike to let them know what it feels like to be over-heated. Do you really feel so hot?"

Martín looks inside. "I could deal with the heat if the guys didn't criticize me for moving slowly. I hate when others see me as the weak link or the cripple."

Franklin turns the truck onto the paved road toward Lake Havasu. "Martín, I'd hardly call you the weak link. You hold important and unique gifts. I think you can do anything. In my dependence upon your gifts, I forgot you live with cerebral palsy and you take longer to master new motor skills. Your strengths outweigh what you consider weaknesses. You overcame so much. I'll get the others to cut you slack. Please realize, I never saw you as a cripple but as someone with his very own growth schedule."

Martín grins in spite of himself. "I develop idiosyn-cratically."

"And exceptionally unique."

They both laugh.

Martín shakes his head. "Thank you for your support, Franklin. But more than physical, I find it hard to work with Mateo."

Franklin speaks. "I direct this operation because your dad, our best agent, demands too much from himself and others. Do you find it triply difficult because as his son, destiny didn't bring you together until you turned twelve?"

"Destiny or Mateo's choice?"

Franklin pulls into the parking lot of a small alternative pharmacy. "Or did it become your destiny Mateo chose to fight in the Resistance? I don't know. But I do know how to plan actions." He gets out of the truck.

Martín follows him. "You planned and led the action ten years ago."

"Yes, and let's change the subject." He winks at Martín, and takes a list out. "Blue Feather, I want you to meet Martín, Mateo's son."

The attractive young woman lurches forward and queries, "Aren't you the curandero from Prescott who moved to Santa Fe? Coyote told me about you. I meant to come see you. You look kind of handsome but not very old." Her speech sounds slightly slurred. She pulled her black hair into a single braid down her back, accenting her dark brown, clear and intense eyes. She stands about 5'2 with a good figure.

Martín blushes, and clears his throat. "Yes, I know that Martín well."

She sizes him up. "You seem intelligent but very small. Just how old are you?"

He blushes some more. "Good things come in small packages. I just turned twenty-two."

Franklin hands Blue Feather the list. "I hope you stock these things."

She glances at it. "Yes, I can find most of these. I distill an antiseptic from cactus."

Franklin leans on the counter. "Do the Mexicans make pulque from it?"

She nods. "Drinking either one will blind you."

Martín sits down on a bench. "May I scan your head?"

She laughs. "Sure. Thanks for asking first. But can I keep any secrets from you?"

"I—I can't read your thoughts," he stammers.

She gathers the items from Franklin's list on the counter. "The knee pads I stock; I ordered for a junior high wrestling team, size small. What do you think?" She holds them up.

"They'll fit fine, right?" Franklin looks at the curandero, who seems far away, scanning Blue Feather.

Martín shakes his head, coming out of his trance. "Oh, knee pads. Terrific. They look great." He turns to Blue Feather. "How did you get the piece of metal near your cerebellum making your speech slur and your movements jerky? Do you feel pain?"

"No. But the way I move gets worse." She looks at Martín, searchingly. "I got shot when the Brotherhood took over Big Pine four years ago."

"Four years ago?" Martín whispers. He looks at Franklin. "Is that near Nevada?"

"Yes, it's in Owen Valley."

"Did you fight in the Resistance?" Martín looks at his feet. "My mother died near Nevada four years ago."

Blue Feather touches Martín's shoulder. She looks thoughtful and sad. "Did people call your mama Sofía? She died so young, and what a warrior! Sofía brought me to safety after I got shot. Then she got blown apart by a grenade. I saw it happen."

"Martín, let's go." Franklin pays Blue Feather and takes their package. "Thank you. See you next time." He takes Martín's elbow and guides him toward the door.

Martín blinks and shakes his head. "Hey, can you come to Santa Fe, maybe in a month or so? I can encapsulate the fragment so it won't give you so much trouble."

Late one night a week later Franklin pulls up to a drainage ditch. Sammy, Mateo, and Martín pile out of the back of the truck. Sammy speaks just above a whisper.

"Crawl through this tunnel. I'll give you two hours and then I'll create a diversion near the front gate. In the meantime, Mateo will cut a hole in the fence near the water tower. Bring Alex there when you find him."

The pipe seems damp. Martín manages without a light until he nears the other end. He feels glad he had practiced and had insisted on knee pads. The tunnel begins to slant upward, and he works a little harder. He hopes he can find Alex and get him to the fence in time. Abruptly Martín comes to the end of the pipe, stretches his back, and glances at the stars to orient himself. He spots the building and takes a step toward it.

Martín sees a guard outside. Hell, he didn't expect the sentry. His whole body tenses. He hates this skulking around. What can he do besides put the guard to sleep? He lowers himself to the ground and scans the soldier's brain and knocks him out. He steps into the infirmary. In the pitch-black hall, he steadies himself against a wall and fumbles for his flashlight. Three doors down, a soldier sleeps. Martín takes the soldier's uniform and closes the door. He tries the next room.

Alex, tied to a bed, lies on his stomach. Martín scans his body. Alex groans. Martín sees his back raw from whipping and one badly bruised testicle.

Martín staggers and falls to his knees. He shields himself from his friend's suffering. After he regulates his own breathing, he whispers, "We'll get you out."

Alex turns his head. Martín sees the pain in his eyes.

Martín cuts the straps securing him. "Can you turn on your side and lie still?"

Alex turns, but he gasps and cries out.

Martín uses his blue light to reduce the swelling and anesthetize Alex's groin. He hears Alex's breath become easier. "There's no time to heal you, but I made it easier for you to walk." He helps Alex sit and looks at the uniform he stole. "We'll put this on you. It's big, but you can't walk out naked. I'll roll up the pants."

Outside they hear an explosion and gunshots. Martín shudders and his muscles tense. He closes his eyes and takes a deep breath.

Alex looks at his friend. "Thanks for coming to get me."

"You would do the same for me." Martín adjusts his body so Alex does not feel so heavy leaning on him. "Come, brother, let's get to the fence by the water tower."

Tears fill Alex's eyes, and Martín modulates his tone to reinforce the blue light he extends to focus Alex's mind. "Help me get you to the fence."

Alex blinks. "Okay."

"Put your arms over my shoulders and lean on me." When Alex hesitates he adds, "Just walk like a drunken sailor."

The two stagger down the hall. Martín opens the door. Gunfire and another loud explosion distract him from concentrating on his balance. He stumbles and they fall.

Martín makes his own voice serious and uses his blue light to help Alex concentrate. "Crawl toward the water tower. Keep crawling no matter what happens."

He takes a step. A force hits his left shoulder and sends him flying.

Martín wakes up in a strange room, well, maybe not so strange—in fact, quite familiar. Alex sleeps in the next bed. He tries to sit up and realizes he can't move. Someone had sandbagged him, quite literally, his whole body weighed down by them.

Coyote walks into the room. "Ah, Martín, you woke. Don't try to move."

Martín shrugs his eyebrows. "How did we get here?"

"Mateo brought you both yesterday. He said soldiers shot you freeing Alex from a prison infirmary. I gave him hell for risking the best curandero. What made you go? You usually show more sense." Coyote puts a hand on Martín's brow.

"For Alex, I'd do anything, but Mateo wanted me to go through a rite of passage."

Coyote shakes his head. "He may be your dad, but he seems mighty strange."

"Does the pot call the kettle black?" Martín laughs, and then winces. "Oh, that hurts."

"You took a bullet through your shoulder. The clean wound heals. With your cerebral palsy I immobilized you. Every time you move, the pain causes your whole body to spasm. We tried hard to get you to relax."

"It hurts to talk. Maybe I should stop speaking." Martín groans.

"Do your best. And only use your blue light on yourself." Coyote lifts a sandbag.

"Why?"

"If you send any outside of your own body, it will take energy from the healing process." Coyote removes another sandbag. "If you promise to keep your body relaxed, I'll take the rest of these off and sit you up."

"I'll do my best." Martín looks at Alex and raises his brows.

Coyote glances at Alex. "Since he's wide awake, I won't speak ill of him."

He groans. "How come you always know when we wake?"

Coyote tries to keep a straight face. "The eyes behind my head tell me."

Alex looks at him. "Martín, thank you for coming after me. I feel sorry they shot you. It hurt me to watch Coyote and his partner working on you." He starts sobbing.

Martín takes a deep breath and tries not to tense his muscles as he speaks. "Alex, those bastards hurt you. I feel just sorry we didn't rescue you sooner."

They hear a knock at the door. Coyote opens it. "Martín, stop talking and focus on your breath. Try doing nothing."

Alex stops crying and wipes his face. Martín, so grateful to rest in a safe place, forgets to concentrate on his own breath and wonders what he can do to heal Alex. But as he leaves his own healing, pain sets in. He'll leave it to Alex to heal his own mind.

Two days later, thirteen-year-old Vela walks into Coyote's backyard, where Martín sits resting in the shade. She kisses him on the forehead. "Coyote thought you'd feel ready for a visitor as long as you stay still. How do you feel?"

He sighs. "I feel tired and hungry, like my body works overtime to heal me. I don't feel much pain as long as I don't move, so Coyote keeps me immobilized with these sandbags. But I haven't seen you since your mother died. How do you feel?"

Vela takes a minute to look inside. "I feel lost, like I can't imagine a future any more. I'm staying with Pedro and Miguel and finishing seventh grade. Their kids are great, but I don't quite belong. Tía Sara spends time with me. I can talk to her. We go for long walks or bake for Pedro's family." Vela opens her backpack and takes out a small package. "By the way, she sent you some fudge."

Martín says, "Give me some before you leave. I felt so lost after Sofía died. Sometimes I would forget that she died and start crying when I remembered again."

Vela frowns. "I did that a couple of times. Tía Sara explained the various stages of grief. Tío Mateo said he'd spend time with me on the land this summer. Pedro and Miguel said I could live with them next year until I graduate from eighth grade. Santa Fe has a better high school than Prescott. I want to come and study there."

Martín feels wistful. "So much can happen in a year. But I'll support you any way I can."

Martín groans. Two weeks after the rescue, his shoulder feels much better, but it still throbs whenever he moves, and he can't find a comfortable way to move. He had insisted on coming to his own space to heal, and though Coyote had advised against moving Alex, they had decided that with Swallow's help, the two friends would stay together. Mateo hadn't said a word on the drive back, though he'd paled when Martín had yelped from the pain of getting out of the truck. He wouldn't look his son in the eye.

Still in bed, Martín goes to the cave at Tierra Oscura in his mind. Part of him doesn't want to enter, but he manages to storm past Superboy and enter a cell where a white soldier stands, his hands attached with duct tape behind his back. Martín picks up a gun and shoots the guy in the right shoulder. Martín hears him howl, and shoots him in the other shoulder. The howling increases in intensity.

Martín feels relieved when he hears a knock on the door, and he decides to come back to the present. He feels surprise and gratitude when his old friend Lark enters and says, "Sammy and the children persuaded Alex to go with them for a couple of hours. I figure you could use a break from him. I'll help you out this morning."

Martín groans as the woman warrior helps him sit up. "Thanks, Lark. Alex appears very attached to me right now. He seems reluctant to let me out of his sight."

Lark eases his T-shirt off and examines his shoulder. "That looks great. It's closed. Shall I help you take a shower?'

He nods at her. "Yes, please, I'd like that."

She steadies him as he walks toward the bathroom. "I heard you met Mary Grey Eyes' daughter, Blue Feather."

He blushes. "Yes, she's beautiful."

Lark supports him as he steps out of his shorts and soaps his body using a wet cloth. "I know her for many years. I feel surprised you two never met."

Martín steps into the shower and shudders as Lark turns the water on for thirty seconds and helps him rinse off. "Well, the few times Mary came to Prescott before Blue Feather's injury, she left her daughter tending the dispensary. After Blue Feather got hurt, Coyote went out to Mary's house, but he left me in charge of his clinic in Prescott."

A little later, while she ties his shoes, Martín inquires, "How's your mother?"

Lark looks up. "She does all right. She felt very sad ever since my dad died, and I tried to get her to move out here and live with us. Last year she moved in with Sammy's mother in San Leandro. Maestra keeps a house full of children and teenagers who lack a home, so my mother enjoys sewing clothes for those kids."

She helps Martín to the kitchen.

Two mornings later, Martín looks around his bedroom. He sees the picture of Abuelo and Abuela, with his mother and Tío Juan as kids, which Martín took from the kitchen of their old house when he left Berkeley. He stares at Abuela and wishes he knew her. A red and gray hand-woven blanket hanging on the wall catches his eye, and he remembers the old man from Taos who gave it to him. Martín healed his granddaughter. A bookcase filled with worn books stands against one wall. He read them all many times. He hears a knock at the front door. Alex yells, "I'll get it."

Martín leans back in the worn leather easy-chair, a gift from a grateful patient.

"Tío Martín, Tío Martín, we came." Swallow knocks at his door and then opens it. "Mama wants to know if she can bring dinner for everyone at six."

He agrees, wondering just who "everyone" is.

She kisses him on the forehead. "I'll go tell her you said yes." She runs out.

Tommy-tres walks into the room. "Hola, Tío, ¿cómo estás?"

"Mucho mejor. I feel much better. Y tú, ¿cómo estás?"

"Muy bien, gracias. Hey, Tío, what does the word 'bully' mean?"

Martín gets even more serious. "What do you think it means?"

Tommy-tres scratches his head. "When someone bigger..."

Martín adds, "Or more powerful..."

Tommy-tres hesitates. "Uses their bigness..."

"Or power..."

Tommy-tres' eyes twinkle. "To force someone less powerful to do what he wants."

"Wow, I find you so smart. And you always question what words mean, the best way to learn. Does someone bully you?"

Swallow and Alex come into the room. Tommy-tres mouths, "Not me."

Alex quips, "What's our plan?"

Martín takes a minute. "Why don't you and Tommy-tres fix us a snack, while Swallow gives my healing a boost? Then I thought we would read a special book together. If three of us take turns and remember to let Tommy-tres keep his finger under the words as we read them, we'll get through most of the book today."

"Okay." Alex turns toward the little boy. "Tommy-tres, you and I will cook." He closes the door as they walk out.

Swallow ponders. "Tommy-tres loves words but doesn't read as well as I do. Is that why you want him to keep his finger on the words?"

Martín considers. "Yes. When I lived in Berkeley I could go to the Public Library and read all I wanted. Now they don't print books, so when I found a box of them at Franklin's, I asked if I could bring them here His children outgrew them. I unpacked them last night, and I plan to donate them to your school." He looks at Swallow. "Shall we get to work?"

"Sure, the same as yesterday?"

"Yes, follow my blue light into my shoulder. Today I'll let you do much of the work of clearing the blood from the bruise, and then I'll show you how to mend a tear in a muscle." Martín leans back and closes his eyes. Silence fills the room.

Swallow goes into a light trance. Ten minutes pass before she opens her eyes.

They sit there stunned until Martín beams, "I feel so proud of you. You learn so quickly. I'll take arnica, and at this rate, tomorrow we can finish mending the tear."

"Remember, you want to stand up and move around. You told me it would help."

"Okay." He groans as he stands and heads toward the bathroom.

When he returns, Alex helps him ease into the chair.

Tommy-tres sits cross-legged on the edge of the bed. "We started some killer spaghetti sauce for our lunch."

Swallow walks over to the bookcase. "Tío, which book do you want us to read?"

Martín responds, "<u>There's a Boy in the Girls' Bathroom</u> by Louis Sachar."

Alex sits down next to Tommy-tres. "Didn't he write <u>Holes</u>?"

Swallow hands Alex the book and sits down on the floor.

Martín feels excited. "Yes, and I enjoyed that great movie. I always identified with Zero because he was mixed race."

"So did I!" Alex agrees.

Swallow settles on the floor. "What's so special about the girls' bathroom?"

"Let's find out." Alex looks at the two children. "I'll read first." He opens the book and helps Tommy-tres find the first line.

Part way into the book he reads a conversation between Bradley, a repeat fifth-grader who is bigger than most of the kids in his class and not so well-adjusted, and Jeff, the new kid.

"I have been to the White House," Jeff admitted. "If you want, I'll tell you about it."

Bradley thought a moment, then said, "Give me a dollar or I'll spit on you."[vi]

Tommy-tres comments, "Oh, so this guy is a bully, too."

Martín answers, "Yes, and before you ask, the president lived in the White House in Washington, D.C., on the East Coast, before the Catastrophe."

Martín reads a passage where Bradley talks with his stuffed animals, his only loyal friends.

He lay on his bed and cried.

"Don't cry, Bradley," said Ronnie [one of the animals]. "Everything will be all right."

"You'll think of something, Bradley," said Bartholomew. "You always do. You're the smartest kid in the world."[vii]

Swallow remarks, "This Bradley seems very intelligent and creative, but weird."

"A lot of smart, creative people seem very eccentric." Martín looks at Tommy-tres. "The word means their behavior is different."

Alex giggles. "You should know."

Tommy-tres looks at Alex. "Would you say Tío seems intelligent, creative, but very weird?"

Alex nods and they all laugh.

Two hours later, Swallow reads a passage where Bradley talks to the counselor, then comments, "I like her. She keeps on saying good things about Bradley even if he doesn't deserve it."

"Doesn't he deserve it?" Tommy-tres inquires. "What did he do so bad nobody should ever treat him kindly again? What do you think, Tío Martín?"

"You ask an amazing question, and you both struggle with some big ideas. Let's keep reading and see what happens."

"The tests *are* easy, he [Bradley] told her. "I could get a hundred if I wanted. I'm the oldest in the class. I answer all the questions wrong on purpose."

"You want to know what I think?" asked Carla. "I think you would like to get good grades. I think the only reason you say you want to fail is because you're afraid to try. You're afraid even if you try, you'll still fail."

"I'm not afraid of anything," said Bradley.

"I think you're afraid of yourself," said Carla. But you shouldn't be. I have lots of confidence in you, Bradley.

I know you'd do so well, if only you'd try. I can help you. We can help each other. We can try together."

It was then that he told her he couldn't talk about school anymore or else he'd die.[viii]

Alex walks into the room. "Come and eat lunch."

Tommy-tres remarks, "That seems weird, doesn't it? I mean that he would think he would die if he talked about school. She knew he felt afraid of himself. I can't imagine that. But sometimes I feel afraid to spar with someone a lot bigger."

Martín groans as he pulls himself to standing, then looks at Alex. "We all hold things we feel afraid of trying."

As they reach the kitchen, Swallow comments, "Tío Martín, you never seem to feel afraid to try anything. What do you feel afraid of trying?"

Martín eases himself into his seat and seems thoughtful as Alex and Swallow serve them spaghetti, squash, and apple juice. "Just before the last action, I met a lovely young woman. I feel afraid to get to know Blue Feather. I feel afraid I like her too much." He blushes and picks up his fork. "And Swallow, what do you feel afraid of attempting?"

She chews a mouthful. "Tommy-tres, this spaghetti sauce tastes great." She sips juice. "When I heal people, I feel afraid I'll hurt them. Y'know, do something wrong."

Martín concurs. "Yes, I feel that way, too. Coyote said when I lose the fear I'll feel too self-confident and then I might hurt people."

Tommy-tres turns to Alex. "Tío, what do you feel afraid of?"

Alex takes a bite and looks down. "Ever since Martín rescued me I felt afraid to let him out of my sight because if I do, the Brotherhood will capture me again."

After a few minutes of eating in silence, Swallow inquires, "Do you think bullies feel afraid of something like us?"

Martín puts down his fork. "Every bully feels fears, just like us. But unlike us, he can't share them with friends or family. You know how it feels to keep things pent up inside. I feel much better when I say my fear out loud; it makes it smaller in a way."

"So do you mean if a bully says what he fears maybe he wouldn't pick on someone smaller?" Tommy-tres asks.

Martín responds, "Yes, but the person doing the bullying would not admit his fears until he felt secure."

They finish lunch and Tommy-tres offers to go for a walk with Alex, who agrees. Swallow and Martín take naps.

Tommy-tres comes back. "Tío Martín, Tío Martín, I want to know what happens next, but I don't want to keep my finger on the words anymore. I got tired."

"No problem. You did that for a long time."

Toward evening, the book nearly over, Carla reassigned to a kindergarten class, Bradley participates positively in school.

> Dear Carla,
>
> Hi, what color shirt are you wearing today? I'm sorry I yelled at you. Guess what? I got a hundred percent on my arithmetic test. Can you believe it? And I didn't rip it up! I would have sent it to you, but I can't because it's hanging on a wall in Mrs. Ebbel's class. Do you like teaching kindergarten? I bet you're a good teacher. Ask them to draw pictures for you. You should teach them how to do somersaults, too. Thanks for giving me back the book which you already gave me. I'm sending you a present too. It's a gift from the heart, so you can't return it.
>
> Love,
Yours truly,
Love,
Bradley[ix]

Tommy-tres sits up on the bed. "I enjoyed this book, and Bradley turned out to be a good guy after all."

Swallow looks puzzled. "I wonder..." She stops.

"What? What do you wonder?" Alex insists.

She continues. "I wonder whether there's a good person inside every bully."

Martín leans forward, "What do you think?"

"I don't know, but I'll work on it."

Tommy-tres stands and begins to jump on the bed.

"Hey, Tommy-tres, take it easy," Alex yells.

"But Tío Alex, they acted like bullies, they acted like bullies. Bradley acted like a bully, and he turned out to be a nice guy. Carla told him he felt afraid of himself."

"Whoa, slow down. Who acted like bullies? What do you say?"

"The white guys, Tío Alex, the white soldiers who hurt you. They felt afraid, too." He jumps down and lands just beside Alex.

Martín holds his breath as he watches the struggle on his friend's face.

Alex whispers, "Yes," and gives Tommy-tres a fierce hug. Alex starts to sob, and Swallow and Martín add their arms around him. They hear a knock at the door.

Swallow disengages from the hug and runs toward the living room. "I'll get it."

Lark follows her daughter back to Martín's room. "Why does everyone cry?"

Martín wipes his eyes. "It's a long story."

Lark shakes her head. "I hope m'ijos didn't make you cry."

Martín looks at her. "If so, we cry tears of joy. Your hijos brought us healing."

Four days later, Alex and Martín walk to the plaza.

Martín looks around the plaza and makes eye contact with two people he knows. He turns to Alex. "I thought a lot about the book, and Tommy-tres' interpretation."

Alex agrees, "Me, too."

Martín continues. "Tolkien got it all wrong."

"Okay, brother. Take me from the bathroom to the Hobbits. Then tell me how Tolkien could do anything wrong. I thought you enjoyed his books."

Martín glances at his friend. "Not anymore. In <u>The Lord of the Rings</u> trilogy, everyone fights the evil orcs. But the orcs don't seem human anymore."

"So Tolkien makes the Other the enemy."

"Right, and the good guys must slaughter the evil orcs. The good guys can't talk to them, and could never learn from them, and forget about trying to integrate them into society. They get labeled the Other so the so-called 'good guys' must annihilate them. But don't you see? If a bully and a good person share in the same body, so do the orcs and Tolkien's heroes."

Alex inquires, "What do you suggest? The Hobbits make friends with those monsters? It couldn't work. It never works. Tons of great writers, like C.S. Lewis, for example, make the same distinction. Why do we even talk about books when the Pure White Brotherhood hold the exact same perspective?"

"Yes, but don't you see? You just said the whole thing. The Brotherhood, who feels they are on the side of good, and we, Alex, we people of color; we are the orcs."

"But if all the great writers always agreed with this split of good and evil..."

"Oh, Alex, we won't get through this by doing things the same old way. We must learn to see things differently. We must stop the division and stop the slaughter."

"You don't mean stop fighting, stop resisting? You can't mean that at all."

"No, of course not. But Louis Sachar held the right idea. What did Jeff and Bradley do near the end of the book?"

Alex ponders. "They become friends."

"And in the middle of <u>Holes</u>, what do Stanley and Zero do which radically changes both their lives for the better?"

"They become friends, too." Alex shakes his head. "But, Martín, how will you become friends with someone from the White Brotherhood?"

"I don't know yet. But many years ago, when I told a good friend Esteban scared me, he said, 'You can catch more flies with honey than with vinegar. Why don't you two become friends?'"

Alex whispers, "I said that a long time ago."

Chapter 19
July 20, 2043

A few weeks later Martín walks across the plaza toward his office. He glances up at the clear blue sky. He enjoys his life although his shoulder still feels sore. He also feels happy because Blue Feather came. He'll see her in half an hour.

He walks through the reception area to the conference room. Tony sits at the table. He glances out the window and sees someone walking into the police annex.

"Hi, Martín. How do you feel, today?"

He walks over. "I feel fine. As a curandero, I can accelerate my own healing as long as I neglect everyone else." Healing himself reminds him of meditating. He scans his body and then focuses his blue light on the red spots and the bruises. Then he does a limited amount of repair work since all healing requires energy. Afterward he feels hungry and very peaceful.

They hear a firm knock that sounds like that of someone used to going to Resistance meetings.

Tony jumps up. "Shall I escort her in?"

Martín doesn't hesitate. "No—I'll do it," and he goes to the door. "Hey, Blue Feather, you made it. Come on in. Come right this way."

Tony raises his eyebrows. "Hi Blue Feather, great to see you. I know Martín can help you. And he sure seems excited."

After Tony takes Blue Feather's history, Martín leads her into his office, where she sees three easy chairs covered with blue quilts and a narrow bed covered by a gray and blue woven blanket. Blue Feather notices Martín had placed a bonsai willow tree in a brown raku bowl, various shells, a rose quartz crystal, a candle, and a photograph of his mother in a blue enamel frame on a low table covered with bright blue silk.

Blue Feather stares at the picture. "She looks so beautiful. I miss her. I feel glad she remains here with you." She surveys the room. "You put so much blue in here; it feels wonderful."

Martín lights the candle on the altar before sitting in one of the chairs. "Do you want anything before we get to work. Water or juice?"

Blue Feather shakes her head. She chooses a comfortable chair and arranges her full blue skirt. She wears a red sash, which looks striking against her yellow blouse.

"All right then, can I begin to scan your head?"

"Sure, what do I do?"

"Relax and just concentrate on your breath." He follows her eyes to the small shrine with a picture of his mother. "Yes, look at her. And breathe." Martín sees Blue Feather grin as he closes his eyes and goes into a light trance.

Twenty minutes later he opens his eyes and blinks, a couple of times, like a waking child. He shakes his head. "I saw the shrapnel, just the way I remembered it, and it will take some time to do what I want to do. I'll see you every day for at least a week."

"What will happen in this week? Will you take it out? Should I worry?"

Martín places his hand on the back of her head where her shrapnel remains embedded. "I'll encapsulate the fragment."

"How can you do that? Will it hurt?"

"No, no," Martín explains. "I'll use our combined positive energy to wrap the fragment. Doing it all at once would wipe us out. A week gives us time to regenerate between treatments.

"You'll want a good night's sleep and a light break-fast each day. You'll feel ravenous after each treatment. I'll form a membrane around the fragment a layer at a time. This procedure will also make the casing stronger than if we did it faster."

Tony approaches the pair as they come out of Martín's office. Martín shakes his head to stop Tony's question. "Can you get Blue Feather a cherry juice, something sweet? Give her a few minutes to recoup after the treatment."

A few minutes later they sit together in the conference room.

Tony comments, "Could you share some herbal healing techniques with us?"

Blue Feather glances at Martín, who nods.

"Sure, I'll gladly do it. Can we make it in exchange for some of the treatments?"

"Absolutely." Martín turns to Blue Feather. "Want to talk about it over lunch?"

"Fine." Blue Feather yawns. "Can you suggest a good place to stay? I'd like to check in and take a nap until lunchtime."

Tony suggests, "Why don't you stay with Susana? Her roommate just moved out." He looks at his watch. "If you go now you'll catch her. She lives four blocks away."

Martín assents. "Yes, great. I also want some time to make preparations and handle any reactions to the treatment."

Blue Feather starts to blush. "That seems fine." She yawns again.

Tony says, "Let me write two messages and I'll walk you over."

"Thanks, Tony." Martín looks at his watch. "Blue Feather, shall we meet at Rubén's at one o'clock?"

A little after one, Martín walks into Rubén's and sits down at the table across from Blue Feather. She still looks tired, but her cheeks are filled with color. "Sorry, I ran just a tad late. I saw many clients this morning and I wanted to swim."

She smiles. "No problem. Susana lives in a lovely place with a cozy room for me."

Rubén comes to the table. "What do you two want to eat?"

Martín looks at him. "Rubén, meet Blue Feather. She trained as an herbalist."

Rubén shakes her hand. "I feel pleased to meet you." He turns to Martín and winks. "Shall I put her lunch on your tab?"

Martín wipes the drip running from his wet hair. "Yes, she'll stay at least a week, so please put what she eats on my bill." He glances at the blackboard. "I'll order the tuna casserole with extra French bread, a large apple juice, and peach cobbler à la mode."

Blue Feather tells Rubén, "I want the same without the extra bread." She turns to Martín. "Please don't feel obligated."

Martín touches her hand. "About two years ago, I healed Rubén's wife. I get free lunches here because he figures he knows a good investment."

"Oh, that's why he winked."

Rubén almost whispers, "And he heals so many people without charging them."

Martín continues. "About this trade we mentioned earlier. I'd like to hire you to give three lectures on herbal healing at the clinic as a trade for your treatments." He pauses. "Of course, I'll provide lunch."

Rubén brings their order. "Buen provecho."

Blue Feather agrees. "That sounds good. What do you want me to cover?" She takes a bite of food. "Mmm, this casserole tastes great."

Martín savors a forkful. "Yes, Rubén feeds me well." He takes a sip of juice. "I'd like your first talk to cover basics. I'll invite my goddaughter, Swallow. She's nine years old and very bright with great aptitude for healing. Base your other classes on the discussion after the first talk, but include why our clinic wants a good herbalist."

Blue Feather sips juice. "I can do that. It sounds like you want me to sell myself."

He blushes and stammers, "Oh no, I didn't mean—"

That afternoon, Tony drives with Martín toward Chimayo. "Sammy said Alex arrived in a blue funk and won't come out of their extra bedroom."

Martín feels exasperated. "Those white bastards hurt him. He seems like a little wounded bird, and I became imprinted as his mother—he won't let me, the first person Alex saw afterwards, out of his sight. It became bad enough when I went back to work, but now when I want my spare time for Blue Feather, I don't know what to do. All his experience, and all his courage, seem gone and he feels helpless without me."

Tony touches Martín's arm. "We'll figure out a way to keep Alex busy."

Martín groans. "I spent so many years healing others; I never learned who I am."

Tony shakes his head. "So Alex isn't the only person who feels helpless. But I don't buy it. You know who you are." He stops the car. "Keep Alex busy while I climb into the spare bedroom through the trap door. Then follow my lead." He leaves the car.

Martín knocks on the door. "Alex, let's go for a walk and talk."

Alex's voice sounds muffled. "Why did you ditch me for a woman?"

Martín hears a loud thud. Tony yells, "But what a woman!" Martín hears a scuffle.

Alex howls. "Tony, you can't do this to me."

The door crashes open. Tony, with two arnís sticks, chases Alex to the backyard.

Strong hands pick up Martín. He glances over his shoulder and yelps, "Sammy, stop! Put me down, now!" struggling as Sammy carries him to the patio.

Martín stands face-to-face with an angry Alex. They each hold an arnís stick.

Tony yells, "Hit Martín if you feel so pissed at him."

Alex mutters, "But," shakes his head, and rushes at the healer.

Martín parries the first three blows. He grunts as the fourth whacks his shoulder, and remembers Maestra taught him to use his blue light to defend himself. Alex dances in and out, striking hard. Martín keeps his focus on his friend's eyes until he sees a lapse in his concentration. As Alex retreats, Martín strikes his left calf with his force and follows with an arnís strike that sends both weapons flying. As Alex stumbles, Martín throws his body at him.

The two go down in a heap. Although Martín weighs less, he can defeat his friend without using his special gift. Already on the ground, he doesn't worry about keeping his balance or falling. In a rush, his body remembers the techniques Maestra and Abuelo taught him. No one can pin him. The two wrestle for several minutes until Martín throws his body against Alex, holding him down for ten seconds. Alex taps out.

They both gasp for breath and smile. Alex speaks first. "Damn, once you get me on the ground, I can never win."

Tony glances at Sammy. "Your ma taught us all well."

Martín laughs. "My Abuelo taught us the fundamentals, but your mother taught me to fight with all my gifts, even my cerebral palsy."

Alex shakes his head again. "I remember when you turned six and Sigún wanted us to teach you to turn over."

Martín hits his friend's shoulder. "We came a long way together. Let's go down to the river and talk." He stands and mouths "thanks" to Tony and Sammy.

The two friends sit on a rock. The sound of rushing water stills Martín's mind. He remembers his dream about the coyote family. Then he looks at his friend, feeling torn.

Alex clears his throat. "Sorry. I sure act strange lately."

Martín frowns. "Yes, those bastards wounded your soul and self-image."

"Can you heal me, brother?"

Martín feels sad. "I wish I could zap your soul with my blue light and presto, you'd return to yourself. I wish I could completely heal Blue Feather's brain injury or my own cerebral palsy, but I can't. I gave it a lot of thought, though."

After a minute, Alex prompts his friend. "And?"

Martín blinks. "Well, as much as I love you, Coyote does this kind of healing better. I saw him work with Juanita. Coyote used her own energy to heal her. She talked and he monitored her. When he finished, she could begin her new life." He stops to look at his friend. "Even after all Coyote's work, Juanita did much more. He taught her to use tools: music, aromatherapy, journaling, and jujitsu, to strengthen the process."

Alex sits. "I want to do something. Would you work with me on this?"

"I'd feel honored, but I won't do it." Martín maintains his boundaries. "Alex, you grow too dependent on me. Consider working with Coyote."

Alex stamps his foot. "No, I'd rather work with you. Besides, if things take off with you and Yellow Feather, this would be our last fling."

"She calls herself Blue Feather. And you jump the gun. I hardly know her."

Alex shakes his head. "But she already changed you."

"How so?"

Alex scratches his head. "I know your energy doesn't seem the same."

Martín laughs. "How did we get on this topic? You distracted me. Let's talk about your healing. What if I went with you to Coyote's and helped you start?"

Alex doesn't look happy. "Well, maybe."

"Use lavender as a great relaxant, both alone or combined with other herbs. You can use it in cooking, in an infusion, or in a sachet for aromatherapy. A drop of lavender oil on the temple will help relieve a headache. I use it for nervous indigestion and for psoriasis and eczema, also as a natural insect repellant. Combine it with almond oil to make great massage oil." Blue Feather takes a deep breath and looks around the room. Her speech sounds clearer than when she arrived in Santa Fe, two days ago.

Twenty-two students listen. More than she expected. Eighteen take notes on her talk. And Tony has promised copies of his printed notes to Martín, Swallow, and Blue Feather's old friend, a curandera from Chama. They'd converted the waiting room of the clinic into a classroom by bringing the large table in from the conference room, where Sammy minds the smaller children. Blue Feather sees Swallow raise her hand. "Yes?"

Swallow scrunches her eyebrows with seriousness. "What would you cook with lavender?"

Blue Feather answers, "You can bake it into sugar cookies to serve with chamomile tea before bed."

The curandera says, "I add it to broth when someone seems quite ill."

Lark affirms. "When my kids act super-rowdy, I add it to their pizza."

Swallow laughs. "Oh, so I can add herbs to almost anything depending on what I want to achieve."

Blue Feather concludes. "The whole point of this class: Go out and use herbs creatively, experiment, and observe. Herbs will affect each person differently in each situation, but use them as powerful healing tools. Thanks for coming. We'll meet again Thursday at seven, and Saturday we'll go for an herb-collecting walk near Velarde."

The students clap, and then talk animatedly. Martín, Swallow, and the curandera from Chama approach Blue Feather. Lark follows her daughter to the front.

Martín feels invigorated. "Great. You got us all excited about using herbs."

Swallow puts her hand on Blue Feather's shoulder. "I learned so much. Thanks for letting me take the class. Except for Tío Martín, most grown-ups think nine-year-olds are dumb."

Blue Feather glances at Martín before turning to Swallow. "I'd never make that mistake, especially now I met you. If you're free Sunday, I'd gladly show you how to press and dry some of the different herbs we'll collect."

"I'd like that." Swallow turns to her mother. "Mamacita, puedo?"

"Sure, hija, as long as you learn to spell the names of the herbs." Lark turns to Blue Feather. "I want our apprentice-curandera to work on her reading and spelling. These days, we can't find many books."

Blue Feather scratches her head. "Then I will work with Tony to develop a written list of herbs, and on Thursday I'll teach the class a scheme for taking notes on their observations."

Lark looks at Swallow. "I like that idea. Blue Feather, why don't you sleep at our place Saturday night? You two can get an early start." Blue Feather acquiesces.

Lark turns to Martín. "I'll even invite you and Tony for Sunday dinner."

He responds, "That'll work if you invite Susana, too."

"Of course." Lark turns. "Hija, we better run and catch our ride to Chimayo. I just saw your dad go out the door."

As they leave, Swallow touches her mother's arm. "Gracias, Mamacita."

Lark responds, "I want you to develop your gifts, and I learned when to bow to the inevitable."

Martín turns to the woman standing beside him. "You are Blue Feather's friend from Chama? And a curandera, too?"

She nods.

"Do you mind if I inquire why you asked Tony to take notes for you?"

The pretty thirty-year-old Hispanic woman hesitates as if she translates. "No, not at all. I live with dyslexia. I want to learn from my friend. I'd hate to get it backwards."

She turns to Blue Feather and reaches down to hug her. Then she pauses before saying, "How long since I saw you?"

"Two years too long. I missed you. Do you remember when my mother banished us from her stillroom for a week?"

Her friend laughs and then stops. "Oh, do you mean because she caught us smoking her medicinal marijuana? How could I forget?"

"I felt compelled to try it." Blue Feather giggles.

The curandera turns to Martín. "Her mother took me on even though I learn differently. She spoke so clearly, and I understood so well, I began to believe she taught things backwards for me. Blue Feather seemed relieved to read the assignments out loud just so I could get them straight. They see beyond a person's difference to her essence."

Saturday night Lark and Blue Feather sit in the kitchen in Chimayo. Swallow and Tommy-tres went to bed. Sammy reads in his office. Lark takes a sip of herbal tea. "This tea tastes delicious. Did you add something special?"

Blue Feather looks at her old friend. "Yes, I added a few secret ingredients. I'll leave some of my special formula with you."

The warrior nods. "Thanks. I'd feel grateful. I enjoy your visit and I hope you will come back soon."

Blue Feather says, "I enjoyed staying with Susana and getting to know Santa Fe better. Monday I'll go back home. How do things go with you and Sammy?"

Lark stares at her tea before answering. "Sammy treats us with great kindness and gentleness. From the beginning, he thought I took too many risks when we do an action. Yet, he remains always there for me but a bit too protective. But he loves us.

"What about you? Are you thinking about moving to Santa Fe?"

Blue Feather looks lost in thought. "Yes, I'd grow if I move away from my mother's and maybe live in Santa Fe for awhile. I want to become my own person, and starting a dispensary would give me an opportunity to do what I love. I already asked Susana to save her extra bedroom for me. She and I have been friends for a long time."

Lark again sounds pensive. "I keep thinking she and Tony will tie the knot when Susana finishes her degree at St. Johns. When she just started in the Resistance she acted too cautiously. Now she acts too carefully with Tony."

Early Sunday morning, Martín hears pounding and answers the front door. Juanita rushes into the house on Galisteo in Santa Fe, followed by her partner, Tomás, carrying their eleven-year-old son on his back. "Can you check him out? Carlos broke his foot." Over twelve years ago, Sammy demanded that Tomás and Juanita be freed when Franklin and Mateo came to rescue him, Lark, and Guillermo from the Marine camp. The couple settled in a small town just south of Albuquerque and maintained a close friendship with Sammy and Lark, as they fight in the Resistance together.

Martín points to the sofa. "Sure, just put him down. What happened?"

Carlos moans softly before saying, "Dad and I run cross-country three mornings a week as part of our training. He led me over the roof of my school and then jumped to a nearby roof. I missed the jump."

Juanita shakes her head. "Running cross-country doesn't usually mean over roofs."

Tomás looks sheepish. "I want to get him ready for anything. After my son heals, we'll work on smaller jumps."

Martín sits in his favorite chair and goes into a trance. He notices three small bones are broken. He reduces the swelling, before he lines up the bones and starts the healing process. He comes out of the trance. "I want to see him in my office tomorrow morning. You can pick up some crutches then. And get him some calcium tablets."

Carlos says, "Thank you. It doesn't hurt so much."

Martín nods. "Stay off that foot and get Swallow to accelerate the healing this afternoon."

Juanita suggests to her partner, "Why don't you get the car while I use the bathroom?"

Once they leave, Martín turns to Carlos and says, "What really happened? You usually show more sense?"

"My dad pushes me too hard and forgets I can't do everything that he can." Carlos looks exasperated.

As Juanita comes into the room, Martín says, "Only you can know when you can do something and when you can't. You will learn to depend on your own judgment and intuition."

Juanita puts her hand on her son's shoulder. "I'll support you saying *no* to your father when he demands more than you can do."

"Thanks, Ma." Carlos grins. "And next time, I'll look before I leap."

Later that morning, in Swallow's bedroom in Chimayo, Blue Feather crushes fresh herbs with a mortar and pestle.

Swallow sits on the edge of the bed, watching. "Strange. My mother gave birth to me after the Great Catastrophe, yet my parents expect me to develop the same skills as a person born before it."

Blue Feather looks up from her work. "I know what you mean about parents' expectations. Maybe the horror made us more capable. Both Martín and I were born afterwards and we became super-people. For starters, we mastered all the old skills of reading, figuring, writing, and using a computer. Then we became martial artists and curanderos to survive."

The eleven-year-old groans. "In this house, it's impossible not to train as a martial artist. Before my sixth birthday, I could take out a two-hundred-pound soldier with just an arnís stick or a piece of wire. My parents and Tío Martín tell me I'll become a curandera. I see uses for numbers. But why read and write when no new books get printed and the internet died a long time ago?"

"Good question. Reading and writing or literacy dies out and soon we will live in a post-literate society. We can still find a few books, and I want you to hold access to as much information as you can."

Swallow furrows her forehead. "Maybe I will hold more options if I can read."

"And write. Yes." The herbalist hears a knock on the door. "Come in."

"Ah, ladies, we will soon serve luncheon. I humbly request your gentle presences." Sammy bows.

Swallow giggles. "Dad, why do you talk so funny?"

"Tío Martín wants to make a good impression." Her father winks, and leaves.

They both laugh. Blue Feather stands. "I'll lend you my copy of Michael Tierra's <u>The Way of Herbs</u> if you promise to take good care of it and read a page a day."

"Sure, I'll do both." Swallow hugs her. "Does that mean you'll come back?"

"Yes, but I'm not sure when."

Blue Feather slides into the chair beside Martín. He introduces her to Tomás and Juanita, freedom fighters from Los Lunas, who drop off their eleven-year-old son Carlos before they go on a mission. Carlos sees Swallow and points to the seat he'd saved for her. "I broke my foot this morning. Martín suggested I ask you to boost the healing this afternoon." He spends time with the Manzanares family, sharing a small bedroom with Tommy-tres. Swallow grins and nods.

Susana winks at Blue Feather. She sits between Tony and Mateo. Tommy-tres catches her eye and points to Tomás. "That's Tommy-dos."

Blue Feather smiles. "Oh, yes, he's Tommy, too."

The little boy chuckles. "That's what I said. I love bilingual jokes."

Blue Feather hears Martín laugh. Before she can inquire about the first Tommy, he and Lark hold Blue Feather's hands as everyone round the table remains silent until someone giggles. Lark hands her a bowl of rice.

Plates of beans, Filipino fish stew, red chili, green chili, baskets of flour tortillas, and pitchers of water and juice get passed around the table. Although food is scarce, each family contributes. Intent on filling their plates, they savor the first few bites.

Seven-year-old Tommy-tres, seated across from Blue Feather, pipes up, "Tío Martín, I heard Don Mateo use the word 'strategy'; what does it mean?"

Martín takes a deep breath. "You know what holding a goal means, right?"

Tommy-tres nods. "Yes, a goal is like wanting to win at checkers."

"A strategy means the steps you take to reach your goal, like when you play checkers with Swallow and she lets you take a checker so she can take two of yours."

Swallow's clear voice interrupts. "So, then, if you don't win, you should change your strategy, right?" Before getting an answer, she looks at Don Mateo and asks, "Don't you think the Resistance should change its strategy?"

All conversation stops as eyes turn to Mateo, who chews a mouthful. His face turns red, but he inquires, "What do you mean?"

Swallow looks around the table. "Since the Catastrophe, the Resistance's actions don't change the situation, besides getting Dad, Tío Martín, and Tío Alex hurt."

Carlos jumps in. "Yeah. My parents go off and blow up more radio stations or rob more banks. Then they rescue their friends from military camps and prisons.

When they get home they complain because nothing changed. The Resistance plays a futile game."

Martín interjects, "Hey, I spend too much time healing badly injured fighters. I just got wounded rescuing Alex. I feel glad I could get him out, but the action didn't change anything."

Mateo shakes his head. "Okay, I feel game. What do you suggest?"

Swallow thinks. "At school, a new kid hurt some of the smaller children, but did it when he knew he wouldn't get caught."

Tommy-tres interrupts. "Do you mean the guy who hurt the third grader kind of bad? I tried to stop him, but he fights dirty and he outweighs me by forty pounds."

"Yes, him." Swallow frowns. "We study in the same class. So I scanned him. I found scars and bruises on his back and an irritated spot in his brain. Over the next few days, I healed him."

She looks at Martín. "Yes, I know I should ask first, but as soon as I started working on him, he stopped injuring the other kids, which seemed like permission enough. Then we talked a long time after school. We made a deal. I told him I'd heal him every time his stepfather beat him up, if he didn't hurt anyone else. I don't know what to do about his stepdad yet."

"So let's see if I understand what you mean." Mateo scratches his chin. "You equate this guy with the white government, right?"

"More like some of the leaders," Swallow affirms. "You could kidnap some and get Tío Martín to scan them."

"And what would I do after I scanned them?" Martín wonders.

Swallow scratches her head. "I don't know that part, yet. But maybe you could learn what makes them hate us and heal them."

"Healing more than one sounds too risky."

"What if you didn't do all the work? What if you healed one, and then sent him back so he could change other leaders' attitudes."

Tomás joins in. "Like when we sent Guillermo back with the computer chip virus, and thousands of non-white recruits from all over California escaped."

Blue Feather laughs. "I remember all those young people pouring into Arizona. Now *that* action did change the situation."

Mateo frowns. "I'll think about your ideas."

Later, Martín and Blue Feather sit on the same rock he and Alex sat on six days earlier.

Martín wonders at the gift that let him cross paths with Blue Feather. "You know," he hesitates, "in Santa Fe, the last herbalist died a year ago. We found no one qualified to replace her." He swallows. "Would you consider relocating?"

With an amused look in her eye, she says, "I will give it serious thought. My still vigorous and healthy mother wants to give me her place in northwest Arizona. Why would I want to move?"

Martín reflects a minute. "Your mother's place sounds pretty isolated. I get the sense you might want to grow in different ways that are more possible in Santa Fe. What did you learn from this past week?"

"I learned from this past week; I enjoy teaching."

"And you teach so well. You'll find plenty of opportunities here." He looks at her. "I can see us healing a whole throng of people together."

Blue Feather grins. "I like your vision. I want time to think it over. Come to my mother's place in a month and ask me again."

The next morning, Martín feels dazed when Mateo walks into the bedroom and opens the curtains. Martín wishes Blue Feather already lived here. He looks at his watch. Darn! Eight! And her ride to Flagstaff left at six. Franklin would meet her there and drive her home.

Mateo's voice startles his son. "I always regret sending Sofía, pregnant with you, to Denver."

Martín, surprised by his father's declaration, sits up in bed.

Mateo continues. "After I got the job in San Francisco, I saw her a lot and I kept my eye on you, but I felt it too risky to tell you my identity. Later, Sofía and

I spent eight great years together here. It's rare to find someone with whom you can share both your life and your life work."

He looks at his father and shakes his head.

"Martín, say something!"

He rubs his eyes. "Way too early."

"Talk to me!"

"What do you want me to say? I feel half asleep, but I listen. I don't respond as quickly as you want. I don't know the answers to all your unspoken questions."

Mateo glares at his son. "Darn it, Martín. O-oh. You mean you know what I'll ask you and your answer is, 'I don't know.'" Mateo nods his head. "You got me good, once again. I suppose you also don't know why a White Brotherhood leader hates us people of color so much."

"Yep." Martín speaks grimly. "I don't know whether they hate us or whether they fear us. Or maybe their leaders indoctrinate them to believe us wholly Other."

"What do you mean? And don't tell me you don't know, again!"

Martín beams. "Oh, but I do know. The whites decided we non-whites are "the Other" and they must destroy us, starting with the Islamic terrorists who supposedly sparked the Catastrophe." He shakes his head.

"Because you seem physically slower I forget you remain miles ahead of me. How did you figure this out?" Mateo looks at his son.

"During my recovery, I did some reading and thinking, and then I got into a discussion with Alex about the Other. But the whites forced us to see them as the Other, in order for us to survive. We robbed them, bombed them, and even killed a few, but as long as we stay enemies nothing will change. Now we want a new strategy."

Mateo counters, "And what would that look like?"

"Dad, I don't know. Maybe Swallow's right. Maybe if you kidnap one of their leaders, I could scan him and figure out what makes him tick."

El curandero puts on his pants in silence.

Mateo clears his throat. "Martín, I want to ask your forgiveness. I pushed you into an action so you would become like me, a physical warrior, and you got hurt. Forgive me for pushing you. You hold too many wonderful gifts to risk them. I want to accept you."

Martín takes a breath. "Dad. I love you, too."

Mateo hugs him.

He continues, "I want to accept myself," even the damn pull toward Tierra Oscura.

Chapter 20
August 28, 2043

After work a month later, Martín rides out to Chimayo and knocks. Swallow and Lark greet him, and he crouches so Tommy-tres can hug him.

Lark inquires, "Can you stay for dinner?"

Martín leans against the wall for a second and straightens up. "Yes, I'd like to, but first I'll talk to Sammy." He knocks on the door to Sammy's study.

Sammy looks up. "Bienvenido, welcome sientaté, sit down, please. ¿Cómo estas? How are you?"

Martín eases himself into a chair. "Estoy muy bien, gracias. ¿Y tú?

"Estoy optimo, I feel great."

Martín looks out the window and then at his friend. "Why do you and Tommy-tres speak so much Spanish?"

Sammy answers. "I love m'ijo. My ma taught me to look at everyone's strengths and weaknesses. My son, with a gift for languages and words, will find opportunities to speak Spanish. With the gift of empathy, like you, he'll never make a good soldier. He feels what his opponent feels, so he won't hurt anybody. So I decided to help him develop his language gifts by speaking Spanish with him and encouraging him to question what words mean. Martín, you didn't come out here to ask me about Tommy-tres. ¿Qué pasa? What's up?"

Martín looks his friend in the eye. "I'd like a favor. I want you to drive Alex and me to Prescott, wait for me there for a day, and then drive me to Blue Feather's. Hopefully, I can persuade her to come back with me."

"Sure, just let me look at my agenda." Sammy opens a notebook. "I'll do a pickup in Durango a week from Saturday. If we leave this Friday, we can do it all. We'll stop in Los Lunas and pick up Carlos. He offered to spend time with Vela on your dad's land."

Martín says, "I'm glad he's going. I don't like Vela staying alone way out there."

Sammy closes his agenda. "Do you mind coming back through southern Colorado?"

"No, I don't mind, and I assume it will be okay with Blue Feather. I hold a little cash. Rubén wanted to buy some jewelry and pottery, and Susana wants to buy some rugs and quilts. Leaving Friday will give me two days to raise the money for gas and expenses. And then I'll talk Alex into going."

"Y'mean you'll talk him into staying with Coyote."

He feels both sad and frustrated. "Yes, you know us both well."

"So unless I hear differently, I'll stop by your place at seven Friday morning and we'll gas up in Albuquerque," Sammy assents.

"Yes, thank you."

They hear footsteps running, and two young voices cry out, "Supper's ready."

"Alex, get in the truck, now. We must get going." On Friday, Martín feels exasperated. He and Sammy tried to get their friend in the truck for ten minutes.

Alex groans. "You'll just leave me at Coyote's and then what will I do?" He's crouched against the door of the house on Galisteo.

"You'll work on your issues," Sammy mutters as he gets out of the truck, marches over to the forlorn figure, and whispers in his ear.

"Okay, move over." Alex gets in, and slams the door. Sammy starts the truck.

On Highway 25 to Albuquerque, Martín glances at Sammy. "What did you say?"

Sammy chuckles, "Y'know, my kids can stay mighty stubborn. So, when something seems important, I make them an offer they can't refuse."

Martín waits a minute. "What did you offer him?"

"Ah, I won't tell you."

Martín puzzles over a scene from his early morning nightmare. Blue Feather lay on the ground bleeding. A Wag soldier shot Sofía over and over with a small pistol. A line like an umbilical cord ran from the soldier to Blue Feather. Martín tried to tear the cord but he couldn't. He felt more and more desperate. Abuelo appeared and hit the cord with a small rock until it broke. The killer ran away.

Martín asks Carlos as he squeezes into the cab of the truck in Los Lunas, "How's your foot?"

"It feels fine. Dad and I returned to training two weeks ago. I tell him when I don't think I can do something. We either discuss it or he lets it go. Ma says that's good training for me in assertiveness."

When they stop for lunch at a truck stop in Gallup, Martín notices Sammy buys Alex a super banana split.

On the way back to the truck, Carlos says, "You seem preoccupied. What's up?"

Martín feels sheepish. "After we drop Alex in Prescott, I want to ask Blue Feather to return to Santa Fe so I can get to know her better."

Carlos comments, "From what I saw, she seemed okay."

"Well, I dreamt strange dreams about her."

"I want to go with you, Martín," Alex whines. On Sunday night, Coyote, his wife, two children, Tío Juan, Tía Sara, and Sammy sit in the living room at Coyote's house.

Martín feels torn. "I understand you don't want to let me out of your sight."

Coyote puts a hand on Alex's arm. "Your fears and anxieties around Martín take up much of your energy. We can redirect this energy, turning it into a healing force."

Tío Juan speaks in a soft voice. "Alex, you and Martín remain such good friends for many years. But right now, you seem stuck. Do you remember when I stayed stuck in the house in Berkeley? I felt so angry and hurt when Sara decided to walk to Prescott." He looks at his wife.

Tía Sara, with tears in her eyes, whispers, "The second hardest thing I ever did meant walking away." Her voice grows strong. "I didn't want to leave my husband and youngest son. But I did what I knew felt right for me, and I couldn't wait for Juan. He had to face his fears and stop using the house as an excuse to stay stuck. I couldn't do it."

She turns to Alex. "Martín loves you. Right now, he must go persuade Blue Feather to move to Santa Fe. And you must stay here and work with Coyote. ¿Entiendas?"

Alex sits there with his head bowed. "Okay, I guess I'll stay here."

Sammy clears his throat. "Alex, that's not enough. Do you want to heal? Coyote can provide you with many tools, but you must commit. Otherwise, you might as well go jump in a lake."

Alex shakes his head. "Sammy, the nearest lake is far away." He looks at Martín. "I'll work with Coyote to heal my inner wounds, I promise." He starts weeping.

Martín holds his friend. "You'll do fine."

After a few minutes, Tío Juan stands and turns to Sammy. "Why don't you and Martín stay at our house tonight? You can get an early start."

Sammy agrees. "Good idea."

Later, Tía Sara comes into the room where Martín will sleep with a small dark blue pouch. "Martín, I found this in your Abuelo's things and I kept it for you, until you seemed ready."

He spills two silver rings into his hands. "They look beautiful."

Tía Sara grins. "They belonged to your Abuelo and Abuela."

Martin gives her a hug. "Muchas gracias, Tía."

Chapter 21
September 2, 2043

Seven o'clock Monday morning, Martín gets ready to leave the house on East Goodwin, now painted indigo. Sammy left to check the tires and fill the truck with gas. Martín suspects he also is meeting one of his contacts.

Pedro bursts in. "I came to tell you good news." He pants to catch his breath and looks around the kitchen. "Buenos días, Martín. Glad to see you.

"One of Estebán's friends just arrived, wounded. He escaped from the prison in Alamosa, Colorado, three days ago. He said Estebán stayed and does okay."

Tía Sara starts crying. "I feel so glad."

Tío Juan jumps up to hold his wife. "We got to get our son out of prison."

Pedro turns to Martín. "Come check out this guy. Miguel's with him now."

Martín turns to Tío Juan. "Please tell Sammy to meet me at Pedro's." He walks out the back door with Pedro beside him.

Tía Sara yells after them, "I'll come there in ten minutes."

Pedro affirms, "We'd just finished breakfast when Estebán's buddy staggered through the front door. So Miguel bustled the horde off to school while I came to tell Mama about Estebán."

Martín strides on. It seems like only yesterday when Pedro and Miguel had bought the Manzanares' house, now filled with their four children and occasionally Vela. Pedro mentions, "When Vela gets out of school at noon, I'll drive her and Carlos out to Mateo's place."

They find the Resistance fighter sitting on the kitchen floor. Miguel clears off the kitchen table, and Carlos washes the breakfast dishes.

He sits down on the floor near the wounded man. "I call myself Martín, the curandero. Where do you hurt?

May I scan your injuries?" He turns to Pedro. "I want clean rags."

The guy raises his eyebrows. "Sure, Estebán told me about you. I took a bullet in my left arm, and walking for miles chewed up my feet."

Martín touches the man's bicep, feeling the heat of infection. He scans.

He comes out of his trance and turns to Pedro, who just returned with rags. "Oh, good. I'll wrap the arm in this old towel while I pop the bullet out." He returns to his trance and within a minute the bullet comes out with a gush of blood. Martín clears out the wound and stops the bleeding. "The bullet didn't do much damage, but the infection became bad." He tears a strip of cloth and ties a pad around the guy's arm.

They hear a knock at the back door. Tía Sara and Sammy join them. The wounded man explains to Sammy, "Estebán could come with me, but he uses his presence to protect a compañera who the guards harass. We agreed I would get word to Pedro. It won't be easy to get them out. Too bad none of the guards will look the other way."

"Just like Estebán to stay when he could come home," Tía Sara cries.

Sammy seems pensive. "We'll go by Franklin's on the way to Blue Feather's, this afternoon. He can plan a job like no one else." He looks at the clock. "Martín, let's go."

Tía Sara steps forward with a cloth bag. "I packed you a lunch." She winks at Martín. "Tell Franklin if he wants anyone to get m'ijo out, he can count on me."

Pedro puts his hand on Miguel's shoulder. "Sí, he can count on all of us."

Sammy and Martín spend the night at Franklin's so they can discuss the action to free Esteban and the compañera. As they leave the next morning, Franklin tells them, "We'll meet at Rubén's cousin's place in Red River north of Taos a week from Friday. I'll get word to Pedro. Tía Sara will drive because she wants to take part in this and no one will suspect her. Martín, your team will stay in Red River, ready to heal any wounded."

"That's close enough for me." He winces. "I still work on recovering from my last encounter."

"Blue Feather, what can I say to get you to move to Santa Fe? You'll soon build your own business, hold an essential role at the clinic, and find opportunities to teach. On difficult cases we'll complement each other and form a healing team for Resistance actions." Martín squints in the sunshine outside her house, the next morning.

Standing in the doorway, she says, "Come inside and meet my mother."

Martín steps inside and shades his eyes as they adjust to the much cooler and darker room with walls covered with hand-woven blankets in browns and reds. He sees three easy chairs. A vase of yellow flowers sits on the dining room table.

Mary Grey Eyes, a striking person of medium height, in her mid-fifties, neither fat nor thin, and very energetic, steps forward and shakes his hand. "Please sit down." She wears a silver and turquoise necklace over a red cotton blouse and long indigo skirt. She pulled her salt and pepper hair into a single braid. "I understand you want to get my daughter to move to Santa Fe."

He sees both mischief and kindness in her eyes. "Yes, ma'am, if she wants that."

"Good answer. Blue Feather strives to remain very much her own person."

He grins. "I come from a long line of people who strive to make their own decisions."

Mary studies him. "What do you say for yourself?"

He looks down at his hands. "I received the gift of helping people heal themselves, and I use it in a way that allows each person to feel good about her or himself. Your daughter's work would complement mine. We'll do good work together, and I'll support her in doing what she wants. We will accomplish so much more together as a team."

Mary turns to her daughter. "And what can you tell me?"

"Martín grows into a good person. He knows he doesn't know everything."

Mary agrees. "You've both suffered deep injuries. Martín, can you let go of any bitterness you still hold about your difference?"

"Cerebral palsy taught me to see the important. I don't spend energy doing frivolous tasks. I want to work on accepting all its facets. I'll work hard not to feel bitter and angry toward the people who caused Blue Feather's wounds."

Mary looks at her daughter. "And you?"

Blue Feather reflects. "We both wobble. Neither of us can do the tasks society says an adult should do. No one can. We'll act creatively as we lead our daily lives. I like seeing Martín interact with Swallow and Tommy-tres — children, yet he listens to them carefully and respectfully." She turns to Martín. "I hope you'll listen to me that way."

He assents. "I'll do my best and you'll remind me. I'd like you to listen to me."

Mary asks, "What's your plan?"

"Sammy and I will spend the next three days helping Blue Feather pack. He wants to go through Durango Saturday morning. When we get to Santa Fe, Blue Feather will stay with Susana and work in the clinic in a suite of rooms she can use both for her own business and for our work together." He looks at Blue Feather. "I hope you'll become part of a healing team. We'll go to Red River a week from Friday to heal people returning from the action." She agrees.

Mary clears her throat. "Sounds like you thought this out well. What about finances?"

He looks at Blue Feather again. "Neither of us saved a lot of cash, but people will always require our work and we'll receive trade goods and bartered services."

She adds, "Both my mother and my friend agreed to contribute to my initial stock of herbs. I also put aside blankets and jewelry to use to trade for cash."

He approves. "So do I. We'll keep our finances separate. But I realize I'll enjoy us spending hours talking about everything under the sun."

Mary clears her throat. "You two made a good start, but you'll work hard. Martín, do you know whether you can generate the energy this relationship will require?"

"I won't know until we try, but we'll go slowly."

Martín notices Blue Feather's mother went into a trance. The young people wait until Mary opens her eyes again. "Before you get to Santa Fe, you will witness an accident. How you both deal with the two people involved will determine much about your future relationship. You may not remember this warning. Take time to purify yourselves. You'll find this test most difficult."

Mateo, his arm cradled by a sling, sits in the afternoon sun, contemplating the view outside his place overlooking a broad valley in Arizona, three days later.

Martín gets out and gives him a hug. "Hey, what happened to your arm?"

Mateo groans. "I got shot during an action in Utah. I feel glad I made it back late last night. Will you look at it after supper?"

Martín nods. "Sure. Hey, we're helping Blue Feather move to Santa Fe. She'll start her own business and consult at the clinic."

Mateo stands painfully, ambles to the truck, and extends his arm to Blue Feather. "Welcome, bright-eyed daughter of my good friend, Mary."

Blue Feather laughs as she gets out of the truck and hugs Mateo. Sammy climbs down, walks around the truck and shakes his hand.

Vela runs out of Mateo's two-room Hogan, greets Blue Feather, and gives Martín a hug. "I'm so glad to see you. Let's talk after dinner."

He nods and turns to Sammy. "Do you know my cousin Vela?"

Sammy answers, "Not yet," and turns to shake her hand.

Carlos walks toward the Hogan carrying two buckets of water. When he notices the newcomers, he puts the buckets down slowly and rushes over to greet them. "It took me a day, but I begin to enjoy the peace and quiet out here."

Vela suggests, "Tío, maybe Sammy can help Carlos and you with the log."

Blue Feather looks at Vela. "I'll come with you so we can talk."

As the two walk toward the Hogan, Vela tells her, "I give him ginger tea every day and use extra turmeric in his food."

Handing Sammy an axe and Carlos the saw, Mateo shrugs. "A tree fell, blocking our path to the river. If you two don't mind, we can chop it up."

Carlos, Sammy, and Martín follow Mateo. Martín remarks, "He means you and Carlos will do the work, Sammy."

"Martín, y'know, I feel glad to do it. My parents taught me to respect my elders. And I'll enjoy the exercise."

Carlos grins. "My parents taught me that, too."

Mateo laughs. "Hey guys, I just got wounded, not old. Please cut this log."

Mateo climbs over the downed tree and motions for Martín to follow. Soon father and son sit by the river.

Martín can hear Sammy's steady swings as the axe bites into the wood and a murmur as Carlos tell him a story. "I love to listen to the river."

Mateo seems content. "Yes, so do I. That's why I live here part of the year." He looks at Martín. "What's on your mind?'

Martín thinks a minute. "Mary Grey Eyes told us we'll see an accident on the way to Santa Fe. How we deal with the two people involved will determine much about our future relationship and we want to purify ourselves before hand. I want to get that right despite the difficulty. Sammy will drive through Durango Saturday. From there we'll go through Chama to Santa Fe. That leaves tomorrow. Can you do a sweat for us?"

Mateo speaks. "Yes, I think so. I know a sweat lodge near here we can use. Sammy, Carlos, and I can set it up tonight so you two can get an early start."

After dinner, as they do the dishes together, Carlos tells Martín, "I enjoyed this time out here accompanying Vela. Every morning, we get up and run. After breakfast I pack a lunch and take long walks. I go exploring. Sometimes I meet up with some guys and we swim or talk together. I come back in the late afternoon. Vela and I cook together. After we eat, we look at the stars and converse."

"I feel glad that you two can build a friendship without any adult pressure."

Carlos interjects, "It helps that we both love to run and that I'm two years younger than Vela, so we don't feel any boy-girl pressure."

Martín dries a spoon. "It also helps that you both seem so trustworthy and dependable. We guys can learn so much from our female friends. Carlos, I hope you treasure your friendships with both Vela and Swallow."

"I do."

Late that evening, Vela speaks to Martín as they sit under the stars and the others set up the sweat. "I feel glad you could help your dad. You two don't always get along."

Martín shakes his head. "No, there's an odd tension between us. I never quite forgive him for not introducing himself sooner. And he seems to want me to fight like a warrior."

"Tío Mateo demands too much from everyone, even himself," Vela comments. "Thanks for <u>A Yellow Raft in Blue Water</u>. I enjoyed reading it. I'm a lot like Rayona."

"Yes, she reminded me of you. Santa Fe has two good used-book stores. So I find it even easier to buy books."

Vela begins to hum with excitement. "Speaking of Santa Fe, Blue Feather seemed very receptive to my coming to Santa Fe to attend high school and study herbs with her. She doesn't know about the living arrangements, but I feel sure something will open up."

Martín chuckles. "I'll wait until Blue Feather brings it up and then give my approval. You'd be willing to work for your room and board, right?"

"Sure, I'll do anything as long as I have time to do my homework."

The next morning, Blue Feather climbs into the truck beside Martín. "I dreamed a weird dream last night about the time I got shot."

Sammy starts the truck. Martín swallows. "Tell me about it."

"I became the person who shot me, but I felt all these compulsions. I did what the officers told me to do. When I shot the person who was me in the back of the head, I didn't shoot a human; I shot a vicious animal." Blue Feather cries. Martín puts an arm around her. They ride in silence until the truck stops outside a small Hogan.

Sammy interjects, "I started heating the rocks last night. I'll pour water on them. I'll stay here all day, reading, if you two want anything. Drink enough water." He puts a water bag plus two canteens inside and carries rocks from the fire to the sweat lodge.

Martín glances at Blue Feather. "The morning we left Santa Fe, I dreamed a nightmare. You bled on the ground. A Wag soldier shot Sofía, over and over. I tried to tear the cord connecting you to the combatant but I couldn't do it. Abuelo appeared with a small stone, which he used to hit the cord until it broke. The Wag fighter ran away."

Blue Feather muses, "Sofía carried me to safety right before the Wag killed her. We already dream connected dreams, which seems more than eerie."

Martín taps her shoulder. "I wonder what our dreams mean."

The pair gets out of the truck. He strips down to a pair of shorts and she to a pair of shorts and a cotton undershirt. They go inside and sit down on folded rugs.

As he leaves, Sammy suggests, "Maybe you both must consider forgiving the person who shot Blue Feather."

The two young people sit in silence as their bodies adjust to the heat.

She clears her throat. "I don't know if I should tell you part of the dream."

Martín looks her in the eye. "Oh." He waits.

"When I still dreamed myself as the other person, I watched a woman drag the person I just shot into a safe house, making me very angry because if I shoot a person I want them to die. So I waited outside the house. When she came out, I followed until I obliterated her with a grenade."

He wonders, "It does seem strange the same person who shot you could kill my mother. Though your dream explains how that could happen."

She seems sad and thoughtful. "But he'd felt compelled to do these violent acts."

To Martín, time seems to slow down. "Many years ago, when I first met Mateo on our trek out from California, he told us the Navajo Night Way Chant. I'll recite a part near the end."

> Happily I recover.
> Happily my interior becomes cool.
> Happily I go forth.
> My interior feeling cool, may I walk.

She teases, "Do you feel too warm, already?" He shakes his head and beams. She continues, "Mateo taught it to me many years ago. I'll say it with you."

They recite together:

> No longer sore, may I walk.
> Impervious to pain, may I walk.
> With lively feelings may I walk.

As it used to be long ago, may I walk.
Happily may I walk.
Happily, with abundant dark clouds, may
I walk.
Happily, with abundant showers, may I
walk.
Happily, with abundant plants, may I walk.
Happily on a trail of pollen, may I walk.
Happily may I walk.
Being as it used to be long ago, may I walk.

May it be beautiful before me.
May it be beautiful behind me.
May it be beautiful below me.
May it be beautiful above me.
May it be beautiful all around me.
In beauty it is finished.
In beauty it is finished.

After a few minutes, Martín muses. "I want to build our relationship in beauty. When I first heard the story I saw myself walk into Dark Cloud House and receive a blessing from Mateo and Abuelo. Now I see us walking into that house together. We receive a blessing from your mother, Mary, and from Mateo."

After a while Blue Feather starts crying. "Anything that beautiful might just make it worth forgiving the bastard who shot me.'

With tears in his eyes, he nods. Two hours later, as the heat continues draining him, Martín wonders whether he bit off more than he can do. He doesn't feel ready to do the hard work of getting to know and supporting another person.

Martín dreams. He and Blue Feather walked in the mountains. The sun shone. They grew warm and thirsty. They came to a stream. Martin lowered himself to his knees and Blue Feather, putting a hand on his shoulder, lowered herself. As they drank, the day turned cloudy and windy. They grimaced. A strange brown snake lept from the water and attached itself to the back of her head. Blue Feather writhed in the water, which wasn't deep. He looked for a knife to detach the snake. He found a palm size rock and used it to hit the snake. He struck the brown snake until it died. Her head bled from a gash.

The next day, Martín comments, "I love seeing the leaves change colors." He sits between Sammy and Blue Feather about twelve miles before Chama.

Sammy continues driving. "Y'know, I do appreciate the drama of the changes in seasons here, unlike California."

She looks out the window. "I enjoy coming this way. My friend's place is across from the old train station in Chama."

Martín gasps. "Hey, I see something wrong with the blue car ahead of us. It weaves a bit."

Sammy seems puzzled. "I'll give it plenty of space; maybe their brakes fail."

"I feel a headache starting from watching it. Martín, would you consider letting someone like Vela live with us, I mean after a while? She's bright and she could attend a good high school in Santa Fe. She wants to study herbs with me. She said she'd work for her room and board." Blue Feather shuts her eyes to quit watching the blue car.

"Yes, I'll consider it. She could work for us, but not too many hours. She's still a kid, after all. I feel glad you connected with Vela. I worried about her since her mother died last year. Her dad died six years ago."

He notices a dark brown pulsating line of energy extending from the car to the back of Blue Feather's head injury, similar to the cord in one dream, and it reminds him of the brown snake in last night's dream. Blue Feather looks very pale.

Martín gasps as the blue car veers off the road and crashes. Sammy pulls over, drags the driver out of the car, tries to beat out the fire, and then helps the driver pull a smaller person from the passenger side. Seconds later the car explodes.

Martín tells Blue Feather sternly, "Don't get out of the truck. I see something strange." He climbs out the driver's side and rushes over to Sammy and the driver. They lay a young boy on the ground. Martín kneels, scans the boy, and then turns his attention to the dark brown pulsating cord. *Bang!* In a flash, Martín sees the stranger shooting a younger Blue Feather. He cuts off the vision. Martín doesn't want to know any more, right now. He vows to help the boy no matter what the father did.

Blue Feather starts to get out of the truck. Martín sees her and yells, "Stop! Please don't get out of that truck."

She sputters, "I can help. I don't know why you are ordering me to stay in the truck. I don't obey orders blindly."

"Please trust me this time. I observe a toxic connection between you and the man." He walks to the truck. "Blue Feather, go with Sammy into Chama. Please bring blankets, water, food, aloe vera, and whatever you use to treat shock. You must leave now."

Blue Feather's face turns gray. "Oh, okay. My mind feels cloudier and cloudier."

Sammy jumps in the truck. "We'll come back. Tenga mucho cuidado and watch yourself."

As they drive off, Martín remembers what his Abuelo did in his dream, and knows he must break the energy between the man and Blue Feather. He grabs a palm-size sharp stone, crouches and strikes the pulsating dark cord with the rock until he severs it. On the last blow, the stranger cries out in pain, grabbing his head with both hands.

Martín takes a couple deep breaths before he goes over to the semi-conscious child and sits cross-legged on the ground beside him. "Rest easy. I can heal you." The man falls on his knees, groaning and holding his head.

Martín closes his eyes and uses his blue light to scan the boy's brain. He repairs a damaged blood vessel. Then he removes the blood collected between the boy's brain and his skull. He scans the boy's body again, noting the bruise on the chest and the broken right forearm. He comes out of his trance and glances at the man, still out of commission. Within arm's reach lies a smooth stick. Martín straightens the little boy's arm, matching up the bones, and binds it to the stick with a clean bandana.

Martín closes his eyes again. He extends his blue light to the bruise on the boy's chest and starts the healing process before turning his attention to the arm. First he makes the splintered bones as aligned as possible before helping them knit together.

The ground vibrates, as he withdraws his blue light from the boy. Sammy jumps out of the truck. "Martín, I drove fast. I didn't want to leave you here alone."

Martín feels too tired to move. "Thank you, Sammy. I appreciate that." He points toward the boy. "Cover him and see that he doesn't get any paler. Watch for sweat, I suspect he's in shock." He gestures to the father. "Blue Feather and I will deal with him."

Blue Feather, with her color regained, steps out of the truck. "I felt awful until we drove away. Then I didn't want to come back. What do you think that's about?"

Martín looks down. "Blue Feather, I saw a strange connection between you and that man. I broke it as you drove away. Now you may want to shield yourself from your memories and any bitterness. He caused your brain injury." He reaches over to touch Blue Feather. "Take as long as you want, but before we agree to heal him, decide whether you can forgive him."

Blue Feather looks at the man and then turns her glance inside. She takes a few deep breaths. "Yes, he did it, and no, I can't forgive him, not yet."

Martín leads her to the other side of the truck, where they both sit on the ground. Blue Feather starts crying. "That bastard hurt me, Martín. My whole life changed. No one can repair me. I don't want to forgive him; I can't." She cries and Martín holds her.

He whispers, "I don't know what to tell you. I love you, the most beautiful woman I know, and I will stay here for you whatever you decide."

She sounds furious. "I wish I could shoot him and he would struggle to learn how to do everything all over again—eat, walk, get dressed."

Sammy's footsteps approach. "Hey, you guys, what do I do? I think this little boy went into shock."

Blue Feather turns to Martín. "We both call ourselves curanderos. I want to let go of my bitterness. Bondage to my anger would drain my energy. I would wound myself."

He murmurs, "I'll care for the boy while you go tell his father you forgive him."

She walks over to the man and takes his head in her hands. He stares back at her with terror in his eyes.

He whimpers. "She whispers, "I know you shot me, and I forgive you." She sits beside him, releasing his head. The man sobs.

She turns to Martín. "I feel so sorry." She looks down at her hands and Martín watches tears drop into them. "You too must forgive him. He killed Sofía."

Martín stumbles then sits down. "I suspected that, but I didn't look until I got the boy stabilized." He takes deep breaths and goes inside himself. "I don't want to forgive the bastard. I want to kill him the way he killed Sofía. I still miss her, every day."

Blue Feather looks at her friend. "I give you back just what you offered to me. Take your time and come back when you can forgive him." Martín walks away.

She kneels beside the unsettled and stunned man, who stops sobbing. She examines the burns on his hands, and then tells Sammy. "Please bring me the aloe vera leaves and tear the clean pillowcase into strips."

As she spreads the salve on his palms and wraps them with cloth, she speaks in a low voice, "I'll smear your hands with ointment from this plant and then bandage them."

As the boy begins to stir, Sammy gets three bottles from the truck. He helps the boy sit, and pours tea. He gives the boy a drink. "I love my two children, a boy and a girl, about your age, very much."

Martín stumbles over. "We did all we can. Never mind our gear. Let's go."

They get into the truck. Sammy drives. No one says a word.

Martín feels a deep rage, but remembers not to use his power destructively. He felt angry before, but not this angry. He realizes Mary Grey Eyes told them about this test. He doesn't want to blow it, but it seems impossible to forgive the man. He gives himself a minute. He wants to get to know Blue Feather and maybe spend his life with her. Yet he doesn't want to face his rage. He says, "Stop the truck; I want to go back."

Sammy raises his eyebrow. "Do you feel sure?"

Martín mutters, "Yes. But I won't heal him."

Sammy turns the truck around. Martín wrestles inside, caught between his anger and his love for Blue Feather. He remembers the dreams again.

It seems like nothing changed and everything changed when they get back. Martín staggers to the stranger. He looks him in the eye. "Even though I feel furious, I forgive you for killing my mother at Owen Valley four years ago I also forgive you for wounding the woman I hope will spend her life with me." Martín sees the connection between this man and his injured son. He can see how much he loves his son and recognizes this man holds some good inside of him. He lowers himself to the ground.

The man extends his right hand toward Martín. "You healed my son full knowing I hurt the woman you love. I thank you."

Martín shakes his hand and sits there stunned. Too much happened too fast. He looks over the mountain valley. The Aspen leaves turn golden. He takes a deep breath. His whole world seems turned upside down and he feels exhausted. He no longer feels furious but sad, peaceful, and more connected to Blue Feather. He feels the pull to enter Tierra Oscura but resists with a shake of his head.

The man continues talking as if some dam released. "I call myself Jason Bateau, and I call my son Jeremy. My family moved to Durango, Colorado, before the Catastrophe and raised me there. After I served my mandatory eight years in the army, I became a guard at the prison in Alamosa. They told me you people were monsters who don't speak English. Yet you treat us well. I wonder about what else they lied." He glances at his son. "Jeremy looks like his color comes back. You saved him. Thank you."

Sammy hands Martín a bottle of tea. He puts a thermos near Jason. Blue Feather notices he can't open the thermos, and does it.

Martín takes a long drink. "What do you mean by 'eight years mandatory service?'"

"The Wholly Aryan Government in Colorado demands eight years of compulsory service. We get drafted right after our fifteenth birthday."

Sammy interjects, "You guys go into the army as kids."

Jason continues, "They divide us into four tiers: leaders, trades people, soldiers, and grunts. Girls can become teachers, nurses, homemakers, or hospitality workers."

Blue Feather looks at him. "Let me guess: a hospitality worker is a fancy word for a prostitute."

Jason nods. "When I was younger, I felt lucky to train as a soldier, but since I raise a son, I realize he doesn't hold any options."

Martín stops wolfing down his sandwich. "Does that mean you don't feel happy with the Wholly Aryan Government?"

Jason takes a few moments to swallow. "Not unhappy. I don't know what to think. They didn't train me to think for myself but to defend our folks from you. You guys seem like good people, so they lied about you as monsters. I begin to wonder what else they lied about." He turns to Martín. "But I owe you big time for healing Jeremy."

Martín looks at Sammy, who clears his throat. "You can do something for us. We plan to get two people out of the Alamosa Prison on Friday night. Will you help us?"

Jason takes a bite. "I'll think about it." He hesitates. "I work that night, and I think I know which two you want. Steve and the Latina, right?"

Sammy answers, "Yes, assuming Estebán Gonzalez is calling himself Steve."

Jason takes a drink. "Okay, I'll consider helping you."

Sammy responds, "We'll take Jeremy with us for two reasons. One, the Wholly Aryan Government's agents can force you to tell them everything. Keeping Jeremy with us will help you stay focused on not leaking anything. And two, when they find out you helped us, and they will figure it out, I don't want anything to happen to your son."

Jason frowns. "I don't have much choice do I? But then with my conditioning, it may be for the best."

Martín feels curious. "Did you say they'd conditioned you?"

Jason nods. "Yes, the government used to put silicon chips in our heads, but twelve years ago they developed a virus and failed. Many recruits walked away to the free territory. Now they do conditioning with shocks, but it doesn't work so well. When I stay focused I can resist."

Sammy whispers, "Martín, it sounds like your cousin Guillermo's sacrifice paid off, but the Resistance didn't follow it up. I can't wait to tell Mateo."

"You can tell him. I'd rather not." Martín frowns.

Jason looks at Martín for a long minute before walking over to Jeremy. "I'll give you an important job, son. I want you to go with these people. I'll come to you by next Sunday. If I don't, Sammy will help you get to your grandmother's in Durango."

Jeremy speaks. "Okay, Dad."

Sammy looks at the sky and sees how much time passed. "We better go."

Blue Feather stands and with great difficulty collects the thermoses and the sports bottle, then gets into the truck. Martín starts to get up, then groans.

Sammy catches him as he stumbles. "Both you and Blue Feather look pale and wiped out. Can I pick you up, put you in the truck, and then put Jeremy in your lap?"

When Martín agrees, Sammy lifts him. He runs back to Jeremy and places him in Martín's lap.

Jason walks to Martín's open window. "I'll go on duty at four Friday afternoon. I'll stop at the bus station on my way to work, around three-thirty. I can't betray you because you hold Jeremy."

Sammy thinks a minute. "I'll stop at the phone box on the other side of Chama and let the patrol know I saw an accident here. They'll come get you."

As Sammy starts the truck, Jason taps Jeremy's shoulder. "I love you."

Friday afternoon, Tía Sara drives her pickup toward the park near the prison in Alamosa, Colorado. She shared the driving with Pedro and enjoyed the opportunity for a long talk with him. They both look forward to seeing Esteban, who has been missing for three years. She spots Franklin at a picnic table and parks the truck.

She shakes Franklin's hand and hugs Juanita, Tomás, Lark, and Sammy. She nods at Pedro and tells Sammy, "We better get to the bus depot."

She buys a ticket for the four o'clock bus to San Luís so she'll have a cover story. Tía Sara finds a spot where she can watch both the main entrance and the door to the buses. She doesn't see anything strange until a very drunk Sammy crashes into a guy in a prison guard uniform. They exchange words, before the guy shoves the drunk away. Sammy staggers toward her and gives the thumbs up.

Back at the park, Tía Sara hears Sammy say, "Y'know Jason passed me a map and told me to bring three more fighters to the prison infirmary." When the warriors study the map, Franklin notices a drainage ditch running from the infirmary to the outer wall.

Tía Sara parks on a hill near the prison. She watches Franklin and Lark create a diversion, while Pedro, Tomás, Juanita, and Sammy climb through the culvert and break into the infirmary. She sees a white guy help Pedro carry the wounded compañera out. Esteban walks. Halfway through the culvert, near the outer wall, they encounter four guards, who start shooting. Tía Sara worries when she sees her people pinned down. She flinches and gets a sick feeling in her stomach when she sees both Esteban and Tomás get shot. Enough! She jumps in her truck and drives to the breach in the wall.

Franklin and Lark cover Sammy's team's escape and the loading of their people on the truck. Sammy carries Tomás and tells Tía Sara, "He took a bullet right through the heart."

Tía Sara feels heartbroken, but she will do her job and get the others to safety. The two prison guards help Pedro, Franklin, and the compañera climb into the back of the white van. Both Pedro and Franklin have been wounded. Juanita climbs into the back of the truck. She wails, "Don't leave me! What am I going to do?" Lark and Sammy climb in beside her and put their arms around her as she holds her dead husband.

The older white guy asks Esteban, "Shall I drive the van, since you're wounded?"

Her youngest son grins. "Sure, just follow my mother in the truck. Dude, I'll shoot you if you do anything wrong."

Tía Sara takes off driving the pickup south and keeps an eye on her rearview mirror to see whether the older white guy driving the van follows her.

Later that Friday, Martín rushes out of the cabin in Red River when he hears two vehicles pull up. Sammy signals him over to the bed of the truck, where Juanita cradles her husband. Martín quickly scans Tomás' body. He searches and searches for a spark of life and doesn't find one. He feels appalled and deeply saddened. He looks Juanita in the eye. "I can do nothing. He's already died."

Juanita screams, "No!" Lark and Tía Sara lead her to the cabin bedroom.

Martín can hear sobbing as he and Blue Feather tend the wounds of the two escapees, three Resistance fighters, and a guard. Lark and Tía Sara stay with a stunned Juanita in the bedroom. A white man, who seems to be a doctor, helps with the first aid. Jason seems to know him. Martín wonders and then glances at Esteban. He feels glad to see his cousin, free and mending. And he feels grief-stricken because Tomás didn't make it back. Blue Feather works beside him. Both last Saturday's and tonight's events bring them together in a rare understanding he never knew possible.

Jeremy curls in his father's lap. Martín knows he did his best to fit into the Manzanares household, sleeping in Tommy-tres' room, attending school, and going on walks with Swallow and then her and Carlos once his parents came up for the action. Lark had put Jeremy's arm in a cast when they'd arrived last Saturday. Martín had checked it, and then he had told Swallow to boost the knitting together of the bone every day. Blue Feather had recommended comfrey tea. Jeremy had felt surprised a broken bone could heal so fast and another twelve-year-old could advance the process.

But Jeremy had felt even more delighted to get to know Tommy-tres. The seven-year-old had gone through Carlos' drawers and had found complete changes of clothes Jeremy could wear. Tommy-tres had explained the rules of the household. The first night when Jeremy had gone to bed he'd felt alone and started crying. Tommy-tres had requested his permission before climbing into his bed and holding him until he'd fallen asleep. Jeremy wonders about these people, as he sits curled in his father's lap. The kids had acted with kindness. Carlos hadn't even blinked when Tommy-tres had told him he had given Jeremy his jeans and t-shirts.

Jason starts talking. "I drove home from my mother's house in Durango last Saturday. The brakes failed and my car crashed. Sammy, Martín, and Blue Feather saved my son and me. In the process, I realized the Wholly Aryan Government lied to us. The people I thought monsters healed my son and forgave me for some very serious violence. But then they took my son with them, which both puzzled and angered me. Yet something had changed inside of me, and I felt oddly peaceful.

"Anyway, soon the patrol came by, took me to the first aid station and put me on the train to Antonito. From Chama I called my buddy, who met me in Antonito."

He looks at his friend, the big burly guard with red hair, who says, "I could tell when you got in the car, you looked more relaxed and hopeful than ever. I knew you changed when I offered to buy you a six-pack, you said, 'No thanks, I want to think.' In the twenty-five years I know you, you never refused a beer."

Jason declares, "I knew him since first grade. We talked many times about our government. I knew I could trust him. So I told him what happened. He agreed to help. He sent his family away because we fear reprisals. My wife left two years ago, and you took Jeremy to a safe place." He glances at the older man by the fire and then continues. "When I went to work on

Monday afternoon, I scoped everything out and formed a plan. Friday, I went to Steve's cell and roughed him up." He turns to Estebán.

"Do you prefer Steve or Estebán?"

"I called myself Steve to survive in prison because it made me less foreign. But I feel proud to call myself Estebán Gonzalez." He laughs. "Imagine my surprise when this guard comes into my cell, spills blood all over me, and tells me to grunt and yell when he hit me. I started to get the drift when I got to the infirmary and saw my compañera already there. She looked like a mess but seemed okay. Today, I felt amazed to see mi mama driving the getaway truck."

The wounded woman interrupts. "With a mother like that, no wonder Estebán acts with such boldness."

Tía Sara comes out of the bedroom as Estebán asserts, "She did more daring deeds than most. Wait until you meet my sister Susana."

She shoots her son a bittersweet grin. "They couldn't keep me away."

Estebán turns to the older man who had helped with the driving and first aid. "Just who are you?"

"I call myself Dave More. I work as a doctor at Mercy Medical Center in Denver. Also, I hid as a sleeper for years. Last week my contact told me to take the temporary position at this prison under an alias. I saved some vacation days; I plan to return to my regular job on Monday." He turns to Martín. "For a year, I've heard about a great curandero in Santa Fe."

Martín frowns. "You didn't answer Esteban's question. Who are you?"

Dave More looks around the room and takes a deep breath. "For years I couldn't trust people. I got a job at Mercy twenty-seven years ago. Two years later, I met my contact, who I call Blue Denim, because he always wears it. He recognized my disapproval of the government and recruited me as a sleeper. I do odd jobs for him: sew people up, take out bullets, and set bones. Back then, his partner gave birth to a little boy, but the kid probably died. He suffered severe brain damage and couldn't suck or swallow. They took him home anyway."

Martín can't contain himself. "If your contact belongs to the Diné, that kid lives and stands before you."

Dave looks at him. "Then you healed yourself even then since you survived. I feel so glad I met you and saw you in action. You impress me."

Martín winces. Dave's words touch his core. He wants time to rethink his whole life; or maybe as he shares his story with Blue Feather, he can reassess his life.

Tía Sara assures him, "If you feel safe going back to Denver, I'll drive you to Antonito Sunday so you can catch the bus. Tomorrow we can get to know you."

Dave murmurs, "Yes, I'd like that."

Franklin turns to Jason. "What do you and your friend plan?"

Jason looks at Franklin. "I don't know. My whole world turned upside down in the last week. What do you suggest?"

Franklin responds, "It will depend on how deeply you two want to get involved. I'll check with my contacts and we'll talk later."

They stop talking when they hear brakes squealing and pounding footsteps. Mateo bursts through the door and looks around the room. "I hoped to find Jason Bateau, but everyone else arrived here, too, except for Tomás. Where did he go?"

Tía Sara frowns. "He died earlier this evening."

Mateo shakes his head. "That hurts. He fought awesomely. And Jason?"

The guard sets Jeremy on the floor. "I call myself Jason."

"I call myself Mateo. I hold a tangled connection to each of you, right, Martín?"

"Yes, Dad."

Mateo avows, "My sources tell me two Wholly Aryans tanks just turned on to Highway 38 at La Questa. They'll arrive here in fifteen minutes. They also watch Jason's mother's home in Durango." He steps toward Jason. "We hold your mother and sister safe with my niece in Arizona. We'll drive them to Chimayo tomorrow." He turns to Tía Sara. "Can you drive our wounded and noncombatants south?"

"Sure."

Franklin looks around the room. "Jason, can you and your friend do some rearguard action?" When they consent, he continues. "Lark, Sammy, you two team with them and help them get back to your place after you ambush the raiding party. Lark, you take charge."

She responds, "I'll slow them down and take out their vehicles."

Estebán clears his throat. Franklin shakes his head. "Your mother would murder me if I took you with us, so help her get everyone into the truck. When you get to Chimayo, you can set up a perimeter patrol. The children will gladly help."

He glances at Mateo. "You and Dave team with Pedro and me. We'll cover the fading back of the team at the pass." He raises his voice. "Let's get moving."

As the room erupts into controlled evacuation, Martín feels a hand on his shoulder. Jason says, "Martín, please keep an eye on Jeremy."

"No problem."

Dave rushes over and says, "We'll stay in touch."

Jason goes to where Lark arms her team. She quips, "They sent two armored cars. Jason, can you carry a mortar tube?"

Martín walks out the door with Blue Feather and Jeremy and climbs into the back of the truck. Estebán follows, helping his compañera. Tía Sara helps Juanita climb into the cab, and before Martín gets comfortable, he sleeps.

Chapter 22
November 25, 2043

Martín finds himself rushing toward Rubén's café, where Blue Feather waits. He feels frustrated. Lately he underestimates the time it takes for him to do things, so he runs late. This causes tension in his relationship with Blue Feather as they do more together.

Blue Feather frowns as he enters the café and takes off his heavy jacket. She looks radiant in her heavy brown sweater and wool pants. She has already started eating. He touches her shoulder. "I regret coming late.

I squeezed in an extra client when I shouldn't have. I feel glad you went ahead and started eating."

Blue Feather looks him in the eye. "You are late again. You do too much so you often run late. I'm starting to feel irritated. My time and energy are just as valuable as yours. I want you to decide whether you want to work on some basic skills like time management and getting places on time. We'll see a family together at 2. I didn't want to be delayed, so I started eating without you."

Rubén rushes up with a plate of food and an ice tea. "I assume you're in a hurry and you want the daily special with extra bread."

Martín says, "Yes, thank you, Rubén," before he turns to Blue Feather. "Because I love you so much, I do value your time and energy. I will change and learn more skills." He looks down at his food and slaps his forehead with his palm. "Darn, darn, darn!"

Blue Feather seems worried. "What's wrong?"

Martín groans. "I just realized that all my life my friends and family have covered for me the way Rubén just covered for me. He saw I was running late and anticipated my desires. Because I grew up nonverbal and then took a long time to communicate when I used a communication device, it became easier for my family and friends, like Tony, to anticipate my requirements. I let things slide, like coming to lunch late, because people will cover for me. That won't work if you and I are building an equal relationship."

Blue Feather grins. "That may be why you lack some basic skills which I take for granted."

He frowns. "I wish you would stop calling those skills basic just because you do take them for granted. Because I haven't developed those skills, your calling them 'basic' feels like a put-down."

Blue Feather thinks a minute as she swallows a bite of food. "You're right. My calling the skills you lack 'basic' is a subtle put-down. I apologize."

Martín looks her in the eye. "Apology accepted. I ask for your help to learn to manage my time better."

"Okay." Blue Feather looks at the clock. "For now, you could concentrate on eating lunch while I walk to the clinic and start an intake on that family."

"Blue Feather, thanks for your help. I do plan to become more punctual." Martín smiles before taking a bite of lunch.

A month later, on Christmas Eve, Tony and Martín sit in Susana's cozy living room with Blue Feather and Vela, whom Susana had invited to come to Santa Fe for the holidays. Susana puts a log on the fire. "Who wants to take a walk and see the luminarios?"

Tony and Vela both shout, "Yes, let's go!"

Blue Feather looks at Martín, who nods, and then she says, "We'll stay here."

Martín listens as Tony, Susana, and Vela leave the house. Tony says, "Luminarios are neat. They are an old custom in Santa Fe. People put a votive candle in a paper bag with sand in it and put them on their roofs and walkways to light the way for the Child Jesus. It's a beautiful tradition."

Blue Feather looks at him. "I hope we are going to open our presents tonight."

Martín gives his at the fire. "No, in our family we open presents on Christmas morning. We'll get up real early and drive out to Chimayo and open our presents with Lark, Sammy, Swallow, and Tommy-tres."

Blue Feather seems to start to get frustrated. "But in my family we open presents on Christmas Eve."

He feels strongly that he is right, but he knows when he feels this way he gets in trouble with the one he cares about. But still. "Well, there are more of us, so you are way outnumbered."

She looks sad. "Being in the majority doesn't make you right. Can we reach a compromise? Can you and I exchange one present tonight and then open presents with the group tomorrow morning?"

Martín holds his breath and takes a moment to think, knowing that he is on dangerous ground. Should he allow the precedent to be set that they as a couple exchange a present on Christmas Eve? He lets out his breath and says, "Okay, let's exchange our presents now before the others come back."

Blue Feather walks to the bedroom that she shares with Vela while Martín goes to his backpack, and they get presents wrapped in pieces of cloth as old-fashioned wrapping paper is no longer available. They return to their seats by the fire.

Martín hands Blue Feather a very soft parcel. Blue Feather exclaims as she unwraps the sky-blue hand-knit muffler and hat. "They're my favorite color! Thank you."

He says, "I got one of my clients to knit them. I know you like that color."

She leans over and kisses him on the cheek before handing him his present. He opens it and remarks, "What a lovely grey flannel shirt!"

She says, "And I got one of *my* clients to sew this. I like the color grey. But we need to talk. I don't like the way the decision to open presents tonight was made as if you had all the power and right to decide. You acted like you were granting me a favor. The way your family always does things doesn't make it the right way."

Martín feels exasperated. "Talking everything through is such hard work. Sometimes I would like just to make a decision without discussing it to the nth degree."

Blue Feather thinks a minute. "It has something to do with power. I want you to see that when you are dismissive of my concerns and make a decision that affects both of us, you are abusing power."

He reflects a minute. "It's a bigger deal than I would have thought whether we exchange presents tonight or tomorrow morning. I see your point. At this stage in our relationship, I don't want to get into any bad habits, nor do I want to abuse my power in either small or big decisions. This relationship takes a lot of energy. Sometimes…"

The front door opens. Vela, Tony, and Susana come rushing in, all cold and breathless. Vela proclaims, "The Luminarios are awesome! I feel so cold, though."

Three months later, the old man's son leads Blue Feather and Martín into a darkened adobe two-room shack, which smells of unwashed bodies and chilies. "When I got back from El Paso this morning, I found my father quite ill, so I came and got you two."

Martín hears a gnarly cough before he sees the man lying in bed.

The son turns on the light. "My dad was skinny before, but now he seems emaciated. He must not have eaten the whole week I was away.

"Here, let me bring you some chairs," he says, and he brings two chairs. Martín and Blue Feather sit down.

"My name is Martín, and this is Blue Feather. We are curanderos. We're here to help you. May I scan your body?"

The old man wheezes and groans. "Sí, it's okay with me."

Martín goes into a trance. The room is silent when he comes out of the trance. He turns to Blue Feather. "His lungs are all congested, and his poor breathing puts a strain on his heart."

Blue Feather stands up. "I'll go to the kitchen and make him some ginger tea with ephedra. I will also look in the kitchen and see what food he has on hand; then I can make a list for his son to go buy at the store. Possibly some chicken soup and lots of juices would be good. If he hasn't eaten for a while we don't want to give him too much food too soon."

Martín looks at her with admiration. "While you do that, I'll strengthen his immune system and start clearing up his lungs." He goes into a trance.

Later in the son's truck, Martín turns to Blue Feather. "I sure enjoyed working with you to help this person. I admire your knowledge of herbs."

Blue Feather grins. "Just think of all the people we will be able to heal together."

Part III

Chapter 23
April 10, 2044

Martín and Blue Feather sit in the plaza across from the Palace of the Governors on a crisp, clear April day. Tony comes jogging up to them. "Hey, I found you both," he says, panting. "Dave just arrived from Denver. He wants to talk to you, and Mateo, too. I'll go tell your dad." He starts to run off but stops. "Susana and I invite you two over to her place tonight. We want to talk."

Blue Feather answers. "We'll come."

They take their time walking back to the clinic. Martín queries, "Do you know what Susana and Tony want to talk to us about?"

"Sure do." She beams as they cross Washington Street, but remains silent.

"Will you tell me?"

They hear two people running. Her eyes twinkle. "No time right now, mi Amor."

Tony and Mateo catch up with them as they enter the door. Martín hugs Dave, who brought Sammy and Lark with him from Chimayo. Susana joins them as they sit at the table.

Dave shakes hands with Mateo. "I raised three children. My oldest, who looks a lot like me, just finished medical school at Denver University. His brother will study a year more of Officer Training in Colorado Springs. And my daughter completed her first year of teacher's training.

"Imagine their shock six months ago, when I told them about my connection with the Resistance."

Dave looks at Mateo. "After I met Martín, I decided to tell them what I do. I felt surprised my confession opened the way to seeing my children and the future differently. I know I broke protocol, but I feel happy I did."

Mateo nods. "I know the consequences of not leveling with children." He glances at Martín. "I didn't introduce myself to my son until he turned twelve. I still regret that."

Dave continues. "My oldest belongs to a secret group of professionals against repression. In the last six months, he made contacts with the Resistance in Denver. At Christmas, I spoke with my other son, who blew my mind.

"My younger son processes information slower than his brother. He likes to think things through and then act. My confession devastated him, until one day, while he swam laps; he realized he must make a choice. He could either continue rising as an officer or he could use the truth to see what went on.

"A group of young officers already invited him to their meetings. He didn't go until last December, when he processed my confession. He felt amazed to find a network of young officers who want to overthrow the Wholly Aryan Government and reestablish a democracy. They hold ties with similar groups throughout the western states.

"In January and February, he got more involved with Young Demos. They call themselves that. He let them know he might find a way to make contact with the non-white Resistance. A big push will come soon, and they want to coordinate their efforts and get rid of all the fascist governments in the western states. So I came here to make contact."

Mateo asks, "How do I contact central leadership? Who coordinates the effort?"

Dave puts up his hands to stop the flow of questions. "Whoa. No, no central command exists, and with so many people here I won't go into details. I do want to make contact with the Filipino truckers. We hope they'll carry an occasional important message."

Sammy answers, "I can help you with that."

Dave speaks, "Right now our people in Seattle, Portland, and San Francisco can't communicate with each other."

Sammy sounds so competent. "I can help you with that, too."

Mateo inquires, "Martín, can I use a room for a meeting with Sammy and Dave?"

"Sure, Dad."

Dave turns toward where Susana, Lark and Blue Feather sit. "A vast network of teachers wants to educate and help people get on with theirs lives once a new government begins. In the last six months, my daughter got more involved with the Denver group. She made contact with women in the barrio. They want a two-woman team to teach them to defend and organize themselves."

Lark looks at Blue Feather and Susana, before saying, "I'll go and I'll invite Juanita to come with me."

Martín suggests, "Juanita still mourns Tomás. You might ask Tía Sara."

Lark confirms. "Yes, she'd do great.

"Sammy will go on the road when he gets more involved with the truck drivers. Martín, would you give Tommy-tres extra attention while I go to Denver?"

He acquiesces.

Lark continues, "Blue Feather, will you take on Swallow as your junior apprentice?"

Blue Feather responds, "I'd love to do that."

Martín looks at her and whispers, "Let's change our living arrangements."

She squeezes his hand, "We'll talk after our dinner with Tony and Susana."

Martín begins to murmur, "Oh," when Tony stands and says, "Lark, Susana, and Sammy, time for a quick conference. Please come to my office." They all troop out.

Mateo glances at Martín. "Son, it looks like I'll move to Denver. I'll sign the house over to you within the next week. I hope Tony and Susana will provide you two with the ongoing physical support."

Dave asks Blue Feather, "Where do Jeremy and Jason live?"

"They moved to Portland. Estebán lives there too, but in his own place. Sammy's ma found both men jobs there," she responds.

Tony leads the group back. As they sit, he announces, "We agreed to invite Tía Sara to go to Denver with Mateo and Lark. We hope they'll form a household in the barrio. We'll ask Tío Juan to live in our spare cabin. Tío Juan can split Sammy's patrol and courier duties with Juanita. Maybe Juanita will agree to share our house. This will free Sammy to act as the roving liaison between the truckers and various Resistance groups."

Dave looks at Lark. "I'll help you find a place to live in the Denver barrio."

As the meeting breaks up, Dave comes over to Martín. "I wish for more time, but we go back right away."

"Yes, me too, but we'll find further opportunities," Martín says. He hugs Dave while watching Blue Feather leave with Susana and Lark.

Martín hugs his dad, and then walks toward his office where he thinks he'll meditate, but first he stretches out on the bed for five minutes. And falls sound asleep.

A knock at the door; Martín doesn't move. He decides he'll ask Blue Feather.

Another knock. Tony says, "Sleeping Beauty, you still nap. Let's go to Susana's."

Martín glances at the clock. "I just stretched out for a minute, two hours ago."

"Do you feel okay?"

He groans again as he sits up. "Yes, I just feel stiff. And Blue Feather?"

"Yeah, she works in the dispensary."

"Please ask her to come in here. And Tony, could you go ahead to Susana's and tell her we'll come fifteen minutes late?"

"Sure, Martín." He winks before closing the door.

Martín brushes his clothes, and runs his fingers through his hair. He opens a drawer and puts the small dark blue pouch in his vest pocket. He hears a rap. "Come in."

Blue Feather walks in. He feels nervous. "Please sit."

With a bemused expression, she sits. "Qué pasa, mi amor?"

Martín takes a breath. "Today, our lives changed, too rapidly. Before events get out of control, I'll ask you a very important question." He uses the arm of her chair to steady himself as he kneels and takes her hand. "Blue Feather, I find you delightful, beautiful, intelligent, and kind. I love you. Will you become my partner and let us weave our lives together?"

Her eyes fill with tears. "Yes, I'd love to."

They kiss.

He fishes the dark blue pouch from his pocket and takes out two matching silver bands. "These belonged to my grandparents. As a sign of our compromiso, will you wear one and put the other on my hand?" He holds them out to her.

Blue Feather takes one and puts it on his hand. "Please, you put it on me."

He does it. They kiss again.

As he stands, she reaches for his hand, "Mi amor, I feel happy you didn't request I marry you. I couldn't stand a traditional marriage."

"I know. We'll make our relationship as equal and unusual as we can." He takes both her hands and helps her stand. "Let's get to Susana's."

She hugs him. "I love you."

An hour later, Martín just finished his last bite of mashed potatoes with gravy and chilito. Susana clears her throat. He pops the last bite of turkey loaf into his mouth before giving her his attention.

"Blue Feather and Martín, when I asked Tony to invite you to dinner, I didn't know the afternoon would turn so eventful or you two would decide to become partners. Tony and I have also decided to become partners." Susana looks at Tony.

Tony seems excited. "We plan a celebration of our union in two weeks, and now maybe you'd like to make it a co-celebration."

Blue Feather looks at Martín and says, "We'd love that."

Martín swallows. "I agree, but everything happens very fast."

Tony speaks. "Martín, I know you desire time to think. While you napped this afternoon, I took the liberty of clearing both of our calendars for tomorrow. I'll gladly drive you to the spot by the Río Grande where you like to watch the water flow."

"Yes, thank you. I'd like that."

Susana declares, "Blue Feather and I will plan the ceremony and the party."

Martín feels a surge of inspiration. "I wonder if we could invite Mateo and Blue Feather's mother, Mary Grey Eyes, to say the blessing."

Susana and Tony agree as Blue Feather affirms, "They'd both enjoy that."

Susana stands. "Tony, will you clear the table while I get dessert?"

"Sure."

Alone with Blue Feather, Martín whispers, "I suppose after the ceremony, you and Tony will switch households."

"Yes, starting that night, I want to sleep with you in our home."

"Oh, good," he smirks. "Mateo will leave for Denver, anyway. I'll request he spend that night in Chimayo." He takes her hand. "Blue Feather Grey Eyes, I love you, and I love your name, a poem to me."

"What last name do you use? In the last seven months you courted me, I never heard you say." Her last words slur together after a long day at the clinic.

He reaches for her hand. "I don't use one."

"Why don't you?"

"As a baby, my mother's husband gave me his name. Then I called myself Gonzalez after Abuelo and because my primos used the name. Then I met Mateo. I could take his last name, True Arrow, but it doesn't suit me. He fights and I heal."

She looks at him. "Well, now you can choose your own. Who do you admire?"

"I think highly of Coyote, who calls himself Yakushi, a Japanese god who heals. But I wouldn't call myself either a minor god or Japanese." He sighs. "Hey, I just thought of the perfect combination for both of us."

"For both of us? Tell me."

"We could call ourselves Martín and Blue Feather Grey Eyed Coyote."

"I like that. Can we hyphenate it into Grey-Eyed-Coyote?"

"According to the woman I love, we can do whatever we want, so we'll hyphenate." He squeezes her hand.

Susana bustles back into the room carrying a tray. "What do you two whisper?"

Blue Feather laughs. "Logistics."

Tony enters with a pot of tea. "Speaking of logistics, Susana and I know you both live with special challenges, and we are prepared to provide long-term physical support."

Martín blushes. Blue Feather admits, "Thanks; neither of us seems coordinated."

"I baked an apple pie," Susana says, and she starts cutting it.

Martín half-mutters, "I've never felt so accepted and accompanied. And I have much to think about, tomorrow."

The next morning, after he meditated and did his Chi Gung form, Martín sits by the Rio Grande on the road to Taos. Events happen way too quickly. A big push will come soon, and he feels pressed to get more involved with Blue Feather. Does he feel ready to make a commitment to her? No, he can't keep his commitments to himself.

Yes, he'd made a promise to himself with Coyote's help. He vowed he'd stay out of the cave. Coyote still lives in Arizona, and he feels the pull quite strongly.

Maybe if he talks to Superboy, he'd gain more insight. Martín shuts his eyes and soon finds himself walking toward the entrance of the cave in Tierra Oscura.

Superboy stands guard. Instead of his usual T-shirt and shorts, he wears khaki pants and a yellow sports shirt. "Hey, how can I help?"

Martín sits on the ground, Indian style. "I came to talk to you. I feel most uncertain making a commitment to Blue Feather, and I feel a strong pull to enter the cave. Changes happen too fast."

Superboy looks him in the eye. "Tell me about Blue Feather. Do you love her?"

He stares into space before answering. "I love her. I want to spend the rest of my life with her. When I see her or when I work with her I feel more whole and complete. Yet we both wobble and find doing certain household tasks difficult."

Superboy says, "Sounds like you love her. We can't control the speed with which events take place, especially in times of war. We can try to steer them in a general direction. You can seize this opportunity to spend more time with her and experiment with living together with both sets of limitations. Where will you start?"

Martín feels more enthusiasm. "At the end of the summer, my prima Vela will come to live with us. Both her parents died. She wants to attend high school and apprentice as an herbalist with Blue Feather. She'll live with us and work for her room and board. I worry she will end up working too many hours."

Superboy quips, "So you'll experiment with more young people living with you and spreading out the work."

He frowns. "What do you mean?"

Superboy becomes more serious. "You know people in the Resistance involved in the next offensive. Their children want a stable home. Also, many other orphans like Vela yearn for a secure place to live and would welcome working for their room and board. You and Blue Feather can choose to live creatively."

Martín hesitates. "With additional young people in our home, how will we find time alone? It hardly seems fair. But I'll discuss it with Blue Feather tomorrow evening.

"But what about the pull I feel to enter the cave?"

Superboy sighs. "First of all, life comes with much unfairness. Think more about building a loving household and giving young people a home. You and Blue Feather will grow more creative about finding ways to spend time together as a couple.

"Secondly, you can enter the cave and indulge in violent fantasies. You decided not to do it today, but you could in the future. If and when you do decide to enter, we'll deal with the consequences. Leaving the cave seems most difficult once you entered."

Martín's mind grows clearer. "I can define my task for this phase of my life as deepening my connection with Blue Feather and forming good relationships with the people who live in our house. I'll feel less alone and less tempted to enter the cave."

Martín starts to stand. "You grow more and more like Coyote."

Superboy extends an arm, which Martín uses to steady himself. "So do you," Superboy says. "After all, I exist as a figment of your imagination, and I gladly serve."

"Anyway, thanks for your help." Martín starts to walk away.

"Sure, come back any time."

By the Río Grande, he thinks about the ways he becomes more like Coyote.

Three days later, Martín, seated cross-legged in his office, hears a knock.

Lark opens the door. "I want to talk to both of you."

Blue Feather follows her into the room. Both women sit in easy chairs.

Martín takes a deep breath. "Lark, what can we do for you?"

She hesitates before speaking. "Yesterday, I talked with Swallow and Tommy-tres. I explained I'd do important work in Denver, their father would travel, and you two would give them attention. I realize you will celebrate your union in ten days and I ask a lot. My two children want to move to Santa Fe and live with you."

He nods at Blue Feather, who tells her, "We discussed this possibility last night. We'll gladly share our home starting August first. We want three months on our own to consolidate our relationship."

Martín adds, "We choose to build an alternative household. We'll both work in the clinic and we both live with limited physical energy and coordination."

"Swallow and Tommy-tres know. As long as they get individual time, they'll feel more than happy to do their share. They'll act like kids, though." Lark shakes her head.

Blue Feather laughs, "I feel certain they'll remind us."

Martín continues, "We also agreed to invite Vela to live with us, starting August first. Swallow will share a room with her."

They hear a gentle rap. He wonders, "Who knocks?"

"Juanita."

Blue Feather speaks loudly, "Come on in."

Martín asks, "Juanita. How do you feel these days?"

Juanita's eyes fill with tears. "I knew I could lose Tomás at any time, but I miss him so much. She wipes her eyes and sits on the floor cross-legged. "I hoped to find you three together. Carlos and I talked a long time. We'll move to Chimayo soon.

"First, I want to congratulate you, Martín and Blue Feather, on your union. I feel excited to see two great curanderos get together. Secondly, I want to make a commitment to helping you build your household."

Blue Feather states, "I thank you. I enjoy living with Susana. She fills in the things I cannot do. I appreciate you helping us out. I wonder if you could commit to two afternoons a week for six months. For the first three months, we'd like an afternoon each to take care of basics like laundry."

"Yes, I can do that."

He notes, "Tony and Mateo looked after all the tasks I could not do myself. I never learned to wash clothes." And he blushes as he adds, "I thought Blue Feather might take over that function. But that won't work in an equal partnership. So I'll feel glad for your help learning basic tasks."

Juanita turns to Blue Feather. "What about the second three months?"

She adds, "I hope you can work with Vela, Swallow, Tommy-tres, and whoever lives with us to learn some chores and help us organize ourselves."

"I can do that. Will they start living with you in August?"

Martín answers, "Yes."

Lark starts to speak, then stops.

He says, "Lark, you can tell us now."

"M'ijo, Tommy-tres, insists you will want two sets of bunk beds in his room."

"And..." Juanita looks at her hands, hesitant.

Blue Feather looks at him and winks. "Let me guess. Carlos wants to live with us, too." She sees Martín's almost imperceptible assenting nod.

Juanita looks at her. "Yes, Carlos wants to live with Swallow and Tommy-tres. He still grieves his dad. After six months, I'll do courier work and I want my son to live in the most stable living situation possible. I want him to stay with you two."

Lark interjects, "All four youngsters should move in at the same time on August first, so no one can claim prior favoritism."

Blue Feather gulps and looks at Martín before agreeing. "Yes, Lark. But this sounds like a load of responsibility for our new partnership."

He adds, "Yes, and at the same time, we belong to a community and can request support." He looks at his future partner. "Would you feel better if we ask Tony and Susana to take our brood from six p.m. Saturday to six p.m. Sunday?"

Blue Feather answers, "Yes that will help a lot. Mi amor, you may not know how to run a washing machine, but you support me well."

"Thanks. This partnership will require our creativity." He looks at his watch. "Excuse me. I want to swim. We'll meet with Mateo and a lawyer after lunch."

While he swims Martín daydreams about the commitment ceremony and what comes after.

Chapter 24
April 24, 2044

The air feels clean and crisp in the late morning when a crowd gathers in the orchard behind the Manzanares Home in Chimayo. Franklin has brought Pedro, Miguel, and their children from Arizona and Maestra Manzanares has managed to come out from California. Pedro, Carlos, and Tommy-tres put the last touches on the gazebo when they hear Vela's flute, accompanied by a guitar, play Pachebel's Canon.

Mateo and Mary Grey Eyes, arm in arm, come from the gazebo and step apart. Tony and Martín amble

down the aisle wearing blue jeans and red shirts. Susana in a bright yellow dress and Blue Feather in a sky
blue dress stroll down toward their partners. When
the two women stand beside their partners, the music
stops.

Mateo speaks in a clear voice. "We bear witness to
the union of these two couples. We welcome you." The
crowd murmurs as Tío Juan arrives, breathless.

Mateo grins at him and continues. "We greet each of
you, particularly those who traveled here from far away
to this happy day in the midst of struggle, a day to celebrate hope in the midst of war and suffering."

Mary Grey Eyes declares, "Not only we the living
bear witness, but also the spirits of those who died in this
war, which never seems to end but will end. The spirits of Susana's brother and grandparents, Blue Feather's
father and brother, Tony's mother, and Martín's mother
and Abuelo bear witness to this magnificent joining
together."

She looks at the well-wishers. "I'll tell you a story,
so get comfortable." At this signal, Pedro, Carlos, and
Tommy-tres bring out six chairs and the wedding party
sits.

She begins. "I got this tale from a storyteller who
got it from his grandmother, a member of the Black
Hawk tribe. Each of us contains a feminine side, which
we want to honor."

Mary Grey Eyes looks each bride and groom in the
eye.

Long ago—so long ago people still lived at peace with each other—many men wanted to marry a very beautiful young woman, but she turned them all down.

Her father asked, "Why won't you marry one of these men? You can marry any one you want."

"I don't want to," she replied.

Still the men held contests, and the bravest and fastest came to her and asked her to marry them. But always she said no.

Her father said in anger, "The finest men asked you to marry them, and you said no. You must love a secret lover."

"No," the young woman said. "I feel sorry you don't trust me. But I know no secret lover. The Sun told me, "Don't marry. You belong to me. I will keep you happy, and you will live a long and healthy life."

"Very well," said her father. "You must do as the Sun says."

Among the people lived a very poor, homeless, young man. Although he was strong and brave, his face was puckered with a terrible scar. People felt sorry for him, and they let him stay a day in one lodge, a day in another, but he lived without a lodge of his own, and no mother or sister to tan a robe for him or sew a pair of moccasins.

The other men liked to make fun of him. They told him, "Look, that beautiful woman won't marry us. But maybe she will marry you, the most handsome and the richest of us all."

The man knew they made fun of him. But he decided to try anyway. After all, she turned everyone else down, he thought. He went to the river and waited until the young woman came to get water for her family.

"May I speak to you?" he asked. "I would like to stand in the full light of the Sun and talk to you openly for everyone to see."

The woman felt so pleased at the way he spoke, she agreed.

"I watched you a long time," the man said. "I saw how you refuse every man who asks. I own nothing. I wear this scar on my face. But it is my face that is scarred, not my heart. The other young men made fun of me. They said I should ask you to marry me. I decided they are right. I own nothing to offer you but myself, but I would like you to marry me."

The woman moved the toe of her moccasin around in the dirt. Then she spoke. "True, I turned down all the richest young men and the handsomest, and those that possess the most courage. But maybe I should marry you. My mother will build us a lodge. My father will give us dogs, robes and furs, and clothes. We will possess everything we require. Yes, I will marry you."

The young man felt so surprised and so pleased, he reached out to hug her and give her a kiss.

"No. Not yet. Just one thing: the reason I never married until now is I spoke with the Sun, who says I belong to him. If you want me as a wife, you must visit the Sun. You must get his permission."

"How can I do that?" the man asked. "No one knows where the Sun lives. No one ever traveled all that way before."

The woman said, "When you reach the lodge of the Sun, you must ask him for some sign, so I will know you spoke to him."

He felt very sad. He sat on the ground and felt sorry for himself.

He recalled an old woman who acted kindly to him. He went to her and said, "I must go on a long journey, farther than anyone ever traveled. Please take pity, and make me a pair of moccasins."

"But why would you travel so far?" the old woman asked.

"I cannot tell you where I go," the young man said.

The very wise woman possessed a kind heart. She asked no more questions. She made him seven pairs of fine moccasins, with thick soles. She filled a sack with pemmican.

When he reached the top of the bluffs which overlooked the place his people lived, the young man stood a long time staring down on the lodge of the woman he wanted for his wife. He felt a great sadness. "I want her to become my wife, but I may never see her again."

Feeling sad and alone, he began his journey. For many days he walked, across prairies, along rivers, in the woods, and over mountains. He ate food he found along the way. But still his food sack grew lighter, and he worried he might starve before finding the lodge of the Sun.

One day he came to the home of a wolf. "Greetings, brother," the animal said. "What do you do so far from home?"

"I search for the home of the Sun. I must speak to him."

"I traveled very far," the wolf replied. "I crossed prairies and climbed mountains, but I never reached the home of the Sun. I do not know where he lives. Perhaps the very wise wolverine knows."

Just as his food ran out, the man reached the home of the wolverine. "Sorry to bother you, but everything went wrong. I ran out of food. It isn't possible to find the home of the Sun."

"Of course you can," the wolverine replied. "He lives on the far side of the Big Water. Tomorrow I will show you the trail."

When the young man reached the edge of the Big Water, and saw how far it stretched, his heart felt very sad. He felt hungry, and the soles of the last pair of moccasins wore all the way through. He traveled so far from home, he felt he could never return. Yet he knew he couldn't go on, to the other side of the Big Water.

He sat by the sea and began composing his death song. And he thought of the woman he left behind. When he asked her to marry him, he almost played a game. But weeks of traveling, he grew to love her very much.

Now it all seemed useless. He would die alone.

He saw two large, beautiful swans swimming toward him.

"What do you do here, so far from home?" they asked.

"It seems I came here to die," the young man said. "I just wanted to marry the woman I love." He told his story. "But I can't cross the Big Water. Now I will die."

The swans felt sorry for him. They took turns carrying him on their backs until they reached the other side of the Big Water.

The man found a trail. Off to one side lay a bundle. The man opened it and found the most beautiful bow and arrows he ever saw, the most finely painted shield, and the most beautifully woven shirt. He closed the bundle and left it lying where he found it.

Down the road, he met a handsome young man with long hair and exquisite moccasins made of colored feathers.

The man said, "Did you see my weapons by the trail?"

"Yes," the traveler replied.

"But you didn't take them?"

"They didn't belong to me."

"I see you are not a thief," the man said. "What do you call yourself? And why did you come here?"

"I call myself Scarface, and I will visit the Sun."

"My father, the Sun, calls me Dawn Star," the man said. "Come visit our lodge and wait for him to return tonight."

Scarface never saw such a fine lodge, the outside covered with beautiful paintings of remarkable medicine animals of the Sun. Behind the lodge hung weapons, unknown to his people, and the most beautiful clothes he ever saw.

Inside the lodge the Moon, the wife of the Sun, the mother of Dawn Star, gave Scarface food and asked him why he came.

Scarface told her his story. "I came to ask the Sun if I may marry this woman who says she belongs to him."

That night, the Moon hid Scarface under robes. When the Sun returned home, he said, "Someone arrived here. I can smell it."

Scarface came out, and Dawn Star presented him to the Sun. "I know he is a good man, father," said Dawn Star. "I saw it in his actions."

The Sun invited Scarface to stay in his lodge and become a companion to Dawn Star.

The next morning when he woke up, the Sun already went to work. The Moon gave them a food pouch and told Scarface, "You may go anywhere you wish, except the Big Water. Never let my son go there, because enormous birds live there. They possess sharp beaks and powerful claws, and they killed many people, including all my other children."

Scarface agreed to avoid Big Water.

For a long time, Scarface stayed with Dawn Star. He wanted to talk to the Sun about the real reason for his long journey, but the Sun is very powerful, and Scarface waited for the right moment.

One day, Dawn Star asked Scarface to go with him to the Big Water to kill the giant birds.

"We mustn't," Scarface said. "Those birds would kill us. Your mother asked me never to let you go there."

Without waiting for Scarface, Dawn Star ran to the water.

Scarface called, but Dawn Star ignored him. Scarface could see the giant birds flying toward Dawn Star with talons out-reached. Scarface ran after him, until he ran ahead of his friend, so the birds would attack him first. He fought them off, kill-ing them with his spear, until none re-mained.

The young men cut off the birds' heads and took them home.

When the Moon learned Scarface saved her son, she wept.

That night, she told the Sun what Scarface did. "Now you too are my son," the Sun said. "Tell me what I can do for you."

Only then did Scarface tell the Sun his story. "The woman I love said you told her not to marry," he concluded. "I came here to ask you to let her marry me."

The Sun spoke. "I made the earth, and everything that exists. I made the mountains and the forests. I made the animals and the people. I made you and the woman you love."

"Then let her marry me," Scarface said.

"The woman you love is a very good woman," the Sun said. "She acted wisely to turn away all those men, because they didn't really love her. She acted wisely to listen to me. Now I give her to you. She will marry you. She will live a long life, and so will you."

The Sun took Scarface outside and showed him the whole world. "I made the raven, the smartest animal," the Sun told him, "and the Buffalo is the most sacred. The buffalo belongs to me, but I gave him to people, for food, for shelter, for clothing."

The Sun told Scarface, "The most sacred part of your body is your tongue. It contains the power of the Sun. It belongs to me."

The Sun continued, "Here is what you must tell the woman who you'll marry. When a man falls ill, or encounters danger, and he recovers, his wife must build a medicine lodge in my honor."

He explained all the details of how to construct a medicine lodge. When the Sun finished, he rubbed herbs on the young man's face, and the scar disappeared. Then the Sun handed him two raven feathers and said, "This is the sign asked for by the woman you love. The husband of the woman who builds a medicine lodge must always wear two raven feathers."

Then the Sun, the Moon, and Dawn Star gave the young man many presents and the Sun showed him a shortcut; the Milky Way. The young man followed the trail, and on the dawn of a hot summer day, he arrived home.

Wrapped in a buffalo robe, he sat on the edge of the bluffs near the village and looked down on his people going about their life. Because of the heat, people passed the day sitting in the shade.

The chief noticed the young man first: a solitary figure, sitting on the bluff, covered with a buffalo robe. All day the chief watched, and noticed in spite of the heat, the figure kept the robe wrapped tightly around him, so the only part of him that showed were the two raven feathers sticking out of his hair.

As the day ended, the chief asked the young men: "Who is that person sitting so still over there? On the hottest day of the summer, he still keeps his buffalo robe wrapped tightly around him. He doesn't eat or drink all day. Invite him to join us in a feast."

The young men approached the figure on the hill and said, "Welcome, stranger. Our chief wants to know why you stayed out here all day in this heat. Come and feast with us."

Then the man threw off the robe. The young men were astonished to see this stranger wearing such beautiful clothes, and carrying weapons they never before saw. Then they looked at his face, and even without his scar they recognized their old friend.

"What happened to you? How did you get so rich? Who took away your scar?" they asked.

They ran ahead, shouting to the village, "Scarface came home."

People gathered around to greet him, but the young man said nothing until he approached the young woman he loved.

From his head he took the two raven feathers and handed them to her. "I found the way long and hard," he said. "But the Sun listened to me. He said I may take you as my wife. He sent you these."

Then the woman knew no one ever loved her so much. With happiness and joy, she married the young man. In honor of the danger he passed through, she built the first medicine lodge.

The Sun smiled and gave the two a long and happy life.

When they grew very old, their great-grandchildren came and said, "Wake up. We brought food." But the two did not stir. Their shadows went away, to the place of the dead, in the Sand Hills.[x]

After the sweet ceremony and a wild party in Chimayo, Sammy drives Martín and Blue Feather back to their house in Santa Fe, happy and tired.

Martín yawns. "Sammy, I feel glad your ma could come out for the celebration. This morning, we talked by the river. She feels excited about the coming events. She'll travel a lot with the truck drivers since she knows so many people."

Sammy hums. "Y'know my ma always acts wisely. She felt so happy when she and Franklin freed Lark and me from the Zombie Marines and I recovered."

"She missed you during your time away." Martín wonders, "Sammy, what do you think about the problem I gave you?"

Sammy laughs. "No big deal; I'll just get behind you."

"Oh." Martín looks at Blue Feather. "You seem quiet."

Blue Feather sounds tired. "Big day. A lot of changes."

Sammy parks in front of the house on Galisteo. They walk to the door. Martín says, "Mateo moved his things to Chimayo. Pedro and Miguel will take Vela with their crew until August." He opens the door, with a flourish, and flicks the light switch. "Blue Feather, my love, I present your humble abode." Sammy steps behind him.

Blue Feather giggles. "Martín, I don't expect you to carry me over the threshold."

Martín laughs. "But I will with a little help."

Blue Feather chuckles. "I won't carry you over any threshold, and this does not mean I'll do your laundry."

"I know. And I love you, too." He picks her up with a grunt. Leaning against Sammy, who supports his elbows from behind, Martín takes a step. Their balance wavers. He takes four steps over the threshold. Sammy leans against the jamb, as Martín releases Blue Feather's legs. She regains her balance and gives Martín a long kiss.

Sammy clears his throat. "I'll leave now." He manages to prop Martín against the wall and shut the door behind himself while the couple still embraces.

Late the next morning, Blue Feather raises herself on one elbow and looks at sleeping Martín. His body lies still. She had never seen him so peaceful. She brushes the hair from his eyes. He stirs and then they kiss.

He murmurs, "It will get even better."

She strokes his face.

He sits up. "Blue Feather, mi amor."

She laughs. "I know you feel hungry."

They put on robes and enter the kitchen. "Wow, someone set up our breakfast."

Blue Feather looks so beautiful. "I thought I heard footsteps earlier."

He affirms. "I hired Rubén's wife to act as our invisible elf for a week." His smile turns into a mild leer. "I figured we could use our energy for other things."

He doesn't realize how hard he'll work on the practical aspects of life with a partner.

Chapter 25
June 15, 2044

Seven weeks later, on a lovely summer day, Martín and Blue Feather shared a ride up to Taos and sit by the river near the Pueblo. She looks at the stream. "I love the sound of the water. I feel something sacred about this place."

"People lived at the Pueblo for a thousand years. Those mountains stood there forever. Watching the water flow refreshes my soul. I do my best thinking near rivers."

She responds, "Working with plants, digging in soil, and even grinding roots up with a metate nourish me. I always enjoyed a green thumb."

He chuckles. "I feel glad you choose work as an herbalist."

They sit in contemplation for a few minutes. She looks at her partner. "Sometimes you seem to go somewhere inside your head. Where do you go?"

Martín thinks a moment and decides to level with her. "When young, I couldn't walk, talk, or move purposely. During that time I invented a character I call Superboy who fought the Brotherhood, protected children of color with disabilities, and stole food to feed the hungry. After my primo Guillermo died, I started indulging in a fantasy where I torture soldiers in a cave I call Tierra Oscura. After Sofía died, I felt so furious, I stayed in the cave too long and Coyote helped me get out. With his prodding, I set up Superboy to guard the cave, under orders to keep me out. I sometimes go to where he guards the cave and we hold long conversations."

Blue Feather seems pensive. "Thanks for sharing that with me. Tierra Oscura means 'dark land.' We each hold areas of darkness. Before I got hurt, I dated a guy in the Resistance. When I woke up afterwards, I found my disability a great shock. I couldn't sit up or feed myself. I felt depressed. It didn't help that my boyfriend visited me once and never came back. Also, I missed Sofía. As an herbalist, I held the means to kill myself and I considered it. Ma and Coyote helped me. He mentioned you felt torn apart by your ma's death.

"Your prima, Susana, stayed with me for six months. Tony and Coyote designed a rehab program, and Susana demanded I stick with it until I began to see real progress. We became good friends and I felt so happy living with her in Santa Fe. We become even better friends. You didn't know we knew each other, did you?"

"No, I didn't, but I feel glad you know Susana, Coyote, and Tony."

She continues, "Sometimes when I feel tired, I get frustrated with my disability. And I think about the option of taking herbs to kill myself, but only as an option."

He moves closer and grasps her hand. "Yes. We both hold areas of darkness, and we will learn to creatively support each other."

They spend several hours sitting by the river near Taos Pueblo.

Later, Martín and Blue Feather catch a ride in the back of a pickup toward Santa Fe. After half an hour, they hear the squeals of tires and a loud crash. The truck driver pulls over to the side of the road. They see smoke coming out of a crumpled car that hit a boulder. Their driver and bystanders drag two people from the wreck.

Martín and Blue Feather rush over to the injured. The woman looks pale and seems nonresponsive, so he does a quick scan of her body. He finds internal wounds and sits on the ground, turning to Blue Feather. "I'll stop the bleeding or she'll die."

She says, "Okay, mi amor. I'll check the guy out."

He goes into a trance and uses his blue light to heal the wounds. About twenty minutes later, he says, "I can't heal her completely without more energy. She'll live if someone gets her to a hospital right away."

One bystander says, "I can take them both back up to Taos."

Blue Feather says, "He'll do okay once his forehead gets stitched."

The driver turns to Martín. "What did you do? She looked like a goner."

Martín tries to stand, but realizes he lacks strength. "I heal, so I used my force to stop the bleeding, but now I want to eat, fast. Look for food." When no one finds anything, Martín asks the driver, "Please help me get in the truck. I feel very hungry."

The driver says, "Sure. And I'll drive you all the way." He helps Martín into the back of the truck and Blue Feather climbs in beside him.

As the truck heads south, Martín groans. "I feel so hungry. I usually remember to carry food to eat after I heal, but this unexpected emergency sprang up."

Blue Feather looks concerned. "What can I do to support you?"

Martín moans. "Maybe if I lay with my head in your lap, I'll relax and get some rest." They rearrange themselves and he falls asleep.

An hour later, Blue Feather asks the truck driver to drop them off in front of Rubén's restaurant and thanks him. Martín stumbles in. "I must eat quickly."

Rubén responds, "I'll make you an omelet with some hash browns."

Martín staggers over to a table. "Great. A car crashed and I stopped some internal bleeding. You know how hungry I get when I heal!"

Rubén brings the food and Martín eats. Blue Feather sits down. After ten minutes he turns to her and says, "Thank you for your support. I'll carry trail mix so I can heal in an emergency without feeling like I'm starving." He returns to his plate.

The next morning, Blue Feather yelps, "Damn, damn, damn!"

Martín rushes to the bathroom door and asks in a loud voice, "What happened?"

Blue Feather opens the door suddenly and seems angry. "Why can't you put the damn seat down after you use the toilet? Do I ask too much? I said quite clearly I want you to put it down, but you don't do it."

Martín feels attacked. "Why yell at me? I hate it when you yell at me, and I could give a damn about the toilet seat. I survived all my life without putting it down."

She seems even angrier. "I'll yell at you if I want to, and I don't know how to let you know how seriously

I take this. Put the damn toilet seat down when you finish."

Martín takes a deep breath. "Let's stop and take a walk and then continue this fight. We both feel too angry."

Blue Feather looks at him. "Well, okay. But I feel very angry."

Later, Martín says, "Blue Feather, I feel sorry I forgot to put down the toilet seat."

She looks at him quite fiercely. "You said that before, and I don't believe you. You keep forgetting. I don't like it. I go in the bathroom either in the dark or forget to look, and there I sit in the toilet bowl. I hate it." Her voice gets louder and louder.

Martín puts up his hands. "Stop. How can we resolve this? I always lived in houses with a male majority and the last four years I lived in an all-male household. I just don't remember to put down the toilet seat. What do you think?"

She scratches her head. "You pay a penalty every time I find the toilet seat up?"

"What kind of penalty?"

"Uhm, how about you wash the dishes every time?" She smiles diabolically.

"Argh. I hate washing dishes…but okay, I'll give it a try. But I wish you wouldn't yell at me when I forget."

"Well, if you'd remember to put down the toilet seat, I wouldn't yell at you."

About six weeks later, Martín and Blue Feather fill a basket in the grocery store. Martín puts a box of granola bars into the basket. Blue Feather reaches in and picks up the box. "Martín, do you really want these? They cost and you pay a lot for the packaging. We could ask Juanita to teach you to bake cookies."

"Argh, I find them easy to eat and they don't cost *that* much." He shakes his head.

"Soon we'll feed four more mouths, and we watch our cash now." She looks at him fiercely.

He groans. "I won't watch every penny or tolerate you questioning everything I put into this cart. We both work hard and earn trade goods."

"We don't earn much cash in the world. We hold different ideas about money and responsibility. Why don't you get the granola bars this time and then ask Juanita to teach you to make cookies?"

"Okay, but we'll discuss this further when we don't stand in a grocery store and when I don't feel hungry."

"When do you ever not feel hungry?" she chuckles.

Twelve days later, Blue Feather and Martín wash dishes in the kitchen. He heaves a sigh, "The honeymoon will soon end. I enjoyed it while it lasted."

She dries a plate. "Yes, the universe gave us the last three months, a gift I will treasure the rest of my life. Yet I look forward to getting to know our new family."

He shakes his head. "I knew each of them since their birth, except for Vela, who I met before she turned four. I don't see so much of her since I moved to Santa Fe."

Blue Feather picks up a mug. "I know Vela best since Mateo often brought her when he visited us. I'll teach her and Swallow to work as herbalists, but Swallow holds other gifts."

He puts his wet, soapy hand on Blue Feather's wrist. "Yes, and I can help her develop her healing powers. She could become a great one, but I just hope her and Vela become friends."

"Oh, no problem; with all the guys around, the girls will become natural allies. But what's Tommy-tres like?"

Martín thinks a minute. "He's a natural empath who seems to develop the gift of foreshadowing, hence the extra set of bunk beds. We must remember he's a little boy."

"So he wants time to play. And Carlos? I hardly know him."

He muses. "I find him the most capable twelve-year-old I ever met. For years, he organizes the kids and cooks a luncheon for twenty. So we'll enjoy his skills."

She emphasizes, "These kids hold many gifts. I'll look for ways to support them as kids." They hear pounding at the door. She yells, "Hold your horses!"

He stands. "How will I find time for myself?" he wonders.

One morning, Tommy-tres whines. "Why clean the fireplace? We'll just get dirty."

"Come on, just go get that half piece of sheet in the rag bag. The luck of the draw means we get to do it." Martín gets down on the floor beside Carlos and puts a hand on his shoulder. "How do you feel these days?"

Carlos frowns. "I don't know. I lived through a rough summer. I miss my dad."

Tommy-tres returns and hands Carlos the sheet. The two boys spread it out in front of the fireplace, and Carlos places the box for the ashes on the sheet. Carlos shovels the ashes into the box. "I can do this job myself."

Martín chuckles. "Yes, but then neither Tommy-tres nor I would learn to do it."

Tommy-tres looks at Carlos. "I sense you feel real sad. What's up?"

Carlos hesitates and his eyes fill with tears. "These remind me of my dad's ashes." He sits down beside Martín, who puts his arm around him. Tommy-tres takes the shovel and less efficiently shovels the ashes into the box.

Martín says, "I remember how sad I felt when my Ma died. My world fell apart."

Carlos looks at the mess Tommy-tres made and says, "Here, let me do that. Go get the broom from the shed in the garden."

Tommy-tres mutters, "Okay," and runs out the back door.

While Carlos scoops the ashes, he asks Martín, "How did you get over it?"

"I didn't get over it. I still miss my mother every day, but the pain doesn't feel as sharp as it did when I first lost her." Now Martín feels sad.

Carlos responds. "Oh, thanks for telling me."

He muses. Only time can heal these kinds of wounds. "What do you want to do?"

The boy thinks. "I want to fight in the Resistance. Ma says to wait until I turn eighteen in five years. Younger warriors fight in Denver. I don't want to wait."

Martín looks him in the eye. "I'll talk to Sammy. He and Lark owe me favors."

Tommy-tres returns with the broom. "We should get a big reward for doing this."

They laugh. "You mean Carlos did all the work and should get the reward," Martín says, looking at the little boy.

Carlos grins. "Tommy-tres can sweep up the fireplace and share my reward, but what about you, Martín? You just sit there." He dumps a few ashes on Martín's head.

Martín yells playfully. "Hey, why did you do that?"

Tommy-tres chuckles. "He anoints you with ashes so you'll share in the grime."

Martín rubs the ash from his head. "Now we'll all take showers, and I get the first one because I make the rules."

Carlos dumps more ash on Martín's head. "By the time you, Martín, put away the sheet and the box of

ashes and Tommy-tres sweeps out the fireplace, I'll finish my shower." He gets clean clothes and heads toward
the shower, seeming to feel better.

After dinner, one evening, Martín washes dishes as Vela
dries them. He asks, "How are you and Swallow getting
along?"

Vela puts down a plate. "She seems cool. I enjoy
getting to know her. We go through all Blue Feather's
herbs, smelling them, and making sure they got labeled
correctly. Blue Feather tells a little about each one. I
take notes but Vela prefers just to listen and then copy
my notes later, which I don't mind."

Martín puts some spoons in the drainer. "We all
learn differently."

"And everyone in this house holds their own opinion
and way of doing things. Do you and Blue Feather agree
on everything?"

Martín reflects. "We try to present a united front,
but, no, we certainly don't agree all the time."

"I notice a slight tension between you two sometimes. Blue Feather seems to enjoy groups of people
more than you do."

Martín scours a pan. "Blue Feather seems to enjoy
teaching groups while I enjoy being alone or talking
one-on-one. How do Carlos and Tommy-tres treat you?"

Vela seems pensive. "Tommy-tres already teases me
in a good-natured way. I like his energy. While Carlos
and I cooked dinner last night, we talked about losing

parents. His loss happened more recently, so I let him know he could talk to me anytime. I'll enjoy this year, and I can hardly wait until school starts."

The following Saturday, Tommy-tres slams the door as he rushes to catch up to Carlos, Vela, and Swallow on their way to spend time with Susana and Tony. Martín sighs. "At last, we get time alone."

Blue Feather sits down on the sofa near Martín's favorite easy chair. "Before we get too comfortable, let's discuss buying these kids school clothes."

Martín frowns. "Must we talk about this now?"

She assures him. "It will just take a minute. Sammy left an envelope for Swallow's and Tommy-tres' expenses, and Juanita gave me a similar one for Carlos. That just leaves Vela."

"Dad gave me money for Vela's expenses." Martín pulls out his wallet and hands her four one-hundred-dollar bills. "That's the benefit of belonging to a community."

"We'll give them one hundred dollars each."

Martín responds, 'Two hundred would be more realistic."

Two days later, Blue Feather remarks, "School starts in two weeks, so this afternoon I'll take the guys out and buy them clothes. Tomorrow I'll take the girls."

Carlos declares, "Good, I grew out of mine this summer."

She sighs. "We'll wash your old ones and save them for Tommy-tres."

Tommy-tres inquires, "What clothes will we buy?"

"What do you think?" Martín feels curious.

Carlos answers, "We'll buy three flannel shirts and three pair of jeans."

"Socks, underwear, and bandanas." Tommy-tres states.

Carlos speaks, "We'll purchase three pairs of shorts and some T-shirts."

"How many T-shirts?" Blue Feather prompts.

Carlos thinks. "Four, no, eight, in case we do gym."

"I don't wear white T-shirts." Tommy-tres adds.

Carlos responds, "Don't worry. My mother taught me to start with the flannel shirts and match the T-shirts to those."

"Carlos, sounds like you know how to buy clothes. What else will you boys buy?" Blue Feather interjects.

He muses. "Since both of us grow fast, we should buy it all one size too big. And we'll buy one vest now, and a jacket and one sweater at the end of October. If we buy them now, we'll outgrow them before we wear them."

"Carlos, would you take charge of the shopping expedition?" Martín probes.

"Sure, I can do that."

"Can we get a treat afterwards?" Tommy-tres requests.

Blue Feather laughs. "Sure, if you don't spend all your money. I figure we'd give each of you, including the girls, one hundred dollars."

Vela sees Martín look at Blue Feather and raise his eyebrows. "But…"

Carlos thinks. "That will work if we go to the Mercantile or the surplus store."

Blue Feather seems pensive. "It sounds like the guys can go alone. Vela, do you want to take charge of Swallow and your shopping expedition?"

Vela looks at Swallow, who nods. "Sure, but can you meet us, afterwards?"

Blue Feather acquiesces.

Tommy-tres wonders, "Hey Vela, what will you girls buy?"

"Most of the same things you guys buy, plus a couple things you don't want to know about for a couple of years."

After the younger people leave the room, Martín turns to Blue Feather. "I thought we agreed on giving each one two hundred dollars."

She looks at him. "Yes, we did. But I thought it over and decided it would be better to give them a hundred now and a hundred at the end of October for jackets, sweaters, and vests like Carlos said. I guess I could have told you first."

Martín sighs. "Yeah."

Martín takes care to arrive home around four that afternoon. He walks into the living room and asks Vela, "How did shopping go?"

"It went fine, but the boys didn't get home yet."

Swallow adds, "We found some great blouses at a second hand store."

The front door opens. Two tired boys walk to their bedroom, their arms full of packages. Martín follows and sits on the floor. They drop their bags and lie down.

Tommy-tres sighs. "I didn't know we'd get so tired shopping. Before today, my mother bought my clothes. They just appeared in my drawers. Presto."

Carlos says, "We bought everything on the list. He bought me ice cream on the way home. He wears smaller sizes which cost less, so he didn't spend all his money."

"Man, he taught me how to match colors so our clothes work together." He turns to Carlos. "I owe you."

Carlos affirms, "I gladly helped."

One evening around eight, a few days later, Blue Feather, Vela, and Swallow traipse into the house, laughing and giggling. Martín demands to know, "Just where did you three go? I worried about you. Us guys ate at six."

Blue Feather thinks a minute before replying. "A special order kept us working late at the dispensary. We started joking around. Without thinking twice, we stopped for pizza on the way home."

Martín feels exasperated. "You three acted irresponsibly."

Blue Feather takes a deep breath. "Stop, Martín. Don't label our behavior that way. Yes, we didn't let you guys know we wouldn't be home for dinner. Next time we will. In fact, we girls will start eating out together once a month. But what you call 'irresponsible' I call 'spontaneous.'"

He mutters, "Well, okay, maybe you should pay a penalty."

Vela comments, "We don't have a phone, so don't blow this out of proportion. I feel sorry you worried instead of trusting us, but that was your choice."

Martín shakes his head sadly.

Chapter 26
September 24, 2044

Seven weeks after the young people move in, just as Blue Feather, Martín, and their household sit down to supper, they hear a knock at the door. Tommy-tres yells, "I'll get it," and runs to the door. He returns. "Hey, Swallow, set a place for Jeremy."

Jeremy drops his back-pack in a corner and sits. "I feel famished." He seems sad.

Carlos wonders, "How did you get here?"

"A long story; can I tell you after I eat?"

Martín responds, "Sure. You look exhausted. Take your time. Do you know Vela?"

As Swallow sets his place, Vela shakes his hand. "I call myself Vela, Martín's prima. I just started high school here, and I study herbs with Blue Feather."

As Jeremy sits, his eyes fill with tears and he starts sobbing.

Tommy-tres puts a hand on Jeremy's shoulder. "You can cry here."

After drinking two glasses of water and eating a plate of food, Jeremy turns to Martín. "Okay, I feel ready to tell you what happened."

"Can you tell all of us?"

Jeremy searches each person's eyes. "I want to tell all of you. It happened two weeks ago." He hesitates, looks around the table again, and begins.

"I walked home from school. We moved to Portland, Oregon, this summer. My dad and I lived together with another couple. The wife never liked Esteban. She said he didn't..." Jeremy looks around the table. Both Martín and Blue Feather murmur reassuringly.

Jeremy takes a deep breath. "She said Esteban didn't look white. Before I left for school, my dad reminded me to check the bathroom window before I approach the house. I could see the high window from the corner. So on the way home from school, I checked the window and I saw it broken, meaning 'run.' I looked up and down the street and noticed several jeeps and a lot more soldiers than usual.

"Last spring, Carlos told me if I want to lose some-one to go to a store and buy underwear, or go to a kids' movie. So I went to Marks and Spenser's and bought some socks, T-shirts, and underpants. My dad gave me one hundred dollars to use in emergencies. I left my schoolbooks, except for my reader and another book, and stuffed everything into my pack.

"From there, I walked through Pioneer Square, watched the skateboarders, and went to the train sta-tion, a meeting point. I didn't know what to do when I got there, but Esteban whistled a signal just before I went in. He looked messed up and hurt. He got away when the soldiers rushed the house. He came there for a meeting with my dad and other Resistance people." Jeremy starts sobbing again.

Martín holds him even after he calms down. Jeremy starts talking again. "The army killed them. When the soldiers stormed the house, my dad ran to the bathroom and broke the window. Once badly wounded, he told Esteban to get away, meet me at the train station. He gave Esteban an envelope for me. Esteban helped me buy a train ticket to Medford and from there to Sac-ramento. He told me to get to Maestra Manzanares in San Leandro. He showed me how to spot a family with children to travel alongside since the authorities don't allow twelve-year-olds to travel on their own. He said he'd stay in Portland.

"I noticed a family getting on the train and once I gave the conductor my ticket, I made friends with the girl nearest my age, went to meals when the family went, and stayed alert. In Medford I spotted another family with a boy a little younger than me and tagged a long. Things went okay until I got to Sacramento.

"I could find no way to get into the train station and buy a ticket. Two soldiers at the entrance demanded to see everyone's identification. I started to get scared, so I hid out under the overpasses. I noticed not many trains passed. As soon as the next train went south, I crossed the trestle over the river and followed the train tracks out of town. I walked until I could see the highway. I crossed a field over to it, and went on south.

"A trucker stopped for me. When I told him I wanted to go to San Leandro, he wanted to know why a white dude like me would go there. I said to get to Maestra Manzanares. Could I tell him what her two grandchildren call themselves? I answered I knew Swallow and Tommy-tres."

"He dropped me at the Manzanares house. She seemed surprised to see me and horrified about what happened in Portland. Maestra said she couldn't keep me safe and arranged with a trucker for me to come to Santa Fe. So I came here." Jeremy seems to run out of air like a deflated balloon.

Blue Feather looks at him. "I feel so sorry to hear about your dad getting killed. Would you like to spend the night here in the extra bed in the guys' room? We can take you to your grandmother's tomorrow."

Jeremy stands up suddenly; his chair crashes to the floor. "I love my grandma, but she's old. My aunt's special requirements keep her busy. Please, can I live with you?"

Martín takes a quick silent poll of everyone at the table. "Tommy-tres, you appear hesitant. What do you want to say?"

He clears his throat. "I chose Jeremy as my friend, and I know I suggested you put two bunk beds in our room. But I don't get enough time alone. I want time on my bunk to sort through the feelings I get bombarded with during the day and time to daydream."

Carlos speaks up. "Tommy-tres, how much time do you want?"

"About an hour." He responds.

Carlos looks from Jeremy to Tommy-tres. "On the days you don't cook dinner you can spend in our room from four to five, and the days you do cook you can daydream for half an hour right after dinner."

"Yeah, I like that idea." Tommy-tres answers.

Carlos adds quickly, "I'll post a schedule on our door so each of us can spend at least half an hour alone in our room every day."

"But I don't get enough time alone with Martín." Tommy-tres blurts out.

Martín looks at him. "I let other things get in my way. I'll do better. You want at least two hours a week, right?"

Tommy-tres thinks before answering. "Yes, but what about the other kids?"

Blue Feather responds, "As part of their training contract, I spend time alone with both Vela and Swallow. They seem okay with that arrangement."

Carlos adds, "Tony spends time with me. We talk. Sometimes we go for a long hike or train together."

Martín looks at Tommy-tres. "Looks like I can become more focused on spending time with you if I take on spending quality time with Jeremy." He sighs. "But I no longer get enough quality time with myself."

Blue Feather quips, "Maybe in this phase of your life, you can choose to learn to enjoy other people more."

Martín groans and everyone laughs.

After dinner, Tommy-tres turns to Jeremy. "Come, I'll show you the bathroom and our room." He opens a door. "Whatever you do, don't leave the toilet seat up."

Jeremy queries, "Why not?"

Tommy-tres shakes his head. "Blue Feather gets angry at us guys, particularly Martín, every time she finds the toilet seat up."

Carlos remarks as he helps the girls put the dishes in the kitchen sink, "Now I know why Tommy-tres insisted on getting two sets of bunks for our room."

Swallow questions Vela, "Don't you think he looks kind of cute?"

Vela laughs. "He's way too young for me, but he looks okay."

Still seated at the table, Blue Feather turns to Martín. "Amor, didn't you grow up in a house full of people? How did you get enough time alone then?"

Martín speaks sheepishly. "I'd go inside my head. I enjoyed my ongoing fantasy about Superboy."

Three weeks later, on a lovely October afternoon, Martín sits cross-legged in his office, dictating case notes to Tony.

Blue Feather knocks on the door, waits for a reply, and opens the door. "We must go to Chavez Elementary School. The principal just sent a messenger. Our four took on twenty seventh graders. I'll get some bandages and antiseptic."

As they go out the door, Tony strides up. "I'll drive. I'll share this responsibility."

Getting out of the car, Blue Feather turns to Martín. "Four out of five got into that fight only because Vela attends high school."

He scowls. "Just wait until I find out what happened."

Tony puts a hand on his shoulder. "Go gently. Your kids grieve deep losses. Two become sensitive healers. Two just lost their dads, and Carlos acts with more common sense than the three of us. Come down on their side in public."

Martín takes a deep breath. "Right. Thanks. I just became an instant parent."

Outside the nurse's office, many subdued twelve-year-olds with minor scrapes and bruises fidget and whisper. The school secretary sees Tony, Blue Feather, and Martín. "I feel so glad you came. Your four sit in the principal's office. Come this way." She knocks on the door and opens it.

Martín sees the four children huddled in one corner. Both Jeremy and Tommy-tres cry and seem upset, but for different reasons. Carlos feels angry. Judging from the energy lines, Swallow heals a bruise on Jeremy's forehead.

The principal, a trim woman in her sixties, waves them toward some chairs. One defiant boy slouches in the other corner.

Once they sit, the principal begins, "This seventh-grade boy and his friends started roughing up Jeremy."

The large Hispanic boy holding an ice pack on one eye grumbles, "Yeah, he's a white honky Wag from Colorado. His dad killed our people, including my Pa and Tío. We wanted to teach him a lesson and hurt him."

Jeremy yells, "Don't call me a honky fag or wag or whatever."

The principal looks at Jeremy. "You're new here. They test you. WAG means Wholly Aryan Government." She turns to Martín and Blue Feather. "The other children from your household defended Jeremy, and many seventh-graders got involved. I found no one seriously hurt, but I confiscated a pair of eighteen-inch sticks from Carlos."

Blue Feather says, "Yes, Jeremy's father, a soldier, did a lot of terrible deeds. He shot me in the back of the head."

Jeremy groans, and the other miscreant sits up straighter.

Blue Feather continues. "When Jeremy's dad found out the Wags lied to him about us, he joined our side and helped us get Martín's primo and some of our people out of a prison at great risk to himself. He joined the Resistance and belonged to a team sent to Portland, Oregon, where soldiers killed him. Jeremy made it on his own to the home of our agent who sent him here. Three weeks ago he joined our household."

Martín turns to the boy holding the ice pack, who asks, "Did you heal my sister?"

"Yes, I did. You can't hold Jeremy responsible for what his father did. You owe him an apology."

The bigger boy bends down ties his shoe, and then grasps Jeremy's hand. "Sorry. I'll spread the word you live with the curanderos."

Jeremy responds, "Thanks, I don't want to get into any more fights."

The principal looks at Jeremy. "I understand the members of your household do chores on Saturday."

Jeremy nods. She looks at the Hispanic boy. "You'll help out for at least two hours soon."

He thinks a moment before looking at Jeremy. "I'll come Saturday at ten."

Jeremy tells him, "Great."

Martín turns to the principal. "My family runs the risk of attack by a variety of agents. We must protect ourselves. If Carlos promises not to use his arnís sticks against other students, may he keep his in his backpack?"

She looks at Carlos. "I find you usually reliable. So if your give me your word..."

He affirms, "Yes, ma'am, I give you my word."

She hands him the arnís sticks and turns to Blue Feather and Martín. "You undertake a lot. I suggest you go home, hold a family meeting, and make sure everyone feels okay." She glances at Tommy-tres, who holds his head.

Blue Feather sighs. "You give us much to discuss."

As they head for the car, Swallow runs to the playground, looks behind a trashcan, and stuffs her arnís sticks into her backpack. She climbs into the crowded backseat of Tony's car. "I hid them when I saw the teachers coming. My dad always tells us, 'Don't get caught with arnís sticks in your hand.'"

Carlos responds, "Right. I fought so hard, I forgot. Where did you put your arnís sticks, Tommy-tres?"

He groans. "I keep them under my bed. I don't like to fight. I get a headache every time I hit someone. It gets worse with sticks."

Martín sits between Blue Feather and Tony in the front seat. "I wish more people got headaches that way. A lot less violence would occur. But Tommy-tres, you'll want to defend yourself, so I'll teach you to shield your-self from the headaches. I trust you not to hurt someone for the heck of it, but still let's look for a better way." He thinks about what he'll do to build people's self-esteem the way Abuelo used to do.

"Hold that thought." Tony stops the car in front of the house on Galisteo Street. "Classes just ended at the high school. I'll go get Vela."

"Good. I want her to take part in this discussion." Blue Feather gets out of the car. "While I make us calm-ing tea, Carlos, will you make us all sandwiches?"

"Sure."

"I'll help Tommy-tres get rid of his headache." Swal-low puts her hand on his shoulder.

"Good." Martín watches the group enter the house except for one who feels upset. "Jeremy, shall we make some chocolate chip cookies?"

"Yes, I'd like to do that with you, but…" Jeremy's eyes fill with tears.

Martín looks him in the eye. "But, what?"

Jeremy sobs. "I want to know when I'll get beaten or sent away."

Martín grabs him and hugs him. "Oh, that's why you felt so worried. We won't ever send you away. You might get some more chores for a while."

Jeremy wipes his eyes on his sleeve. "When I arrived, Blue Feather told me you both would never hit us when I asked her, but I got everyone into a fight."

"No, we don't hit kids; it promotes more violence. Did your dad beat you?"

"No, but the teachers at school did. Once my second-grade teacher beat me so bad my dad rushed me to the hospital."

"I feel sorry that happened to you." Martín shakes his head at the emotional and physical scars borne by these kids. He steps back and looks Jeremy in the eye again. "And you did not force the others into the fight. They choose to watch your back. Tell them you feel grateful when you get a chance. Now, go wash your face and hands and meet me in the kitchen."

Ten minutes later, Swallow pours tea while Carlos passes out sandwiches as the household gathers at the kitchen table.

Tony walks through the door. Vela strides in. "Wow, I heard you guys beat up the whole seventh-grade class when I left my last period. My high school buzzed about it."

Swallow responds, "One of the bigger guys and his friends started beating up Jeremy and we defended him. Things sort of escalated, but we didn't hurt anyone."

Blue Feather clears her throat. "While we never condone violence, this seems a matter of misunderstanding and self-defense. So we'll give no penalties beyond Jeremy's acting as a good host on Saturday. How do each of you feel about what happened?"

She looks at Jeremy, who glances at Martín before saying, "I feel angry at myself for getting into a fight, and I thank you all for guarding my back. I feel amazed that you would get into a fight for me. I want to learn how to defend myself. But I never knew how much the WAGs hurt this family and people in this town."

Swallow blurts out, "And you know less than one tenth of it."

Martín interrupts. "Swallow, will you go next?"

"Sure, I hate fighting but I saw Jeremy way outnumbered, so I did my best to stop people, like hitting their shins without causing lasting damage. I'd rather heal a bruised leg than an internal injury."

Tommy-tres goes next. "I don't like fighting at all. I don't think I'll like it even when I know how to shield myself from the headaches. I feel glad I know how to defend myself and my friends." He smiles at Jeremy.

Carlos clears his throat. "My parents taught me to defend myself well. I want other skills, but I don't know what to call them. Like when I saw the fighting start, I ran and got my arnís sticks. Before I returned, things escalated out of control. Maybe if I stayed and I knew what to say, I could stop the fight."

Vela jumps in. "Yes, do you mean non-violence and peacemaking? We read a book on Mahatma Gandhi in government. He defeated the British Empire with his non-violent strategies. This new guy from California suggested to the teacher Gandhi held relevance to our situation. The teacher listened and assigned us the book. I'd like to learn more about applying those strategies. The other day, I witnessed a fight in the girls' bathroom. I didn't feel afraid, but I wished I could stop it."

Tony holds up his hands. "Whoa, slow down. I hear a lot of different things. Let's see if I got this straight. Jeremy wants to learn how to defend himself. Tommy-tres wants to learn to shield himself from headaches. Carlos and Vela want to learn about peacemaking. Vela also wants to learn about nonviolent tactics. Swallow, what about you? What do you want to learn?'

She takes a minute to look at each person in the room. "Our extended family will draw attacks, so we each must learn to defend ourselves better, even Martín and Blue Feather. I agree with both Carlos and Vela; we want to learn peacemaking and non-violence. I'd like to learn how to put people to sleep."

Martín responds, "I can teach you to put people to sleep and Tommy-tres how to shield himself from head-aches. Tony, will you give us all classes in self-defense?"

"Sure." Tony grins wickedly. "I can do one class a week, maybe on Thursday afternoons. Will you and Blue Feather train then?"

Martín looks at Blue Feather, who nods and won-ders, "How we can tackle the training in peacemaking and nonviolence?"

Vela jumps in, "We could ask this smart white guy in my government class, who suggested we all read about Gandhi. Anyway, he calls himself Will Anderson.

His family lives near here and they call themselves Quakers. Maybe he could talk to us."

Martín responds, "I like that idea. Will you go with me to ask him?"

Vela avows, "Sure! He seems cute."

Blue Feather suggests, "Go tonight, while we still feel gung-ho about this."

Vela inquires, "Yes. Shall I go by his house and ask if they'll see us?" Both Martín and Blue Feather acquiesce.

That evening, Vela and Martín approach a well-lit adobe house and knock on the door. A forty-year-old man, dressed in brown corduroy pants and a flannel shirt, opens the door. "Hello, I call myself Lou Anderson, at your service. Please come in."

They walk into a warm, cozy, but male-oriented living room. Will, a handsome fifteen-year-old, strides in. He takes off the apron he wears over his black cords and dark gray flannel shirt and wipes his hands on it. "Dad, Vela shares my government class. And I believe Martín serves as her guardian." They shake hands.

Martín clears his throat. "Thanks for inviting us in. We request Will's help. Four young people in my household got into a fight at the elementary school today, a misunderstanding, and no one seemed badly hurt. We spent the afternoon discussing what happened, and Will came up as a possible resource because we want to learn more about peacemaking and nonviolence. We wonder if he'd teach us."

Lou adjusts his wire-rim glasses. "Can you tell me more about your household?"

Vela responds, "We formed an alternative household. Both Martín and Blue Feather, differently-abled curanderos who recently got partnered, took on five of us kids between the ages of nine and fourteen, either orphans or our parents serve in the Resistance. We do chores and we all pull together. But we bear scars from our pasts. Will shares my government class and I got the idea he knows a lot about peacemaking and nonviolence, so I thought he could teach us, maybe once a week?"

Lou looks at Will, who nods. "My son would feel honored to serve you. We call ourselves Quakers, and he could do this project as his community service."

Martín questions, "I recognize you Quakers believe in nonviolence, but can we exchange a class on self-defense for the classes on peacemaking and nonviolence."

Lou looks at his son. "Yes, the White Brotherhood killed both my wife and youngest son two years ago in California. They protested the lack of educational opportunities for students of color. We moved out here this summer when I got a job teaching history at St. John's. A self-defense class might help him process his anger and make friends. I can trust him to know when to use his new skills. Will, I'd like to help you prepare the classes on peacemaking and nonviolence."

"Sure, Dad, I'd like that, since adults will participate in the class."

Martín assures him, "Both Blue Feather and I will come, and maybe Tony."

Lou states, "Will sometimes teaches the younger people in our meeting and seems to enjoy it. So he'll do fine."

Will sounds excited. "The early Quakers spoke their truth to power and went to prison for it. Gandhi introduced nonviolent civil disobedience in India."

Lou adds, "And in the United States, Martin Luther King Jr. used nonviolent tactics in the Civil Rights Movement."

Martín suggests, "Wasn't King a Southern Baptist?"

Will asserts. "Yes, but Quaker activists like Bayard Rustin influenced him."

On Saturday, Martín overhears Jeremy talking to his new friend in the yard.

The bigger Hispanic boy inquires, "Is Will the new weird white guy from California?"

Jeremy responds, "Yes."

The friend comments, "He seems real smart but not a snob."

Jeremy sits down. "What makes him weird?"

The bigger boy responds, "When he first came, my cousin tried to pick a fight with him. Will avoided the fight and offered to tutor my primo in algebra. Now

Will tutors three other guys, too, until Christmas. He asked them to spread the word he's okay but he won't fight. My primo flunked algebra last year and he wants to get into a mechanical drawing class, so he worried, but with Will's help he earned a C so far."

Chapter 27
October 21, 2044

Lark jogs up the second flight of battered steps and down the clean hallway with walls scarred by bullet holes and tire irons. She gets back into shape but finds it rough after two kids. She feels glad to fight on the frontline, here in Denver. She scans the hall before unlocking the three heavy locks on the metal door. She resets them after entering the tiny apartment.

Doña Matilda, heavy-set and in her sixties, bakes the bread she sells mornings at the bus stop. Latinos rushing to work buy her sandwiches and snacks. Her customers return yesterday's bottles before grabbing new ones filled with café con leche.

She looks up from her kneading. "¿Cómo le fue? How did it go? Would you like some warm tea?"

Lark agrees. "Yes, I'd love a cup. I feel so cold. Just let me put my things away." She takes off her wool pea jacket she'd bought one size too large so it would fit over many layers. She walks to the one tiny bedroom, hangs her jacket and shrugs out of her heavy sweaters.

The toilet flushes and Tía Sara comes into the room. "Lark, I hope it went well."

Lark sits at the kitchen table and cradles the warm mug in her hands. "The women seem so eager to learn, they soak up everything and a lot of them got over their initial soreness and begin to build agility and coordination."

They hear a sharp knock. Doña Matilda hurries to answer.

A too-skinny ten-year-old girl bundled in several layers of much-too-large clothing enters the kitchen, panting. She catches her breath. "Don Mateo sent me. The Wags go toward the Residencia de Colores with tanks and a bulldozer. Create a noisy diversion in front of the grammar school so he can get the old people out." She turns to Doña Matilda. "He also wants you to bring thirty bag meals to the church in about two hours. He said to put them on his account. He doesn't want los ancianos to feel hungry while he figures out what to do with them."

She acquiesces. Tía Sara and Lark rush to put on coats.

Lark wraps a muffler around her neck. "Tía Sara, can you go by the houses of our people and tell them to meet us at the school while I get Mollies from the depot?"

The girl turns to Lark. "Shall I round up las Tigres?"

Lark looks serious. "Yes, but tell the girls to take care. The Wags shoot to kill." Lark shrugs into her backpack. She hears Tía Sara and the girl shut the door and start jogging down the hallway. She shakes her head as she runs down the steps. Tía Sara always keeps in good shape. Lark runs five blocks into a seemingly abandoned building.

She holds up five fingers, signaling the sentry, before winding through the rubble until she comes to another metal door she opens with a key. She fills her pack with Molotov cocktails. Five boys who look younger than their average age of twelve enter the munitions room. Lark turns to José, the leader of los Leones, a scrappy small fourteen year-old in an old army jacket. "While we create a diversion at the school, can you build a barricade on Mercer three blocks before la Residencia de Colores? Don Mateo said to slow the Wags down but don't risk anyone on your team getting hurt."

José assents. "We'll slow them way down and take out their lead vehicle. Mi Abuelita stays at la Residencia, so we'll give Don Mateo all the time we can. We'll stay super-cautious. I lost two soldiers last week." He looks sad and wise for his years.

Lark puts two grenades in her pocket before handing two to each boy.

José looks at her. "We'll make each one count." He leads his team out.

Lark shakes her head as she relocks the metal door. José and his team don't seem much older than Carlos. She nods at the sentry and jogs to where others wait.

Lark leads them into the deserted hallway. "I feel glad each of you could make it. We'll divert the tanks and bulldozer from la Residencia de Colores so Mateo can evacuate los ancianos, the old ones. José's team sets up a barricade on Mercer to delay them. Mateo said to delay them without taking casualties."

She turns to the younger girl. "You and las Tigres will lead the Wags this way. I'll give you some Mollies. Throw them at the lead tank and take off running. Station the next Tiger about two blocks further and repeat the drill."

The skinny ten-year-old agrees. "Sí, sí, we can do that."

Lark passes out the Molotovs. Las Tigres dash off; Lark turns to Tía Sara. "Take two compas to the roof of that building. Use the Mollies and rubble you find to slow down the lead tank. When they get past, get to Mercer and cover José and los Leones when they fall back."

"Will do." Tía Sara looks concerned. "But what do I use to cover the boys?"

Lark frowns. "Use stones and your own ingenuity. I wish I could give you more."

She leads her team to another rooftop. As the women get into place, they hear an explosion, shots and vehicles. The din grows louder until the two tanks and the bulldozer arrive beneath them. Las Tigres did a good job. Lark and her team drop Mollies and rubble down, then duck as the lead tank takes aim at their rooftop. The shooting continues for five minutes before the command tank rumbles on. As Lark and her team race down the stairs and over to Mercer, she feels the two grenades in her pocket.

Los Leones stop the head tank. Lark lobs both grenades into the rear tank's hatch when a soldier peeks out. She drops to the ground as the grenades go off. She stands and notices her left hand hurts a lot, cut by shrapnel. While the bulldozer driver, enclosed in bulletproof glass, radios for help, the medic starts disinfecting her hand.

José runs up. His shoulder bleeds. "Let's leave before their reinforcements get here. I'll tell everyone to vanish."

Lark concurs. "Yes, we bought Mateo more than enough time."

The medic, a competent, petite, thirty-year-old with a long black braid, catches José by his good arm. "Meet me behind the post office in ten minutes so I can dress your wound." She looks the tough fourteen-year-old in the eye. "That's an order, soldier."

José salutes her. When the medic finishes bandaging her hand, they run through the area to make sure no one remains besides the driver bulldozing his way past a tank.

The medic stops Lark. "Medical personnel can give their commanders orders. Go home, rest and drink clear fluids. I'll come tomorrow to redress your hand."

Lark salutes her with a lopsided grin. "Yes, sir." She walks home.

Two hours later, Tía Sara shakes her awake. "Doña Matilda will serve dinner in half an hour. If you want to take a shower, I'll wrap your hand in a plastic bag."

Lark starts to sit up and then groans. Her whole body feels stiff and sore, especially the wounded hand. "I'd love a shower, but..."

Tía Sara interrupts. "I'd feel glad to help you. After four children and living with Martín, I can handle caring for family."

Half an hour later they hear a knock. Tía Sara steps toward the door.

José, in worn clean clothes with his arm in a sling, walks into the apartment. "With so many Wag patrols out; your power-hungry medic sent you these." He hands her an envelope. "Take one green pill every four hours for infection, and take two white ones for pain before bed."

Lark grimaces. "Thanks, and I know what you mean."

Doña Matilda offers a worried smile. "The young people without families can't find enough to eat. Come by any evening around seven; just let me know before-hand."

She hears a knock at the door and answers it and leads Mateo, wearing a red flannel shirt and heavy sweater under his usual denim jacket, into the room.

He looks around. "Because of all our hard and dangerous work, all thirty-three ancianos from la Residencia de Colores got out before the Wags bombed and bulldozed it this afternoon."

The tired fighters respond with quiet smiles and one "Hurrah."

Mateo looks at Tía Sara. "I can't find a place for six ancianos who use wheelchairs and walkers in the community. I saw at least four empty apartments on the ground floor of the building next door. We'll refurbish two apartments and put the old people there. We want someone to care for them. Will you do that for us?"

She sighs. "You could persuade me. I have... three conditions."

He raises his eyebrows. Tía Sara looks at him. "I train the wonderful medic to take over as manager."

"Done. She agreed to monitor the residents and wants to work with you."

She tells him, "We'll redo four apartments, open two to the street children and let each anciano act as the foster grandparent to two children."

Mateo agrees. "I love that idea. Both ancianos and street kids will gain. Sure, we'll fix all four apartments. And what's next, mi jefe?"

Tía Sara starts to blush then clears her throat. "The barrio lacks food. La gente suffer hunger and starvation. Let's figure out how to get people the basics."

Mateo thinks a minute then turns to Doña Matilda. "We'll rob some warehouses — dangerous, but no more dangerous than a barrio full of starving people. Write a list of what to try to steal and set up a distribution system."

She takes a deep breath. "I can set up a distribution center and times people can pick up food, but we'll adapt to what you find. No use passing up a shipment of corn beef hash because we look for rice and beans."

José looks at him. "Don Mateo, how did you know the Wags would hit la Residencia? They could hit anywhere in the barrio."

He responds, "My source saw the order and got word to me before they arrived."

Lark cradles her wounded hand and asks Doña Matilda, "Do you find this winter worse than usual?"

Doña Matilda replies, "Yes, with our increased actions outside the barrio, the Wags know something changed and want to crush us once and for all."

Mateo stands. "José, do you want to spend the night at my apartment? I found an extra mattress."

José smiles and nods. They leave. Tía Sara turns to Lark. "Shall I pour you some tea so you can take your pills and then help you get in bed?'

She nods, too tired to speak.

Later, Tía Sara starts drying and putting away the dishes. "I worry because these street kids fought all their lives. They don't know about eating enough, receiving presents, or just playing and doing silly things."

Doña Matilda looks up from wiping the counter. "M'ija, I know what you mean. We can only teach them kindness as we help them survive."

Lark falls asleep wondering about Tommy-tres and Swallow.

Chapter 28
November 3, 2044

On a November evening, a crowd sits in the living room of the house on Galisteo in Santa Fe. Tony came, along with Will and Lou Anderson.

Vela wonders, "Did you always call yourself Quaker?"

Lou looks at her. "My wife's mother raised her Quaker, but I converted. Before she married me, she asked if we'd send our kids to First Day School, and I agreed. She always treated me so respectfully and with so much kindness, I grew curious and started attending First Day Meetings with her. The other Friends involved me in their activities. Four years after we married, I became a member of the San Francisco Meeting."

Martín sees Will glance at Vela with a broad grin on his face. "So, Will, what would you consider the basis for your non-violence?"

Will looks at his dad. "Well, Quakers look for a divine spark in each person. People can call it by different names, the Tao, Jesus or even the Force."

Tommy-tres interrupts. "Do you mean 'the Force be with you' in Star Wars?"

Will nods. "We'll do nothing to quench that spark in another."

Vela jumps in. "You mentioned before the Religious Society of Friends. Is there a connection? When that guy at school wanted to beat you up, you turned things around and became his friend?"

Will asserts, "Yes, what better way to deal with conflict than to become friends?"

Vela turns to Will. "How do the Quakers differ from the Wags' Christianity?"

Will puts down his mug. "We believe the divine spark dwells within each person and requires nourishment, and trying to force people to act like Christians from the outside can never work. From the beginning, Quakers stood in opposition to the government, who put them in prison for not worshiping the way the British mandated."

Tommy-tres interrupts. "What does 'mandated' mean?"

Will blushes, "I apologize for sounding too much like a textbook. It means to order. You know some Spanish, right?"

The smaller boy nods.

Will continues. "It comes from the same root as the Spanish word 'mandar.' Anyway, Quakers opposed slavery in the former United States and played an active role in the Underground Railroad helping slaves escape to the North. We also opposed the draft during the three World Wars and became conscientious objectors." He looks at Tommy-tres. "That means they did some alternative service like working with people with developmental disabilities instead of becoming soldiers."

Jeremy comments, "The Wholly Aryan Government says its religion is the only right one, and it doesn't allow for objectors."

"Neither does the White Brotherhood on the West Coast." Will seems upset.

Lou whispers, "Will and I grieve. The White Brotherhood killed his mother and younger brother."

Blue Feather says, "Sorry for your loss." She pauses and looks around the room. "This war took away so much from each of us."

Martín looks at Lou. "How do Quakers remember the dead?"

"We hold a service where we tell stories about the person who died."

Will perks up. "I like stories. Could we do it?"

Lou catches his son's excitement. "A great idea, son. We'll hold a service in two weeks, so these friends can prepare their accounts."

Vela wonders, "I'll invite my Uncle Mateo."

Jeremy interjects, "Wouldn't telling those old stories make people depressed?"

Lou responds, "We run that risk, but a good memorial service heals people. I'll reserve the Meeting House for that night so you can invite your families."

Will speaks up. "I'd like to plan the music. Will you work with me, Vela?"

"Sure, maybe I could play the flute."

Tommy-tres clears his throat. "Some of us, like Martín and me, might want help writing stories."

Will looks at Martín. "Why would you want help writing? Oh, sorry, I forgot."

Lou jumps in. "Let's meet next week at our house. Will and Vela can plan the music, and I'll help people write their stories."

The following Tuesday, Blue Feather says, "I gave this project a lot of thought."

Martín shakes his head. "Here comes trouble. I'll bite. What do you think?"

She playfully taps him with her foot. The tap turns into a caress.

Will looks at Vela, who whispers, "They partnered this summer, and they aren't even nine years older than we are."

Blue Feather continues. "With so many hero types who died fighting, we may decide to honor our loved ones who we lost in less dramatic ways."

Lou puts down his glasses. "Could you give an example?"

She looks down. "My mother's younger brother, Big Bear, kind and gentle, won many friends and dated a woman who lived in Flagstaff. He fought in the Resistance. Twelve years ago, Franklin brought him home badly wounded. Mother couldn't control his pain. I remember how he screamed at night.

"My uncle talked two friends into driving him to Ciudad Juarez, near El Paso. Before he left, he gave my ma his savings. Big Bear never returned from Juarez. Within a week, he died of an overdose of heroin. His friend stayed with him until the end."

Jeremy shakes his head. "I wouldn't equate dying by your own hand with dying in a gun battle."

Carlos looks at him. "Sí, a lot people around here call themselves Catholics, and the Catholic Church condemns suicide."

Lou says, "I would never encourage suicide; but people are much more than their final act. We can remember each person's whole story."

Tears in her eyes, Blue Feather says, "In desperation, my uncle suffered pain."

Martín reaches for her hand. "The damn white governments murder our people."

Tommy-tres looks at Martín. "Do you mean like my uncle, killed by the Pure White Brotherhood because he lived with a developmental disability?"

He whispers, "Yes."

Lou passes out paper, pens and pencils.

Jeremy asks, "Who knows how to spell 'tragedy'?"

Swallow beams. "Martín can spell anything."

"A-n-y-t-h-i-n-g; that's easy." Martín smirks, and then, seeing Lou's quizzical look, explains. "For years, I used a communication device which required I spell correctly in my head.

Will says to Vela, "I want you to hear a CD with The Four Seasons by Vivaldi."

Lou puts a hand on Tommy-tres' shoulder. "Let's go to my study."

The next night before bed, Tommy-tres climbs into Martín's lap and reads to him:

"My parents called me Tommy-tres in memory of my mother's older brother. Carlos' father, Tomás, sometimes called himself Tommy-dos. Mama told us her older brother acted with kindness, gentleness and great strength. He didn't read and add numbers because of an injury at birth. Some of his friends from school used wheelchairs, and Tommy-uno liked helping them out. On a school trip, Tommy-uno pushed his friend's wheelchair. The two got separated from the group and missed the bus back. Tommy-uno didn't know the way; the other boy knew but couldn't move his wheelchair or even talk. So the boys formed a team. While his friend pointed out which way to go, Tommy-uno pushed. They went like that for miles. They made it back, safe and sound.

"The next year, the Brotherhood killed both boys with developmental disabilities."

Martín sighs. "That great account reminds me of another story. Mateo told us The Night Way, a healing chant on the way from California. In that story, Talking God visits his sons, nine-year-old twins. One becomes lame and the other becomes blind. The blind twin carries the lame one home while the lame one guides the other."

Tommy-tres says, "Oh, I get it. Tommy-uno played the role of the blind twin guided by the one he carried. Maybe we all help each other get home."

Martín gives Tommy-tres a hug. "Time for bed, O wise one."

The next afternoon, when Blue Feather and Martín arrive home from the clinic, they find Tommy-tres, Jeremy and Swallow huddled in the kitchen with their jackets on and the oven door open. Tommy-tres blurts out, "We all feel so cold! There's no electricity. Vela and Carlos chop wood in the back yard for the fire place."

The two come through the back door with logs and kindling. Vela says, "The company turned the electricity off because no one paid the bill. I removed the notice from the front door and put it on the kitchen table." Carlos follows Vela into the living room, where they start to lay a fire.

Blue Feather turns to the three in the kitchen. "Swallow, please heat up that soup in the refrigerator and make some peanut butter cookies. Tommy-tres and Jeremy, please make us sandwiches. Be creative and use whatever you find. But check the weird combinations out with the others." She looks at her partner.

Martín, blushing, says loudly, "Yes, I blew it. I didn't pay our electricity bill. Last Monday, on my way to pay the bill, I ran into an elderly patient. I gave the money to her to get her current turned back on instead of paying our bill. When I returned to the clinic, I found two people requiring emergency care. I promptly forgot about paying the bill. Tomorrow morning, I'll sell some trade goods and pay the bill, first thing."

"I admire your generosity to your patient and I'll refrain from labeling your spontaneous act of kindness as irresponsible." Blue Feather grins.

Her partner sputters, "At least I want to change and grow."

The next Tuesday, Martín takes off his jacket and looks at the faces in the Quaker Meeting House. He sees a fire in the fireplace, warming the room after the cold night air. He squeezes Blue Feather's hand. Jeremy sits beside his grandmother. Tony walks in with Susana. Tío Juan and Mateo find seats together. Martín feels surprised seeing his dad in town. Vela watches her uncle but continues playing a flute solo.

As the music ends, Will stands. "I welcome each of you to a time to remember our loved ones. In a Quaker memorial service, we sit in silence. Each person stands when they feel moved to speak. After someone speaks, we allow at least a minute to reflect before the next person stands. At the end my dad will give a reading."

After a few minutes, Lou rises. "I will tell you about my son Vincent. Just as my oldest son shows great leadership potential, Vincent showed great artistic potential. Eighteen months old, Vincent would draw on anything he could reach: sidewalks, walls and even his own diapers. My wife and I made a deal with him. We would supply him with colored chalk, crayons and newsprint, if he would draw only on sidewalks and paper. Once he understood, he agreed. By the age of five, Vincent's drawing became very realistic and advanced.

"Vincent loved colors. For a while, he would take off all his clothes until Will figured out — by looking at Vincent's drawings — his brother would only wear certain color combinations. We managed to get him a set of watercolors. He spent hours painting, experimenting, figuring out how to make the colors more vivid.

"I found Vincent too single-minded and difficult to discipline. But I miss him fiercely." Lou sits down. The room remains silent until Tommy-tres reads about his uncle. Then Blue Feather talks about her uncle.

Martín feels amazed to see Tío Juan stand. "After the Catastrophe, my father never spoke about my mother, Elena Tuan Gonzalez. Born in Vietnam, her family escaped on a boat. They made it to the United States, where they settled in Sacramento.

"My mother loved languages. She learned English in kindergarten and soon found herself translating for her parents and others in her community. Living in California, Elena learned Spanish and dreamed of translating for the United Nations.

"My parents met their junior year at Cal Berkeley in a Spanish literature class on Gabriel García Marquez, arguing about surrealism. They fell madly in love. After graduation, they spent a year studying Latin American literature at the University of Mexico City.

"They stayed madly in love, even when they moved back to Berkeley; both worked part time, and raised two children, me and Sofía. We grew up, moved away. Not until I married Sara and we started raising our own children did I realize how close my parents remained, and how much they loved each other.

"After the Catastrophe, it took me a year to prepare for the trek back to Berkeley from Portland. I got everyone good shoes, helped my children train and gathered enough supplies. When we arrived, my dad seemed severely depressed and wouldn't answer any of my questions about my mother. He got a little better after we moved in and he started his kung fu school. He loved mis hijos. Not until Sofía and Martín moved back and he discovered Martín's gifts did my father recover.

"When he knew he'd soon die, my dad told me right after the Catastrophe, white soldiers killed my mother in a skirmish. My dad lamented his inability to keep her safe. He missed her until the day he died. So will I." Tío Juan sits down.

Martín finds himself weeping, feels stunned and vaguely aware other people speak, but he feels his Abuelo's loss and his own loss.

Soon Tío Juan holds him. "Your Abuelo loved you so much."

Saturday, Blue Feather and Martín relax in the living room. Everyone else went to Susana and Tony's.

She puts a gentle hand on his arm. "By the end of the evening, I didn't see a dry eye in the Meeting House. The memorial service brought healing to all who attended. I noticed Jeremy grows calmer the last few days."

"I feel lighter and less burdened." He grins.

"You and Tío Juan talked for a long time that night."

"We achieved a breakthrough in our relationship." He feels content.

"But what kind of a breakthrough?"

"I realized I always resented Tío Juan for not being who I wanted him to be, instead of enjoying him." He sighs.

She smiles at his happiness and then sobers. "Who did you want him to be?"

"At first, I wanted to call him 'my dad.' I envied my primos for their father. At the age of eleven, I wanted him to do active and adventurous deeds like Mama and Tía Sara, but he got stuck taking care of the house in Berkeley."

Blue Feather says, "And who did you want him to act like lately?"

He stares at her. "How did you know? Ever since Abuelo died, I miss him so much, I felt angry at Tío for not doing what Abuelo did."

"I knew, because you use one tone of voice when you talk about Abuelo and Tía Sara and another when you talk about Tío Juan."

"Oh." He sighs. "Tuesday, I told this to Tío. He confessed he resented how much Abuelo loved me and, when he died, his spirit came to me and not to him."

"Maybe now you two can get off to a new start." Blue Feather queries Martín, "Speaking about new starts, I wonder whether you feel ready to start our family?"

"Mi amor, we already raise five kids." He holds out his arms to her. "We'll discuss this tomorrow when we'll feel less tired and more rational. But for now, I want to love you with protection." He smirks now.

She blushes. "Oh, okay. Is that a grin or a leer?"

Martín stands and leads the way to their bedroom. "Come, find out."

The next morning, still in bed, Blue Feather brushes the hair from Martín's forehead. "Amor, what do you want to do today?"

He stretches and yawns. "We'll meet Mateo at the plaza at noon."

"Maybe we can give this baby starting a try." She slips her hand under the covers and squeezes him. "We could try now."

Martín reaches down and grasps both her hands. "Hold on a minute. I love you, but why this sudden desire to start a baby?'

She looks him in the eyes. "The memorial service showed me life's fragileness again. I want to try now while we can."

He holds her. "I plan to stay right here, but I won't make love to you without protection. I want to work on becoming a better father to the kids we already raise."

She frowns. "I disagree, but I sense something you don't say. What is it?"

He takes a deep breath. "Two issues. First, the war continues. So many children lack homes. I don't want us to give birth to a child who becomes an orphan.

"Secondly, I already told you about Tierra Oscura. Sometimes I struggle hard to stay out of the cave.

The face I show to the world appears more stable than what I feel. I want you as my partner to know."

She takes his hand. "Thanks for leveling with me. I'll respect your decision. I reserve the right to bring it up from time to time. But Martín, no one shows all they feel to the world."

"I know, but I struggle." He sits up, and walks toward the bathroom.

Just before they leave, Martín hears a yelp and rushes toward the bathroom. Blue Feather yells, "You forgot to put down the toilet seat. I feel angry at you! How many times are you going to forget?"

Martín takes a deep breath as Blue Feather comes out. "I feel sorry. I work hard at remembering, and I do much better. I'll do your dishes this week. Can we just go to Mateo and not argue right now?"

Blue Feather sighs, "Well, yes, you do better, so if you do my dishes for two weeks, I'll let it go."

He groans. "Okay."

When they arrive at the plaza, Mateo already sits. "How's the special pair?"

Martín collapses onto the bench beside him. "We work hard to become a couple."

Mateo tells them, "The memorial service Tuesday felt powerful and healed people. We can learn from Quakers. I hope Vela doesn't get too attached to Will."

Blue Feather turns to Martín. "At their age, all the teenagers form attachments. Will Anderson will treat her more respectfully than most boys. But I will talk to Vela again."

He thinks a minute. "She seems kind of young to act sexually. I assume she knows about contraceptives." When Blue Feather nods, he continues. "I guess I'll talk to the guys about their sexuality. Did you start talking to Swallow?"

She smirks. "Yes, I did."

Mateo says, "Martín, the boys function at different levels. I suggest you speak to Carlos on his own."

Martín shakes his head. "I didn't know raising kids involved so much work."

Mateo comments, "Abuelo did a good job, but I wish I took a more active role in your upbringing."

The three sit in companionable silence for a few minutes. Martín turns to Mateo. "You don't say much about my grandmother. Can you tell me about her?"

Mateo draws an old photo out of the breast pocket of his worn brown corduroy shirt. "I knew that question would come, so I brought this picture."

He holds the photo where both Martín and Blue Feather can see it. "She called herself Annabelle Tso from near Chinle. My dad met her at a dance in Crown Point, where she taught at the Maryknoll Mission School. Your grandmother earned a master's degree from UNM in anthropology. Dad felt surprised she allowed him to court her. No slouch, he still worked on his degree in police science from Arizona State. Later he studied law and became a civil rights attorney in Prescott, where your grandmother taught American history and social studies at the high school.

"My fierce, goodhearted ma kept me on my toes. She helped us do more than we could ever do without her. They bought the house on East Goodwin Avenue."

Martín can't stop himself. "Do you mean that house belonged to you?"

Mateo nods his head. "Yes, when I knew our family moved to Arizona, I found Tía Sara after she arrived in Prescott with the guys and gave her a deal on the house she couldn't refuse. I knew you'd come to Prescott, and I wanted you to live in our house."

Martín looks at Mateo. "Several years before we walked to Arizona, I dreamed about living there."

Mateo says, "Well, they raised us three children in that house. Things went well until someone bombed Teheran and infuriated Muslims around the world. Things got worse and worse. One morning we found my dad a hundred yards from the back. Judging from the trail of blood, shot in the back, he bled to death crawling home.

"About ten years later, we decided to go south. My ma and sister took the bus to Mexico City, where they found an apartment. But white supremacists bombed it to keep 'the non-white hordes' from invading the splendid United States. They both made it back to Prescott. My sister died right away, while Ma passed from cancer six months later. Coyote and Mary Grey Eyes eased their deaths as much as they could."

Blue Feather recounts, "I met them once or twice. Mother told me Coyote came to her for substances to alleviate their terrible pain. My dad and Tío went to El Paso to get morphine for Annabelle, before my dad disappeared and my Tío died in El Paso.

"Hey, Mateo, I never before connected that first trip to Tío's overdosing there."

"Yes, those years brought our families much pain and loss. And I feel so glad you and Martín got together. It feels like a resolution to that suffering."

Martín looks at his partner. "How did your dad disappear?"

"During the turmoil and chaos, people just disappeared." She sounds sad. "Roving vigilantes in armored jeeps murdered non-whites. My dad went to get supplies in Flagstaff and didn't return. We never found out what happened."

Mateo puts down his empty glass. "Franklin and I retraced his route, but we found scattered burnt bodies and car wrecks."

Martín puts his hand on Blue Feather's. "I don't believe we survived. The government tries to exterminate us."

Mateo holds a core of anger under his calm. "They still actively murder us. Yet we survive and even thrive."

"How long did you know Franklin?" Martín inquires.

Mateo savors a spoonful. "I know both Franklin and Blue Feather's mother forever. Franklin, Blue Feather's mom, some others and I started the Northern Arizona branch of the Resistance during the chaotic time. First we watched the California-Arizona border near Needles and following the vigilantes coming across on Route 66.

"I developed a gift for undercover work and for recruiting people. I even recruited Sofía out from California and got her to move to Flagstaff, where we fell in love. She got the Hispanics to trust us and connected us with the Filipino truckers. Franklin always planned actions, and I functioned as chief observer. I could see details no one else saw."

Blue Feather almost whispers, "You still do."

Carlos will soon receive a rare opportunity.

Chapter 29
December 24, 2044

Sammy and Tía Sara walk into the living room. Pandemonium breaks out as everyone hugs the newcomers. Lark follows carrying a too-big Tommy-tres. People redistribute themselves. Carlos and Jeremy sit on the floor. Swallow insists on sitting next to her dad.

Martín takes advantage of a pause. "So glad to see you. How did it go in Denver?"

Lark grimaces. "Growing up in San Leandro, we always scavenged enough food — not a lot, but an adequate amount — so I didn't realize how repressive starvation could feel. The Wags kill us in the Denver barrio and keep us from getting provisions. And it got worse in the last four months. When Sammy came through on Wednesday, Tía Sara and I decided to take a break and come down for a few days. Tía Sara trained a medic from the barrio to run a residence for ancianos and street kids."

Tía Sara jumps in. "I wanted to see how well our medic could do on her own, to see if I can start another residence for children."

Sammy announces, "We'll get ready for a big offensive this spring with major actions in California, Oregon, Nevada and Colorado on the same day. We linked to groups in every Western state except Utah. The Wags in Colorado ship food and weapons to Salt Lake City, another reason they keep supplies from our people."

Carlos asks, "Do you think the Mormons will join forces with The Wags?"

Sammy looks at him. "They already did. I think after we gain control in Colorado, California and Nevada, all the hardcore white supremacists will move to Utah."

Jeremy speaks from the floor. "What's going on in Oregon?"

Sammy looks at Tía Sara. "Estebán does a great job at linking with already existing progressive groups. Oregon, like Northern California, was a radical place before the Catastrophe, so I don't think many people from either place will move to Utah."

Tommy-tres speaks from his perch on Lark's lap. "Carlos, please answer the door."

They hear a knock, so Carlos runs to open it. He hugs his mother, and leads her into the living room.

Sammy looks around. "We want to meet with Carlos. Vela, will you take the young people to Tony and Susana's? They expect you early. We'll come by for supper."

She consents.

As people reconfigure, Martín moves to his favorite chair. Blue Feather raises her eyebrows, inquiring, "What's up?"

He shakes his head. "I don't know."

But she knows from the twinkle in his eye Martín is far from innocent.

Soon Carlos sits by his mother, Juanita. Lark sits by Sammy and holds his hand.

Tía Sara begins, "Carlos, we'll invite you to do something, and we want you to make your own decision. How old are you?"

Carlos speaks soberly. "I lived thirteen years."

Tía Sara tells him, "We want you to come to Denver for three months and organize the street boys. We think you could teach them how to run their household."

Juanita states, "The job holds many risks. You'll prove yourself to the guys by taking part in actions. I came here to make sure you feel free to say 'no.' Your dad and I never involved you in our work, but we made sure you trained to defend yourself. Like us, you hold many practical skills. I hoped to wait until you grew older, but you hold the right skills for this job."

In the quiet room Carlos takes a minute to think, but no one feels surprised when he speaks. "I feel honored you invite me to join the Resistance. I worked hard to learn many skills so I can do a lot. I want more information."

Lark watches his face. "I like your response. I found the barrio a rough place. The Wags starve us out of existence. If you decide to take this assignment, I'll act as your superior officer. You'll work with a core group of five street boys between the ages of ten to fourteen, called los Leones. Another six boys do their share of observing. José, their leader, turned fourteen but looks smaller than you, so you'll want to win his confidence without challenging his authority. Like him, we'll give you the privilege of eating supper every day in our apartment.

"The guys fought all their lives. Two can read and do some basic math, and one doesn't know the alphabet. I'd like you to find ways to improve those skills and teach basic things like cooking a meal or doing your wash regularly. First, we want you to just get to know the boys and learn your way around the barrio."

Carlos inquires, "What kind of actions will I do?"

Tía Sara seems angry. "I feel uneasy. Los Leones do a lot of scouting and observation. But I saw José take out a tank with grenades and rocks. The Wags shoot to kill, and two Leones died. I don't want you getting hurt."

Carlos takes another minute. "Yes, I'll give this assignment my best shot."

Juanita hugs her son. "I feel proud of you. Your dad would feel proud of you, too. I hope you don't neglect your education."

Martín looks at the boy. "You study diligently, and we'll hire Will to tutor you when you return so you don't lose the year."

Carlos shrugs. "I just hope the guys accept me."

Juanita puts her hand on his shoulder. "Just give it your best shot. I'll sell some jewelry and rugs, and get you some cash."

Martín adds, "So will I. You never know when it will come in handy."

Carlos winks at Martín. "Thanks for everything. Someday I'll pay you back."

Two weeks later, after the younger people leave for school, Blue Feather answers a knock. "Tía Sara, Lark, come right in. I'll get Martín."

Lark announces, "I want to use your bathroom," and rushes past.

Tía Sara says, "Lark and I will leave in a week. Juan and I will make some big changes this summer."

Martín enters and sits. He feels curious. "Oh, what will you change?"

Tía Sara continues. "Going to the barrio opened my eyes. I want to work with the orphans and street children. After the big push, we'll move to Denver and start a home for these children. Dave More looks for a big house near the barrio."

Martín scratches his head. "But all those youngsters will require a lot of work. We raise five and they keep us very busy."

Tía Sara frowns. "Five kids require a lot of attention. I thought only four."

Blue Feather shakes her head. "Jeremy moved in officially in October. The Brotherhood killed his dad, and he managed to get himself here. Esteban helped him leave Portland. But five keep us occupied."

Tía Sara turns to Martín. "I thought you should know, we want to sell our house in Prescott to finance our new home. Do you feel okay with that?"

Martín takes a minute to look inside. "I feel fine with it. But why ask me?"

Tía Sara responds, "When I bought the house, Mateo requested I put your name on the title along with m'ijos' names. You are entitled to ¼ of the sales price."

Martin glances at Blue Feather and raises his eyebrows. Blue Feather nods. He says, "I didn't know. Please sell the house and use my share to buy a house in Denver. What did my primos say?"

Tía Sara grins. "Thanks. Susana and Pedro said what you said. I didn't ask Esteban yet."

Lark comes into the room and sits down smiling. "There's a funny sign on the wall behind the toilet: 'Put the toilet seat down if you value your penis!'"

Martín blushes. Blue Feather says, "Only certain guys leave the toilet seat up. It became a pet peeve."

Lark grins. "I know neither m'ijo nor Carlos would be so arrogant, and Tommy-tres would tell Jeremy. So who keeps forgetting?"

Martín clears his throat and turns to Lark. "How do things go for you in Denver?"

Lark reflects, "I learn a lot about the wounds and scars with which the oppressive white government leaves us. While m'ijos thrive and develop their gifts, several kids in the barrio starve to death. I talked a long time with Tía Sara and Doña Matilda. They helped me see that ever since my brother died, I got stuck in survivor mode.

"These past two weeks, Sammy and I talked late into the night. Once this phase of the war ends, we will get counseling both as a couple and as a family. I want to leave the Resistance, switch from surviving to thriving, and finish my education. We will rebuild our family after this time apart. I can't expect m'ijos or my husband to feel or act the same way they did last fall. I don't."

Blue Feather responds, "Wow, what big changes! What would you like to study?"

Lark shakes her head. "I don't know, maybe community organizing or maybe something different. I just know I want to stay open."

Tía Sara clears her throat. "Blue Feather, how do things go for you?"

Blue Feather takes a minute to reflect. "This last a year and a half I made big changes. I moved to Santa Fe and started my own dispensary. Then we celebrated our commitment ceremony, and I moved in with Martín. Then I started teaching two apprentices and raising five children."

She looks at Martín. "I find becoming Martín's partner the most challenging part. I love him dearly, but we want more alone time both to enjoy each other and work out our differences."

Lark speaks up. "And Martín, how do things go for you?"

"I agree with Blue Feather; we'll work on our relationship. I want more time just for myself, too. I don't feel comfortable as the father of five. I'd like to start out with one or two and maybe add some of our own. Blue Feather feels ready to get pregnant. I hope I'll feel ready after the big push, when the house becomes less crowded."

Lark looks at her watch. "Sounds like you two will work hard. It gets late. Shall we drop you two at the clinic?"

Chapter 30
January 17, 2045

Carlos shivers as he gets out of the car and shrugs into his backpack.

Lark kisses Sammy before he drives off. She puts on her pack, picks up a duffle bag and turns to Carlos. "We'll walk for a half an hour."

Carlos feels glad he bought food to fix tomorrow's breakfast on the way. He follows Lark and Tía Sara as they pick their way through rubble and into a culvert. Once through, he sees Lark wave at a rooftop. Within minutes, a scrawny figure joins them.

Lark puts down the duffle. "José, I want you to meet your new recruit, Carlos. Please show him the ropes and take care of him. You'll teach each other a lot."

José extends his hand. "Pleased to meet you, 'Mano."

Carlos shakes it. "Likewise."

José picks up the duffle bag, and they continue walking through a group of apartment buildings. Lark stops and points. "We live with Doña Matilda on the third floor of that building, apartment 369. I will expect you there tomorrow night at seven for dinner. And los Leones live on the first floor of that building. José will show you."

Carlos follows José, who jogs toward a building carrying the duffel bag. He hears Tía Sara call out, "Suerte!"

Soon José opens a door. The apartment contains two rooms: one with three bunk beds, the other with a kitchen table and refrigerator.

"The guys went out on patrol. You can meet them later." José points at a lower bunk. "That's your bed. Did you bring a sleeping bag?"

"Yeah, sure." He shrugs out of his pack and unrolls his sleeping bag. He opens the duffel bag and takes out a bag of food. "I got us some stuff to make breakfast. Where can I put this to keep it cold till tomorrow?"

José opens the window. "You can keep it in this box outside for now."

Carlos puts the bag in the window box and looks around the very sparse apartment with no furniture besides the kitchen table and three chairs and three apple crates. The stove looks like a mess, and the refrigerator doesn't seem to work. José points. "The bathroom's in there." Carlos steps in and finds it spotless, to his surprise.

Coming out, he wonders, "Who cleaned the bathroom?"

José grins. "One guy knew how, so I asked him to teach us. Put on your jacket and I'll show you around."

The next morning Carlos takes a minute to remember why he wakes in this cold apartment. He hops out of bed and dresses. He opens the window and gets his bag of food. He notices a skinny ten-year-old following him as he goes down the hall to an older woman's apartment. He had met her last night and had asked her if he could use her stove this morning. So now he knocks on the door. The ten-year-old boy follows him as he walks into the apartment. "Hello, can I use your stove?" He finds a bowl and breaks two eggs into it, adds milk and a little cinnamon. He finds a frying pan and adds a little lard. As he waits for the pan to heat, he starts a pot of coffee.

The Hispanic woman enters the kitchen. "M'ijo, where did you get the coffee?"

Carlos shows her a small jar. "I bought some on the way into town. I'll leave you a couple spoonfuls. I used some of your lard."

She pats his head. "I'll enjoy it."

The kid watches Carlos as he dips slices of bread into the batter and fries them up. He puts the finished French toast in a pan in the oven to keep warm. The boy wants to know, "How'd you learn to do all that?"

Carlos washes the pan. "My mama taught me a lot of practical stuff. Also, my dad cooked a lot, and now I live in a household where we all take turns." He hands the kid the pan of French toast and leads the way with the coffee pot and a pot of warm milk.

The guys rush to the table. Carlos suggests, "I'll trade you a great breakfast for half an hour of elbow grease each."

José grabbed a piece but swallows before mumbling "Okay." The boys murmur "Yes." Carlos passes out the French toast. He feels glad he took time the night before to wash plates, cups and forks. The boys devour the food.

The skinny ten-year-old looks up. "Tell us about your household."

Carlos thinks. "An alternative household means a family group that doesn't fit the old traditional pattern of a mother, father and their natural children. I know two gay men in Arizona who adopted four kids. The blind dad understands his children in a different way. They can't get away with saying they can't do something."

Roberto, a scrawny twelve-year-old with dark curly hair, comments, "With so many dead, lots of people live in non-traditional family groups in our barrio."

José takes a sip of café con leche. "Carlos, why do you live in an alternative household?"

Carlos swallows a bite. "Even before my birth my parents worked in the Resistance. When they both went away, they would leave me with Lark and her family. I grew close to her two kids, Swallow and Tommy-tres. They both decided to join a brand new household when they found out their parents would go away this year. When my ma told me she would do a lot of traveling for the Resistance, I joined the same one."

Roberto puts down his mug. "Who are your parents?"

Carlos murmurs, "Juanita and Tomás Yamamoto-Rodriguez."

José says. "They're legendary! Your dad died last year, didn't he?" Carlos nods yes. He feels sad. José changes the subject. "When did you join the Resistance?"

Carlos finishes his café con leche. "Lark said you would show me the ropes on my first assignment."

The boys nod and then the kid wonders, "I turned ten and I ran errands for two years and fighting for a year. Both Roberto and José started fighting before they turned eleven. You look like you turned fourteen."

Carlos sighs. "No, I just turned thirteen."

Roberto continues, "How come you just now begun your first assignment?'

Carlos' face gets red. "I don't know. My parents wanted to keep me safe and I wanted to fight for years.

They figured something big would come soon. I feel ready, and you guys could get me started."

José looks dead serious. "I'll obey orders, but you'll prove yourself."

Carlos swallows. "I will."

When they finish eating, Carlos inquires, "Who can fix things?"

Roberto looks up and says, "I can fix anything."

Carlos stands. "Okay. Can you help me fix the stove up?"

"I'll give it a try."

Carlos points to a pile of clothes on the bedroom floor. "Hey José, do you know where we can find the nearest washing machine?"

José looks at him. "I saw a washer and dryer, which still work, in the basement. But not all the clothes seem worth washing. Shall I sort through them?"

Carlos helps Roberto start on the stove. The ten-year-old starts the dishes. Twenty minutes later, Carlos and José run down to the basement. They each carry a load of dirty T-shirts plus underwear, and Carlos, a box of detergent. Someone else uses the dryer but not the washer. Carlos sees a pile of quarter-sized slugs on top of the washer. He puts the clothes in the washer and adds detergent. "I bet I can use those slugs for the machines." He starts the wash.

Later at the main gate, José tells Carlos, "We'll stay on duty until six. I'll introduce you to our people. Roberto wants to check out the refrigerator." Carlos nods and José continues, "Tomorrow, when Roberto goes out to scrounge parts, he'll know what he wants to fix both appliances."

Carlos looks at the wasteland outside the gate. "You guys don't miss a beat."

"Neither do you. Do you miss your home?"

"No, since I'll see Lark later today and I spent a lot of time at her house. I welcome this opportunity to see what I can do on my own."

José inquires, "What's your current assignment?"

"Lark told me the first phase: to get to know you guys, teach you any skills you want to learn and get to know my way around the barrio. Tell me about yourself."

José takes a minute to think. "There's not much to tell. The whites killed both my parents before I turned seven. Wags shot my Tío Gil a couple of years ago. His leg never healed right, so he feels angry and bitter, not the fun guy he used to be."

Carlos keeps his eyes on the area outside the gate. "He might be suffering a lot of pain. Let's get a medic to look at him. Too bad your uncle can't see a curandero like Martín, the man I live with."

José shakes his head. "Other guys suffer pain and they don't act mean like Tío Gil. I ran messages for my uncle, who watches our storage depot. An older guy found me reliable and requested I join his team. When he moved on and two guys died, Don Mateo promoted me to lead los Leones." He sees runners coming toward the gate. "Let's cover our people." He hands Carlos a bottle with a rag in it.

Carlos sees three people with heavy packs run toward the gate. The rear one carries a semi-automatic pistol. She turns to cover the retreat of the other two. José hands Carlos a lighter and runs down to open the gate. Carlos lobs mollies.

The three make it through the gate. The four pursuers start taking shots at the tower, but Carlos ducks and they retreat. José sprints upstairs.

Lark appears and shrugs out of her pack. "Carlos, you throw well."

She continues, "Our medic wanted medical supplies, so we robbed a pharmacy."

Two more enter the tower room. José clears his throat. "Don Mateo, our new recruit, Carlos Yamamoto-Rodriguez."

"Hey, Carlos, welcome to Denver. I enjoy seeing you in action." Mateo turns toward the third person. "Please meet our most valuable medic."

Carlos shakes her hand.

Mateo inquires, "I hope los Leones treat you well."

Carlos nods and José adds, "He knows how to do all this cool stuff like throw a molly right on target, cook French toast and read."

Mateo grins. "I know Carlos, a person of many talents, all his life.

Lark steps forward. "I see José shows you the ropes. I want you to attend my arnís classes weekday mornings at ten. José will show you the place."

Carlos salutes. "Yes, sir."

Lark looks him over. "Do you want anything?"

Mateo and the medic raise their eyebrows when they hear Carlos say, "I want a place and primers to start a reading class."

Lark responds, "Tomorrow after arnís practice, we'll check out the supply room and a classroom at the school."

The medic looks at José. "When we noticed they followed us, we decided to use the main gate rather than compromise one of our less obvious entrances."

José asks, "What sort of medical supplies did you, uh, secure?"

The medic steps toward José. "Things for wounds like antibiotics, pain relievers and sterile dressings."

Carlos nudges José, who says, "I'd like you to check out Tío Gil again. Carlos thinks his leg hurts him."

"I'll do it if you come with me. I won't tackle your Tío on my own." She looks at her watch. "I'll come by here at six, and we'll walk over to the warehouse together."

José agrees. "Okay, but I want to get to Doña Matilda's by seven."

Two weeks later, Carlos feels glad he has eaten a good breakfast and has stretched well as he spars with another student, a young man in his twenties, strong and agile but lacking control. He ducks a wild swing and gives his opponent a sharp tap on the shoulder with his arnís stick.

Lark comes up to him. "Let's show them a good fight."

Carlos sighs, knowing he'll get hit hard. He turns and salutes his former opponent before saluting Lark. He decides to try a different strategy. He runs forward, kicks Lark in the stomach and follows with a flurry of strikes with both arnís sticks. He gets hit a couple of times, but he doesn't let it bother him. He keeps up his attack, remembering to add a variety of strikes, kicks and wild blows that keep Lark off balance.

The eighteen students in the old grade school gymnasium watch the match, cheering both adversaries. After fifteen minutes, Lark signals time out. The others clap and resume sparring. She bends double with her hands on her knees, panting. "You fought so well. What got into you?"

Carlos wipes his forehead with his sleeve. "When a friend got knifed yesterday, I realized we don't train people to play games but to get themselves out of life and death situations. I spent the last few classes ducking wild blows, but I realized I can use them. I thought I'd incorporate them in my sparring and throw you off balance."

Lark looks at him. "You did challenge me, and I encourage you to add the unpredictable. Would you like to take a shower before you teach your reading class?"

Carlos salutes Lark then the whole class before grabbing his pack with clean clothes and running toward the boys' locker room.

Later, Carlos follows Roberto through a culvert. Heavily armed young men give them a hand into the back of a van. The van takes off through the streets of Denver.

One hands Carlos a bright pink marker. "When we get to the warehouse, you'll go in with Roberto and mark the boxes of food, mostly protein. We'll follow and load them into the van."

Two soldiers put ski masks over their faces and jump out. Carlos copies Roberto as he ties a bandanna over his face, bandit-style. Soon the van backs into a loading bay and the two boys run into a large room with large boxes and bags of food on shelves. Roberto stays alert as Carlos walks through marking boxes of spam, corn beef, Crisco, bags of rice, beans, sugar, raisins and flour. Carlos feels happy when he finds several cartons of milk powder.

The two boys round a corner as a white soldier with an automatic rushes through a door. Before the man's eyes can focus, Carlos takes a flying leap, kicking him in the stomach, and follows up with a blow to the temple with his ever-handy arnís stick.

Roberto snags the pistol, the wallet and the extra ammo from the man's pocket and puts them into his backpack. "He's the same size as José's uncle. Help me strip him." The two boys take off the soldier's boots, pants, vest and heavy shirt.

Roberto hands Carlos a Swiss Army knife. "I found this in his pocket. I figure you could use it." He stuffs the boots and clothes in his pack.

Carlos fills his pack with boxes of protein bars. "Thanks." He hears the whistle. He points to a box of chocolate bars. "Take these." The boys run for the van.

The young men packed every inch of the van with food. A young man motions them to the front, where they climb in beside the driver.

Carlos inquires, "What about you guys?"

The young man grins, "We'll make it back. Don't worry."

Back at the culvert, José waits with a group of people. In minutes they empty the van and carry supplies through the culvert to the warehouse where Doña Matilda and three women distribute everything.

Carlos picks up a carton and follows Roberto from the van to the warehouse.

As they catch their breath, people leave carrying food boxes. Roberto climbs to where Gil Sanchez guards the warehouse. "I figure these clothes would fit you."

The soldier examines the clothes, and his face relaxes. "Muchas gracias."

Roberto crouches near the guard. "I saw an empty studio apartment next door to us. Could you move in there and eat with us?"

Tío Gil thinks. "You 'manos live on the first floor, right?" He looks at his crutches.

Roberto states, "We'd help you move your things."

Tío Gil looks at him. He remembers losing his wife and stepson and wonders how much he wants to get involved. "I'll think about it." Roberto runs back down stairs.

Doña Matilda puts several extra chocolate bars in the box she packs and hands it to José. "Take this for your household." She hands Roberto a box. "Please take that to the older woman who lives across the hall." She gives Carlos a box. "Please take that to my place."

The boys agree. "Sí, Doña Matilda."

She waves at Tío Gil as she and Carlos leave the building. She puts a hand on his shoulder. "You think fast, and you did well."

Walking to her place, Carlos hopes the big push succeeds and his friends survive.

Chapter 31
April 10, 2045

Tío Gil looks fierce as he stares at Carlos. "What do you mean, you know a guy who can heal my leg?" He visits the boys, still pondering if he wants to move next door.

The other guys hold their breath as they wait for Carlos to respond. He knows Gil heard him, and doesn't repeat himself, just looks at the older man.

Tío Gil growls, "Who said my leg is a problem?"

José jumps in. "Tío, we see you pop pain relievers when the medic can get them."

Roberto says, "I heard about this guy. He healed some serious injuries, but isn't he a cripple himself?"

Carlos glances at Tío Gil. "I don't use the word 'cripple.' I saw Martín take out a ninja from California using his kung fu."

Roberto looks at the wounded soldier. "Sorry." Tío Gil shrugs.

Carlos continues. "Yes, Martín, born with severe cerebral palsy, wobbles when he walks and shows coordination problems. He says he lives with a 'physical difference.'"

Tío Gil seems pensive. "I raised a stepson with severe cerebral palsy whose mother called him Martín. His mother took him to California because the Wags scheduled him for termination here. He'd be twenty-four. I wonder if it is the same guy."

Carlos responds, "You could ask Mateo. He'd know."

Tío Gil looks at Carlos. "I'll think about seeing him, but other people seem stupid about me now that my wound doesn't heal. It's their problem when they think I can do less or think less intelligently. And anyway I can't get to Santa Fe right now." He wonders whether his stepson still lives. He'll ask Mateo.

Carlos speaks. "Sammy said he or my mother would drive me back to Santa Fe sometime in May. You could come with us then."

A week later, on guard duty, Carlos feels surprised to see Alex and other Resistance fighters he knows. He shakes their hands but gives Alex a hug.

Alex says, "So, they finally recruited you. We came to Denver for the big push."

Carlos speaks with pride. "I worked with José's gang for the last three months. I have learned so much from them."

That night, Carlos arrives and starts setting the table. Doña Matilda makes tortillas. "Please set four additional places."

Tía Sara stirs chocolate in a pot. "I make pudding for dessert. I seldom see Alex. He seems like one of my own."

They hear a knock at the door. Carlos calls out, "I'll get it."

José arrives, then Mateo, Lark and Alex. Doña Matilda announces, "Supper's ready."

As Carlos sits between José and Lark, he notices Alex hug Tía Sara.

Halfway through the meal Mateo clears his throat. "José, starting this Friday at six p.m., you'll take charge of patrolling the perimeter for at most a week. I'll put las Tigres under your command. Gil Sanchez will take command of the wounded vets. Should you detect an assault or any other problems, get word to him or Doña Matilda, who will take charge of logistics. Every able-bodied fighter over fifteen will attack key positions in Denver."

José looks him straight in the eye. "So the big one begins at last."

Mateo tells him, "Yes, and we count on you to protect our base. Carlos will act as your second in command. Use his skills and make sure you both get enough rest. Our fighters will come back wounded and exhausted, so get any injured to the clinic."

José salutes him. "Yes, sir." He looks at Carlos. "We'll begin planning tonight."

Carlos concurs. "I'll start a list of people left to protect the barrio."

José adds, "And we'll meet with Tío Gil, tomorrow."

Doña Matilda looks at José. "I'll come to the meeting, and bring the medic."

José looks chagrined. "Yes, shall we aim for two at the warehouse?'

She responds, "Yes, that will work."

Lark turns to Carlos. "Tomorrow we'll hold our last arnís class and your last reading class. We can say goodbye to our students and rest on Thursday."

Carlos feels sad. "Yes, sir. We won't say 'goodbye,' will we?"

Lark looks at him. "No, we'll mark the end of one phase and the beginning of another."

Carlos feels relieved. He realizes he grew attached to people in the barrio.

The next day, Lark hears a knock on the door before dawn. She and Tía Sara dress in dark clothing and put on their packs.

As they head out, Doña Matilda hugs them one by one. "Do your best and stay alive."

They walk downstairs. Tía Sara speaks. "Remember Sammy always tells us..."

Together they both chant, "We can't fight back if we died."

Lark hugs the older woman and then watches as Tía Sara walks toward her rendezvous point at the elementary school for a few seconds before Lark starts jogging. The medic, Alex, and then four other guerrilleros join her as she moves through the aqueduct. Once on the streets, several small groups of fighters join Lark's group until their numbers swell to thirty.

Lark sees Dave More's youngest son. He gives her the signal and leads the way to an arms depot guarded by soldiers with red arm bands. Many combatants add red bandannas to their necks and red markings to their helmets.

While the rebels outfit themselves with vests, helmets, cell phones and arms, he leads both Lark and her commander, a seasoned twenty-five-year-old, a slight wiry warrior, to the officer in charge. Soon their unit heads toward the northwestern edge of the city in army trucks.

The officer deploys Lark's unit of six fighters farthest north, past Westminster, where the road narrows. Using abandoned cars, she closes the road to one lane and then positions her two best shooters where they can hit drivers or at least tires.

A silver Mercedes-Benz approaches the road-block and stops. A young officer opens his door and gets out, hands in the air. Lark searches the Mormon Bishop of Denver. She recognizes him from a billboard. In the trunk, they find a well-stocked cooler, a brief-case of gold bars and a cache of arms. They empty the trunk.

Lark walks over to where the wife stands. "Can you drive the Mercedes?"

A tall, elegant blonde in her forties answers. "I can. I drove before I married him."

Lark watches as the woman and two children climb into the car and drive north.

Two days later, Estebán wakes up, excited. He showers and dresses in rain gear and takes the light rail out to the Portland airport, where he joins his unit. Most high government officials had left yesterday, headed toward Utah, but patrols had seen isolated pockets in the outlying towns. His unit receives orders to go to Dunthorpe, where they overcome an armed group. They begin a house-to-house search.

Four fighters approach an elegant two-story house with a garage for four cars. Estebán hits the ground as he hears a shot. He confers with the other men and sends two to the rear door; then as he and another guy approach the front door, shots ring out again. So they take cover. He yells, "Throw your weapons out, and come out! We surround you!" More shots ring out, so he throws a smoke bomb.

More shots. A voice yells, "Don't shoot!" A fragile woman throws the guns out the door. "I hit my husband with a saucepan to get him to stop shooting. I know it's over."

The unit enters the house, and using duct tape, they secure the officer. Estebán radios in, "Please send a truck to 7501 on Billy Graham Avenue. We hold an officer, his wife and four children. No one's hurt, except the officer suffers a bad headache." He laughs.

As it grows dark, two days later, Estebán and his unit approach Pioneer Square and check in with their commander. Estebán feels tired, wet and hungry, but he salutes his commander. "We finished checking that district, and all seems clear."

The commander salutes back. "At ease. When the last unit reports in, I'll call the whole city clear. Estebán, how would you feel about acting as a policeman for a while?"

"Permission to speak freely, sir?"

The commander nods. Estebán continues, "I fought against the system for too long to become a good cop. However, I'll help restore order."

The commander, with a twinkle in his eye, says, "Yes, I realize that. Report tomorrow morning at seven sharp at the central police station."

Sunday, Carlos sees people with red bandannas around their arms headed toward the main gate. He alerts José to open it while he aims a mortar at the tank following them. Whoosh. He scores a hit, and the tank stops moving. When the two fighters reach the gate, they turn and cover the medic and Alex, who carry a wounded woman.

The medic sets up a first aid station just inside the gate, and examines the injured woman. Soldiers take advantage of lulls in the fighting to get minor wounds bandaged. Alex follows her directions. Carlos feels surprised to see how tenderly Alex cleans a wound.

Carlos and José stay alert as fighters come and go. Near noon, Mateo arrives with fighters in a jeep. Exhausted but elated, Mateo announces, "The high command has left for Utah. Their elite squads covered their retreat. Everyone else surrendered to the young officers' group. They set a perimeter patrol. Dave More took over the hospital." He wipes his forehead with a bandanna. "The final push went much easier than I expected. I wonder how it went on the West Coast."

The very next day, on a drizzly morning, Estebán's patrol inspects a warehouse near the river in Portland. They had received an anonymous tip. The lead soldier, just ahead of Estebán, trips over a wire. The building explodes, killing Estebán and five others.

Four days later, after supper, Martín hears a quiet knock at the front door. Tommy-tres already strides to answer it. Tony follows the little boy into the living room, where members of the household read, study or play checkers.

Tony looks around the room. "Everyone, Maestra called our house when she got word a warehouse explosion killed Estebán. A setup, the police received an anonymous phone call. The building blew up, killing Estebán and most of his patrol."

Jeremy bursts into tears. Estebán, a good friend of his in Portland, helped him get out of the city after his father's death. Tony and Tommy-tres sit on either side of the bereaved boy and hold him.

Martín feels great rage. "I thought the war ended. Are they sure he died?"

Tony nods. "Yes, they made sure."

Blue Feather speaks from great sadness, "No, the war didn't end by a long shot. The time to maintain most vigilance is when we think the war ended. We will find both buildings and human beings rigged to explode."

Swallow wonders, "How can they rig a human to explode?"

Blue Feather responds, "I don't know for sure, but white soldiers received conditioning to hate people of color."

No one speaks on the long drive to Denver, two days later. Martín uses the time to remember Esteban, their history, the difficult spots and their adventures. He recalls how Esteban seemed to grow up overnight and had decided to pull his own weight. He remembers the time they got punished for robbing the food depot, their trek to Arizona and the time they went to see Mateo but took a detour, so Esteban could visit some girl. He'll miss his cousin and he feels a deep anger that Esteban died after the push ended.

As the car passes Colorado Springs, Martín decides to visit the cave in Tierra Oscura. He walks up to Superboy feeling fiercely determined to enter the cave.

Superboy, wearing black pants, a solid black T-shirt and a black headband, seems sad. "Ho, Martín, stop! Think twice before going inside. I know Esteban died, but you'll want your energy for healing in Denver." He steps, blocking the path.

Martín snarls, "Get out of my way! I feel angry at those white bastards for killing my primo! I want to teach them a lesson." He tries to shove his way past.

Superboy puts his hands on Martín's shoulders, stopping him without knocking him over, not easy because of Martín's unpredictable balance. "Whoa, Martín, you don't want to go in that cave. You don't want to use your energy that way! You'll heal the wounded soldiers in Denver much more effectively if you don't go in there."

Martín collapses and Superboy lowers him to the ground. "I do want to go in my cave, but those warriors wait for me to heal them." He begins to weep.

In the car entering Denver, the fighter sitting next to him holds him as he sobs.

Chapter 32
April 30, 2045

That same day, Tío Gil sips his tea and mutters, "We fought so long; I don't know what to do now. How do I build a life?" He looks around at the others. "Well, at least I don't feel alone. Let's stick together. Carlos can come visit us in the summer."

Carlos nods. "I'd like that."

Roberto swallows. "After my mother died, I made up this fantasy about getting adopted by a Hispanic couple, somewhere peaceful."

José giggles. "No kidding. I enjoyed the same day-dream."

Tío Gil adds, "We all did, even me."

Roberto continues, "Then I met Carlos. When I heard he chose to live in an alternative family, I realized I could do the same. For now, I choose you guys."

They hear a sharp knock at the door. José runs to answer it.

Lark follows him into the room. "Gil, José and Carlos, each of you, pack a bag for several days. You pulled special duty at Mercy Medical Center. Your transport will come in twenty minutes. Roberto, please go with Gil and give him a hand."

"Why?" Tío Gil shrugs, stands and salutes. He and Roberto leave to pack his bag.

Lark follows José and Carlos into the bedroom and shuts the door. Both boys get gym bags out and start packing. Lark informs them, "I give you two a difficult assignment. Dave More set up a hospital ward and invited Martín Grey-Eyed-Coyote to heal those whom traditional medicine doesn't seem to help. Carlos, you'll become Martín's aide, taking care of the details and keeping him nourished."

Carlos shakes his head. "Keeping Martín supplied with food when he heals will require ingenuity, but I know the drill."

"Take some money for extras." She hands him an envelope and turns to José. "I give you a much harder job. Martín will work with six wounded fighters. You and Alex will act as their gofers. You'll also keep an eye on them, spending time and supporting them as they won't rest easy in a hospital. Carlos will help your team whenever he can."

"Yes, sir." José salutes. "I just feel glad Martín will see Tío Gil. Who'll tell him?"

"I'll inform him now." Lark leaves.

An hour later, José and Carlos watch Tío Gil get down from the jeep and follow them into Mercy Medical Center. The man at the desk sends them to the third floor.

Alex comes up to them. "The front desk called. Martín just arrived." He turns to Carlos. "Why don't you and José go get him while I get Sergeant Sanchez settled."

José asks, "Where shall we put our bags?"

Alex responds, "Just drop them inside Room 3059. The three of us will share it."

Carlos spots Martín, runs and gives him a hug. "I feel so glad to see you."

Martín gives him an extra squeeze. "I missed you Carlos. We all missed you. Tommy-tres and Swallow send you their special love."

Carlos makes sure Martín catches his balance. "Please meet my friend José."

José shakes Martín's hand. "Es un gran placer."

Martín bows. "El placer es mío."

Carlos hands José one bag and picks up the other. "I'll lead the way."

"My mother gave birth to me in this very medical center, but I don't remember."

Martín half runs, half stumbles over to Alex. He seems to fall into his arms. "I feel so glad to see you, bro."

They hug and Alex laughs. "Hey, I missed you so much. With Coyote's guidance I healed myself."

Martín gets settled and finds José at a nurse's station. "Do you know Tía Sara?"

José smiles. "Yes, of course! She cares for all us street kids!"

Martín feels aware of great sadness. "I want to talk to her this afternoon. Can you ask her to come to the medical center around five?"

"Sure."

That afternoon, Martín sits cross-legged on a pad on top of the desk Carlos and Alex had pushed into a corner, to make more room in the small office so Martín can lean against the wall. When Tío Gil enters, Martín can't believe his eyes. "Aren't you my stepfather? You treated me with such gentleness when I lived with you."

Tío Gil approaches. "Yes, if your mother called herself Sofía?"

Martín nods and they hug. Tío Gil asks, "What happened to Sofía?" He lowers himself into a chair.

Martín feels sad. "About six years ago soldiers killed her in Owen Valley."

Tío Gil shakes his head. "I missed both of you after you left. You've grown up and you can do so much more than you could before. I've heard you've become a great healer."

Martín blushes, then responds, "I remember your kindness. But let me check your wound."

Five minutes later, Martín comes out of his trance. "While I can't turn you into a long-distance runner, I can help you with your pain."

"I want to get off pain relievers. I'm addicted to them, though."

Martín gets serious. "Then can you make a commitment to do certain things today and the next six days?"

"Like what?" Tío Gil inquires.

Martín looks him in the eye. "Stay off that leg, get plenty of rest, drink lots of fluids, see me twice a day, and let José, Alex or Carlos know when you feel bad pain."

Tío Gil adds, "And don't take any meds on my own."

"Yes, but you can put one of these arnica under your tongue every two hours. This herb reduces swelling." Martín hands Tío Gil a bottle.

Tío Gil puts it in his pocket and takes a minute to think. "From what I heard about you, I could gain a lot, so yes, I'll make a six-day commitment to do those things."

"I'll jump-start your healing and see what I can do about those cravings. While I work on you, I'd like you to meditate. Do you meditate?"

Tío Gil queries, "Do you mean like following my breath and using that as an anchor? Our medic taught me."

"Yes, and I want you to picture the healing happening in your own thigh as I work and at other times."

"Sure, I can do that. I want to take an active role in my own healing."

Martín sighs. "That's the only way it will happen." He goes back into a trance.

Twenty minutes later, he shakes his head. "That's all for now, but I'll try to do a little more than I thought at first. I'll know more in a few days.

"I feel so glad to see you again and have a chance to thank you. I'll see you again this evening. On your way out please tell Carlos to bring me a smoothie." Martín shuts his eyes before Tío Gil can add anything.

Tío Gil uses his crutches to go to the door and open it. He shuts the door. Martín hears him speak to Carlos.

Carlos enters. "I brought the smoothie. I hope you like it. I bought the ingredients to make more and put them in the staff refrigerator." He holds the container for Martín.

El curandero takes several sips. "Thanks, Carlos. I feel glad to work with you here. I hope you didn't spend your own money." He continues drinking.

Carlos responds, "No, Lark gave me more than enough money, so just let me know what you want."

Martín thinks. "I want a pile of brightly colored cotton T-shirts. I saw three patients, and this shirt feels soaked."

"For now I'll get you one of mine." Carlos puts the container on the desk. "Martín, thank you for helping me get this opportunity to serve in the Resistance. I learned a lot and I feel closer to my dad. He fought so people of color could live better lives and the Wags couldn't exterminate us."

Martín gives him a hug. "I felt glad to do it. You become more and more like your dad." As the boy leaves the room, the curandero removes his wet T-shirt, and stretches.

Carlos knocks again and enters. "I wear an adult medium, so it will fit a little big."

Martín puts on the dry shirt. "Thanks again, Carlos. Did Tía Sara come yet?"

Carlos puts the wet clothing in a plastic bag. "Yes, she did. It will take me about an hour to buy the shirts. Shall I go now?"

Martín acquiesces. "Yes. Just tell Alex where you go, and please send in Tía Sara."

Tía Sara strides into the room and gives Martín a hug. "I feel so good to see you."

He says, "Please sit down. I'll tell you some very sad news." She frowns and sits, and he continues. "Just before I left Santa Fe we got word Estebán died in Portland."

Tía Sara cries out, "Oh no!" and he holds her as she starts sobbing.

She asks, "What happened?"

He responds, "His patrol received a tip about a warehouse in Portland, and when they went inside the whole building exploded."

Late Friday Mateo comes to the med center. He waits outside the office until the last wounded warrior leaves, and then knocks. Martín, seated cross-legged on top of his desk, grins. "Great! Hi, Dad. I wondered if I'd get to see you before I returned home." He stands and gives his father a hug.

Mateo says, "Well, I meant to come sooner, but I work a lot. I'll dine with Dave More. We wonder if you'd come with us."

"Sure, I'd like that. Say, Dad, do you remember Gil Sanchez, the guy who provided a home for mama and me here in Denver twenty years ago?" When his dad nods, Martín continues, "Well, I treated him all week."

Mateo says, "I feel glad you can help him. He took care of you and Sofía years ago and now suffers a lot of pain.

"Martín, please sit down. I want to tell you something before dinner."

"Okay, Dad."

Mateo clears his throat. "I don't know where to begin. I'll move to Provo and establish a deep cover identity. With so many people arriving in Utah, I'll go now and use the turmoil. Quite a few Utes work with the Mormons. I'll pass as a half-caste. I can fool any white person but not another Indian.

"My team leaves tomorrow. If all goes well, I'll stay two years."

Martín blinks and takes a breath. "I wondered what you would do now that peace came to our area."

His dad taps his foot. "Well, yeah, I worked undercover all my life. Except for you and Vela, those white racists killed my family, my wife and many of my friends. I won't stop fighting until we vanquish them or until I die."

Martín stands and gives him a hug. "I love you and I'll send you positive thoughts every day. I'll miss you."

Mateo releases his son and looks at his watch. "Let's go meet Dave. I left a package for you with Tony. Use those resources to help our people rebuild their lives and get educations. I also left an envelope for Vela."

Tears fill Martín's eyes. "Okay, Dad, I will."

Still at the med center, Saturday morning, Carlos knocks on Martín's door. "Hey, you wanted me to wake you up at eight."

He groans. "Come on in."

Carlos walks in. "Shall I open the blinds?"

Martín sits up in bed. "I bow to the inevitable. Yes."
"How do you feel?"

He swings his legs over the side of the bed. "I feel very tired yet I still do good work, but I feel ready to go back on Monday." He walks toward the bathroom.

Carlos shakes his head. "I don't want to leave these friends."

Martín turns. "You did a better job here than anyone else could do. You'll work hard to readjust to our home and Santa Fe. But I'll make you a deal. What do you want?"

"Can Roberto come to Santa Fe with me? He's quick, and I told him I'd help him get ready for junior high."

"Sure, you can study together. And Will can tutor both of you." Martín walks into the bathroom, takes off his shorts and T-shirt, and steps into the shower.

Over the sound of the water, he hears Carlos say, "Thanks, Martín."

Martín feels worried and realizes he cannot heal everyone.

Chapter 33
May 7, 2045

Monday evening, Sammy pulls up to the house on Galisteo and parks. "Y'know, I feel strange not hiding the car."

Lark stands outside, "You should hide it. This lull doesn't mean the war ended."

Sammy responds, "Y'know, I trust you. I'll go park it."

Martín, Carlos and Roberto get out of the car. Blue Feather, Swallow, Tommy-tres, Vela and Jeremy rush out. Pandemonium reigns as they hug each other.

Blue Feather beams. "We waited for you to eat."

Roberto turns to Carlos. "How did they know we would arrive this evening?'

Carlos tugs a nine-year-old kid over. "Roberto, he calls himself Tommy-tres."

Roberto and Tommy-tres shake hands. Carlos continues speaking. "He can sense what people feel and when certain people he knows approach the house."

Tommy-tres nods. "Sunday, I got Jeremy to help me put clean sheets on the extra bunk bed."

Roberto shakes his head. "But Carlos didn't invite me to come until Saturday night."

The house seems crowded and chaotic. Sammy clears his throat. "I called my ma just now." All stop talking. He continues, "She said the White Brotherhood fell on the West Coast. The higher leaders fled to Utah. Those staying formed a legislative assembly with representatives from all groups. They invited my mother to act as the mayor of San Leandro. She agreed to do it because she wants to promote reconciliation."

The next morning, Martín wakes and stretches his arms toward the head of the bed, careful not to disturb Blue Feather resting beside him. But she woke before he did and now kisses his cheek. "I missed you so much. Do you feel ready for breakfast?"

"When do I ever not feel ready to eat?" he teases.

She hits him with a pillow. "When you wanted to make love to me."

"Did you just issue an invitation?"

Blue Feather kisses him more passionately and slides her body on top of his.

After they make love, Martín kisses her. "Now I feel more ready for breakfast."

Carlos and Roberto drink café con leche, when they amble into the kitchen.

Carlos asks, "Hi, sleepyheads, I volunteered to be the official egg scrambler. Shall I make you some?"

Martín leans against the counter. "Where did everyone go?"

Carlos whisks the egg mixture. "Vela said she'd take care of the dispensary. Swallow went with her. Tommy-tres and Jeremy went to the plaza to ride their skateboards. They didn't want to wake you. Tommy-tres invited Will to stop by."

Roberto hears a knock at the door and raises his eyebrows. "Shall I answer that?'

Martín, who still stands, says, "No, thanks, Roberto. I will." He heads for the door and opens it. "Hola, Will. How do you feel? Come to the kitchen." He leads the way.

"I feel fine." Will sees Carlos. "Welcome back."

"Carlos hugs Will and turns. "My friend calls himself Roberto."

The two shake hands very hesitantly.

Carlos asks, "Will, shall I scramble you an egg, too?"

Will seems pleased. "Yes, thanks. I understand you seek a tutor."

Blue Feather answers. "Yes, and we'll pay you cash."

Carlos puts a plate of eggs on the table. "I want to finish the seventh grade."

Roberto looks at Will. "I never attended school and I'll start in August."

Carlos adds, "He learns super-fast. I taught a basic reading and math class these last three months, and Roberto took to reading like a duck to water."

Will agrees. "I can work with you two from nine to twelve every day. Shall we start tomorrow?" They nod.

Blue Feather clears her throat. "I wonder if you three would include Jeremy and Tommy-tres. Jeremy, who mourns his father, didn't pass his seventh grade math exam. And Tommy-tres wants to hang out with you guys."

Will looks at the other boys before indicating yes.

As they finish their eggs, Carlos answers a knock and Tony enters the kitchen.

Carlos looks at Tony. "My friend from Denver calls himself Roberto." He pauses. "Tony manages the alternative clinic where Martín and Blue Feather work."

Tony shakes Roberto's hand, nods at Will and then turns to Martín. "Several families arrived from southern Colorado, and we want you both in the office now."

Martín stands up. "Ah, yes. We see the beginning of a flood of people coming now that we opened the borders. Just let us take a quick shower and get dressed." He glances at Blue Feather, who follows him out of the room.

Later, Tony drives down Galisteo toward the plaza. Blue Feather comments, "First, we three will come up with a formula for triage."

Martín stretches his shoulders. "And then I'll talk to Swallow," he says. "She can handle the minor wounds while I deal with those with life-threatening and chronic conditions.

Tony drives along the plaza. "Shall I call Coyote and his wife and see how soon one of them can come?" He sees Tommy-tres, honks, and points toward the office.

Martín assents. "If they don't feel swamped, maybe one can come help us here in Santa Fe." He turns to Blue Feather. "Can Vela take medical histories?"

She states, "I just taught her and today she can practice. And I'll supervise her."

Twenty people wait lined up on the sidewalk. Tony stops the car in front of their clinic. "The line grew in the last half hour. Many families with kids arrived."

Martín holds the door for his companion, who spots Jeremy and Tommy-tres on skateboards and calls them over. "Please help us."

The two boys agree with a nod. She continues. "Tommy-tres, can you take some of these kids to the plaza and play games?"

"Sure."

Tony turns to Jeremy. "Please run to Rubén's and tell him we want to feed lunch to fifty people. Make sure he knows these folks can't pay."

Jeremy consents. Martín exclaims, "Fifty people!" He glances at Tony, who nods yes and turns to Jeremy. "Tell Rubén we'll work something out."

"Wait until you see the waiting room." Tony turns back to Jeremy. "After you talk to Rubén, go to Lou Anderson, Will's dad, and tell him we want his help. Afterward, can you help Tommy-tres with the kids in the plaza?"

"Sure." Jeremy takes off on his skateboard.

Vela rushes over to them when they enter the crowded waiting room. "It just looks daunting. I put the one urgent case in our conference room. But, Martín, prepare yourself for a shock." She turns to Blue Feather. "Three families wait in line to see you. I'll take their information."

Blue Feather sighs. "Fine. Show me the case histories when you finish." She looks at Martín walking toward the conference room. "I'll send Swallow to you."

He glances back. "Gracias, mi amor." He takes a deep breath and enters.

A white soldier dressed in fatigues turns to greet him. He sees another seated who appears wounded in the calf. The older standing soldier looks desperate. "Please, please don't turn us away. They conditioned us to kill non-whites. Now we want to live in peace. In Alamosa, we worked as guards at the prison and we knew Jason."

Martín stumbles to a chair, feeling stunned. He feels deep anger for friends, like Tomás, his mother, and two

primos, Estebán and Guillermo, who died. He decides
to put his grief aside.

Swallow enters, and sits on the floor. Martín looks
at the girl. "Swallow, I'd like you to examine his calf
wound and clean it up while I take a look at the other
guy."

She turns to the younger soldier. "When did you get
hurt?"

His voice trembles. "I got shot two days ago. We
hassled an older Hispanic man, and his daughter chased
us away with a gun."

His friend adds, "I know many like us in southern
Colorado."

Martín frowns. "I want you to tell Tony about the
problem. In the meantime, I'll scan your brain."

Ten minutes later, they both blink, and glance at
each other. Swallow starts. "The bullet went through
the calf, so first I cleared out two small areas of infection and removed some dead tissue. Then he started
bleeding, so I stopped the flow and healed the capil-
lary. Tomorrow, I'd like to check for infection again
and then start mending the muscle. Do you want to
check it?"

He shakes his head. "No, I trust your work. Unless I
teach you something new, I won't check it. Please go get
Tony and Lou." He turns to the men. "They gave you
an addiction to violence triggered by frustration. It will
take me a few days to decrease it."

Soon Tony and Lou enter, and he feels relieved. "Hi, Lou, I feel glad you could come on such short notice. Over the next few weeks we'll get a flood of people from southern Colorado. Some will stay for a few days, and others, a week at most. I'd like you to ask the people in your Friends Meeting to open their houses to these families and feed them in exchange for doing chores and whatever payment they can give."

"Sure. Shall I coordinate with Tony?"

"Yes, please." The healer glances at the two men in fatigues. "Could you and Will take in these two men?"

Lou looks at them. "No, but I will ask my neighbor to take them for tonight to help you out of a jam. But don't ask me to do it again. Even us Quakers have learned to set limits. With limited resources, ex-Wags don't appear on my priorities. Require them to change their clothes before they leave. I don't want a lynching on my hands."

Tony leads a Hispanic couple, the woman carrying a small child, into the room. Swallow follows them and puts a milkshake on the table near him. Tony announces, "Martín, we could use Swallow's help in the waiting room healing some injuries."

Martín looks at Swallow, who nods an eager yes, before responding, "Sure, Tony, but make sure she goes to the plaza for a while after lunch."

"Thanks, Martín. I'll make sure she takes plenty of breaks."

Martín turns to the couple. "Please sit down. What can I do for you?"

The man, in his mid twenties and wearing clean work clothes, chokes up and gets tears in his eyes.

The wife, neatly dressed, looks at her husband before stating, "We live near Chama. The herbalist, or curandera, there sent us. Our two-months-old son can't keep anything down. The first month he seemed okay with breast milk. When I got a breast infection, I switched him to regular milk. He started vomiting more and more. Now he seems only to keep down water." She hands Martín the infant.

Martín cradles the baby in his lap. He does a thorough scan of the baby's gastro-intestinal tract, relaxing some muscles and healing several irritated areas. Coming out of his trance, he muses, "I find this challenge a tough one, and I can make no promises. Let's try rice water. I want you to see my partner, Blue Feather, an herbalist. She'll explain how to make rice water and suggest herbs to soothe his digestive system. I want to see him tomorrow. Can you stay a few days?"

The father agrees. "Sure, we'll do anything, but we couldn't earn cash in Colorado to pay for food or housing."

"And you'd work for your room and board?" When the couple responds affirmatively, Martín hands the infant to his mother. "Let's see what we can do."

That evening Martín sits down in the living room. He feels beyond exhausted. He breaks the silence. "I thank each of you for helping us out at the clinic today. And Roberto, you jumped right in and helped serve lunch, played with the children in the plaza and cooked dinner."

Roberto confirms. "I felt happy to help, so I just followed Carlos' lead most of the time. I didn't want to meet the white soldiers, so I stayed here."

Martín sits up straighter. "You acted on your convictions. I felt uncertain when I saw them, and I regret not taking the time to think it through."

Swallow pipes in, "I felt uncomfortable healing the ex-Wag, but I didn't know I could refuse to heal someone."

Martín says, "Yes, you can decline to heal anyone, but consequences happen either way. I feel sorry I didn't explain that sooner. When we get beyond this flood of people, perhaps you, Blue Feather, Vela and I can discuss this issue." The three herbalists nod in affirmation.

Blue Feather speaks. "I'll change the subject. The next week or so will feel hectic. And yet let's not get sidetracked from our goals. I think Vela and Swallow should continue their apprenticeships." They nod in agreement. She continues. "Martín and I feel grateful for Vela and Swallow's work in the clinic."

Martín adds, "Yes, we can use the present crisis to teach you."

"I feel sure you two will." Vela grins. "But I don't think what you call a crisis means a crisis."

He mentally braces himself. "Oh?"

Vela's grin gets bigger. "Everything seems pretty much under control, and we hold an opportunity for us to pull together and repair some of the damage the Wags did."

He wonders at her vitality. "I never thought I'd say, 'Every cloud contains a silver lining.'"

Blue Feather asserts, "Since we choose to see this as an opportunity and not a crisis, Carlos, Roberto, Jeremy and Tommy-tres will study with Will starting tomorrow."

Jeremy blurts out, "Why me?" He swallows. "Oh, yeah, I forgot I didn't pass a math exam to get into eighth grade."

Martín continues, "And we ask Carlos and Roberto to do dinners, Tommy-tres to do childcare, and Jeremy to run messages in the afternoons." The four acquiesce.

Later, as Martín gets undressed, Blue Feather, in bed, comments, "You worked hard today and look exhausted, but you also seem troubled by the ex-Wag soldiers."

Martín, silent as he lies down beside his partner and pulls the cover over himself, sighs. "Yes, Lou and Roberto taught me today. I don't want to heal those killers. Ever since Estebán died and even before, I felt this rage. So many people come to me for healing; why did I spend our energy on those murderers?" His voice gets louder.

She interrupts him. "You can choose not to heal anyone you don't want to heal. In fact, I'll support you if you don't want to let them into the clinic."

The curandero sits up and turns, facing his companion. "Thank you. Years ago, Coyote mentioned I can heal only those I choose to heal. I get so absorbed in what I do, I forget. I told Swallow this evening she can choose who to heal, but I forgot that applied to me. I choose not to heal those killers. Whew! What a relief!" He bends and kisses her.

She adds, "But think about not making the ex-Wag soldiers the Other."

Martín groans, laughs and then kisses her again.

The next morning, Martín, Blue Feather, Swallow and Vela walk into the conference room of the clinic, where Tony and Coyote converse.

Martín hugs Coyote. "I feel glad to see you could come."

The three herbalists start toward the door. Martín sees Blue Feather wink at him as she leaves the room.

Coyote rests his hands on Martín's shoulders. "I always feel happy to see you, and the world changes faster than we can keep up. I can help you for two days and then Sammy and I will tour through southern Colorado and stem the flow of ex-soldiers."

Martín breaks in. "After today, I will not work with the ex-Wag soldiers. I feel too much rage to do a good job. Ever since Tomás and my primo Esteban died, my old fury against white soldiers rekindled, I want to honor those many loved ones who died and my own grief.

With so many people coming for help, I decided to set that boundary."

"I respect your decision. You matured enough to know your limitations. Do you mind if I continue to work with them?" Coyote lets go of Martín and steps back.

"No, of course not; that's your choice. I will not treat them and I no longer want them to enter this space," Martín responds.

Tony interrupts. "Which leads me to three questions. Does Blue Feather support this? What do I do with the two soldiers waiting in the bathroom because I didn't know where to put to them? And what do I do with any additional ex-Wags who come?

Martín looks him in the eye. "Yes, Blue Feather supports my decision. On the way here, we stopped at the Zen Center. A woman said they'd provide a room for Coyote. Within two days they'll put a team in place so we can send the ex-soldiers there.

"I'll introduce you and then you can take them to the Zen Center." Martín sighs.

He turns to Coyote. "What's the best way to undo this conditioning without causing a lot of anxiety?"

Coyote thinks a minute. "I'll look at how the conditioning affects brain cells, but I'll find ways to support the ex-soldiers as they go *through* the anxiety rather than try to decrease the anxiety."

Martín says, "Yes, that makes sense."

They hear a knock. The soldiers come into the room.

Martín turns and addresses them. "My teacher will work with you from now on." They both seem anxious but otherwise okay.

They murmur, "Pleased to meet you," before the younger, wounded one, blurts out, "Lou's neighbors treated us so well, I almost forgot they were Hispanics."

The older one seems surprised. "They appeared kind and generous until they asked us to pack our things and bring them. We won't return there tonight, will we?"

Coyote frowns. "No. You won't go back there. I'll take you over to the Zen Center. Their people will put you up tonight."

The Wag soldier responds, "Too bad. The neighbor and I talked as we did the dishes, and I see things differently. Our government told us, their own people, a lot of lies and never let us think for ourselves."

Coyote shakes his head. "Any time a government manipulates the truth to stay in power, any time they tell even a tiny lie to their citizens, they do evil. I'll travel through southern Colorado and meet people conditioned by your old government."

The older one jumps right in. "I'd like to go with you. I know many ex-soldiers."

Coyote assents with a smile. "Great. But for now I'll take you to the Zen Center."

They nod and pick up their packs. One turns to Martín and extends his hand. "Thank you for everything."

Martín stands awkwardly, avoiding shaking his hand. "I did what I could. I just begin to realize the extent of both the damage done and the healing required."

"Yes, I'll see you later, Martín." Coyote leads the two ex-Wags out.

Tony sticks his head in. "I hate to interrupt, but another group of ex-Wag soldiers arrived and I sent them to the Zen Center with Coyote. Several new families also arrived from Colorado. It got crazy out here."

Martín looks at Tony. "Did the family from Chama come?"

"Yes."

"Please send them in." Martín takes a deep breath.

The mother walks in carrying her son. Her husband follows. They both grin. She states, "Blue Feather put together a special blend of herbs to add to the rice water."

The father says, "Lou Anderson let us stay at his house. I felt shocked; he's white. But he took us right in. He and I spent the afternoon painting his house. He calls himself a Quaker, and they look for the Divine Light in each person regardless of color. He gave me a lot to think about."

The woman says, "I spent the afternoon in the kitchen with one of Lou's neighbors and her daughters. We prepared the rice and herb mixture and we took turns dribbling it into his mouth. He slept much better last night and his color improved."

"Please give him to me and I'll check him out."

The mother places the baby in his arms. Martín checks out the little one's digestive tract, relaxing muscles, calming irritated places and making tiny adjustments. He murmurs, "Yes, I see an improvement, and we still will do more. Your son experiences a severe allergy to dairy, so we'll figure out a diet that will meet his requirements. Today I'd like you to add chicken broth to the rice mixture. Bring him back tomorrow and we'll see how much he progressed."

As they leave, Tony pops his head in. "I ordered thirty lunches from Rubén and sent him the pottery he likes. He says our credit is good and he feels happy to help."

Martín murmurs, "Thanks, just send him plenty of trade goods. He gave us so much over the years."

Tony scratches his head. "Shall I send you the next client?"

Martín sighs. "Yes." He ponders when he will get a break and get to spend more time alone with Blue Feather.

Chapter 34
July 15, 2045

Eight weeks pass. Late one afternoon, Martín wanders around the empty clinic. He feels hot, hungry and tired. He hears a noise and finds Vela reading <u>The Bean Tree</u> by Barbara Kingsolver and sipping a cold drink. "You stayed late," he says. "What's up?"

"Would you like some ice tea?" Vela pours him a glass after he nods. "Both Swallow and I want time alone. On the afternoons neither of us cooks; I stay late here while she spends time alone in our bedroom."

Martín takes a sip. "This tea hits the spot. Is that a good book?"

"Yes, I like Taylor Greer, the main character. She seems wise, practical and funny. She looks for her path and finds an abused tiny Indian child named Turtle, who seems cool. I know that some Indians use drugs and alcohol to self-medicate. The tribal council placed a girl at school with an older couple after she came to school with bruises. They work very hard to protect us kids from abuse. I still let one of them know where I am, and I check in with her once a month. This summer, I'll spend time on our land. Pedro said he'd drive me out."

Martín speaks softly. "I feel glad you maintain that connection and that the tribal elders protect and look out for their young people."

Vela says, "I do enjoy this book, and Taylor holds good priorities. I look forward to spending a week alone at the Hogan to think about my priorities. I find it hard to balance school, work here at here and at home, a social life, and Will. I want to get more exercise, so next year I'll try out for track. I enjoy long-distance running. The team runs before school.

"Do you want to borrow this book when I'm done?"

He nods yes. "I'll read more when the house empties for a month. Like you, I'll use that time to reflect on my priorities. I want more time to meditate. I signed up for a one-week retreat at that Buddhist place near Taos."

Vela asks, "What about you and Blue Feather?"

Martín pauses before answering. "I'll spend more quality time with her. Between you and me, I find our relationship daunting, requiring more energy than I have. But I want to plan to do more fun activities together."

A week later, three shirtless guys sit on a rock watching the Rio Grande flow. They wear shorts and hiking boots. Will says, "I figured we could celebrate Carlos passing into eighth grade. And Roberto, you made phenomenal progress."

Roberto declares, "You both taught me well. Carlos, thank you for this opportunity. I discover how to study, which means I can learn whatever I want."

He turns to Will. "Thank you. You surprised me. You are the first white guy I got a chance to get to know, and you're okay."

Will grins. "And you're the first guy from Denver I ever met."

The three laugh. Carlos tells them, "I always wanted to teach and now I know I can do it well. But Will, what do you want to do?"

Will watches the river. "My dad expects me to go to college, and I want to know more about history and sociology, from an alternative viewpoint. I want to organize people in the barrio who want to make things happen, yet don't know how. I want to marry Vela and raise a family with her. How do I weave these threads together?"

Carlos looks at him. "You'll work it out, but Vela doesn't call herself a Quaker. Don't you want to marry a Quaker?'

Will sighs. "In the old days, Friends married Friends, but in the last fifty years that changed; we became less strict. Still, I define my dilemma as I want to marry a Quaker and raise our kids that way, but I want to marry Vela at the same time."

Roberto stares at the rushing water. "Couldn't Vela become a Friend?"

"She could." Will says. "I wouldn't want her to do it just to marry me."

Carlos interrupts. "I know her well. She wouldn't do anything just to please someone; she'd only do it if she thought it right for herself. What would she do to become one?"

Will throws a stone into the river. "She already believes in a divine spark in each person, and she does many kind deeds. But she doesn't believe in non-violence."

Carlos admits, "I don't understand that myself."

Roberto interjects, "What does 'non-violence' mean?"

Will hesitates. "Because a divine spark exists in each person, we don't kill anyone or harm them."

Roberto looks sharply at Will. "I trust you don't joke! When the whites tried to exterminate us, we fought back to survive."

Will's eyes fill with tears. "And they shot my mother and brother for protesting the lack of education for children of color."

Roberto puts a hand on Will's shoulder. "I feel horrible."

The three boys sit watching the river and sipping their cold drinks.

Carlos turns to Roberto. "What do you want to do?"

He continues looking at the water. "I never expected to live long enough to grow up or get an education. I want to learn about building things like radio towers and bridges, particularly bridges. How do you plan them and know what materials to use?"

Will muses, "Maybe you should study structural engineering and design. You already do math well, but you'd want to draw."

Carlos interjects, "The dude draws well."

Will looks at Roberto. "When you can, take a mechanical drawing class, maybe in high school, and see how you like it. Then when you get to university you can study either architecture or engineering."

Roberto shakes his head. "How could I go to university without money or parents to support me?"

Will interjects, "A dude who learns as fast as you do will get scholarships and work study. You and Carlos want to talk to my dad. He'll tell you how to plan."

Carlos looks at the sun. "We better start back."

As they stand up, Roberto glances at Carlos. "I still will study another week with Will. Now you passed your exams, what will you do?"

Carlos says, "Since I don't know when the Resistance will give me another assignment, I'd like to continue studying with you until our household breaks up."

"That feels fine." Will frowns. "I keep forgetting the war continues in Utah. It will take years to heal the scars. But what do you mean your household will break up?"

Carlos looks at the river. "Lark and Sammy sold their place in Chimayo and bought a house here in Santa Fe with my mother. Tommy-tres, Swallow and I will move there at the end of the month."

Will adds, "Vela told me she and Jeremy will go to Prescott to stay with Pedro during August. She wants to spend time at the old Hogan."

Carlos draws a circle in the dirt with his foot. "Yes, when they return for school they'll live with Martín and Blue Feather, who both look forward to the month of August with no kids. Our household as well as Tony and Susana will give them ongoing support. They survived a difficult year as a newly partnered couple."

Roberto looks at the sun. "Let's start back."

Two days later, Martin sees Alex, Gil and José Sanchez, and two other wounded freedom fighters he treated at Mercy and feels happy and relieved when he walks into the clinic just before ten. He hurries to greet them and then introduces Blue Feather.

Alex hugs him. "If Mohammed won't come to the mountain, we would come to you. We figured people from Colorado would swamp you."

Martín feels glad. "You know me. I felt torn between keeping my commitment to Tío Gil and the other soldiers and my commitment to this clinic." He glances at Blue Feather. "I'd like you to meet my stepfather, Gil Sanchez." The two shake hands.

Martín looks at Alex. "How long can I work on these people?"

He answers, "These three heal so well; three days tops. The others didn't come. We'll take Roberto back with us, if he agrees."

Blue Feather replies, "He draws well. I'll get Vela to show you where Lou and Will live. Roberto and most of our boys study there this morning. Tío Gil and José can squeeze into our place, but the rest of you will want to inquire whether Lou can find you a place for three nights in exchange for a few hours' work."

Martín walks to Tony's office and inquires, "Does my schedule look crowded? I'd like to fit these three from Denver in today. Alex and I did intakes on them already."

Tony looks at the book. "You can see one now, one at three and one at four."

Martín turns to the two freedom fighters. "Please go with Vela and get your housing arranged." He turns to her. "Ask Carlos to come get José before lunch."

He says to Tío Gil, "I'd like to start with you. Will you and José come to my office?" Tío Gil swings on his crutches. Martín hears Alex tell one warrior first thing

to do is take Roberto aside and ask him if he agrees to
return to Denver.

José closes the door and sits down cross-legged on
the floor. Martín takes his favorite seat, on top of the
day bed. Tío Gil eases into a chair. "I do the exercises, meditate with José, take calcium and stay off the
leg. Since the second week, I stopped feeling so much
pain and I sleep an extra hour or two every night. I
also crave eggs. The medic said, 'Eat them. Your
body requires the protein to heal.' So I do, but it gets
harder to stay off the leg. José helps by encouraging
me."

Martín looks the boy in the eye. "Thanks, José. Healing means a long slow process, and we want all the allies
we can get."

José looks serious. "Thank you, Martín. Over the
summer, Tío Gil became less grouchy and more fun,
more like his old self. He seems to feel less pain."

Martín says, "I feel glad I can use my gift to start the
healing process in people, but only they and their allies
can continue it. With more serious injuries, we may not
achieve a complete healing, but we can make life easier.
What did you do this summer?"

José speaks. "School begins in two weeks. Dave
More's daughter started a summer school in the barrio
for us kids who never attended. She thinks I can go into
an accelerated third grade class, which will cover the
third and fourth grade in one year. I hope Roberto will
help me now that he comes back."

"Make him an offer he can't resist," Martín says, turning now to Tío Gil. "I want to scan your leg." Gil agrees and Martín goes into a trance. José and his uncle both begin meditating.

He scans the thigh bone and feels delighted by what he senses. The femur looks strong enough to bear weight. He checks the muscle which he smoothes, easing out a contraction and removing pockets of lactic acid.

He comes out of the trance and rests a minute. "Tío Gil, your femur looks strong. You worked hard. Will you try bearing weight?"

Tío Gil exclaims, "Oh, yes."

Martín tells him, "Use your crutches and bear weight on your leg as you step."

Tío Gil takes a couple steps and then starts walking more smoothly. He grins.

Martín motions José to stand behind his uncle. "Now, pick your crutches up, and take four steps without them."

Tío Gil takes four steps then puts his crutches down and grimaces. "My thigh muscles spasm."

"Then sit and rest." Martín goes into a trance. He relaxes the spasms and breaks up the lactic acid. "Drink lots of water, use arnica ointment and a hot water bottle. I'll spend two more days working on those quadriceps."

Tío Gil looks at him. "I feel so much less pain, and I never thought I'd bear weight on that leg. Thank you."

Martín nods. "Before you leave, I'll give you a different set of exercises and a set of canes. Use your crutches the first few weeks for long distances, and when it snows. Try using a cane and a crutch, or two canes. Experiment; you may want crutches on busy days and a cane or two on quiet days. Take it slow and keep your quadriceps warm."

Tío Gil gets teary. "Thank you. I made more progress than I ever expected."

Two weeks later, Blue Feather watches Martín wake up. "Hi, sleepyhead."

He looks at her. "Hola, mi amor. The house seems so silent. I enjoy the peace."

She brushes hair out of his eyes. "Yes, I enjoy it too. I feel sure just Vela and Jeremy will stay quieter than the five, though I'll miss Carlos' handiness."

Martín yawns. "I will miss my talks with Tommy-tres, but he moved just about six blocks so we will see him regularly and I can still spend special time with him."

She smiles. "And now, we can talk to each other. We can't hide behind the chaos of all those young voices, at least, until we raise one or two of our own. What do you want to do today? We can choose."

"Well, after breakfast, we'll catch a ride to Velarde, sit by the river and talk."

"Okay with me. Let's stop by Rubén's and pick up a picnic lunch." She kisses him.

"Great, I always feel hungry."

i   Washington Matthews, <u>The Night Chant: A Na-vaho Ceremony</u>. Original publishing New York 1902 by Knickerbocker Press, Re-issued in 1995 by The University of Utah Press in Salt Lake City, pages 212-265.

ii   <u>http://score.rims.k12.ca.us/score_lessons/treaty_greenville/pages/night_chant.html</u>, Section 1.

iii   Washington Matthews, <u>op cit.</u> page 245.

iv   <u>http://score.rims.k12.ca.us/score_lessons/treaty_greenville/pages/night_chant.html</u>. Section 1.

v   <u>http://score.rims.k12.ca.us/score_lessons/treaty_greenville/pages/night_chant.html</u> Section 4.

vi   Louis Sachar, <u>There's a Boy in the Girls' Bathroom</u>, Alfred A. Knopf, NY, NY. 1987, page 5.

vii   <u>Ibid</u> page 17.

viii   <u>Ibid</u> page 78.

ix   <u>Ibid</u> page 194.

x   Susan Hazen-Hammond, <u>SPIDER WOMAN'S WEB: Traditional Native American Tales About Women's Power</u>, The Penguin Putnam, Inc. NY, NY. 1999, pages 187-195.

Made in the USA
Charleston, SC
12 October 2011